THE TABIT
GENESIS

THE TABIT GENESIS

TONY GONZALES

The right of Tony Gonzales to be identified as the author of
this work has been asserted by him in accordance with the
Copyright, Designs and Patents Act 1988.

First published in Great Britain in 2015
by Gollancz
An imprint of the Orion Publishing Group
Carmelite House, 50 Victoria Embankment, London EC4Y 0DZ
An Hachette UK Company

This edition published in Great Britain in 2016 by Gollancz

1 3 5 7 9 10 8 6 4 2

A CIP catalogue record for this book
is available from the British Library

ISBN 978 0 575 09323 2

Printed and bound by CPI Group (UK) Ltd, Croydon, CR0 4YY

The Orion Publishing Group's policy is to use papers that are natural,
renewable and recyclable products and made from wood grown in sustainable
forests. The logging and manufacturing processes are expected to conform
to the environmental regulations of the country of origin.

www.orionbooks.co.uk
www.gollancz.co.uk

To Ben

1

ANONYMOUS

20 January 2809

Dear Amaryllis,

I apologise for not writing sooner. It's been a difficult time.

I never had the chance to tell you about my parents. My life is so different now that I have trouble believing I was ever their son. They lived in Bangor, Maine, which was then the largest city on the Atlantic seaboard. Every day of their existence, their generation lived under the threat of nuclear annihilation.

Mom and Dad had come to terms with that fate. Decided they would rather die at home than struggle to survive in the wastelands beyond the city walls. Then one day everything within a ten-mile radius of Broadway Park vanished in a fireball as bright as the sun. The Fourth World War had begun, and I never heard from them again. When it happened, I was aboard an UNSEC shuttle on my way to Lunar Base Hadfield, staring at the orbital shipyards where the Genesis motherships were once built.

Most of us were too shocked to grieve. We had made our choice to leave, but it had been reassuring to know our families were still there. One flash of light changed everything. I remember thinking of you and the colonists who boarded those magnificent vessels years ago, lost in cryogenic dreams of wondrous new horizons, the dawn of alien worlds, and the faith that your loved ones were safe at home.

The *Tabit Genesis* and *Tau Genesis* were to be the interstellar seeds of mankind, the arks that flung us across the cosmos to pollinate new worlds. Wars bring sobering perspective to civilisation, at least for a while. For the first time in hundreds of years, the human race joined hands to build something that would take generations to complete. My parents spent their entire lives constructing the Genesis ships, as did their parents before them. And they did so knowing they would never be among the voyagers who would fly those ships to the stars. Their sacrifice was the epitome of selflessness: they built Genesis for us.

Before the wars choked the Earth's skies with ash, the stars Tabit and Tau Ceti had only ever been seen from the highest elevations, and then solely from the northern hemisphere. After a century's worth of observation, those two insignificant specks in the night sky were confirmed to harbour planets just as habitable as Earth, or as Earth used to be, before man ruined it.

My parents' generation was born in the devastation left by the Third World War. Apart from a notorious few, they all understood that Earth could never recover from the damage humans had caused. This realisation was the birth of Genesis. For a brief time, there was a golden age even for the damned. I remember endless conversations between my parents about the 'privilege' and 'honour' of enabling the first humans to set foot on an extrasolar world. Failure was not even a *thought*, let alone an option.

In fairness, there must remain the slightest sliver of hope that the *Tau* reached her brave new world, just the way my parents envisioned. But the more time passes, the less likely it is that we will ever know. I can only speak for the *Tabit*. The fate of that mothership would have broken their hearts.

What may well have become the *last* human beings in existence left a dying Earth, and travelled for decades only to arrive at another dead planet. Imagine being a passenger on the *Tabit* and discovering that the blue-green paradise of your dreams – the world they called Eileithyia – had been transformed into a furnace resembling Venus.

And while *Tabit* pressed on its voyage to nowhere, Earth continued to rot. Those lucky enough to survive the war retreated inland, away from the glowing embers of the coastlines. But anyone with the means travelled north, to Greenland, where UNSEC stood victorious: the last viable geopolitical entity of civilisation, with the strongest military, in the most coveted land on Earth.

That was where the Raothri struck first.

It was just three years after the Genesis ships left Sol space. By now you've probably seen the footage of the Raothri landings at the Arctic Circle fortifications. There are worse. I have clips from the desert interior of Brazil, the shores of Niger, the Appalachian coastline, the European Isles, the Himalayan badlands, and every city left standing in between.

We had discovered our human brotherhood too late. Not that it would have mattered. The Raothri were superior – *are superior* – to humans in every way. After seven hundred years of wireless broadcasts, the last recorded human transmission from Earth was a dire warning to never return. Our world was irretrievably lost. Can you even imagine what horrors would convince you that *all* humanity was doomed? Every religion was wrong about the Apocalypse. Tribulation, Qiyamah, whatever the prophecy or creed, none could bring a worse fate than the one we suffered. The end of the world had come, and not even God could stop it.

Mercifully, my parents had already died. This may sound cruel, but I hope your parents also met their end without remorse or fear. *You* probably grew into someone they would have been proud of. My parents, I accept, would have been ashamed of me.

Why? Because I believe the Raothri may have unintentionally saved mankind. By taking Earth from us, they compelled the *Tabit* voyagers to find a way to survive.

Two hundred years have passed since the end of days. And still, somehow, the human race endures. When the people of Orionis Colony look towards Sol, they no longer see a home they can return to. Instead, they see a harbinger of what may come.

I don't know when I'll write next. But I hope it's soon.

Love,

- *A*

3

2

ADAM

Pulling himself through the cockpit hatch, Adam twisted in the micro-gravity to orient himself with the seat above. Today he felt neither fear nor apprehension, having lost count of his descents into Zeus. Even though he was just eleven years of age, the experience of falling through the atmosphere of a gas giant had become routine.

Settling into position, Adam scanned the controls before him, cycling through his pre-flight checks. Most days he was excited to pilot the old Pegasus M2 mining mech. Not that he was naïve to the dangers – he just preferred the freedom of roaming on the rig's sprawling platform to the cramped metal tubes of the trawler.

But today his heart was heavy with sadness. For the longest time, Adam had believed his father would recover from the 'accident' that had left him maimed. Now he had finally accepted that would never be.

The old depressurisation mechanism sighed a weary *hiss* as the young pilot sealed the hatch. Clad in a loose-fitting flight suit, he lifted his knees to fit custom metal scraps over his boots. Without them, his feet couldn't reach the mech's actuator controls below.

Dad's voice scratched through his helmet.

'Mining's all about understanding pressure,' he said. The only thing Adam's dad loved more than troubleshooting atmosphere harvesters was teaching everything he knew about them to Adam. 'Start with the intake gauges and work your way towards the scrubbers …'

Ever since the accident, Dad had been prone to repeating things. The monitoring systems on the rig platform had been inoperable for

4

two years, yet Adam was still making several trips down per week. He knew its machinery as well as any prospector in the Belt.

As Dad continued explaining what needed to be done, the mech began powering up. Volumetric displays flickered on, greeting Adam with pixelated warnings of malfunctioning subsystems and neglected repairs. There wasn't much more that could break on the old machine.

Another voice cut through: his sister, Abby.

'Alright Brat Face, radio check,' she muttered.

'Brat Face copies all,' Adam answered. Abigail, five years his senior, tormented him with all the ferocity of a rival sibling, frequently with alarming hostility. She was fiercely competitive and bright, especially skilled at mathematics. Sadly, she still aspired to an Inner Belt corporate career. But Adam knew that could never be. Whatever her qualifications, she was no firstborn, and only they qualified for those opportunities. As the offspring of parents who were born through amniosynthesis, Adam and Abby were both 'ghosts'; unrecognised and thus unentitled to any of the benefits afforded to firstborn citizens of Orionis that would, among other things, keep them alive past the age of twenty.

But Dad's accident had changed Adam's role in the family from dependant to provider. Abby, however grudgingly, had conceded respect for him, acknowledging that his natural-born skill at mech piloting was now more essential to their survival than being able to reconcile an inventory ledger.

'Winds are 130 at the tropopause,' she said. 'Mining depth is sixty knots and steady.'

Adam smiled. It was a nice day on Zeus.

'How's Mom?' he asked.

Mother was always distraught when he visited the rig, unable to bring herself even to speak with him during sorties. But their family owed steep debts to bad people, and this was the only way to repay them.

'She's freaking out,' Abby replied. 'There have been Arkady sightings.'

Adam saw these elusive, deadly creatures all the time. Officially called 'zenomorphs', he never reported them unless other miners were nearby. There were hundreds of trawlers prospecting on Zeus, all engaged in cut-throat competition to set the market price with their

5

bounty of noble gases. Miners only shared information that might save lives, and even then, would treat the warnings with scepticism.

But the nearest trawler was tens of thousands of kilometres away. His mother had probably heard about a random Arkady sighting on the mining net, which could have happened days earlier and been anywhere. If she knew how often Adam really saw them, she would never have let him leave the trawler again, even at the cost of the business, and perhaps even their lives.

'How many?' he asked.

'Not enough to kill this drop,' his sister answered. 'I'm opening the doors.'

Across the hangar from where Adam was seated, the orbiter's outer bay doors pulled away from each other, and the swirling reddish-grey cloud bands of Zeus greeted him from six thousand kilometres away.

'The tanks should be full by now,' Abby said. 'We need this. Hurry!'

Adam adjusted the exterior cameras to view the mech's rear, visually inspecting the clamps locking its chassis to the drop sled. In just a few moments it would propel him down one of the trawler's four carbon nanotube fibre cables to the mining rig below.

'I'll be fast,' he promised.

'You'll be *careful*,' Abby said. 'Would hate to lose that *Three*.'

'Thanks, I'll be fine,' Adam said.

'Whatever,' she said. 'You're good to go.'

With an abrupt jolt, the drop sled pushed through the bay doors. Adam looked up through the mech's canopy at the underside of the orbiter looming overhead. From this vantage, he could barely see where the ship ended and space began.

'Adam, did I ever show you how to replace a faulty check valve?' his father asked.

Adam sighed, switching on the music player. For this trip he had picked out a mix of seventeenth century classical music, along with some twenty-second century electronica.

'Can't hurt going over it again,' he answered, pressing the release button.

When the *Tabit Genesis* arrived in 2638, the first order of business for the colonists was to survey their new neighbourhood for resources.

The nearby Eileithyian moons Amnisos and Lucina provided ample sources of water ice and raw ores. Helium-3 was also present, mixed into the upper layer of regolith on both lunar surfaces. The mothership had come prepared to harvest those sources immediately, bringing with them spooled space elevator cables to expedite the transfer of materials to orbit. But mining the precious gas was time-consuming and costly.

The sixth and largest planet of the system, officially designated Pi^3 Orionis-f by UNSEC, was thus targeted due to the favourable composition of its upper atmosphere – primarily hydrogen and helium, the essential fuels for the fusion technology of the era. Beneath that layer, swirling in an organic soup of methane, water vapour, ammonia, carbon, oxygen, nitrogen, sulphur, and phosphine, were abundant concentrations of Helium-3, or just *Three* as it had been known on Earth. Then and now, it was the critical isotope that made spaceflight possible.

Gathering enough of it from the Sol system to launch the Genesis motherships had required the colonisation of the moon, the asteroids Vesta and Ceres, Mars, and a tenuous alliance of superpowers to protect the corporations capable of harvesting it. Helium-3 remained a precious commodity, though its abundance at Pi^3 Orionis-f was the only reason why any colonists bothered settling beyond the Great Belt at all.

Prospectors took to calling the planet Zeus, after their beloved Jupiter back home. The gas giant was smaller than its Sol namesake, and lacked a defining iconic characteristic like the Great Red Spot. But its cloud bands were thicker and darker, containing far more water vapour and thicker concentrations of organic compounds. Of the Tabit system's fifteen planets, none was more menacing, or majestic, than Zeus.

Adam was immersed in his music, almost in a meditative state, as the sled plummeted through the atmosphere. At this stage of entry even the most hardened miners would be nervous, if not outright sick. Metal groaned and the cockpit shook as hurricane-force winds slammed the mech in its harness. But Adam *knew* that nothing bad was going to happen – an instinct that always kept him tranquil during these descents. He had skirted danger before it could happen hundreds of times, and was well past the survival odds for a trawler miner with his level of experience.

He didn't think anything of it, believing that all people shared his prescience. And so onwards he plunged, deeper and deeper into the roiling bowels of Zeus, strumming his fingers to Bach as the mech dived through the rattling pelt of an ammonia crystal downpour.

The oldest orbital trawlers ran a minimum of four cables to the platform rig dangling below. The newest corporation models dropped eight times as many. In theory there was no limit to the number, as long as the orbiter thrusters could compensate for the atmospheric drag of the platform. The rig could rotate its horizontal orientation so that it always faced the prevailing winds, and sat upon enormous helium bladders to maintain buoyancy. Arrays of intakes and scrubbers isolated the bounty from Zeus air into tanks that, once filled, ascended the cables to be consumed by the orbiter or transported away for sale.

By the time the ammonia showers ceased, yellow-orange skies were visible between breaks in the clouds. The altimeter was broken, but Adam could tell that he was about a thousand kilometres away from his target.

Adam switched off his music player and keyed the radio.

'Orbiter, Brat Face,' he said. 'Touchdown in two mikes.'

'Yeah, yeah,' Abby huffed. 'Just get on with it.'

As the roiling clouds rushed towards his feet, the sled's thrusters fired, slowing his descent. The rig grew until his downward view was overwhelmed by its rust-coloured features. Hovering for just a moment above the landing gantry, the sled slammed into position.

'I'm in,' Adam said, checking his displays. Everything that absolutely needed to be working was online. 'Radio checks at five-minute intervals.'

'Hello, Adam, it's Dad.'

Adam cringed at the sound of his voice.

'Make sure you hook up the refuelling hoses for the sled or else it'll take forever to get back topside.'

'Okay,' he said, as the mech detached from the harness. With a subtle leg movement, he stepped the machine onto the platform. The rig itself was several football fields in length and nearly as wide. It was windy, just like Abby had warned, but still not dangerous for a mech that weighed six tons.

The fuel hoses were right where he had left them, attached to tanks with compressed hydrogen inside. Using the mech's arms and tri-pad 'hands', he expertly attached them to the sled, making sure the transfer was under way. If necessary, he could gently grasp an egg or hoist a crate of tungsten I-beams. The Pegasus was old, but in the hands of a skilled pilot, it was still a capable machine.

As Adam turned to make his way towards the scrubbers, a sudden wave of premonition froze him in his tracks.

There was danger ahead, but not enough to make him turn back. The subliminal warnings were abstract, never betraying details. The only clarity they offered was in their urgency, informing whether he should flee or be extra vigilant.

He needed a moment to catch his breath.

'Time's wasting,' Abby warned. 'Come on, Adam.'

'Okay,' he said, trekking towards the large air intakes at the leading edge of the rig. There were eight of them, each with their own scrubbers plus a myriad of pipes, regulators, distilling tanks and machinery in between. Finding the problem could take minutes or days.

So with one heavy metal step after the next, Adam stomped on, relishing the view. Two of Zeus's ninety-one moons were visible through a clearing in the skies overhead; soft rays of white sunlight fell like marble columns upon mountains of amber clouds that stretched beyond the horizon. Dad had once said that his ancestors would have given anything to see this just once in their lifetimes.

It distressed Adam to remember how his father had once been. Though his mother had explained what happened, he knew she was concealing the truth. The Ceti bastards who owned the rig were aboard when it happened. Adam was certain they had played a role in the 'accident'.

By the time he reached the first intake, Adam had become unfocused by anger.

Then suddenly, the events of his premonition began to unfold.

A pack of Arkady sturgeons darted over the windward side of the rig; then an entire school of them followed. Adam stepped back in awe as thousands of translucent, flattened creatures accented with black streaks soared by. Each was more than five metres in length and awash in countless bursts of bluish-green light. Numerous gill slits along their bodies regulated the airflow coursing around and through them, allowing them to cut through the wind's currents with a preternatural ease.

Adam was thankful the rig's radars were broken. Abby would not keep this a secret, his mother would panic and, one way or the other, they would find some way to hurt these magnificent creatures.

Watching the zenomorphs made Adam forget his anger. He studied the swarm until they vanished back into the clouds, then, feeling invigorated, he returned to the task at hand, bending the mech forward to check the intake's gauges. Squinting at the numbers, he didn't see the great shadow descending on him until it was too late.

With a terrifying bang, the Pegasus was knocked onto its back. Adam's helmet slammed into the head guard, disorienting him. He reflexively threw his hands up in a guard position, preparing to fend off more blows from whatever it was that had struck him.

The actuators reacted just in time; a loud *snap* brought Adam out of his stupor. His face was just centimetres from the severed tentacle of an Arkady hunter, its serrated hooks dangling off the mech's tripads. The rest of the animal was partially trapped in the maws of Intake One amidst a stream of smoke, flailing wildly.

Adam realized that the animal's severed limb was wrapped tightly around the Pegasus. Had he been standing a metre to his right, the creature would have pulled him over the side.

'You're a minute past your checkpoint, Brat Face,' Abby complained.

Adam nearly overloaded the mech's power core trying to get the machine back onto its feet.

'Sorry,' he said, backing away from the frenzied creature. 'I'm concentrating.'

'Whatever, just hurry up.'

Adam was mesmerised by the hunter's struggle. The only sounds he could hear were the howling wind, his own shallow breathing, and the muted strikes of cartilaginous flesh on metal. But the creature was no longer lashing at him with its deadly limbs. From ruthless killer the Arkady hunter had become desperate victim; just another living thing fighting for its very life.

Adam was trapped between compassion and caution, though only for a moment.

Moving beyond the reach of its flailing tentacles, he clamped the mech's tri-pads onto the regulator that would shut the damaged intake down. As the turbines ground to a halt, the shape-shifting beast writhed in pain, unable to free its limbs from the machine.

Dad's voice cut through the radio.

'Gas mining is tedious, but it's dangerous work,' he informed. 'But there's always a buyer for your harvest. That makes it all worthwhile.'

Adam took a step towards the hunter, willing himself to ignore the radio completely.

'Did you know that every Orionis citizen will use several *million* cubic litres of compressed hydrogen fuel over the course of his lifetime?' his dad informed.

The desperate hunter, its strength depleted, was fading away. Taking a deep breath, Adam marched directly towards it.

'What are you doing down there?' Abby demanded. 'You missed another checkpoint!'

Adam was within ten metres when the hunter lashed out at him; its tentacles, now coruscating in angry bursts of yellow and green, made a futile attempt to latch onto the mech. Instead the limbs collapsed onto the rig, splayed out like strands of discarded cable. Gill slits along its body began twitching. Adam sensed it was dying. Time was running out.

He climbed deftly on top of the intake. The exhausted creature was heaving besides him, close enough to touch. Securing the mech's footing as best he could, Adam set to work removing the intake's cowling to examine the inside.

'Radio check,' he mumbled.

'Did you find the problem?' Abby demanded.

'You could say that,' he answered. As the cowling came loose, he carefully set the metal sheet down and peered inside. Two of the creature's limbs were badly mauled and tangled in the turbine fans. The Pegasus was strong enough to pull them apart, but he would have to step up and over the leading edge of the platform to reach.

So that's what he did, trying not to think about what would happen if he slipped.

'Well, how long will it take to fix?' Abby asked. 'The offloaders are en route.'

'Intake One can't be fixed,' Adam said, plunging his tri-pads into the ruined machine. 'It has to be replaced.'

He clamped on tightly, transferred as much power into the arms as he could, and began pulling.

'Are you serious?' Abby asked.

With an abrupt, sickening *snap*, the fans came apart unexpectedly, and the sudden surplus of momentum carried the mech off the edge.

'*No!*' Adam shouted.

He thrashed out with both arms to grab onto something, anything. The first arm grabbed nothing but Zeus air; the second found the edge of a flotation bladder. Adam transferred all the power to the grip, dangling over oblivion as he brought his second arm up.

'Really?' Abby fumed. 'What's your problem?'

Adam thought of some choice words, but instead:

'No, I mean, *yes*, the intake is ruined,' he said, plotting a vertical path to reach the platform rail.

'What the hell can ruin a turbine intake?' Abby demanded.

'Did I ever tell you the story about how I got this rig?' his father asked.

'I didn't think you ever wanted us to know that,' Adam muttered, thankful for the interruption. The Arkady hunter was gone. He hadn't seen what had happened to it. Given his efforts, he hoped it had flown away instead of falling to its death.

'Yes, that's right,' his dad said. 'It's probably best you don't.'

With full power diverted to a limb, the Pegasus was capable of pulling several times its own mass. But he would have to overload the reactor's output in short bursts, timing each one with the grips he needed to reach safety.

In the hands of a lesser pilot, it would have been impossible. By the time Adam stepped over the rail, the reactor was overheating and doing permanent damage to the mech. Grateful to be alive, he limped back towards the drop sled, covered in Arkady remains.

Abby was relentless the entire time.

'So not only did we miss the cut-off, now we produce less than every other rig. Wonderful.'

'I'm finished down here,' Adam said, unlatching the fuel hoses. 'The *Three* tanks are full and ready to go on Cable Four. Cables Two

12

and Three are on schedule for H and O deliveries. I'm coming up on One. Lift off in ten.'

'Fine,' Abby grumbled.

Exhausted, Adam very much wanted to get back into orbit. He just didn't have the energy to explain that the Pegasus was likely ruined as well. Yet much as he wanted to avoid her, Abby had every right to be upset: the load coming up now wouldn't reach the market before the other trawlers sold off their inventories. The cost of these equipment failures would far exceed whatever pittance they received for the harvest, and they would fall deeper into debt.

Their Ceti overlords were tiring of excuses. The last visit had made that clear.

Adam stowed the fuel hoses away and backed the ailing mech into the sled cage. When the harness locked into place, he keyed in the launch sequence.

As the countdown commenced, he gazed down the length of the rig. Somehow it seemed much longer than usual.

Adam's heart stopped as it began to move, undulating in the wind currents, rising above the rest of the platform.

A colossal zenomorph, wider than the entire platform, was gliding towards him. He had never seen an Arkady like this before. Its skin was pitch-black, its winged shape masterfully controlling its position in the gale.

The sled began ascending, all too slowly. Closer and closer the beast approached, unfurling tentacles many times longer than the hunter's, all within easy striking range.

It would be no effort for the creature to kill him. But instead, as the sled ascended, a pattern of blue flashes danced across the Arkady's ebony, liquescent skin. Symmetrical and deliberate, unlike the chaotic life energy that radiated from schools or hunters.

Adam sensed the signs were intended just for him.

3

JAKE

I was lying face down in my own vomit when the Minotaur showed up.

There must have been a binge, and a bad one. I had the awful feeling I was falling, but I couldn't be since the mess was spread out instead of floating around in puffy blobs. This was good, insofar as being preferable to a micrograv crash. Beyond that, I had no idea where I was or how I got there. With considerable effort, I managed to lift my head and look around. But my eyes wouldn't focus on anything, except for ... the Minotaur. And I decided there was nothing unusual about a horned, bull-faced humanoid and just let my head fall back onto the deck where it belonged.

Which may have offended him, since he kicked me so hard I threw up again. Then he began to laugh-snort through his formidable nostrils.

'What do you want?' I gasped.

'I'm here for Jake Reddeck,' the Minotaur said.

'Don't know him,' I managed. The bile in my throat tasted like some twisted narcotic concoction.

'I'll help you remember,' the Minotaur said.

He kicked me again. I was beginning to wonder if there was a non-lethal exit from this. Bad enough I had no recollection of my evening, but who was this animal? Either I owed him money, in which case this was a simple misunderstanding, or he was *the competition,* which meant I'd have to kill him. I have no patience for Belt-trash amateurs trying to muscle their way into my business, even if I used to be one of them myself.

There are twelve million lawful firstborn human beings in Orionis, and they would all love to shove me out of an airlock. Mostly, that was because I was guilty of doing to countless others what the Minotaur was about to do to me. It's the nature of the drug trade; the old Ceti saying is 'Success scales not with the customers you serve, but with the enemies you make.' After whatever evil I committed last night, I was sure I deserved a promotion.

But the more I tried to remember, the more my head hurt. Whether from injury or product or both, there was a black hole in my memory. I've seen some crazy augmentations in my time, but this Minotaur … *damn*. Mutants aren't hard to find in the Zeus colonies, but this guy was a *fucking aberration*, easily the most disfigured one I'd ever seen. I mean, there were *heat waves* radiating off the man. Just being in the same room as him was giving me cancer.

Considering the circumstances, I thought it best to remain civil.

'Have we met?' I managed. My sinuses felt like someone had scrubbed the inside of them with steel wool. 'Whatever this is, I'm sure we can work something out.'

'Here's the best deal you're going to get,' the Minotaur said. 'Bring me to Jake, and I won't kill you slowly. How about that?'

Everywhere I looked, the rest of my surroundings took a few moments to catch up. As reality blurred across my vision, I heard this wailing sound, like screaming children over the groan of old, bending metal. The fog was palpable; I was only *peripherally* aware of my own existence, just watching myself from the edge of consciousness.

That meant I was *dangerously* intoxicated, even for a hard bastard. The crash was coming, and I needed something to soften the landing.

'I can help with that,' the Minotaur sneered.

I don't know if I asked for a fix out loud, but the mutant obliged with another kick to the gut. By the time I finished wheezing, the floor was coated in blood.

I know how it looks: my consumption habit is killing me. That's fair, because I've tried every drug there is. It's expected of me in this profession, which is running a distribution network for Ceti. From Tabit Prime to the House Worlds, I vend chemical pleasures to people of all statures. What kind of sales rep would I be if I didn't sample the product? That's the kind of enthusiasm clients want to see. It's made me very rich and, consequently, very sociopathic. Like any successful businessman, I defend my interests fiercely, with no regard for the laws of governments.

The downside: I do very bad things when I'm high. Because of the drugs.

Which I do because the profession demands it.

I guess the infinite loop of denial means I've reached rock bottom. What a view.

'It gets worse,' the Minotaur said. The room was spinning *around* him now, like he was the centre of the universe. 'You have no idea.'

The mutant had bright yellow eyes criss-crossed with purple capillaries. Every time he blinked, one of the irises changed colour.

'Jake was mindful of these things,' the Minotaur said. 'Where is he?'

'Look, man ...or whatever you are: I don't know who you're talking about,' I repeated, turning myself over.

The Minotaur reared up an iron hoof for another kick, and I cringed. But he held back at the last moment.

'Is your name Jack Tatum?' he asked.

'That's right,' I said. 'Who are you?'

The Minotaur snorted a puff of hot smoke.

'What do you do for a living, "Jack"?' he asked.

'I work for Ceti,' I answered, hoping the mere mention of the most notorious cartel in Orionis would make him recoil in horror. But no such luck.

'Tell me something, *Jack*,' the Minotaur asked, kneeling so his hairy face was very close to mine. 'What happened to your hands?'

I hadn't realised that my knuckles were shredded and bruised. They reminded me of the more despicable things I've done in my life. But *not* what had happened last night.

The Minotaur was now holding a gun.

'Do you want to know?' he asked.

His question provoked a powerful revulsion in me, like some primeval, autoimmune response to danger.

'No,' I answered.

He pressed the weapon against my temple. Deep down I could feel this whimpering urge to do something about it. But my limbs were

16

limp, unresponsive dead weights. I had a reflex to deal with this. The muscle memory was there because I'd practised it a thousand times. It just wasn't listening to me.

I guess I didn't care.

'You swore an oath,' the Minotaur said, snorting through flaring nostrils. 'Remember?'

I didn't, but began surrendering to the possibility.

'Lie to yourself all you want,' the Minotaur said. 'The truth is coming.'

'Is that why you're here?' I spat.

Steam poured from his nostrils.

'Something like that.'

Maybe the high was wearing off, and the adrenaline was wresting back control of my sanity. But a voice rang out that I hardly recognised, and it used my mouth to speak.

'I do what I do for the job,' I muttered.

The Minotaur roared a slow, throaty laugh.

'How's that working out for you?' he quipped, tapping the gun against my head. 'Is it worth this?'

Strangely, the cold sensation of steel against skin reminded me of someone who once gave me strength.

But I had to try harder to forget.

'The job,' I said, driving the memory out, 'is absolutely worth it.'

The Minotaur spat onto the floor. His phlegm burst into flames on contact, making the place stink of sulphur.

'This is the last time I'll ask,' he warned. 'Where is Jake Reddeck?'

My patience ran out.

'Look, friend,' I said, 'I really don't know who he is.'

He struck me once, then again when the first blow didn't open a deep enough gash.

'Guess you're telling the truth,' he growled, leaning in close to admire his handiwork. 'Danna wouldn't recognise you, anyway.'

The name made my skin boil. Lesions bubbled out, oozing necrotic slime that dripped over every inch of me. The world spun with the ferocity of a Zeus cyclone.

'Tell me,' the Minotaur sneered, 'was Danna worth the "job" as well?'

I snapped.

'*Fuck you!*'

'What do you care?' the Minotaur roared, centimetres from my face. 'She was Jake's problem, not yours.'

Violent shivers wracked my spine.

'I have to see this all the way through,' I heaved. 'Especially now that ...'

I couldn't bring myself to say it.

He stepped back, shaking his long, pointed horns back and forth.

'You think she deserved what happened to her,' he said.

'I didn't say that!' I whined.

'I think she died for nothing,' the Minotaur said.

'That's not true!' I shouted back.

He pressed up against my face.

'Show me why it isn't.'

Furious rage ran with the toxins in my veins. But I was the Minotaur's captive. And, goddamn him, he was right. I could never justify all the wrong I've done.

'Once you're in, you go all the way,' I muttered. 'That's how it is.'

His eyes were crimson.

'You broke your oath last night,' the Minotaur growled, pushing his gun past my teeth. 'You know what that means.'

I shut my eyes, ready for the end, when an ear-piercing ring silenced the snarl of the Minotaur's breath.

A second ring, twice as loud, made him step back.

The room's spin was starting to slow.

'Too bad,' the Minotaur snarled. 'See you around, Jack.'

Familiar settings began taking shape. Of all places, I was in my own apartment.

'Jack! I know you're in there,' I heard. 'I'm breaking in.'

It was my friend Dusty, and I couldn't answer him because I was holding a gun in my mouth. It fell between my legs as the door slid open.

His frail, ungainly silhouette appeared in the doorway.

'Holy shit,' he breathed. 'What's with the cannon?'

I decided against mentioning anything about the Minotaur. He'd be back soon enough.

'What are you talking about?' I croaked.

The shadowy figure lifted the weapon slowly, like a bomb technician, gently placing it beyond reach.

'I brought stuff for a hangover,' he said, 'but not … this.'

Jack Tatum would never admit how good it was to hear Dusty's voice.

'… could use some water.' My voice was a bare rasp.

'You've never been this bad,' he said. 'Better get your mind right, real fast.'

'Why?'

'Jack,' he said. His voice was more subdued than usual. 'You are the *toast* of Ceti today. You're practically a hero.'

I tried to focus on the clock resting on the night table. The number said 17:49.

'When's the last time you saw me?' I asked, bracing for the answer.

'Seven thirty,' he said. I felt a cup pressed against my lips. I had no pride left at all. 'Yesterday morning.'

I gulped the water. It went down like cold fire, refreshing and excruciating all at once.

'Yesterday?'

'Someone realised you were missing,' he said. 'They sent me to find you.'

I had a vague memory of being with some big-time Ceti officers, personnel way up in the organisation who reported directly to Vladric.

The closest I've ever been to the top.

'Where were we?' I stammered, taking a moment to spit out bile.

'You really don't remember, do you?' Dusty asked. 'Jack, you were at The Helodon.'

The most exclusive club this side of the Belt, run by Ceti, for Ceti personnel only. Just getting a glimpse of it was an achievement most operatives never reached in their careers. The kind of moment you'd remember, unless you came close to overdosing.

If I was that close to senior officers – and still alive – then I would be connected to their most crucial importers: Inner Belt agents embedded in government, the corporations, you name it. People with the power and means to bypass Navy dragnets and Customs stings. They were the key to the whole Ceti network, the most sought after prize of undercover police work.

And by all accounts I was about to screw it up.

'We have a run to make?' I blurted out.

'Yeah,' Dusty said, rummaging through his satchel. He never went anywhere without it. 'They're keeping us mobile. For our safety, they said.'

'Safety?'

'The bounty on you is worth as much as Vladric's now,' he said.

'Oh.'

Dusty offered some pills. It looked like he was holding three hands in front of him.

'I took care of everything,' he said, pushing them into my mouth. 'The *Breakaway* is ready to fly.'

What was once an abandoned freighter was now an armed speed rig that could outrun House Obyeran corvettes, all thanks to Dusty. He is the most talented engineer and skilled pilot I've ever met. He could easily pass the technical qualifiers for a Navy command – and then fail the part that required interaction with people. Dusty was a social introvert, and under no circumstances was he allowed near my clients. Physically, most people mistook him for a mutant: short, lanky build, with bony, hunched shoulders and a twisted face that was scarred from the way he was treated by Ceti before he became useful to them.

That was how we met. Like many other privateers working the Outer Belt, his family owed Ceti a lot of money, and I found him getting stomped by a few thugs sent to collect his debt. Since Jack Tatum was a newly minted associate in the organisation, I saw this as an opportunity to assert myself. After all, Ceti operatives will just as soon steal from each other as they do from everyone else. So I challenged them to a friendly bout of hand-to-hand combat – no weapons. If I won, his debt to Ceti became my problem. I didn't offer terms if I lost. They accepted anyway.

Crippling them sent a clear enough message. The event bought enough time and space for us to start producing revenues. Between my way with people and Dusty's ability to convert junk into high-performance machinery, we began climbing the ranks.

I've met all kinds, but Dusty is unique – not because of his skills, but because of his outlook. Those Ceti punks left him for dead. He's permanently disfigured; children are literally frightened of him. But if you ask, he'd say that if he could go back in time, he wouldn't change a thing. He says that beating was the wake-up call he needed to get the right attitude about life. If not for those three thugs, he'd be dead by now.

I'd walk through fire for him.

The room stopped spinning almost the instant the pills reached my stomach. Dusty got up, walked to the sink and poured another glass of water. I could feel a bit of my strength returning, and with it the clarity of recognising that I had been about three pounds of trigger pressure away from blowing my own brains out. Dusty had just saved my life, but for the moment I wasn't convinced that was a good thing.

Slowly, I managed to stand up.

'You said the ship is ready?' I asked.

'I did,' he answered.

I walked over to my gun. He looked away as I wiped the blood and spit from it.

'Thanks,' I said, hoping he'd never mention this again. I felt better – still horrible overall, but at least functional. It was about a twenty-minute trip to the spaceport, and I needed to piece together exactly what had happened last night before we got there.

'Change your clothes,' Dusty said. 'You're not stepping onto the *Breakaway* smelling like that.'

4

VLADRIC

The most powerful crime syndicate in history was named after the destination star system of the *Tau Genesis*. While the fate of that mothership remains unknown, Vladric Mors used the tragedy of Eileithyia to make his cause immortal. Ceti was founded on his belief that the highborns who travelled to Tau Ceti today inhabit the pristine new world that the *Tabit Genesis* travellers were denied in Orionis. The name 'Ceti', once synonymous with hope and humanity, today embodies Vladric's bitter hatred of highborn culture and the government that empowers it.

Eighty-five years since its founding, the strength of Ceti has grown to rival the House worlds. Its settlements are concentrated in the Great Belt, with the most strategically vital of these being Lethe, the largest moon of Zeus. Business at its main spaceport was always urgent, but now the scene was chaotic. Angry travellers queued in the shuttle boarding areas, quietly cursing the official reason for the departure lockdown. Sig Lareck, the Governing District Officer for the Lethe settlements, eyed the crowd. No one dared to meet his gaze as he paced behind the chair of a young, nervous spaceport technician.

'How much longer?' Sig demanded.

'His gunship just left Brotherhood,' the technician answered. 'Flight time is eight minutes.'

On any approach from the Great Belt, Brotherhood Station emerged as a tiny, bright spool suspended between the banded hues of Zeus and the glittering canyon settlements of Lethe. Only one of the station's four torus-shaped rings was rotating; the others were wrecked shells defiled by acts of war. Home to nearly two hundred thousand people, it was the largest station in the Outer Rim, and the epicentre of regional trade among the Zeus colonies.

Twice that number resided in the Lethe settlements themselves, the population composed mostly of miners, engineers, merchants, and geoscience professionals with their families. They lived comfortably, but worked hard for their earnings. Dropships hauling goods and personnel came and went every few minutes at the spaceport, serving the immense mega-industrial complex.

But the unplanned visit by the Ceti founder had thrown the clockwork operation into disarray. Anticipating flaring tempers, Sig had brought a formidable contingent of guards, with several mutants among them for maximum intimidation.

'Tube traffic has been cleared,' the technician said. 'You'll have a straight run to Delta Lab, no stops.'

With the transit system halted, the unexpected visit from Vladric Mors was now affecting the entire colony.

'There'd better not be,' Sig warned, straightening out his collar. 'He's in one of his moods.'

A coalition of corporations had spent nearly three decades building Brotherhood Station and the Lethe settlements. But it had taken less than five hours for it to fall under Ceti control. The Battle of Brotherhood transformed the drug cartel into a regional sovereignty, exposing the limits of Navy power beyond the Belt. It inspired a mass rejection of Orionis governance over the Outer Rim worlds by the Houses and privateer corporations, both of which renounced their citizenship. The lawless period that followed spawned skirmishes between Ceti, the Navy, corporations and privateers throughout the Belt. They called these the Independence Wars, the first armed conflict of the Orionis Age.

So began the legend of Vladric Mors. Sig Lareck had been by his side long before then.

'Do you know what this is about, sir?' the flustered technician asked. Sig could hear someone shouting through her earpiece. He empathised – a dropship pilot with a heavy load never wanted to be told he couldn't land. But orders were orders.

23

'That's not your concern,' Sig answered. 'I don't advise asking about it, either.'

'Yes, sir,' she answered.

Sig used his reflection in the armoured glass to straighten his uniform. The grey-black canyons beyond were hundreds of kilometres long, awash in the lights of settlements carved into the stone walls. By conquering Brotherhood, Vladric Mors had not only seized the richest known stock of metal ores in the Outer Rim, but he had preserved what was essentially unregulated, unrestricted colonialism in Orionis. The resulting explosion of privateer settlements turned Lethe into the crown port of call for the Belt. There were nineteen districts, each the size of a city and interconnected by a subterranean rail system that stretched across a third of the moon. The spaceport was District One, the capital, where Sig governed on behalf of Ceti.

Officially, the prestigious post was awarded in recognition of his decades of loyal service to the cartel. Sig wanted to stay at the helm of a corvette, but this was where Vladric needed him. The people who lived on Lethe and on Brotherhood owed their allegiance, willingly or not, to Ceti. In return, they lived in a free society where bloodlines offered no entitlements. There were no restrictions on breeding, nor any distinction between firstborns and ghosts. Vladric offered the people who lived here discounted food (plundered from corporation convoys), free radiation therapy (provided with equipment stolen from government clinics), and all the honest work they wanted (by threatening the corporations who bid for Ceti projects).

Sig noticed a bright blue light on the horizon.

'Is that him?' he asked, pointing.

'Yes, sir,' the technician said. 'They're cleared to land.'

'Good,' he said, facing the guards. 'When he arrives, we'll move directly to the tube entrance. Anyone gets in the way, disable them. No killing.'

As the gunship's vectored thrusters settled the imposing craft onto the landing pad, Sig considered whether he was blessed or cursed to know Vladric Mors. On one hand, the relationship had made him a wealthy man. On the other, he always felt one misstep away from losing everything. There was a price for Vladric's 'friendship'. Whether that meant taking life or a bullet to keep it – Sig had done both – Vladric Mors expected nothing less of him.

The legend emerged from the airlock alone, wearing no protection other than the sheathed, crescent-shaped knives at his hips. He was a tall, dark man, with a shaved head and a long goatee that hung beneath a square jaw and sharp cheekbones. His black overcoat concealed broad, muscular shoulders, its upturned collars emblazoned with the insignia of Ceti. But for all his menacing appearance, his baby-blue eyes seemed absurdly out of place, more apt for a child than a king; perfect for concealing his intentions.

'Brother,' Sig said, crossing his chest with one arm.

'Governor Lareck,' Vladric growled, returning the salute. 'Hope I'm not interrupting.'

'Never,' he answered. 'Welcome to Lethe.'

Vladric grunted, ignoring the technician offering magnetic boots to aid navigation in the low-gravity environment. He had come wearing his own. 'Let's move.'

'Right this way,' Sig answered, as guards formed a spearhead in front of them. The halls connecting the buildings were lattices of transparent armour, providing a spectacular view of Zeus rising on the horizon. 'The researchers have quite a show for you.'

'So I heard,' Vladric answered. People on the tram platform crowded closer for a glimpse, only to be shoved aside by the guards. 'There's been a change of plans.'

'We're ready for anything,' Sig assured, as the group stepped into the waiting tram car.

Vladric withdrew into himself as the car accelerated. Sig knew he was troubled but didn't press for an explanation.

After several minutes Vladric finally spoke.

'Do you trust the men in your command?' he asked.

'With my life,' Sig answered.

'As did I,' Vladric said.

'"Did"?'

Vladric smiled weakly as the tram zipped underground.

'We've been compromised,' he said.

Sig's heart sank.

'Who?' he asked. 'How bad?'

'Two fleet commanders, both with deep knowledge of the Plan.'

Sig nearly flinched as the tram rattled a bit.

'Were they mine?'

'No,' Vladric assured. 'I doubt you've ever met them.'

Sig could barely hide his relief.

'Then who were they?'

'It's unimportant,' Vladric muttered. 'They've been dealt with.'

The Ceti leader demanded that everyone who signed onto the Plan had to be willing to die for it. As it was, the odds of surviving an attack on the most powerful ship ever built weren't good to begin with.

'What did they disclose?'

'Our true numbers, and that we mean to attack the *Archangel* in port,' Vladric said. 'So much for surprise.'

'Can we launch earlier?'

'That depends on what your scientists have to show,' Vladric said.

The Orionis government had approved funding for the Archangel project almost a century earlier. Its goal was to continue the Genesis mission by constructing a mothership capable of reaching Tau Ceti. At 21 light years away, the system held the only other known habitable world for humankind, and was the presumed settlement location of the original Tau Genesis colonists. The difference now was the real chance of encountering hostile alien civilisations, notably the Raothri. While people generally agreed on the importance of reuniting the last of Earth's survivors, many believed it was beyond reach, and considered the *Archangel* a costly waste of valuable resources.

Building a ship that could withstand a Raothri attack was impossible. Yet the Navy argued that by the time the *Archangel* was ready to launch, human weapons and defence technology would have progressed enough to give the ship a fighting chance – at least against the capabilities the Raothri were known to possess when they took Earth.

Or so the rationale went. At first, the practical result of this theory was the biggest arms race since the Third World War, in which corporations used the *Archangel* as a test bed for new technologies that quadrupled construction costs. Many believed the money would have been better spent fortifying Inner Rim settlements and expanding central governance to the

Belt. It was the most contentious political issue of a generation, almost as divisive as the One Child rule imposed by the Orionis government.

But the Battle of Brotherhood silenced the debate. The Navy's inability to enforce Orionis law in the Outer Rim changed the *Archangel's* mission. Instead of constructing a mothership to reunite humanity, Orionis was building a weapon that would cast a long shadow over the entire system.

'You think they'll attack us first?' asked Sig.

Vladric's eyes answered the question.

'We will take that ship,' he said, 'or die trying.'

Slowing its breakneck speed, the tram approached the platform of Delta Lab. The sprawling facility was sixteen hundred metres beneath the surface, built inside an ancient magma chamber. This was the heart of Ceti's research and development; it was also where most of the narcotics it sold were manufactured. Long assembly warehouses crewed by men and machines loomed beside the group as they exited the tram; many of the captains charged with hauling the product to distributors hovered nearby, supervising how the contraband was packaged before being stowed on their ships.

One of them broke away from his companions and began marching directly towards Vladric. The guards quickly intercepted, but he persisted.

'Commander Mors, may I have a word?' he said.

'Mind your tone and stand aside,' Sig snapped, catching a faint whiff of alcohol.

Vladric raised a hand.

'What's your name, *captain*?' he said.

'Lazrel, sir,' the dishevelled man said. Desperation was in his eyes. 'Atticus Lazrel.'

Sig would have warned that this was a bad time, but it was too late.

'Well, Captain Lazrel,' Vladric said. 'How can I help you?'

'Sir, I've served Ceti for years,' Atticus said. 'I've never questioned anything asked of me. Not until now.'

'What have we asked that imposes such a burden?'

Released by the guards, Atticus straightened up.

'There's a food convoy en route to Ironbound Prospect,' he said. 'I've been given orders to raid it.'

The Prospect was an asteroid colony on the Inner Rim side of the Belt. Although Navy patrols generally thinned the further one travelled from Eileithyia, any sortie inside the Belt was risky. The burn time from Zeus to Hera was three weeks; the return trip could take twice as long, depending on what was stolen and how much fuel remained. If Atticus Lazrel was instructed to target this convoy, it was either because he was a highly skilled captain, or because his commanding officer was intentionally setting him up to fail.

Sig had a strong suspicion it was the latter.

'Ironbound,' Vladric began, 'is the property of Merckon Industries, correct?'

'Yes, sir,' Atticus said. 'They get three shipments per year. The first was lost to privateers, the second to engine failure. I've been ordered to take the third … Ironbound can't produce its own food. I have family there. They've been rationing for weeks and will starve if that shipment doesn't get through.'

Atticus waited for sympathy.

'Sir, my *firstborn* is there,' he implored. 'Vladric, please.'

Sig held his breath.

'You realise those supplies are needed here,' Vladric said, without a single trace of emotion. 'And that Merckon refuses to negotiate a trade agreement with us?'

'They can't resupply,' Atticus insisted. 'That should be enough reason to consider other options.'

A smile surfaced beneath Vladric's blank stare.

'You see, Sig?' he said. 'Do you trust the men in your command?'

'With my life,' Sig repeated.

'Would you trust this one?'

'No,' Sig answered.

Vladric turned his glare back to Atticus.

'Don't despair, Captain,' he said. 'We'll bring your family here, and share their firstborn food with us ghosts as well.'

Atticus looked relieved.

'Thank you, Command—'

'I'll also send more firepower to ensure our victory and the safe transport of your loved ones to Brotherhood, where they will begin their new lives with Ceti – after you've been executed for treason.'

28

The blood drained from the man's face.

'*What?*'

Sig nodded towards the guards. Two of them forced Atticus's arms behind his back.

'I was trying to help my family!'

'You've had the means to help them for some time,' Vladric growled. 'Since you can't, I will.'

'Then I'll raid the convoy!' Atticus protested. I'll do what you—'

'A Ceti captain follows orders without question,' Vladric said. 'He finds a way to honour his duty to family and our brotherhood.'

'Please, I beg your forgiveness—'

Vladric's face turned from indifference to anger.

'Governor Lareck!' he snarled. 'Get this traitor out of my sight before I kill him myself. Seize his funds and property. The ship is ours, the rest belongs to his children.'

Sig glared at Atticus, who was now sobbing.

'Guards,' Sig said quietly.

It was best never to look back. Bystanders, even the few who might have been searching for the courage to intervene, all returned to their business as the guards dragged Atticus back towards the tram platform.

Sig knew that word of his sentence would spread quickly.

'"Ready for anything", eh?' Vladric sneered, marching towards the lab. 'Not with cowards like that in our ranks. Root them out *now*, Sig. It'll make all the difference in this fight.'

Dr Ilya Tallendin, the chief researcher in Ceti's weapons division, emerged from the main entrance to the complex.

'Welcome, Commander,' he said, giving the salute. 'You're just in time.'

'That implies good news,' Vladric said.

'Oh, it is,' Ilya replied, leading them inside. 'Right this way, please.'

The weapons lab hall was an enormous cavern burrowed deep beneath the magma chamber itself. Dr Tallendin led them to an observation deck that ringed the highest elevations within; the bottom was nearly two hundred metres down and sectioned into staging areas crowded with heavy machinery. The scientists working inside wore survival suits, as the environment mimicked a pristine vacuum, with temperatures well below freezing.

On one side of the cavern floor, Sig recognised the menacing contours of a frigate's railgun; its turret was securely bolted into the rock. Opposite, just fifty metres away, was a segment of ship armour.

Dr Tallendin cleared his throat.

'For this test, we're using an authentic Navy MK50 railgun, and firing it from point-blank range into the same plating used on most Ceti corvettes. The MK50 fires a slug at speeds in excess of eight kilometres per second, presenting a kinetic energy challenge, or more specifically the amount of force transferred at the point of impact, which is the output of mass times velocity—'

'Move along,' Sig interrupted.

'Right. Quantum particles attain their mass through interactions with the Higgs field, "absorbing" mass via the Higgs boson. We sought to block that interaction, by either preventing the absorption itself, or by cancelling the field oscillations. As it turns out, there was a third way to—'

'Ilya ...' Sig warned.

'We can reduce the mass of any projectiles that travel through our shield barrier by at least ninety-five per cent,' the doctor said.

Sig felt his jaw drop.

'Ninety-five?' he repeated.

'That's correct,' the doctor said, looking towards the cavern floor. The scientists working within had exited, and yellow warning lights were ablaze in the test area. 'We may be able to increase that somewhat, but not much further—'

'Show me,' Vladric demanded.

'As you wish,' the doctor said.

After a few moments, Sig thought the lab had exploded. A fireball erupted from the railgun which engulfed the target, and from that range the armour plate should have been obliterated. Instead, a sizable dent crowned the crosshairs painted onto it, and the slug itself had broken into countless white-hot fragments.

'How ...?' Sig asked, incredulous. Vladric remained motionless throughout, his face impassive.

'The round which struck the target had only five per cent of the mass it had when it left that railgun,' Dr Tallendin explained. 'Standard tungsten-based alloys with carbon nanotube layering can withstand the reduced kinetic energy transferred at impact.'

'How long can you hold that shield up?' Vladric asked.

'The energy cost is low, but it takes some time for resonance generation to recover from impact,' the doctor answered. 'Unfortunately, the degradation penalty is high, to the order of thirty per cent per second or so.'

'So three seconds to fully recover from a direct hit?' Sig clarified.

'From an inert round, yes. And explosive warheads will still detonate on contact with the shield barrier. But with the MK50's low rate of fire, the odds of successive rounds striking the same location during combat are very low, assuming the Navy doesn't know how this defensive system works.'

'They don't know,' Vladric interjected. 'How soon can you equip the fleet with this?'

Dr Tallendin looked at him as though he were kidding, which Sig could tell he regretted almost immediately.

'The *fleet*?' he croaked. 'I can deliver a corvette or two with the equipment we have here, but setting up a manufacturing line for the generators would take—'

'I'll give you *total* control of Ceti's resources to make this happen as soon as possible,' Vladric said.

Dr Tallendin was sceptical.

'I am honoured, but ...'

'Ceti's shipyards, Lethe's mines, the Belt's labs, every ship in our fleet, every manufacturing plant we have, and my personal word to procure anything else you need,' Vladric insisted. 'All you'd have to do is ask.'

Sig knew nothing of the technology, other than the fact it had been stolen. But the corporations that built up Lethe had done so with a mega-industrial output in mind, and Ceti had managed to attract smart people who knew how to use its infrastructure to maximum effect.

'I'll find a way,' Dr Tallendin finally said.

'Now that's an attitude I can admire,' Vladric said. 'Succeed, and you'll keep some of the power I'm giving you now to make this work.'

Dr Tallendin knew better than to ask the price of failure.

31

5

VIOLA

There was white water on the Danube this morning, and Viola had to push herself to keep pace with its swift current. She raced off the pathway marked for joggers and into the brush parallel to the river, vaulting over and under obstacles that had once left her bloody. As much as she loved the challenge, it was the sound of the running, churning water that invigorated her most. There were few places like this, and soon it would be truly unique in Orionis. The station engineers had warned residents about the speedier currents as a consequence of a larger eco-engineering effort to introduce fish stocks, a first since the colonisation of Orionis.

The 'Danube River', named after its ancient ancestor, ran through the entire nineteen-kilometre circumference of the torus-shaped station Luminosity. It wound through forests, orchards, and grass-lands grown from original seeds and reconstructed genotypes that had arrived with the *Tabit Genesis* in 2638. Viola felt a surge of invigoration as she leapt over a rock outcrop, propelling herself even faster through the course. The air was thick with scents of natural vegetation growth and decay, so unlike the scrubbed, sterile gas of most ships and stations.

Curving far ahead and above her, she could see a radiant beam of reflected sunlight illuminating the darkness beyond. Were there such a thing as paradise, it would look like this. Bounding through a small stream, Viola relished the splashing of water beneath her soles, knowing it would be some time before she felt it again. Such was the price of curiosity.

For today she would begin a comprehensive study of the Arkady species on Zeus, under the sponsorship and supervision of Merckon Industries.

This could well be the greatest day of her professional career. It had started well – her morning run had been exhilarating. But on approaching her flat, Viola saw her father waiting at the front door.

The sight of him made her bliss evaporate.

'What was your time?' he called out.

She glanced at her watch.

'Twenty-nine minutes.'

The course was ten kilometres long. A personal best.

Her father, Dr Klaus Silveri, was unimpressed.

'*And* twenty-eight seconds,' he added. 'A pathetic effort by any measure.'

It was just past 0600. Viola knew why he was there, and decided she would pretend he wasn't.

'I'm going to be late,' she muttered, walking past him. Dressed in colonial highborn attire, her father's back was straight as iron, and ancient lines etched a permanent scowl upon his face.

'Are you surprised I'm here?' he asked, following her inside.

'I'd be pleasantly surprised if you left without another word,' she answered, shedding her shirt.

'Manners, child,' her father scolded. 'I wanted to tell you—'

'Excuse me?' she interrupted, motioning for privacy. Glaring at her, he slowly turned as she began removing the rest of her soaked garments, letting them drop onto the floor. Completely bare, she took a protein drink from the kitchen and made her way to the shower.

Klaus followed and stood right outside the bathroom door.

'I wanted to offer my congratulations,' he said. 'This is an honour for the Silveri name. You make me so proud.'

Viola was practised at ignoring his bitter sarcasm. Gulping the sustenance down, she relaxed for a moment under the gush of water, willing her body temperature to cool.

'That's kind of you,' she said, throwing open the shower doors. Viola locked onto his cold, grey eyes to make sure they didn't wander. 'Out of my way.'

Drying off quickly, she picked a maroon-coloured business skirt, opting against anything too revealing. The collar was high and oversized, but the rest was snug enough to flaunt her athleticism. Disregarding the impatient tapping of Klaus, she inspected the cut on her knee, which she had opened up a day earlier on the same running course. What had been a deep, serrated gash was now almost completely healed. The people of Orionis had regenerative powers far more robust than their ancestors, but her firstborn genetic modifications gave her even more of an advantage.

'Since I know you won't listen to reason,' her father said, inspecting her final appearance, 'I've come to warn you instead.'

Viola's grandparents, Drs Thieron and Alexia Silveri, had been bio-engineers aboard the *Tabit Genesis,* tasked with maintaining the 'slush tanks' that stations and long-range ships could not function without. The tanks were an essential component of a microbe-driven distilling system that dissolved organic compounds into reusable components. For every form of human waste – septic, manufactured, even toxins – a microorganism could be engineered to transform it into fuel for another process that was useful to man. The journey from Sol to Orionis took three decades, and the thousands of slush pits the Silveris had maintained did as much to keep the *Tabit*'s passengers alive as the hulls separating them from the vacuum of space.

'*Another* warning?' Viola dismissed, adding some eyeliner. 'Sounds serious.'

'I never discouraged your interest in exobiology because, quite frankly, I underestimated your passion for it,' Klaus said, raising his chin. 'Had I known you would take it this far, I would have derailed your ambition much sooner.'

Viola never planned on telling him about her commitment to Merckon Industries. As a man with deep corporate connections, he would inevitably find out. But the longer the secret was kept, the less he could do about it. Or so she hoped.

Abandoning her make-up, she started for the door.

Klaus intercepted her. Her physique was much more imposing than that of the 164-year-old man in her path. Yet she stood paralysed in the space between them.

'I say that because I'm more interested in your preservation than your career,' he said, looking up at her. 'I don't mean to understate your accomplishments, but let's be honest: genetically speaking, you

34

are *perfect*. All the challenges most people struggle with you conquer with ease. Your success was never in doubt. Not until now. I do fear you're on the wrong path.'

Viola stepped around him.

'I'll try not to let you down,' she said, walking outdoors. The commuter platform was just half a kilometre away, but Klaus stayed right on her heels.

Viola's late grandparents were pioneering biologists who had ensured mankind's survival by passing their expertise on to the first generation of humans to be born beyond Earth.

Hydroponically-grown food was the only sustenance for the original Tabit settlers, and their lifespans averaged 120 years of age. Population limits were tied to agricultural yield and the scarce availability of living space. In anticipation of this, the male voyagers of the *Tabit Genesis* had their seed frozen and were all sterilised before their journey from Earth began. But a gene bank containing a diverse genetic sampling of the human population was also brought with them.

When the Tabit settlers finished building the second torus ring about the spine of the *Tabit Genesis*, the first sweeping act to expand the human population was passed: 'One Child.' Females were encouraged to birth a single offspring via a government-supervised in vitro fertilisation pregnancy, using either pre-approved genetics from the bank, or any partner from the Tabit.

The original Firstborns thus came into the world, and among them was Klaus Silveri. One decade later, fate would steer his path to an original Tabit settler – or "highborn," as they were known today – by the name of Mace Merckon, founder of the corporation that bore his name.

Viola lengthened her stride, glancing about to see who was witnessing the spectacle of her father giving chase.

'Why are you giving your talents to commercial interests?' he demanded loudly. 'For generations, we have pursued science essential for the survival of mankind. Where do the Arkady fit into that?'

Other commuters were making their way to the platform. She focused on the gardens alongside the pathway, glittering beneath a veil of mist, distracted momentarily by their beauty.

But Klaus was relentless.

'They're *pests*, Viola,' he spat. 'The entomological equivalent of roaches. What possible good can come from this?'

'I'd have to study them first to answer that,' she said.

He grabbed her hand, and she stopped.

'And what if there *is* no good?' he challenged. 'Have you considered that? Are you that selfish?'

Viola felt her cheeks redden.

'*Please* not here—'

'Our generations have never walked the surface of a world without a mask,' he scolded, 'and you're fixated on gas giants? Viola! What are you doing to help bring us *home*?'

Of all things, *dirt* was the product that launched Merckon's fortunes. In Orionis, topsoil was among the most precious substances known to man, without which it would be almost impossible to grow the seeds brought from Earth. The fate of Eileithyia left the Orionis colony with none, and the sustainability of the population was endangered. Klaus Silveri made his own topsoil from crushed asteroid regolith, supplemented with organic waste from the *Tabit* and seeded with microorganisms grown in its slush tanks.

From the lush ecosystems built into stations like *Luminosity* to the orbital farms that produced food for millions, Merckon soil or slush pits were nearby, and both were the brainchild of the Silveri family.

Viola wanted to respond, but Klaus continued his rant.

'Travis Mareck only wants to know if zenomorphs can make him money,' he continued, referring to the Merckon CEO. 'He couldn't give a damn about the science. Did you consider that?'

Viola drew in a deep breath.

'Merckon is one of the few powers that can fund a study like this,' she said calmly. 'They own several rigs and have the means to protect—'

'Nobody owns anything past the Belt!' Klaus scoffed. 'Not with Ceti scum prowling about. More to the point, this isn't science. It's greed.'

'There was a time when you would have called it "capitalism",' she growled, resuming her walk.

Viola had begun working for Merckon when she was just twelve, the usual path for someone with firstborn lineage. Specialising in microbiology, she effected numerous improvements to the same agri-cultural and waste reprocessing technologies that made Merckon its billions. Her obsession with the Arkady began with a passing fancy; a random conversation she overheard about the miners of Zeus, and the strange tales many believed were the fables of delusional, sick men. Upon discovering that the alien life forms were real, she devoted every moment of her spare time to learning more about them.

But she knew how the funding game was played, and her father was right to challenge her on the ethics of her decision. Her proposal was light on language describing her personal fascination with the creatures, and heavy with verbiage on how they represented a potential goldmine of undiscovered advancements in everything from bioengineering to materials science.

'An academic grant is one thing,' Klaus insisted. 'That at least keeps the findings transparent. This is entirely different. What you discover, should there be anything, belongs to Travis Mareck. You know he won't use them for anything beyond his own benefit, let alone the greater good. Viola, what's happened to you? I didn't raise you to think like this!'

Viola hoped her father would desist before they reached the plat-form entrance. But she had no such luck, and Klaus stayed with her as she walked inside.

'I suppose it's asking too much to just trust me,' she said, marching into the elevator. Klaus made a scene of not allowing another hurrying resident in as the doors shut. They were alone, and he stood much closer to her than necessary.

'Viola,' he said. 'I admit there were times when I pushed you too far. I did it to prepare you for many things, but not for this. Please listen: you do not understand what you've gotten yourself into.'

She chose to look past him, watching the landscape fall away as the elevator ascended higher and higher. A moment of disorientation passed as they reached the station's central hub, where she could feel the gravity reduce.

'Travis Mareck is ruthless,' Klaus warned. 'He'll never let you leave Merckon. You know he'll send you to Zeus, and you cannot control when – if ever – you return.'

The lift stopped, and the doors opened at the shuttle bay level. Her personal craft, a sleek new Legatta RX model, was latched in dry dock directly across the platform.

'This is my choice,' she said.

Viola left without looking back. And this time, Klaus didn't follow her.

'Then remember everything I taught you,' he called out. 'Protect yourself always.'

According to the latest census, there were 1.8 spacecraft for every registered human being in the Orionis Colony. That meant there were approximately 36 *million* of them darting about the Inner Rim, and at present it seemed like they were all converging on Merckon Prime. Civilian ships – everything from high performance shuttles like Viola's Legatta to mining skiffs resembling insects – were cramming the flight pattern for the main station hangar. From kilometres away, freighters with their distinctive modular shipping containers lumbered towards ports connected by cable to the main station. A pair of Navy frigates, resplendent in their white reflective plate, sat idly outside the station as military police corvettes with flashing blue lights patrolled the lanes to keep everyone on course.

As much as the Legatta flew itself, Viola alternated between cursing at the congestion – this was *space*, after all – and losing herself in thoughts about the Arkady. The species took its name after the Helium-3 prospector Arkady Vostov, the highborn who had first encountered them more than a century ago, when the first mining expedition sent by the *Tabit* dropped its cables into the Zeus atmosphere. The urgency of building a reliable energy pipeline for the Inner Rim colonies had left little room for scientific expeditions, and so the alien species had remained an enigma all this time.

As the gaping hangar bay of Merckon Prime filled her view, Viola wondered what it must be like to see them up close. Her father was right: to unravel the mysteries of the Arkady, a journey to the gas giant was inevitable. There was little more to learn from the frozen fragments of specimens that miners returned to the Inner Rim with.

Soaring past the outer barrier, the Legatta turned toward a cluster of long, half-transparent columns jutting out from the bay walls. Each was lined with docking collars set at even intervals, with groups desig-nated for different shuttle classes. Almost every one was occupied, and even more craft were taxiing in behind her. As the autopilot rotated the craft to align with an empty spot, she noticed an older woman in busi-ness attire waiting for her near the airlock. Short and sturdy-looking, she wore a Merckon ID badge, and her jet-black hair was slicked into dreads fastened to her broad shoulders.

Viola glanced at a mirror one last time, then activated the hatch. As it rushed open, the woman thrust her hand inside.

'Dr Silveri,' she said. Her eyes were vacant and cold. 'I'm Mighan, your new assistant.'

Viola took her hand firmly.

'Hello, Mighan, nice to meet—'

'Right this way please,' Mighan interrupted, stepping aside and leading with a hand towards the dock tram. 'Mr Mareck is waiting for you.'

Viola's heart skipped a beat, although she was becoming annoyed with the curt demeanour of her new 'assistant'.

'What else is on the agenda?' she asked, as the tram began racing towards the main concourse.

Mighan seemed completely uninterested in making conversation.

'After your meeting with Mr Mareck, you have a blood transfusion scheduled for 0900. At 1100, the CFO wants to discuss your budget proposal. You're expected to begin your work immediately after.'

The tram slowed inside the main concourse. Like Luminosity, Merckon Prime was a Stanford torus design, only instead of orchards and rivers there were buildings and avenues, with the occasional tree or garden to break the arch of city blocks curving high overhead. Three of the station's four district arcologies were Merckon property; much of the corporation's manufacturing capacity and business operations was located here. The fourth district was devoted entirely to housing, and was where many of the company's employees lived. The tram had taken her directly to Merckon Centre, the tallest building in the station; its ornate pinnacle nearly reached the central hub. Towering waterfalls cascaded down either side of the stairs leading up to the main entrance, where a statue of Mace Merckon stood.

Everywhere Viola looked, people hurried about. Men in suits discussed projects with engineers dressed in sterile scrubs and EVA gear. A teacher led a group of young pupils away from the platform, as more tram cars filled with commuters arrived. Pairs of security guards milled through the crowds, offering friendly greetings and the occasional direction. As the door opened, a series of personalised advertisements for cosmetics and shuttle craft appeared in mid-air; Mighan marched right through them, motioning for Viola to hurry.

By the time they reached the top steps, the Merckon assistant was laboring with breath but still pressed on urgently. The lobby was an arboretum; lush vegetation hung from sculpted containers suspended at varying heights from the ceiling. They had just reached the glass elevators when a voice called out from behind them.

'Dr Silveri?'

Viola turned to find a familiar face that always took a moment to process. Wegan Lark, a maintenance administrator whose sole responsibility was to keep the Merckon facility clean, had set aside his equipment to speak with her. He was a mutant, and a severely disfigured one. Old Wegan had spent his better years aboard a gas harvester orbiting Zeus, and all that belt radiation awoke the dormant cancers within him. Boils the size of lemons deformed his brow, pushing his eyes apart from one another. If not for the blood transfusions and gene therapy that every firstborn was entitled to, he would have died long ago.

He went out of his way to greet Viola every day, and she thought him very sweet and kind.

'Good morning, Wegan!' she beamed. It was difficult to know which of his eyes to address.

'I heard about your promotion,' Wegan muttered, with a hint of sadness. 'I just wanted to wish you the best of luck.'

Viola flushed with appreciation.

'Aw, thank you!' she said. 'Don't worry, I'll still—'

'Stop wasting your breath on him,' Mighan interrupted. 'Keep moving.'

Viola shot her a glance that might have pierced steel, and Wegan slunk away.

'If Mr Mareck learns you were late because you felt a mutant's time was more important than his, it won't bode well for you,' Mighan warned, her arm extended. 'This way, please.'

Wegan didn't dare turn back. Mutants were never treated well, but this was outrageous. Viola held her tongue, but by the time they reached the elevator, she could no longer restrain herself.

'Mighan, what exactly is your problem?' she fumed, as the car rocketed up. 'Your attitude is completely unacceptable, and it needs to change right now.'

Viola waited for a response, but none came. The elevator came to rest and Mighan stared at her, expressionless, for a few long moments.

'This way, please,' she said, as the doors opened. 'Mr Mareck is waiting.'

Viola's temper was ready to boil over when a man's deep voice rang out.

'Dr Silveri,' Travis Mareck said, stepping in front of them. Tall and muscular, he wore a beige-coloured, tight-fitting sweater that exposed much of his neck and chest, and charcoal slacks made from fine linen. His eyes were light green with flecks of grey in them, and they were blatantly drinking her in.

'Mighan's role is to supervise and assist your production of zeno-morph research,' he said. 'She reports to you but answers to me. Her small talk is awful but you'll find her more than capable. Will that be a problem?'

His eyes never left hers as, cautiously, Viola took his hand.

'No, sir,' she said.

'Good. That suit isn't flattering,' he said, 'though it's more inter-esting than the lab scrubs you usually wear. Let's see your new office.'

Despite being a household name in Orionis, few people had ever seen Travis Mareck in person. Until now, Viola had considered herself fortu-nate for the privilege. But there was an allure to him that transcended the simple fact that he was extremely powerful. He was presenting her with a different sort of challenge, she realised, and that provoked her own competitiveness. A mix of ancient ethnicities predating the forma-tion of UNSEC flowed through his veins; he was as close to a living, breathing person of Earth as it was genetically possible to achieve.

To some, that made him a god. Most people saw huge projections of him on virtual adverts or speaking on the news net, metastasising his larger-than-life stature. Somehow he seemed even more magnificent – and pathetic – in person.

Mighan was first into the office, which struck Viola as under-whelming. It offered an impressive view of the curving cityscape, but little else; a burgundy-coloured desk and an ergonomic chair were the only furnishings.

'I know what you're thinking,' Travis said. 'But looks are deceiving.'

Mighan stood behind the desk, and with a subtle hand movement raised a volumetric display. Then the room erupted with more of them. There was barely anywhere left to stand that wasn't awash in imagery or data.

'Welcome to your virtual lab,' he said, sitting casually on the desk. 'Everything you could possibly need to perform your work is located right here, in this room. And if we've missed anything, Mighan will take care of it in short order, isn't that right?'

'Yes, Mr Mareck,' she answered.

'What about working with physical samples?' Viola asked.

'Also done from here,' Travis said. 'Your lab clearance was revoked. From now on, a machine will hold the scalpels for you.'

Viola was taken aback.

'Revoked?'

Travis flashed a broad smile.

'You represent a large investment for me,' he said, motioning for her to be seated. 'These steps are necessary to protect it. There's been a plague of industrial espionage. In my experience, proactive measures are the best defence.'

As she took her seat, Mighan left the room, and the door shut. Travis shifted so that his legs were just about touching the armrests on her chair.

'I'll be watching you closely,' he said. 'It's for your own good. From here, all your work will be meticulously logged. So I'll never have any reason to suspect you of any mischief that happens, in the lab or anywhere else.'

'I'm grateful for the opportunity,' Viola said, 'I believe very strongly in the potential of this research.'

'As do I' Travis said, checking his immaculate fingernails. 'I've known your father for many years. He's a good man, and I can see the same devotion in you. Both of you have served Merckon well, and for that I am … satisfied. For now.'

The Merckon CEO leaned in closer.

'No doubt he warned you about the sacrifices you'll have to make,' he said, his eyes moving up and down the length of her. 'I'm sure old Klaus left you well equipped to deal with challenges. He always was thorough.'

Viola held his stare for a few moments.

'Thank you, Mr Ma—'

'Travis,' he said, rising as the door to the office opened. 'Just call me Travis. But only when we're alone.'

6

WYLLYM

'Captain Lyons? It's time.'

The words startled Wyllym from a deep, dreamless state, and the sudden movement sent his sleeping bag churning in the microgravity until the restraining tether pulled it taut. He could feel himself being tugged gently towards the bridge; the ship was slowing down.

'You're welcome to the view from up here,' the intercom continued.

'Alright,' he grumbled, unzipping the bag and wrestling out, brushing against other restraints floating in the cabin. The trip to Corinth Naval Yards was a sixteen-hour burn from Tabit Prime, and Wyllym had slept for most of it. Squinting through a weary haze, he spotted his mag greaves clinging to the metal deck, fastened to a small travel case with his personal items. Everything he owned might have fit inside. Other than uniforms, medals for valour and some harsh memories, he had little else to show for his long career in the Orionis Navy.

The Gryphon training regime was a brutal affair, exhausting him and his students to the point of collapse. Even though he resented Admiral Hedricks for calling him to the *Archangel* in person, the respite was welcome. Wyllym's greying hair was cut too short to need combing, and white stubble spread across his gaunt jaw like a dusting of snow. Every bone in his thin, angular frame ached and the whites of his steel-grey eyes were splotched with patches of blood. The flight manoeuvres he led with the Gryphon cadets were taxing enough even once per week, but the stress of multiple sessions per day was literally killing him.

The mere act of pulling his greaves on was painful. But for his own healing abilities and the genetic therapy the Navy administered to speed recovery he could already be dead. Every evasive manoeuvre unleashed crushing G-forces that, depending on the skill of his target, could last for minutes on end. Worse still was having only peripheral awareness of the damage his body was absorbing during the exercises. Only when the helmet was removed, and the Gryphon technology that blocked his brain's ability to process pain was disengaged, did the full agony reveal itself. Most pilots lost consciousness, and all needed to be carried from their craft.

Wyllym swallowed his pride and opted to float towards the bridge instead of walking. He would never let his students see him like this, but here on the ONW *Belgrade*, it made no difference. The crew had been courteous when he boarded, but he had caught their stares and muted conversations. He was the first Gryphon pilot they had ever seen, and not at all what they were expecting.

Reaching for the painkillers that he had abused for too long, he wondered what this crew of privileged firstborns would think of the Gryphons after seeing a few more of their battered pilots. The programme was just one of many curses from the Archangel, and Wyllym had hoped to never board her. But Admiral Vadim Hedricks cared as much for Wyllym's personal preferences as he did for malignant tumours. Wyllym could think of no reason why the Admiral had summoned him in person. At worst, it was showmanship, a pathological need to demonstrate total command over everything.

At best, it was to relieve him of command.

The wishful thought accompanied a burst of narcotic inhalants, sending a rush tingling down Wyllym's spine. His legs floating freely, he pulled himself into a narrow passageway that ran the length of the corvette's centreline. The *Belgrade*'s engineering officer was clomping her way back to the engine room in greaves when Wyllym emerged.

'Ten, hut!' the engineer proclaimed, snapping a crisp salute.

'As you were,' Wyllym mumbled, coasting forward. The young woman opened her mouth to speak, then thought better of it. Wyllym was grateful; he was in no mood to converse but did not want to be rude. He passed by without another word, gliding over the thick bulkhead separating the engine room and its fusion reactor from the main compartments.

The *Belgrade* was a Keating-class corvette, the workhorse of the Orionis Navy fleet. From above, she looked like a long, flat arrowhead; at the end of each of her 'wings' were oversized, cylinder-shaped vectored plasma thrusters that could swivel in almost any direction. She was eighty metres long from bow to stern, and less than half as wide, covered in a quilt of grey and white armour plating all over her hull. Beneath her keel was the main drive, an ion pulse engine that could push her to velocities approaching a quarter of the speed of light. Her smooth contours tapered into the hangar at the stern, large enough to house a boarding tug or a rear-facing point-defence gun turret.

Wyllym remembered when there were just a few of these magnificent ships in existence, long before cruisers or even frigates existed. The Inner Rim was teeming with warships now, and it was near impossible to pass by a station or outpost without seeing one. In Wyllym's mind, Orionis had been better off when there were fewer ships flying around, before men like Vadim Hedricks rose to power.

The corvette was more of an interceptor than anything; excellent at chasing down speedy shuttles or mid-burn heavy freighters and disabling them with virus bombs and mass driver cannons. Maybe it could chase off a few light gunships or another corvette. In those scenarios it came down to the skill of the crew and their pain threshold. Against a frigate, if the captain was very talented and could get in close, she might even last a few minutes.

But if a corvette engaged a Gryphon, she would be obliterated without ever knowing what hit her.

The bridge hatch slid open before Wyllym could knock on it.

'Please.' Captain Yoto Ishiin gestured. 'Take the engineer's seat.'

Like most of the crew compartments, the bridge was crammed into a tight space. Captain Ishiin stood before the projected viewscreen, surrounded by volumetric ship telemetry. There was barely enough room to accommodate his height, and he wasn't an especially tall man. He had Eurasian features; thick, dark, perfectly combed hair, dark narrow eyes and a lean, athletic build. His smooth, cleanly shaven face seemed incapable of growing a beard.

Wyllym lowered himself into the seat as the hatch closed behind him.

'If you don't mind my saying,' Captain Ishiin remarked, taking his chair at the head of the bridge, 'you look like hell.'

Wyllym's eyes did a casual sweep of the instrumentation, absorbing the ship's data without even being fully aware of it. His mind sensed that the *Belgrade* was operating normally, but the ship's velocity was too high for an approach to Corinth. But he decided not to ask questions just yet.

'It's the mileage that gets to you,' Wyllym said, stretching out. 'Not so much the years.'

The *Belgrade* captain regarded him thoughtfully. Judging from his appearance, Wyllym guessed he was three times the man's age.

'The crew would love to speak with you, but I've ordered them to respect your privacy,' Yoto said. 'When they heard you were coming aboard—'

'When they heard *who* was coming aboard?' Wyllym interrupted, deciding he didn't care for the young captain. 'Hedricks warned you not to say.'

'They recognised you at port,' Yoto said, with a slight smile.

'Didn't realise I was famous,' Wyllym grumbled. 'I'll talk to anyone you want, but I can't answer questions about the Gryphons.'

'Oh, they know that,' Yoto said. 'They just want to meet the highest ranking ghost in the Navy.'

Wyllym narrowed his eyes at the man.

From the day it was founded, the Orionis Navy had run a strict firstborns-only culture – until the elected government forced them to allow lowborn recruits. Reluctantly, they accepted, restricting promotions to administrative roles only. Captain Wyllym Lyons, however, had broken down one heritage barrier after another, becoming the first lowborn officer on a combat ship, the first to be awarded a command, the first to record combat kills, and the first to receive Navy medals for valour. But his promotions drew the ire of a culture programmed to mistrust anyone who didn't represent a direct link to Old Earth.

By the time the original wave of firstborns reached adult age, the colony was capable of supporting a much larger population. A third torus had been constructed around the *Tabit Genesis*, and the lunar camps on the Eileithyian moons were now producing their own food. To encourage growth, the Orionis government passed the Heritage Act. Highborns were urged to have more children, and incentivised their eldest sons or daughters to spread out beyond the space now known as Tabit Prime.

Under the new law, the Orionis government guaranteed firstborns and their children access to basic necessities such as food, healthcare, education, and employment as a fundamental right of citizenship. To encourage exploration and development, each was granted access to emerging technology, manufacturing capacity, ships and specialised equipment suited to their area of expertise. This was a debt-free loan: a single chance to wield these assets in the creation of a sustainable enterprise that could help Orionis expand.

The policy was intended to promote the growth of communities, commerce, and self-reliance. Some of the largest corporations now existing began with the Heritage Act in 2665. But even with no restrictions on breeding, the rate of growth was still too slow for ageing highborns who wanted to see a stronger resurgence of the human race. An impassioned plea to repopulate the species was heard throughout Orionis, driving the commitment of scientific resources to find ways to accelerate human reproduction. By 2667, amniosynthesis was created: the ability to grow human embryos to term inside a machine.

The passage of the Amniosynth Charter decreed that the technology and access to the human gene bank of the *Tabit Genesis* be made available to any firstborn on the condition that they demonstrate the means to raise children responsibly and to provide the same basic rights that Heritage granted to firstborn citizens. Some corporations took this charge with great care. Sadly, many others did not. Failed ventures, accidents, and outright neglect or abuse left a generation of amniosynths orphaned, and the resulting humanitarian crisis taxed the resources of Orionis and corporations to breaking point.

Many amniosynths, particularly those created beyond the planet Eris, were born with defects. Without basic rights, they were unable to procure the blood transfusions they needed to recover from the radiation damage sustained by working in space, particularly around Zeus and the Great Belt. The government could not – or would not, depending on the political perspective – amend the Heritage Act to include them. They became known as ghosts: human beings without a true biological mother or father, with neither rights nor place in a society ruled by last living connections to Earth.

But the lowborns fortunate enough to be taken in by noble corporations thrived. Some banded together and formed the first privateer corporations: those with no ties to Orionis, free of government taxes, able to conduct trade with any party they chose.

Wyllym was the third child born to ghosts who owned property on the agricultural moon Peleus, where he spent his childhood in vast subterranean caverns excavated beneath an airless surface. Water drawn from underground streams and reservoirs irrigated crops grown on imported Merckon soil. Sunlight harvested from orbital solar arrays powered artificial illuminators in the caverns below, nourishing the fields and prized livestock commodities that thrived there.

The workdays were long and backbreaking. But Wyllym never complained, and his own aspirations were never more ambitious than to own his own farming outpost someday. His brother Rob was of similar demeanour, a simple man who loved getting his hands dirty. But with the blessings of his parents, his sister Amie sold her share of the business and moved to the Inner Rim to pursue a corporate career in finance; her gift for numbers would have been wasted tilling soil on a Heran moon.

For Wyllym, life on Peleus was fulfilling. And it came to a horrifying end all too soon.

'Where I'm from, the word "ghost" is rude,' Wyllym growled. 'But your ship, your mouth, your rules.'

'My sincerest apologies,' Yoto said, sounding like he meant it. 'Truly, I meant no offence. Forgive my ignorance, but what is the correct way to address—'

'"*People*".' Wyllym glared. 'Human beings who weren't born with privileges. I'm sure that's what you meant.'

'That's what makes your accomplishments all the more impressive,' Yoto said, leaning forward as though fascinated by the musings of a toddler. Wyllym sighed. The crew's order to stay mute didn't apply to the captain, it seemed.

'The competition to make the rank of captain ... how did you ...?'

Wyllym knew he was trying bait him into talking about the Gift.

'By earning it,' he said.

Captain Ishiin was undeterred.

'But *how*, exactly, were you able to defeat so many of your—'

'I was better than all of them at one thing,' Wyllym said.

'Fighting?'

'Teaching,' Wyllym said. 'By taking heritage out of the mix and training my squadron to work as one.'

Captain Ishiin seemed disappointed at first, then his face brightened.

'What was it like, battling Ceti?' he asked. 'At Hera's Deception ... when Brotherhood was lost?'

Wyllym was certain that Captain Ishiin had never fired a weapon outside of a training sim. He had been promoted simply because of the blood in his veins.

'You don't think about fighting for your life,' Wyllym said. 'You just move from one decision to the next.'

Captain Yoto Ishiin frowned as he mulled this answer.

'They say you shot down six Ceti corvettes and many more gunships before ...'

'Before I died?' Wyllym said.

'Yes. Is that true?'

Wyllym had been barely a month into his own command then, patrolling the privateer outposts in the Hera Belt when Ceti descended upon his corvette *Santiago*. They attacked in packs of three, indiscriminately destroying civilian and military targets in the rings. As the Navy rushed to divert ships to Hera, Wyllym battled against odds that should have killed him instantly. Instead, he somehow knew where to manoeuvre the *Santiago* to avoid hull-shattering cannon fire, and he was doing it impossibly faster than any computer.

It was strange enough that he seemed to know what the enemy was going to do before they did themselves. But while he fought, Wyllym declared that the Ceti fleet attacking the Hera outposts was a diversion, and warned Navy Command that Brotherhood Station was in danger even though it was millions of kilometres away.

This was the red flag the Navy was looking for. The telemetry of what

Wyllym Lyons was accomplishing – singlehandedly mauling one Ceti ship after the next – triggered a secret protocol whose urgency exceeded the outcome of the battle itself: the captain of the *Santiago* had to be recovered, dead or alive, because it was clear that he possessed the Gift.

'I remember a rock the size of a frigate tumbling towards me,' Wyllym said. 'Next thing I knew I was in a medbay with a bunch of doctors telling me six months had gone by. They said I died a few times. I have no idea. You'll have to ask them.'

Captain Ishiin shook his head.

'You must possess extraordinary skill,' he said. 'They've never gone through such trouble to bring a man back before.'

'Might wish they hadn't, depending on how the Gryphons turn out,' Wyllym said.

'I doubt that,' Yoto said. 'Is it true your students are all as … *Gifted* as you?'

'It's a classified programme,' Wyllym said. All his students had the Gift, though some used it better than others.

'My crew really does admire you,' Yoto said. 'I confess, I am somewhat envious. There are few enough opportunities for a captain to accomplish what you have.'

'A crew has to respect you before they'll admire you,' Wyllym said.

In spite of the insult, Captain Ishiin smiled pleasantly while the sound of hydraulics and metal gears rumbled through the bridge.

'We're almost there,' he said, strapping on a five-point harness. He flashed one of the belt straps towards Wyllym, gesturing that he should do the same. Then all the seats on the bridge rotated to face the rear of the ship.

'You're accustomed to Gryphon braking manoeuvres,' Captain Ishiin said. 'So this should be no bother.'

Wyllym felt the impulse drive beneath the *Belgrade* ignite, and the bridge instruments indicated the wingtip vectoring thrusters were doing the same: the ship was executing an emergency high-G burndown. With barely enough time to fasten his own straps, unrelenting pressure mashed him into his seat, pushing him to the brink of unconsciousness. Crushing agony stretched seconds into hours and stamped the breath from his lungs; waves of bone-crushing pain tested his will to survive. After what seemed like an eternity, the pressure finally let up.

'I hope that wasn't too unpleasant,' Captain Ishiin announced, as the bridge seats all resumed their forward positions. 'The Navy requires us to perform these burndowns to maintain combat readiness. It couldn't be avoided.'

'I'm ...sure,' Wyllym stammered, as the tunnel vision subsided. Captain Ishiin was slightly out of breath, but appeared no more the worse for wear. A burn that aggressive should have left him incapacitated ... unless the Navy had given him the same genetic augments that kept Gryphon pilots alive for their own combat manoeuvres.

Then it dawned on Wyllym all at once: Admiral Hedricks had insisted on seeing him in person to make the subtle point that neither he nor his Gryphons were that special any more. It was a threat, and Captain Ishiin was the messenger.

'Ah, she's in range,' the captain said. 'Let's look upon her with our own eyes, shall we?'

Shaking, Wyllym unbuckled his straps as segments of armoured plating retreated from the *Belgrade*'s bridge, revealing viewports that offered an unaided view into space. Even from their distant vantage, the *Archangel* was breathtaking and foreboding all at once. Her construction resembled nothing else in the Navy, and for several ethereal moments Wyllym had difficulty believing he was looking at something built by humans.

He had heard about her dimensions: a kilometre longer than the *Tabit Genesis* and nearly twice as wide. Captain Ishiin set the *Belgrade* on wide approach pattern, no doubt so he could admire the beast himself. Every metre of the *Archangel's* hull was a reflective ebony sheen broken only by the glare of construction lamps and navigation beacons. From above, the hull resembled an elongated pentagon with two superstructures cutting through her beam like oversized keels. The front and rear of these structures housed recessed thruster nozzles wide enough to accommodate a cruiser. Her cross-section was hundreds of metres thick, lined with docking bays that could take a frigate aboard. Docking ports for corvettes lined her dorsal and ventral surface areas, with launch and recovery systems for the Gryphons built into the twin superstructures.

But her most startling feature was the four vertical columns rising through the centre of the ship, extending all the way through the decks.

If their endpoints were connected, they would form a perfect cube, at the centre of which was ... nothing. A massive circular gap whose diameter matched the distance between the columns was cut into the main body of the ship. The towering walls lining this gap were buzzing with construction activity; arrays of instruments and machinery ringed the cross sections of unfinished deck levels, the only segment of the ship not doused in black.

As the *Belgrade* closed range, Wyllym scoured the hull for signs of more traditional weapons, like turrets or missile bays. But all he saw was the reflection of engines and welding sparks against the onyx curves of this mysterious ship.

'Magnificent, isn't she?' Captain Ishiin whispered.

Wyllym snorted, motioning towards the four towers.

'Is that the drain for this money sink?'

'Rumour is that's Raothri technology,' Captain Ishiin said.

'Civilians can spread rumours,' Wyllym said. 'Soldiers can be court-martialled for it.'

Captain Ishiin smiled again as the *Belgrade* changed course.

'The people who live there must know the truth,' he said, pointing to the torus-shaped station adjoining the construction yard of the *Archangel*. Within it lived thousands of lowborn employees, all skilled labourers plucked from the general population. Many would spend their entire lives there, building this ship and nothing else, with little to no contact with the outside colony. The station was as finely equipped as any built in Orionis, even Luminosity. They lived more comfortably than most, and in many respects were like the generation that built the *Tabit Genesis* centuries ago.

But to Wyllym, they were slaves in all but name.

'I bet they don't even care,' he muttered.

The captain's expression changed to frustration as the *Belgrade* approached one of the open hangar bays.

'Why do you hate the *Archangel* so much?' he asked.

'Because we could have built a dozen stations or terraformed a moon with what it cost to build this,' Wyllym said. 'For millions of people, this is home. The *Archangel* was never going to bring them all to another system, let alone a new world. We should keep building here.'

'Or we find the right world now, instead of trying to change one that will never be what Earth was,' Captain Ishiin said. 'With the *Archangel*, we can link with the Tau Ceti settlers, build more ships like her and find another pale blue dot to colonise. Who knows? Perhaps someday we can return to Earth—'

'That will never happen,' Wyllym said.

Captain Ishiin looked at him thoughtfully.

'Admiral Hedricks believes it will be possible someday,' he insisted. 'If we had a fleet of *Archangels*, he'd point them—'

Wyllym had heard enough.

'If he thought it'd make him a hero, Hedricks would point a gun at his own mother.'

Captain Ishiin was stunned.

'That's classified, of course.' Wyllym added, fighting through the pain in his limbs to stand. 'Best kept secret in the damn Navy.'

7

THE PATHFINDER

Two gladiators, a man and a woman, clashed in a blaze of combat, unleashing a furious symphony of strikes and parries. Powerful muscles bulged beneath the milky-white flesh of the combatants as they danced, their bare skin exposed to the frigid cold from the waist up, save for the narrow strap that pressed the breasts of the female tightly to her muscular chest. Both combatants were armed only with Obyeran skythes in each hand: part knife, part plasma torch, the indispensable tool of spacefarers for centuries converted to deadly melee weapon.

Worn on the wrists, the skythe was a retractable amorphous alloy blade with an edge of nanoscale-sized teeth that could saw through metal as easily as bone. At the tip of the weapon was a suspended plasma arc designed to cut through wreckage or weld breaches shut; they carved white-hot arcs through the air as the fight raged on. Beneath the armoured hexglass dome high overhead, the crash of weapons sent menacing echoes across the rock amphitheatre; a deep, sizzling shriek that sounded like heavy cloth being ripped apart. The arena basked in soft beams cast down from orbital solar mirrors, each one a sun in the hazy night-time sky, as the bluish-yellow face of the ice giant Heracles gazed down on the spectacle.

Hundreds had journeyed to the surface to attend the match in person, and thousands more were viewing on the local net. The cameras capturing the event split their time between the combatants and the man who sat at the highest seat in the arena: King Masaad Obyeran, the Pathfinder, founder of the House that bore his name. The Rites, revered as they were in this culture, had drawn more eyes than ever before, since the warriors battling today were the King's own son and daughter. To claim a Lightspear command, an Obyeran had to pass the warrior trials, and his children were no exception.

Masaad was old but unwrinkled, his pale flesh stretched across an iron jaw and high cheekbones that held the cradles of his amber-coloured eyes. Beneath his hood was a shock of thick hair, white as snow, long to the sides and back. He sat expressionless, gauntlets gripping each arm of the stone seat, unmoving since the contest began. The cadence of air exiting his mouth in long icy wisps gave the only hint that he was alive. He did not flinch, nor even blink, no matter how hard his children struck one another. He simply held his gaze, watching his bloodied, weary progeny back away from each other, circling, studying, anticipating each other as only twins could do.

It was his son Maez who erred first, feigning a kick and then launching a savage overhand that would have cleaved his sister from neck to crotch. But his daughter Myrha countered with a spinning back-strike, avoiding the blow and meeting the base of her brother's skythe near the ground. The blade sliced clean through his wrist, and both hand and weapon caromed away. Yet even as streams of blood spurted out, he swung his hips and shoulders towards her in a continuous, fluid motion. Now his other skythe had a clear path to her neck, and she had no way to parry or dodge. All she could do was snap up the closest blade towards his heart, and hope it reached there in time.

But The Rites allowed no deaths, and the arena technology linked to their weapons ensured that striking a mortal blow was impossible. Just milliseconds before biting into flesh and artery, the blades vanished back into their sheaths. Blinding spotlights flooded over them as guardians converged to break the siblings apart. The contest was over.

King Masaad exhaled slowly, watching as a medic clamped a clear tube over his son's haemorrhaging stump. When the blood made contact with the gelatinous substance inside, the container filled with pinkish-white foam. Maez grunted in pain, though his pride hurt more than his wound. The same was true of Myrha, who was furious with herself for losing what should have been a decisive victory. According to Obyeran Code, the siblings now shared the honour. Facing the podium, the combat master grasped their wrists, and raised them high overhead.

King Masaad rose slowly, nodding his approval, as those in attendance crossed their fists in the Obyeran salute. The deeds of his son and daughter had been witnessed by all. Maez and Myrha climbed the stairs, steam rising from their bare skin. Both were orders of magnitude stronger than he had ever been. They were perfect creations; the unsurpassable specimens of humanity.

'I am the proudest father who ever lived,' King Masaad said. 'You honour me.'

Guardians placed heavy cloaks over the shoulders of the twins as they approached. Myrha quickly bundled hers up.

Maez turned his away, motioning towards his stump.

'"Honoured?"' he growled.

'The honour is ours, my King,' Myrha said, ignoring her brother and bowing from the hip.

Over two hundred and fifty years of age, Masaad Obyeran was the oldest living survivor of the *Tabit Genesis*. He and his brothers, Al Khav and Alim, had been the founders of Arcwave Technical, an ancient corporation that had helped fund the Genesis project. The signature achievement of Masaad, a renowned nuclear physicist, was the invention of scalable aneutronic power. All industrialised machinery, from exomech suits to the *Archangel*, used Obyeran technology to produce energy. The breakthrough is considered the most critical enabler of sustainable habitats beyond the mothership and the human exploration of Orionis.

But thirty years after his arrival, Masaad, his wife Lyanna, and his brothers vanished from civilisation. They reappeared another three decades later, reborn as the self-appointed rulers of the icy moons of Heracles. Their settlement remained the most remote in the system, located some five billion kilometres from Tabit Prime. Masaad and Lyanna declared their independence from the Orionis government, stating themselves free both of rights and obligations to the colony.

House Obyeran was thus born, then just several dozen followers strong. The brothers established a dynasty by leapfrogging through time, entering hypersleep for decades on end as one brother after the next carried forward their mandate to build a culture free from the corruption of Orionis. Masaad ruled from the inception of their House in 2701 until the reign of Al Khav began in 2731; thirty years later, the reign of Alim began. Through it all, Masaad and his beloved Lyanna slept for sixty years, their lives entrusted to technology that placed their bodies in deep hibernation, slowing their metabolisms to a standstill.

King Masaad was now eighteen years into his second reign. All the brothers were loved, but Masaad's return was heralded the most by the citizens. Al Khav was generous and a fearless warrior, but he lacked Masaad's charisma. Alim was a brilliant strategist, but was known more for his temper than his intellect. Together they both deserved just as much credit for the colony's prosperity as Masaad himself. But there was only one Pathfinder. And of the three brothers, only Masaad had taken a wife.

Every Obyeran knew that this contest between his children had become important for more reasons than just a mere starship command.

'Call me "Father",' Masaad addressed Myrha. 'Lightspear captains or not, you are my daughter and son. You both achieved your goal, no matter the cost. Even in death, you were both victorious. That is the Obyeran way.'

'I'm not proud of my performance,' Myrha muttered. 'You fought well, brother.'

'Have you named your spear yet?' Maez asked, as the medic checked the tube covering his stump. The device would keep the nerve endings, bones, and tendons nourished and free of infection. A new hand would be grown in bioreactors and reattached within a month. '*Vindictive Bitch* seems fitting.'

Masaad had watched his son dominate every opponent in every contest, physical or mental, during The Rites, remaining almost blasé throughout. The same was true of his daughter, though she made less a show of it.

'The Rites reveal weakness,' Masaad said. 'She exposed yours as no one else could.'

'Think it's worth losing a limb over?' Maez asked, flexing his formidable arm at the elbow. The medic left without a word. 'I suppose I'm fortunate to have kept my head.'

'With one arm you proved your strength beyond measure,' Masaad said. 'Most would have crumbled, but you recovered and salvaged victory – a costly one, but victory nonetheless. Men will follow you, son. The House was witness. A limb is nothing for the respect you've earned.'

'I took his skythe,' Myrha brooded. 'I should have won outright. What does that prove?'

'You were flawless, right until the end,' Masaad said, placing an arm around her waist. Her shoulders were too high for him to reach. 'Strong as you are, no one expected you to win this contest. Yet you remained valiant.'

'My "victory" would have cost more lives than my own,' she said.

'That is true,' Masaad said. 'A desperate enemy can summon great force in a final bid to save himself. The Rites have taught you to never relinquish, not until the outcome is certain. Be thankful you learned that lesson here, and not in real combat.'

'Yes, now she'll lop off a man's cock to win an argument,' Maez sneered. 'They'll be queuing up to serve on your command.'

'Next time I'll take both his hands,' Myrha growled.

'You won't have another chance,' Masaad said. 'From here on, you will both fight as one.'

'I'm not so sure,' Maez said. 'Seems our lady Obyeran forgets we're siblings.'

'Seems you're only half a sibling now,' Myrha quipped.

Maez smiled, as he always did when he was enraged.

'Sweet sister,' he said, 'if not for the safeties, there would be no *heiress* now.'

'*Maez*,' Masaad blared, loud enough to make the guards flinch. 'Mind your words.'

'Did that offend you?' Maez asked, turning his towering frame to look down upon his father. 'Tell me, what if I had done the maiming? Would you be carrying on about how she learned something important then?'

'Stop it,' Myrha demanded.

'No,' Maez said, holding his father's glare. 'I don't think you would.'

He turned and walked away, towards the tunnel leading into the throne catacombs beneath the surface.

'His pride will get him killed someday,' Myrha muttered. 'I shouldn't have provoked him.'

'Three minutes,' Masaad fumed. 'Three minutes separated your births, and you would think it was three decades.'

'He's still twice the man of anyone else,' she said.

'He needed to be humbled,' Masaad scoffed. 'I knew this would bring out the worst in him.'

'Precisely what The Rites are for,' she said, 'I have no regrets.'

Long shadows followed the pair as they moved from the arena grounds. The landscape beyond the dome was barren, serene and mystical; a soft glow fell over the icy mountains, valleys and canyons, all glistening from the heat of the orbital mirrors. Works of art cut from the native rock jutted from the surface, lining Strength's Path like ghostly giants; a crowd wearing survival suits had ventured beyond the safety of the dome and gathered around the work entitled Creation, depicting the old gods suffering at the hands of the Raothri; forbidding stone effigies of Christ, Buddha, and Mohammed shielded themselves from the four-winged demon towering above them, reaching down to take Earth.

The population of native Obyerans numbered just under forty thousand, yet they produced the industrial output of a colony ten times its size. Their pale, tall, muscular physique was unique to their genetically engineered amniosynth bloodline, a stark contrast against the diverse privateer population living among them. Many of those outsiders were staying over from voyages that took years to complete. Trade, the colony's only connection to Orionis, was as much for information as goods. House Obyeran worked only with reputable privateers, refusing all business with Inner Rim corporations and cartels. Freighters arrived with ores, soil, Helium-3, and some manufactured goods like armoured glass and thruster modules. They left with Obyeran fusion cores, carbon nanotube cables, some luxury foodstuffs, and solar production technology.

But the real power of House Obyeran came from her fleet, which boasted none of the heavy warships that the Orionis Navy favoured so much. Instead, Masaad Obyeran had created the Lightspear. By itself, the corvette-sized starship was a technological marvel, built for resilience and adaptability. It could fly for a limited time without electronics; the ship's vectoring engine pylons could be manoeuvred manually from the inside, and its Obyeran microfusion cores, unjammable in their dormant states, could provide thrust and power if need be. Redundancies were built into layers that accounted for almost any contingency; every Lightspear was built to serve a mothership's mission.

Most importantly, the Lightspears were modular complements of each other. Two or more could physically link together, combining resources to serve a single purpose; to multiply engine thrust to push a disabled freighter, or to compartmentalise the functions of a larger starship to travel great distances; to fight as a single weapon; or to pool their manufacturing capability to repair a crippled ship more quickly.

Lightspear captains were required to be just as versatile as the vessels they commanded. Competition among native Obyerans to become crewmembers began in academies that pushed their genetically enhanced mental and physical endurance to its absolute limits, and those who persevered attained a near spiritual devotion to their ships. This competition was called The Rites. At the beginning of the programme, a cadet was introduced to the ship they would later call their own – if they passed. They trained with the vessel, learned her inside out, and by graduation every crewmember could operate every part of her, just as her modular design required.

A Lightspear was crewed by just seven, and The Rites decided who among them would be its captain. Every two years, the captains would compete against each other for the right to be called a lance commander. Among those, Myrha and Maez were the latest to earn that rank.

'He was right about one thing,' Masaad admitted. 'If he had hurt you … that might have been more than I could stand.'

'Best keep that to yourself,' Myrha cautioned.

'I know,' he said, as they approached a statue that was taller than all the rest. 'But you remind me too much of *her*.'

Reaching nearly as high as the armoured glass ceiling was the likeness of a beautiful, robust woman with long, flowing hair. Surrounded by Lightspears, her muscular arm pointed towards the stars, leading them into the heavens.

'She would have been so proud,' he said.

Myrha gazed up at the likeness of her mother.

'I wish I had known her,' she said.

'You have her courage,' Masaad continued, with sadness in his voice. 'And her strength.'

Though her death was served by pirates, it was House Alyxander that Maez and the rest of House Obyeran blamed for the murder of Lyanna Obyeran. She died the way she always lived: nobly serving others. Pirates had attacked a privateer outpost on KC-185, an asteroid between Zeus and Heracles, and Lyanna's ship – a pre-Lightspear corvette called *Dauntless* – had been the closest vessel that could assist. Ever the bold and fearless captain, Lyanna destroyed two pirate corvettes and led a boarding party inside the outpost to rescue survivors. But she took a serious wound during the battle, and refused treatment while civilians remained aboard. By the time the last one was evacuated, Lyanna had slipped into shock.

As the Dauntless crew worked furiously to stabilize her, more pirate ships closed in pursuit. The nearest outpost with the necessary surgical facilities was owned by House Alyxander, which had brokered a fragile détente with those same pirates, who had an affiliation with Ceti. House Alyxander considered Obyeran a weak House of little relevance; certainly not worth incurring the wrath of bloodthirsty criminals who had just watched Lyanna Obyeran cut down many of their own.

Under a pretext of keeping the peace, House Alyxander refused to allow the *Dauntless* to make port, leaving Lyanna Obyeran to die of her wounds in space. Her crew also died, fighting the pursuing pirates to the last man.

Masaad was certain that his wife would still be alive had she been aboard a Lightspear. Every Obyeran wanted a war to avenge their queen, and Masaad yearned to give them one. But he refused. Soon, they would finally understand why.

'Whenever Maez comes here, his heart grows darker,' Myrha said, really feeling the chill now. Even with the solar harvesters illuminating the dome, the ambient temperature inside was hovering at -15 Celsius. 'He dreams of leading the fleet against House Alyxander.'

'To avenge the mother he never knew,' Masaad said. 'Vengeance is a convenient outlet for violent tendencies.'

'You don't trust him.'

King Masaad drew a deep breath.

'Maez is a weapon whose power can be harnessed for great good,' he said. 'Yet I fear the day we should ever unleash it. Without guidance, his wrath could be ruinous. He has loyalty and compassion for those he trusts, but he is too quick to anger. That is why I intend you to succeed me.'

Myrha gasped.

'Father, I—'

'Don't act surprised,' Masaad scoffed. 'No one else will be, least of all Maez. He will stand by your side as the protector of our House, but all Obyerans will call you Queen.'

She felt as though the ground were shaking beneath her feet.

'Near the end, much of Earth looked like this,' King Masaad said, waving towards the lifeless mountain ranges beyond the dome. 'I was born on a world with no hope. Look at us now. We live in bubbles and tunnels and caves … we were not meant for this.'

Myrha was stunned to hear him say it. Hyllus alone was home to thousands who called themselves Obyerans, and this was the only world they had ever known. Far beneath the ground where they were standing was breathable air, flowing rivers, and lush fields where grains and vegetables grew under the glare of artificial sunlight. Masaad Obyeran had broken from the pack all those years ago to build this great House, and today provided them with a life that was inspiring and worthwhile.

She would never mention it to her father – he was ever the atheist – but she felt a spiritual bond to the place.

'For us, Earth is a myth,' she said. 'Hyllus is our home.'

Masaad shook his head.

'I am old,' he said solemnly. 'The machines say I'm in good health, yet I sense I may not wake from my hypersleep.'

He faced her, reached up with both hands, placing them on her shoulders.

'Myrha, by the time Alim rises, I promise that you will be walking the shores of another world and breathe its air with no mask. When we reach it, I will leave you to carry on the work I have begun.'

Myrha took a breath, staring into her father's amber eyes.

'Are you saying … you've found—?'

'Nothing else would stop me from taking revenge on those who murdered my beloved wife,' Masaad said, his eyes glistening. 'Our Lightspears must carry us to a new world … not to war. That mission is greater than me … greater even than her. She made me swear it before my brothers. We all did. *Nothing* must come between us and our new home.'

'Who else knows?' Myrah brought herself to say.

'Your uncles, and now you,' he said, resuming his stroll.

'Where?'

'Ch1 Orionis AB,' he said. 'Ten light years from here, twenty-eight from Earth.'

Myrha knew it: a binary system with a yellow-orange main sequence star very similar to Sol, which was orbited by a red dwarf companion every fourteen years. No planets, not even torch companions, had been detected, at least not the last time that anyone looked. The gaze of Orionis was locked on the Tau Ceti system, pinning its hope on the *Archangel* as a means of reaching there and joining the other human colony.

'You know for sure there's a habitable planet there for us?' she asked.

'Al Khav has been there for twenty years,' Masaad said.

Myrha stopped in her tracks.

'By *himself*?'

'With his crew. They are building a colony, laying the groundwork for our arrival.'

With a wave of his hands, a bluish-white sphere appeared, suspended in the cold air. Huge white continents with specks of green and brown peeked from behind swirling white clouds, all surrounded by vast blue oceans.

'Our new world,' Masaad said. 'I wanted to name it Lyanna, but your uncle has more than earned the right to name it himself.'

'Did he get there on a Lightspear?'

Masaad beamed.

'The Lightspears can take us there. *This* is what they were made for.'

'Have you been in contact with him?'

'Every day for the last eighteen years,' he said. 'But each message is a decade old.'

And so much could have happened in that time. The passengers of the *Tabit Genesis* could certainly attest to that, Myrha noted.

'But you have enough information to make a decision?' she asked. 'We're really going to leave here?'

'Alim believes we should,' he answered. 'The world is a closer fit to Earth than Eileithyia ever was. And so far, we're the only humans who know for certain it exists.'

'And Al Khav?' she asked, fearing the answer.

'There are no intelligent civilisations, the air is breathable, and he supports a mass migration, all at once, with no notice to Orionis or anyone else.'

'And you?'

'I see no reason why any of us should remain, except to protect our holdings against the unlikely event any of us have to return.'

It was tempting. So tempting, in fact, that Myrha was certain it was a mistake.

'Your silence is telling,' Masaad said.

'To be honest,' she admitted, 'I'm terrified.'

'You should be,' he said, 'because now you must continue The Rites.'

The siblings had earned their lance commands in the arena, but the test of a Lightspear Fleet Command was voluntary and the most brutal trial by far. It was called The Voyage Home. A captain was towed in a disabled Lightspear to a random location with no functioning instruments or crew. The experience simulated survival conditions in extreme emergencies; explosions, EMP bursts, collisions or engine failures could leave a crew incapacitated in a ship tumbling out of control. Recovering one's bearings under a high-G spin, often with no reference point, took special skill that only a worthy captain could master.

Many unravelled just trying to stabilise the ship. Others could not find their way back to Hyllus. There was no time limit; a captain could take a lifetime if he chose. The Lightspear was equipped with a beacon they could activate at any time to declare surrender, at which point Obyeran ships would come for them.

But for those who returned under their own means, there was no greater honour, and no greater respect among the people of House

Obyeran. To date, only two captains had succeeded. One was Al Khav. The other was King Masaad himself.

'The Queen who leads us to the new world must prove she can find her way home,' he said.

'And if I cannot?'

'Myrha, I love you so much,' he said. 'Never doubt yourself again.'

8

ANONYMOUS

22 February 2809

Dear Amaryllis,

Since my last note, I have participated in some rank atrocity.

My actions were so cruel they made me think of you, as I do whenever I despair. That is testament to your power, your absolute control of me. I only wish you could see my barbarism for yourself, so that you might understand the true nature of the universe.

I'm often asked what similarities there are between Orionis and the homeworld some of you remember, specifically how humans have changed since the Apocalypse. My answer is they haven't. Ignorance blinds them. Greed kills them. Pride compels them. After all that's happened, they still struggle to make the right choices. How can a species continue on that path? And I answer: because humans are inherently selfish. Their design is flawed; the attributes of free will and intelligence all but ensured their destruction.

Yet nature still tolerates them. *Still!* My colleagues introduced me to the poem 'Do not go gentle into that good night', citing its relevance to humans, whose resilience astonishes them.

Even *me*. I'm beginning to wonder if other forces are conspiring to keep you alive.

Once upon a time, a charismatic minority with inordinate political power preached that a higher power created the universe and all life within. For centuries, men amassed armies to kill one another in the name of some creed or deity. I always believed such thinking contributed more to humankind's destruction than anything else. But given Earth's fate and the Raothri invasion, I've come to realise the zealots were necessary. That their actions, twisted and despicable, played a crucial role in keeping the species alive.

You see, a curious thing happened to the human population when it was culled from fourteen billion to fewer than fifty million people in just a decade. When that happened, humans were about to join the legions of extinct species that once lived on Earth. Over the long view, catastrophes – self-imposed or otherwise – are no rare occurrence. The most effective ones throw out the old variables for survival and introduce new ones. For instance, you owe your charmed life to a rogue asteroid. Before then, you were just a rodent living beneath massive reptiles who were indifferent to your existence.

But subtle attributes make all the difference when the system changes. An insignificant creature clinging to life in a remote corner of a world begins to thrive once the prevailing conditions become more favourable. Nature always hedges its bets, placing varieties of creatures with exotic combinations of attributes at the boundaries of ecosystems. The strongest of those are the ones that survive.

So it seemed that nature had failed to spread its risk with humans. The primates were all but extinct by the twenty-second century, and humans were the last of the hominidae. Evolution takes time, and the species that don't have it expire.

Yet, uniquely, humans evolved *three* characteristics in a *single* generation. One person in three hundred thousand born after World War Three had at least one major mutation. By the time the Genesis motherships were finished, it was down to one in fifty. Unlike your ancestors, you have some tolerance to radiation thanks to an evolved DNA mismatch repair system orders of magnitude more effective than the one they had. Because of it, your body's cells can fully repair damage from low doses of ionising radiation ninety-nine per cent of the time. The blood transfusions that are a regular part of your privileged first-born regimen are merely an additive to scrub away what your own defences cannot, making you all but impervious to radiation sickness except in the most extreme exposure conditions.

Next is your body's ability to heal from wounds. From initial hemostatic response to resistance to infection, every stage of cicatrisation is quicker and less prone to complications than ever before. Combined with the regenerative biotechnology advances of the last five decades, your species has within its grasp the means to end all disease and extend lifespan by centuries for every member of its population.

But the third change isn't really a mutation. To call it such would imply we can find it in the human genome. It's the *Gift* we've heard so much about, Amaryllis, and it has been hidden in plain sight for the entirety of human existence.

After the Third World War, the number of reported paranormal experiences increased by a factor of *twenty*, despite the drastic reduction in population. It was as if nature foresaw what was coming to mankind, and, in a desperate bid to save it, designed a new type of clarity: a sixth sense. To be clear, no one can *see* into the future – as in witness events forward in time and then report them back to the past. But one *can* reach a hyper-consciousness of an inevitable future based on *observable* conditions and information available *now*, at this moment – not unlike forecasting the weather.

Those endowed with the Gift reach an unparalleled level of awareness of the universe around them, down to details transcending the five physical senses; they sense every dimension of causation; they are attuned to the frequency of matter itself, able to glimpse all the possibilities at this nexus in the universe in an instant.

The Gift is powerful. It conveys information to possessors in different ways; it finds some in their dreams, others moments before combat; some just before it's too late and others with time to spare. Not all Gift bearers are the same; speed, skill and intelligence make all the difference. The most talented among them react the fastest to information they receive – with the *right* course of action.

As far as I know, humans are the only species in the universe that possess it. Again, you can run a Gift bearer's DNA side by side against someone who lacks it, and you would see nothing amiss. In rare cases, active brain scans will catch a premonition episode in progress – for a fraction of a second. The regions that are most active when humans dream illuminate like supernovae whenever the Gift whispers to them.

Of course there are sceptics, and I'm sure you're one of them. Evolution takes time, and grants no preference to species no matter how dire their situation. That should have also applied to humans. But it did not, there is no explanation why, and that is deeply unsettling. The Gift is a mystery that has made me consider the possibility that a higher intelligence exists. For the first time in my deranged life, I am uncertain. The more I see of the universe, the less it makes sense. I suppose that distinguishes me from the zealots.

But I now think they are right to say that not everything can be explained away by science. Your notions of what real is, or ought to be, are biased, constrained by the limits of perspective from a single world. If you knew what I did … if you could see what I've seen, you would agree.

The Raothri are not the only intelligent race that humans have encountered. There are others, some with technology just as advanced, and possibly with the same intentions. One of them stalked the *Tabit Genesis* on its journey from Earth for years, hovering in its wake, blinking in and out of sensor range in a ghostly jeer that screamed *we are watching you*.

That precious ship, holding what may have been the last humans, as vulnerable and insignificant as a mote of dust between the stars, was *allowed* to pass.

Please excuse me. I've more atrocities to commit. More lives to curse. I hope I haven't offended you. But again … you know so little.

- A

P.S. I've never seen Lunar Base Hadfield. UNSEC didn't take us there.

9

ADAM

A spinning globule of high protein, nutrient-rich slime floated untouched before Adam's eyes, his appetite ruined by the confrontation under way. Tonight's dinner originated from the discarded tube tumbling nearby: a single serving of survival rations stamped with a faded Merckon logo and overdue expiration date, its contents divided evenly among the Lethos family. Abby eyed his portion, clutching her straw, waiting for the chance to impale the neglected sustenance when he wasn't looking.

His crippled father was smiling, and the corners of his mouth were crusted with residue that his mother had yet to clean. Instead she focused on Adam, glaring as she waited for an answer that would infuriate her more.

The spectacle of his parents filled Adam's heart with sadness. They were gaunt and sickly, with ominous dark splotches covering their pale, mottled skin. Neither had received blood transfusions in months, and that was a death sentence in such proximity to Zeus. Dad's hair, once a thick brown mane, was all but gone, and his sunken cheekbones seemed incapable of holding his dark eyes in place. Mom was the healthier one, but hardly looked any better. She had been beautiful, once. Now her hair was falling out in clumps, and what few strands remained floated on end like wisps of vapour.

'*Adam*,' she snapped for a second time. 'What were you thinking?'

He had Abby to thank for the betrayal, though it had been wishful thinking to believe he could hide the truth forever. The rig was no longer producing *Three*, not least because Adam had been unable to visit

71

the platform since his near deadly encounter with an Arkady hunter several weeks earlier.

His claim was that turbulence, not direct Arkady contact, had damaged the old machine. It was a plausible lie, since it wasn't unheard of for bits of Arkady residue to collide with mining platforms, especially on the equatorial rigs. The trouble was there were a *lot* of entrails stuck to the Pegasus, including an intact hunter tentacle that Adam had managed to hide from them. He had heard from other trawlers that on occasion, freight captains would pay for Arkady samples. So he thought of a clever scheme to get rid of the evidence and raise the money he needed for repairs.

When the fuel tanker arrived to collect their meager gas harvest, Adam offered to sell the tentacle instead. The captain readily agreed to his price, and as a deal sweetener, included some spare mech parts as well. Both parties felt very good about their exchange.

Of course, Abby learned about the trade from the money transfer. When she discovered how little Adam had received versus what the sample was actually worth, she snapped. Adam was made to realise his ignorance during a profanity-laced tirade on how he had effectively traded the value of a bumper Three harvest for a handful of scraps.

'Why wouldn't you tell us?' Mom demanded. 'More to the point, why would you lie?'

Adam knew that his sister's unpleasantness scaled with her hunger, and times were lean. The truth came out, not by accident, when they were down to their final crate of rations. The comment launched an investigation led by Dad, who still knew his way around a mech's datacore, where the truth of what really happened that day was stored.

'Because ...' was the only word Adam could mumble.

Abby finished the sentence for him.

'... you're selfish?' she offered. 'Or just dumb?'

'Abigail, shush,' Mom snapped. '*Because* ...?'

'I knew you'd get mad,' Adam said.

Mom struggled to control her exasperation.

'It's not anger,' she explained. 'It's concern for your safety. The Arkady are deadly creatures – you know they've killed miners before! At the first sign of them, you have to—'

'Abort, I know,' Adam said. 'But I don't … I don't think they mean to harm us.'

Abby snorted, and Dad just kept smiling.

'Never, ever presume to understand *any* animal's intentions,' Mom said, 'let alone an alien species.'

'It was a stupid risk,' Abby said. 'You should have let the thing die.'

Adam let the thought linger before answering.

'Well, you kept going on about how important the harvest was,' he challenged.

'Oh, don't you dare,' Abby warned. 'I said we were going to starve if we didn't get a decent yield, but I never said to take any chances down there.'

'If I don't take chances, we can't eat. Here,' Adam said, nudging the floating globule across the table, 'you'll make more sense on a full stomach.'

'Stop it, both of you,' his mother said. 'Abby, you're excused.'

Abby stabbed the food with her straw and sucked until it vanished.

'Whatever,' she said, launching herself out of the room.

Adam sighed.

'We don't know much about the Arkady,' his father said, beginning another oft-repeated lecture. 'We're the aliens in *their* world. It's always best to stay clear.'

'I did try to stay clear,' Adam snapped. 'It landed right in front of me. What was I supposed to do?'

His father's smile faded, and his head began shaking in erratic jolts.

'When you're young … lying seems harmless,' he was stammering. 'But it gets grown men into serious trouble.'

The look on Mom's face made Adam's stomach drop.

'The logs show that you literally walked off the platform edge,' she said.

All information about the mech's movements, including the orientation of its gyroscopes, was recorded in its datacore. If you played that information back – how many steps it took, when it used its appendages, and – most damningly – *how* it used them – and transposed that information over a map of the rig platform, it was just as revealing as recorded video.

'For God's sake, the thing knocked you over!' Mom exclaimed. 'You're lucky to be alive!'

'It was stuck in the intake,' Adam protested. 'How else was I supposed to fix it?'

'You weren't supposed to fix *anything* under those circumstances!' Mom snapped. 'Do you have that little regard for your own life?'

Adam shrugged his shoulders.

'It was dying,' he said.

Mom stared at him incredulously.

'Please tell me you understand that it tried to kill you,' she said.

'No, that's not true,' Adam said. 'It was just … scared.'

'*Scared?*' Mom repeated.

'That makes it even more dangerous,' his father said, still shaking. 'You've got a big heart, but we don't want to lose you.'

'You mean we can't *afford* to lose the dumb ass,' Abby yelled out from the next room.

'Go to the hangar, please!' her mother shouted.

'Mmkay, Mom,' Abby sneered.

'The mech is fixed,' Adam said. 'We can start harvesting again.'

'You're not going back down there,' Mom declared.

'Uh, yeah he is,' Abby called out again.

'*Abigail!*' Mom shouted.

'If I don't, how are we going to survive?' Adam asked. 'Dad's hurt, you don't know how to pilot, and Abby won't try prostitution.'

'Eat shit,' his sister yelled, just as the door leading to the hangar closed shut.

Mom looked as if she might explode.

'The old saying is that a good *Three* miner is one with a pulse,' Dad said.

'You are not going back down,' Mom repeated. 'Not until the radars and turrets are fixed.'

'Mom,' Adam said, looking at her thoughtfully. 'Even I know we can't afford that.'

'I don't care,' was the response. 'The answer is no.'

Adam felt anger taking control of him.

'What about the people who hurt Dad?' he said. 'We could always ask them for money again.'

His mother lurched across the table but stopped short of hitting

74

him. Adam's reflexive flinch launched him off his seat, hurtling him backwards in the microgravity until he struck the bulkhead. She fell back into her seat, her clenched fists trembling, despair and frustration on her face.

After a few long moments, Adam finally spoke.

'You can't stop me from going,' he said. 'Excuse me.'

Adam pushed off the wall in a slow drift. He left the small room, leaving Thomas and Dawn Lethos to themselves.

Both waited until the hatch to Adam's cabin closed before speaking.

'I can't believe it,' Dawn said. 'I've lost them.'

'Not yet,' Thomas reassured, his head shakes calming somewhat. 'But we're close.'

'We can't provide them with anything,' she spat. 'Not even food.'

'It's time to let them go,' he said. 'Past time, really.'

'Go? To whom? What would they do?'

'They'll find their way,' Thomas said wearily. 'They won't outlive us staying here. They've paid for our sins long enough.'

Dawn reached forward and wiped the corners of his mouth.

'We had friends, connections,' she said. 'Someone must still be willing to help us. We're firstborns, for God's sake!'

'Shh,' Thomas hushed. 'It's too dangerous for them to know.'

'It's their *right* to know!' Dawn snapped. 'They have privileges with corporations and government—'

'We've been through this so many times,' Thomas said, his mouth reaching for the tube that allowed him to control his wheelchair. After a few puffs, the machine withdrew from the table and rolled into the corner. 'They lost their rights the moment we changed their names.'

'Their real names may be all that saves them the next time someone comes here demanding money,' she insisted.

'That's just as likely to get them ransomed or killed,' Thomas said, as the overhead light flickered. 'We sold our souls. Sooner or later, the devil gets his due. Adam is safer working a rig than he is anywhere in the Inner Rim. And if any of the roughnecks around here discover that these kids are firstborns ...'

The only record of the Lethos family's existence was in the Orionis Navy archives, and it had been forged by Ceti hackers who created a fictitious biometric signature designating them as Outer Rim ghosts. In truth, Tomas Straka was descended from the highborn founders of Titan Industries, where both he and his wife Dayla had been executives just ten years earlier.

Titan was the leading producer of synthetic biology, specialising in the creation of artificial life forms. On the *Tabit Genesis*, biocybernetic organisms cleaned slush tanks, performed hull repairs, processed radioactive waste, and helped manufacture some of the first gas giant trawlers when the *Tabit* arrived in Orionis. But on Earth they had levelled cities, enslaved populations, and performed surgical assassinations in the Third World War.

Synthetic organisms were most often created by combining elements taken from 'The Catalogue', the non-human gene pool archive that the *Tabit Genesis* had brought from Earth. It contained sequencing data for every native species of life that remained in the twenty-second century. As the colonisation of Orionis expanded, parts of the Catalogue were opened for privatisation and corporate investment. With the horrors of war still fresh in the minds of highborn officials, the government acted as both broker and auditor of all sequencing sales, scrutinising every transaction with vigilance.

House Alyxander, notorious dabblers in genetics and biocybernetic technology, made no secret of their intent to acquire a *complete* copy of the Earth gene pool, including the sequences used to produce biocybernetic weapons. They were especially active in the black market, always the highest bidders for illegal sequences that could create designer mutations in humans or in exotic creatures to sell as pets. Because of their ties with Ceti and other privateer cartels, Inner Rim corporations were forbidden from conducting business with them.

Ten years earlier Tomas Straka, then the President at Titan, had stumbled upon a dark discovery: the very corporation his own ancestors founded had obtained the biocybernetic weapon sequences. And the CEO at the time – Argus Fröm – was directly implicated by the evidence. Weighing the ramifications, Tomas had taken the moral high ground and reported his findings to the Navy Police.

Arriving home an hour later, he had found Abby and Dayla – then eight months pregnant with Adam – bound and unconscious. Before he could take another step, he had been forced to his knees and restrained. Tomas didn't see the intruder's face as a gun was pressed to his head. He relived the experience often.

'Did you tell anyone else what you found?' a voice asked.

'No,' Tomas said.

The gun pressed harder.

'I'll shoot your daughter first.'

'No!' Tomas shouted. 'I didn't tell anyone else!'

'I believe you,' the voice said. 'If I didn't, she'd be dead already. We need to talk.'

'Who are you?'

'The messenger,' the voice said. Tomas heard the footsteps of other men in the room. 'When you wake up, you'll be on a freighter. You'll find out your options on board.'

'My options?'

'You have enemies. The life you knew is over. This is the only way to save your family. Do you understand? It's highborn's luck you aren't dead already.'

Those were the last words he heard before awakening in orbit around Zeus. Adam was born soon after, on the Ceti outpost where the Straka family vanished from existence. The cartel had been paid by an anonymous donor to move them from the Inner Rim and to keep their true identities secret.

Little else about the deal had turned out favourably for the Lethos family ever since. Tomas would never know for certain who had betrayed him – or who had rescued them from danger.

'I didn't sell our souls,' Dayla snarled. 'You did.'

'If our children survive, it will be because of their natural gifts, not what a plutocracy says their name entitles them to,' Tomas said. 'They'll have to make their own names here.'

Dayla was despondent.

'I hate your damned altruisms,' she growled. 'I always have.'

Tomas's head began to shake erratically again.

'What kind of people do you want your children to become?' he asked.

'Not like us!'

'Exactly.'

'I mean not like *this*! Living in poverty, when by rights we should be living like—'

'Criminals,' he said. 'We would be criminals, Dayla. Titan has the weapons which nearly annihilated mankind. We would be guilty of—'

'We are *not* criminals,' Dayla snapped. 'You had nothing do to with it.'

'I would have been guilty of not stopping the inevitable atrocity while I had the chance.'

'Look at all the good your guilt has done for us!'

The shout rang throughout their metal home, striking every bulkhead, smashing her anguish upon everything they owned.

The echo took forever to subside.

'I wanted our children to have a conscience,' Tomas said finally, his voice wavering. 'I wanted them to have a father who stood for what was right.'

Dayla pushed away from the table.

'I just wanted them to have a good life,' she muttered, gliding towards the door.

10

WYLLYM

Corinth Naval Yards was a bulbous monstrosity distinguished by its four spinning 'onion' habitat domes, each over a thousand metres in diameter. Wyllym was seated in the observation tower high above them, at the end of the structural 'z' axis that formed the centreline of the station. Reserved for the supervision of fleet training exercises, the deck had been cleared for him; he was alone in a vast hall glowing with volumetric displays of ship telemetry. Four large transparent blisters gave him an unobstructed view of space, though from this vantage point the *Archangel* and her construction yard were out of sight, some twenty kilometres below.

Confirming Wyllym's own suspicions, Grand Admiral Hedricks had indeed recalled him to assert his control over the Gryphons. Not only that, but he had also moved the entire training infrastructure to the proving grounds at Corinth, integrating them with Navy fleet exercises without waiting for a recommendation from Wyllym to do so. The fighters, equipment and support personnel had arrived days after he did. The Admiral never apologised, explaining that the move had been kept confidential for security reasons. Furthermore, he was expected to continue in his role as flight instructor, only now he'd be doing so under the scrutiny of the entire Navy command structure.

That was fine with Wyllym. They were welcome to relieve him anytime they wished.

With the naked eye he could only see the sporadic blue pulses of ship thrusters and the white blossoms of explosions as live rounds struck their targets far downrange. There were three proving grounds outside Corinth, each one a cube five hundred kilometres across. The largest objects in the ranges threw reflections of sunlight that might have been mistaken for dust. But these were the profiles of cruisers, frigates, asteroids, and eerie-looking structures called The Red Graves: kilometres of twisting, turning stone and metal walls modelled after the deadly, semi-aware Raothri protostruct swarms.

The AR controls allowed him to slip into the cockpit of any Gryphon and observe the action through the eyes of the pilot. Wyllym was watching several of the fighters at once; a gruelling mental exercise in command multitasking, only marginally preferable to the physical ordeals of being inside a Gryphon. The disadvantage was that although he could experience the decisions of his pilots, he couldn't sense how they were using the Gift to guide their choices. For that, he needed to physically be there, in combat alongside of them.

It was why the Gryphon needed a human pilot in the first place. No drone could react faster than those with the Gift, and no code could simulate what the Gift could provide. But when two fighters armed with such talent met in combat, the advantage was neutralised, and the result was a brutal exhibition of raw physical endurance. Wyllym switched into one such dogfight; the two Gryphons were turning in tight circles just under a kilometre in diameter at blazing speeds, their manoeuvring thrusters turning, firing, turning, firing, struggling to get the craft's weapons to point in a direction ahead of where their target would be. In another exercise, a pair of Gryphons were dismantling a capital ship – in this case, the ONW *Monmouth*, a Navy cruiser. Her long-range guns failed to bring the fighters down from afar; the nimble craft seemed to know the exact moment when the dummy shell would be fired, thrusting laterally or vertically to foil the targeting solution as they closed to within range of their own weapons.

Then he switched to a pair of pilots flying through The Red Graves, the most dangerous exercise by far because of the very real collision hazard. Some Raothri technology behaved like it was alive; physical structures that seemed to 'grow' quickly from a synthetic proto-material and assemble into the latticework that could later become a ship, a station, or an obstacle designed to protect another structure. That information was as classified as the technology of the *Archangel*, and no one with his level of clearance knew how it had been obtained. Wyllym experienced a rush as the pilot deftly weaved through the structure as it tried to kill him, changing its shape and closing off course solutions as he adjusted. The Gryphon eventually made it through, successfully managing to take down each of its targets in between turns.

But the pilot behind him made a critical mistake. Wyllym switched into his cockpit just in time to see – even feel – one of the fighter's three 'wings' get pulverised as it clipped an obstacle. Recognising there could be no recovery from this catastrophe, a series of automated disaster mitigation systems engaged in picosecond succession; a hardening crash foam solution filled the cockpit to protect the pilot from further trauma as the Gryphon shut itself down.

The pilot – his name was Lieutenant Trace Vanders – was rendered unconscious by the impact, his body thrashed by wicked G-forces as the fighter careened out of control. An ice-cold plasma solution packed with anti-inflammatory agents was injected into his bloodstream, slowing his heartbeat and halting his body's potentially pathogenic response to the trauma. Flash-frozen and encased in a tomb of foam that included the seat, he was ejected from the Gryphon. Rocket motors ignited to stabilise the seat's spin through space as it hurled away from the crippled fighter, blasting distress beacons for rescue ships to follow.

'Lieutenant Vanders's day is over,' a gruff voice said, startling Wyllym. 'How many fuck-ups is that for him now?'

Wyllym backed his mind out of the doomed pilot's link, feeling a moment of vertigo. Even the virtual experience of being ejected from a spacecraft travelling a few hundred metres per second was unpleasant. Clearing his eyes, he saw Orionis Navy Police Chief Augustus Tyrell standing at the room entrance.

'Who let you in here?' Wyllym demanded.

'The same fool who promoted you to captain,' Augustus said, striding in on magnetic greaves and offering his hand. Wyllym took it, bracing for his hand to be crushed. He wasn't disappointed.

'Good to see you,' he said, trying to remember the last time they'd met.

'Likewise,' Augustus said. But he was all business, nodding towards the displays that were tracking Lieutenant Vanders's life pod tumbling through space.

'So how many is that?' he repeated.

'This makes three,' Wyllym said, leaning back in his seat. The pilot's vitals were weak, but within an acceptable range for someone in early stage cryosleep. 'I have to expel him. Assuming he lives.'

Chief Tyrell grunted.

'If he wakes up, he's mine.'

'Admiral Hedricks said the washouts are still assigned to the *Archangel*,' Wyllym said, stifling a yawn. He'd lost track of how long he'd been up there.

'I don't give a shit what he wants,' Augustus said. 'Your trash belongs to me, not him.'

Wyllym lifted an eyebrow. His friend was among the most divisive figures in the Navy, despised by corporations, privateers and criminal cartels alike. But he was feared by all. Augustus had been the figurehead crime fighter in Orionis for the last twenty years, and his brand of justice was essentially martial law. In the Inner Rim, which was all the space up to Hera and her moons, Augustus had almost singlehandedly established a fortress of peace and order. The police presence around population centres was intimidating; no matter where a person ventured, a pair of formidably armed officers was patrolling nearby. He was an evangelistic believer that deterrence was the most effective peace-keeping tactic, and that force, when necessary, must always be brutally decisive.

But where he had earned the named 'Tyrell the Tyrant' was in his relentless pursuit of criminal activity past the Belt into the Outer Rim. Economists called him 'an enemy to commerce' thanks to his interdiction mandate: Navy police reserved the right to force any ship to burn down from intersystem freight speeds and be inspected at the Hera Transit, no matter who the owner or how much fuel it cost them. He also made sure the Navy maintained an active presence around Zeus, protecting its *Three* mining operations and sharing security resources with Inner Rim corporations. Most controversially, he sent undercover agents into privateer stations, even cartel hideouts.

He spent a large portion of his budget on espionage, and gave his officers unlimited discretion to extract information from criminal operatives. ·

Feared, loathed, or admired, enough people believed that Orionis needed someone like him. Like Wyllym, he was the product of a generation whose brotherly innocence had been shattered by the Independence Wars. The urgency to maintain law and order for the last bastion of mankind gave him licence to embrace tactics which valued the pursuit of justice by any means. To a fault, he was loyal to the Orionis government, and mortally opposed to all those who were not.

Fortunately for Wyllym, the man considered him a close friend, and he knew better than to let himself get baited into a conversation about their favourite Admiral.

'Lieutenant Vanders is a good man,' Wyllym said. 'Talented too, in spite of this debacle.'

'So what happened then?'

'Exhaustion,' Wyllym said, stretching out his own carcass. He hadn't flown in days, and it was doing miracles for his recovery. He almost felt human again. 'We're finding their limits.'

Augustus – Wyllym had called him 'Ty' since their days in the Naval Academy – took a seat across from him. His leathery face was criss-crossed with age; much of his scalp showed beneath thin strands of white hair.

'I thought the Gift prevented this sort of thing from happening,' he said.

'Knowing what's coming is one thing,' Wyllym said, rubbing his eyes. 'Reacting to it is something else. The lad's not "trash", Ty. This is a highly competitive pool for a small number of spots.'

'I know, stop being so damn sensitive,' the old man growled. 'A pilot with skills like that belongs on a belt runner chasing down Ceti corvettes.'

'Hedricks isn't going to let that happen,' Wyllym warned.

'*Fuck* Hedricks,' Augustus snapped, loud enough to make Wyllym concerned about the deck entrance being open. 'He's taken enough already.'

Wyllym lowered his voice.

'I agree, but I wouldn't be so vocal about it. You're not untouchable, Chief.'

'Neither is he,' Augustus said, defiant as ever. 'I'm not sure I understand where it says that his post lets him appropriate the best resources in Orionis for a science project.'

'I don't like it either, but I keep my head low. This is the Navy, right?'

'Not the one I joined. The priorities around here aren't what they used to be. Years ago someone like you would have earned a cruiser command by now. Now you're a classic example of government waste.'

Wyllym stared at him for a moment.

'Is that what you think of the Gryphons?'

'No offence, Wyll,' Augustus said, 'but there must be a horse somewhere in Orionis, because its shit is all over the show you're running here.'

'Thanks for your support.'

The police chief leaned forward, his eyes blazing.

'You just slammed a good pilot into a wall, and for what? To prove he can't fly through real morph razors? That's stupid. The red bastards can't be beaten. You know it, I know it, anyone with a functioning brain knows it. All this nonsense does is let Hedricks trick Chancellor Jade and those Senate idiots into thinking there's hope. Hell, you've seen what the SPECFOR freaks have found. The *Archangel* is a political toy that's good for just one thing: bullying humans, that's it.'

'The Gift makes those Gryphons especially deadly—'

'And there's just what, eighteen of them, less the one you splattered in a training exercise. So what if they can dodge cannon fire? This *Archangel* business is giving the cartels a strong incentive to launch an offensive, and I mean a real one. Not isolated outpost raids but a serious push on the Inner Rim.'

'Isn't that a little conspiratorial?'

'Wyll, you're not some rookie with a hero complex any more.'

'I've never had a hero complex.'

'Whatever. *Think*, Wyll. When the *Archangel* leaves, the most powerful deterrent we've ever had is leaving with it, along with our most capable commanders and soldiers.'

'It's my understanding that our fleet strength is completely unaffected by anything the *Archangel* is doing,' Wyllym said, surprised that he was becoming defensive. 'There will be just as many Navy warships here as before.'

Augustus was indignant, reddening as he spoke.

'The government bankrupted itself to build that fucking thing, so we can't afford to replace any ships we lose. Or did you forget we depend on the Outer Rim for resources, like cheap fuel? You don't think Ceti is aware of that?'

'It always comes back to Ceti with you,' Wyllym said, deciding that he'd had enough. 'Did you come up here just to be a jerk? I don't have time for it.'

Augustus frowned at him, surprised by the query.

'Katrin left,' he said, matter-of-factly. 'Thought you'd want to know.'

Wyllym felt a pang in his stomach.

'Are you kidding?'

'A month before you got here. No note or explanation. I came up here to say hello and ask if maybe you've heard from her.'

'I'm sorry, Ty, I haven't,' Wyllym said. He had introduced them during their graduation ceremony nearly thirty years ago. 'I don't know what to say.'

'Bah, it was a long time coming. People change.'

'That's true enough.'

'It's been five years since we lost Danna,' Augustus said. 'We kept it together longer than anyone thought we would. That's something, right?'

Danna Tyrell had been nothing like her father, and everything like her mother. A pacifist, an aspiring bioengineer, she'd been happily married to a promising young police cadet named Jake Reddeck. While he was away on assignment, Ceti marauders had raided her shuttle and tried to extort a ransom for her safe return. After a failed rescue attempt the pirates had killed everyone on board. Danna had been carrying their first child.

Augustus was staring at him, waiting for an answer.

'You still had more than most people ever get,' Wyllym said carefully. 'Are you sure you just want to throw it away?'

'She's the one who bailed out.'

'You have no idea why?' Wyllym asked, with a dangerous level of sarcasm in his voice. 'She stood by your side through the darkest times. Katrin didn't change at all. You, on the other hand—'

'I don't have to take this shit from you,' Augustus said, standing up. 'What would you know about having a partner, anyway?'

'You don't like hearing the truth, especially when you're wrong.'

Augustus thumbed his own chest.

'I'm never wrong.'

'Well that part of you hasn't changed. How goes the war on Ceti?'

'The numbers speak for themselves, Wyll,' he returned, his face darkening. 'Inner Rim crime is down, illegal trade is down. We've got brave men and women fighting a covert battle to dismantle the cartels. I'd say the war has never gone better.'

'That reminds me. There was an article in the Orionis Net, about this so-called war you're waging.'

'About some undercover agents that were executed?'

'That's the one.'

'You really don't want to know.'

Wyllym lowered his voice again.

'Everyone knows about the gift-wrapped heads you received from Vladric Mors, and they want to know what you're going to do about it.'

Augustus held his glare.

'It was Jake.'

Wyllym felt a wave of nausea.

'You mean, his head was in …'

'He's the one who sawed theirs off,' Augustus said. 'Our understanding is that Jake sold them out, then tortured and killed them.'

Wyllym was speechless. He had met Jake several times. The lad was a good man, had been a good husband. This had to be a mistake – but Augustus would never joke about something like this.

'Did Katrin know?'

'It's better for her she doesn't. Besides, I just put a large bounty on him.'

'He's your son-in-law.'

'Was. Now he's a top dog at Ceti with Navy blood on his hands. I don't know what compelled him to kill those cops, and I don't care. What he did was despicable. Dead or alive, Jake is coming home.'

'You put him in that position,' Wyllym pressed. 'Was it worth his life?'

'Undercover work is dangerous. He knew the risks. We put soldiers in harm's way to protect Orionis. You weren't overly concerned whether Lieutenant Vanders survived.'

'It's not the same and you know it,' Wyllym countered. 'If you came up here looking for someone to tell you you're doing the right thing, you're out of luck.'

The police chief nodded, ever so slightly, never once blinking. Wyllym only saw this face when Augustus was furious – it was passive, hiding his true intentions.

'Why do you do this?' Augustus asked quietly.

'Do what? Confront you with the truth?'

'*Sacrifice*,' he said. 'For the Navy. The Gryphons. Hedricks. What did you turn into, the day half the people you loved were buried alive?'

'That's low, Ty.'

'Sixty years old, no wife, no children, no home to call your own. Look at you, back from the dead, and for what? What did you come back for? What reason do you have for actually living?'

Wyllym regarded his friend with cold, grey eyes.

'When the *Archangel* has her Gryphons, I'm retiring,' he said. 'I was happiest when I was growing things. Nurturing life. I thought I'd lease a plot on Eris. Go back to being a farmer.'

'Alone?'

'Yes.'

'So all you live for is dirt and solitude,' Augustus said. 'All I ever wanted was to be a grandfather. I lived for Danna. But to each his own, I guess.'

Wyllym took a deep breath, and exhaled slowly.

'I won't put Vladric Mors in front of a judge,' Augustus continued. 'I owe her that much.'

'If you want to understand why Katrin left,' Wyllym said, 'think about what you just said.'

A soft tone interrupted the tension, followed by another. Someone from the rescue operation was trying to reach Wyllym. He plucked the headset floating nearby and put it back on.

'Lyons.'

Augustus began making his way to the exit.

'Just received word that Lieutenant Vanders will survive,' Wyllym announced, raising his voice. 'I'll send you his files, but if anyone asks, you didn't get them from me.'

His friend stopped at the door.

'Keep them,' Augustus said. 'Might be he's safer on the *Archangel*. Lord knows what I'd ask of him.'

11

VIOLA

There was no place left to hide, and Travis stalked her like a relentless predator, his eyes full of murder. She fought against him with primal desperation, but he laughed at her struggle, toying with her before one final shove sent her hurling through the airlock, falling into the atmosphere of Zeus. As she plummeted towards oblivion, the ship faded from view, swallowed up by the clouds. Terrible gusts of wind pummelled her. She tried not to scream, for there was no air to breathe. But her lungs betrayed her and she began to choke, clutching at her throat, thrashing to face the direction of her descent.

That was when she heard it: *music*, of all things, beautiful and dark and hauntingly hypnotic. And then they emerged from the red clouds beneath her – breathtaking, luminescent swarms of Arkady hunters; thousands of intelligent beings acting as one, enveloping her, offering comfort, singing her death song ... Viola, Viola, *Viola!*

'*Viola!*' Mighan shouted, her voice thundering through the ammonia clouds.

The dream collapsed and Viola's eyes blinked open, focusing on the puddle of drool on her desk.

Mighan was standing just a metre from her.

'Wake up!' she demanded.

Viola sat abruptly, pulling strands of spittle-dampened hair from her mouth and tucking them behind her ear.

'The hazmat crew would like a word,' Mighan growled with blistering annoyance.

The time was 21:52. Viola had no idea how long she had been asleep.

'What for?' she mumbled, her voice dry. Reaching for her water jug, she tilted the end to her lips, but it was empty. So she held it out towards Mighan.

'Do you mind …?'

Nostrils flaring, the assistant snatched the container from Viola's hand.

'Answer the damn call!' Mighan bellowed.

That cleared the fogginess somewhat, and Viola returned fully to her desk at Merckon Prime.

'Silveri,' she said.

'Hi, finally. Sorry to interrupt, but the sample we just brought in is enormous. It won't fit in the lab unless we cut it.'

'No!' Viola shouted, wide awake now. 'Don't you dare! Let me see it.'

'Yes, ma'am,' the hazmat crewman said. The camera display showed a large shipping container, one of the standardised ones that were stacked inside the modular nodes of freighters.

Normally, Arkady tissue samples came back in crates barely larger than her chair.

Dressed in airtight survival suits, the hazmat specialist and his colleagues began opening the container door. It hissed as cold air leaked out, and the camera began panning inside.

Viola gasped.

'May I present one slightly decomposed, structurally intact hunter tentacle,' he said. 'It's six metres long and weighs eighty kilos. The business end is missing, but it still has some of the thorax attachment tendons.'

'Where did this come from?' she breathed.

'A Vulcan Dynamics freighter called it in. The captain said he bought it off a trawler operator at one of the Zeus exchange outposts. Apparently it changed hands several times before he acquired it.'

'But you don't know which trawler?'

'No, ma'am, I do not. The captain mentioned that whoever was on the receiving end of that tentacle must either be dead or the toughest roughneck in Orionis.'

Viola would have given anything to interview the miner who had come face-to-face with a hunter. Getting close to one and coming out alive was considered miraculous. Surviving actual physical contact was unheard of.

'Leave it right there, and keep it under guard,' Viola ordered. It was so annoying that she couldn't just go down there herself, but those were the rules. 'Nice work, gentlemen.'

'Thanks—'

'Mighan!' Viola shouted, whipping her hands about to manipulate new data imagery projections. 'I need you to extend AR coverage to the freight container downstairs. There's a specimen inside I'll need scanned and modelled. Talk to engineering about getting drones in there, I don't trust human hands for this. How soon can we run a preliminary—? What?'

The exasperated assistant was glaring at her.

'It is almost 22:00,' Mighan said in a calm, composed voice. 'You haven't left the building in three days, and you've been in this office for the last twenty hours.'

'So?'

'So get a life,' Mighan snapped. 'I'm shutting the office down.'

And with that, all of Viola's airborne telemetry vanished. Before she could protest, Mighan held up a large hand.

'My job is to protect your work, or more specifically Merckon's work, and unfortunately that means safeguarding your well-being,' Mighan said, tossing a tiny keycard onto the desk. 'Take that and get out of here so I can leave.'

Viola eyed the card suspiciously.

'What's this?'

'Unlimited VIP access for you and a friend to Sirkus,' Mighan said, strolling towards the door, her feet cutting a path through crumpled wrappers of empty food containers and energy supplements. The accumulated detritus from working non-stop was alarming, but then Viola's fascinating discovery several days earlier made all the sleep deprivation worthwhile. There was just so much more to learn that it was easy to block out everything else.

But Sirkus was an enticing distraction. It was the most exclusive nightclub at Merckon Prime, a playground for the rich and famous.

'Why are you giving me this?'

'Because Mr Mareck thinks you're in danger of burning out,' Mighan said. 'Everything you order is on the company account, no questions asked, including transportation. He also said to take tomorrow off.'

'I don't want the day off, that specimen needs to be catalogued—'

'It is *not* negotiable,' Mighan spat. 'The building won't let you in. Find somewhere else to go.'

'Why wasn't I informed of this before?'

'Because you didn't ask,' Mighan said. 'Now get out before I remove you myself.'

The lights went out, and Mighan crossed her arms impatiently. Viola felt helpless for a few moments. Then she reached for her corelink and placed a call.

'*It seemed like a good idea at the time*' was the last thought Viola recalled before a ringing corelink reminded her that she had made plans for a late evening. There were no Arkady dreams – just blackness, and a disorienting inability to remember how she ended up in the women's locker room at Merckon Prime. Her friend Carrie found her half asleep on a bench, and had to drag her into the shower to wake her up. The physical toll of so many hours and so little sleep was evident, but Carrie would hear nothing of it: no one passed up an opportunity for Sirkus, especially, as she described it, 'a nobody that works in legal'. A fitness fanatic like Viola, the two had become acquainted in the Merckon gym; similar routines and schedules created opportune circumstances for them to become friends.

An hour after Carrie had helped her get dressed, they sat with eyes wide open within the opulent dreamscape of Sirkus, two cocktails and a potent psychostimulant into a fierce conversation about work. Their balcony table overlooked a dance floor packed with swank socialites who were partying without a care in the world. The bar itself was a fusion of twenty-first-century cyberpunk melded with French neo-classical architecture and matching burlesque attire for the employees. Volumetric light shows featured largely naked male and female dancers, performing on poles, soaring through the air on cables, and offering drinks, drugs, and sex to patrons in secluded rooms that could be rented for a small fortune.

It was an anything-goes party for the bourgeois at its finest, and darkest. Viola and Carrie had been thrice propositioned already – by professionals of both sexes, and one intoxicated executive. But Viola, now wired on the stims, found herself talking incessantly about the Arkady, oblivious to the temptations around her.

'Music!' Viola exclaimed, between sips of her third cocktail. 'Don't tell a soul this, but I think they actually compose music!'

'Oh, really?' Carrie said, her deep brown eyes twinkling at some male specimen offering drinks to the women at the adjacent table. 'Like what, club, techno, classical—?'

Viola stifled a giggle.

'I mean, I haven't mapped the patterns to musical notes yet, but the point is only the most advanced kinds of intelligence can do this … like, communicate for reasons that aren't directly relevant to survival.'

Carrie gave her a blank expression, and Viola set her drink down to gesture freely.

'Okay, so, on Earth, birds – you know what a bird is, right? Well, most of them used a variety of songs to serenade potential mates, protect their territory, and so on. I observed different groups of Arkady sturgeons within swarms emitting identical light sequences at regular intervals … It was actual *tempo*, like notes in a measure, not the frantic pulses we usually see when they converse individually—'

Carrie snapped away from her indulgence.

'Wait, wait, wait. You mean those things *chat* with each other? Conversationally?'

'*Yes*,' Viola said, taking an enthusiastic sip from her drink. 'Well … strictly speaking, that's just a theory.'

'What makes you think they can?'

Viola's eyes darted sideways, and she leaned forward again. Carrie rolled her eyes and followed suit.

'I've seen footage from trawlers all over Zeus. Some of them are violent, even tragic … but it's fascinating. You can see the Arkady trying to outsmart point defences. They work together, use tactics, even diversions. They are far more intelligent than anyone knows …'

Carrie looked past her and frowned.

'I swear that hot waiter keeps looking over here,' she said.

But Viola was on Zeus now.

'Only miners think they're intelligent creatures,' she said, gulping down the rest of the cocktail. 'Isn't that ironic?'

Carrie's face paled.

'Oh my God, look who it is.'

'Who? The waiter?' Viola stammered, holding up her glass. 'Oh, good.'

Her friend straightened up and spoke through her teeth.

'No – Travis Mareck is heading this way.'

Viola's muscles tightened as Carrie smiled uncomfortably. The Merckon CEO approached and looked down at them, resplendent in his form-fitting attire, his eyes a dreadful mix of greed and desire. Accompanying him were two bodyguards – augmented mutants, judging from their size, and the hardware covering their eyes and ears.

'What a pleasant surprise,' he remarked. 'I hope you find these arrangements satisfactory?'

Viola's heart was pumping in her ears.

'Yes, sir,' she mumbled. 'Thank you for this.'

'I should be thanking you,' he said warmly. But his charm dissolved as his eyes shifted to Carrie. 'I'm afraid we haven't met.'

'I'm sorry,' Viola said. 'This is Carrie—'

'Lin, who works in my legal department,' Travis said. 'I know *who* she is. I just said we haven't met.'

Carrie cleared her throat.

'Hello, Mr Mareck,' she said, extending her hand. 'Nice to meet you?'

Travis regarded her with disdain.

'Has Miss Silveri told you anything you weren't supposed to hear?'

Carrie's cheeks flushed as red as a rose.

'Excuse me?' she staggered. 'No, sir, not to my knowledge.'

Travis shook his head.

''Tsk, tsk,' he said. 'Bad enough you indulged her, Viola. Now you've made her a liar as well.'

Suddenly, Carrie winced and clutched at her temples. As Travis looked on, she began shaking violently, her eyes rolling upwards, her hands clawed and locked in a seizure. Viola stood to help her, but was forced down by a heavy hand on her shoulder. She watched in horror as Carrie locked up one final time, then slumped onto the table – alive, as far as Viola could tell, but unconscious.

Viola noticed one of the guards slip something into his pocket.

'Too much to drink,' Travis sighed. 'Happens to a lot of people their first time here.'

Some staff approached and scooped Carrie off her seat, hauling her away quietly. Travis sat in the vacated chair.

'What did you do to her?' Viola demanded. 'Where are they taking her?'

'In a few hours she'll awaken in her home with a fierce headache and some amnesia,' he shrugged. 'Which, as it happens, is necessary to protect my intellectual property. You *did* tell her too much, Viola. I find that upsetting.'

'I didn't say anything of consequence,' Viola said.

'That isn't yours to judge,' he said, leaning back into the seat. 'You and I have a mutual interest in maintaining the widespread belief that our research subjects are mindless, savage beasts. It isn't like you to be so careless. That's a sign you're working too hard.'

Travis rose abruptly, offering his hand.

'Come,' he said. 'We must remedy this.'

Viola got up slowly, catching herself from losing balance. The alcohol had done its work. The floor wobbled beneath her as alarm bells blared through her impaired mind. Travis led her from the VIP area towards the dance floor, moving through the frenzy until they were completely surrounded by the celebration. He turned, grasped her by the hips, and began moving to the rhythm, eyes ablaze.

'Let yourself go,' he urged.

A burst of adrenaline compelled her to resist.

'No!' she protested. 'Where did … what have you done … to Carrie?'

But for some dark reason, her willpower was overwhelmed.

'*Let go,*' he commanded.

Her body obeyed, gracefully matching his movements, grinding against him even as the skin on her neck tingled with anger. How could she feel so physically attracted to someone she loathed?

'Your work is important to me,' he said, so close that she could taste his breath. 'But you need a release.'

His lips made contact with her ear lobe.

'I can help,' he said, running a hand up her back. Every fibre of her being was battling a primordial instinct to run. She gasped as he took her hands with a firm squeeze and led her off the floor, towards the restricted area of the club, where muffled sounds of pleasure rose above the thundering music. The host at the entrance smiled without making eye contact, as a couple brushed past them half undressed.

The world was spinning as Travis led her to a room at the end of the hall. When the door slid open, a waft of sterile air with hints of antiseptic fragrance assaulted her sinuses; the only furniture inside was a lush bed with reflective comforters and dozens of pillows.

Her stomach churned, and for a moment she thought she might be sick.

His hand slid lower from her back.

'Now,' Travis said, 'about your indiscretions …'

Viola froze in the doorway, muscles tight as steel, contemplating escape scenarios, when the voice of an old woman called out from behind them:

'I'd move that hand away from there if I were you.'

Viola saw Travis tense up, gritting his teeth.

'Cerlis,' he hissed. 'Did you just threaten me?'

'No, that was advice,' the woman said. 'She's not interested. Every guest here can see that. Isn't that right, honey?'

Travis turned around, removing his hand. Viola followed suit, and was shocked to see Cerlis Tarkon, the CEO of Vulcan Dynamics, standing there with a tall, buxom blonde on each shoulder plus an entourage of security personnel behind her. Barely a metre and a half tall, she looked to be a century old. Yet her features were striking, and her posture was as rigid as the ladies glued to her hips.

'This is my room,' Travis snarled.

'I outbid you for it,' Cerlis said, stepping forward. 'Seems you're not on the best terms with the management in your own club, so they were more than happy to break the agreement. So if anyone's panties drop in there, they'll be mine. Miss Silveri, may I buy you a drink? I'd love to have your company.'

'Um,' Viola managed to say.

Cerlis read her thoughts.

'This won't hurt your career,' she said, casually looking towards her entourage. 'Will it, Mareck? Speak up now, *boy*. Damn club music makes it hard for an old lady to hear.'

Travis was standing perfectly straight, his expression impossible to read. But his eyes were simmering orbs radiating with malice.

'Take care to remember our NDA,' he said pleasantly. 'Cerlis likes to intrude on matters that don't concern her—'

'Oh, fuck the formalities,' Cerlis muttered, storming forward and taking Viola by the hand. 'C'mon girl, let me show you a good time.'

Viola was yanked away from Travis, nearly tripping over her heels. Cerlis's grip was a lot stronger than she expected.

'I don't want to cause any trouble, ma'am,' Viola said.

The old woman gave her a scolding look.

'What?' Cerlis demanded. 'Are you apologising for being *groped*? Bloody hell. You ought to be thanking me instead.'

'Excuse me, I meant to thank you,' Viola said, before suddenly remembering. 'Oh my God, Carrie!'

'She's fine,' Cerlis assured, hobbling back up the steps leading to the VIP area. 'My people had her home safely before those two meatsacks knew what hit them.'

'The bodyguards?'

'If that's what you call them,' Cerlis said, as one of the blondes helped her onto a barstool. She looked like a child seated at the counter. 'The shits used a synapse jammer on her, gave the poor thing a seizure. So we cranked the level up a few notches and turned it on them. Looks like they mutated a few genomes in the wrong direction now. *Bartender!* Do I need to show my tits to get a drink around here?'

Viola blushed scarlet as the blondes giggled. One of the scantily clad male bartenders rushed over.

'Vodka, no ice,' Cerlis snapped. 'The lovely lady here will have a glass of water. And look here, you greasy pec moron, have someone else bring the drinks. If I catch you eavesdropping on our conversation I'll have your balls stuffed into your ears. Got it?'

The bartender nodded eagerly and rushed off as Viola's jaw dropped a few centimetres.

'One of Merckon's imbeciles,' Cerlis said. 'Most of the staff are augments, fitted with all kinds of sensory enhancing crap to make them better spies. Watch what you say around here. Everyone's on a payroll and they're all listening. My ladies here are running some interference of their own to make sure no one hears what I have to say.'

Cerlis pushed a pill towards Viola. 'This will sober you up. Swallow it.'

The two blondes, Viola realised, were scanning the crowd. One beamed a smile at the waitress who brought the drinks.

Viola took the pill and chased it down with the water.

'Let me explain something to you,' Cerlis said. 'When I was your age, women were worshipped. Not for our brains, mind you, but for our vaginas. And not because of what men like sticking in them, but for what comes out nine months later. When humanity faced extinction, anything with a uterus was sacred. Now, I've never met you before, but I know a consensual fling when I see one. That wasn't. What Travis did back there would have got him killed on the spot. Today, I'm not even sure it gets him fined. Why did you let him do it?'

Viola shook her head, disgusted with herself.

'I don't know,' she said honestly.

'Makes two of us,' Cerlis said, taking a gratuitous sip. 'A strong woman like you should know better. That pig isn't half the man who used to run Merckon. Times have changed, and not for the better. Looks like prosperity on the surface, but really we're heading backwards. Your father would agree, I'm sure.'

'You know him?'

'I sure do, though he'd probably deny it.'

'What do you mean?'

'We worked together for decades and argued about everything. Smartest fool I ever met, he is. He chose to have one child, I chose to have ten. Mine all came out from between my legs. But you were born from a synthetic uterus, lucky you.'

Viola blinked.

'Excuse me?'

'What, he didn't tell you? Well, isn't *that* just like him.'

Either the pill was working very quickly, or the shock of what

Cerlis Tarkon had just revealed had blasted the drunken fog away with sobering clarity.

'You're telling me I'm an *amniosynth*?' Viola stammered.

'Oh, stop acting like that surprises you,' Cerlis waved, taking another sip. 'You're not just *any* old amniosynth dear. He's treated you more like an experiment than a daughter your whole life. Don't tell me otherwise, I know. Thanks to him, humanity doesn't need a woman's plumbing to procreate any more. So use that genetically polished IQ of yours and tell me you can't fathom how your father and I might have our differences.'

'My father made topsoil for Merckon,' Viola said. 'He doesn't know anything about—'

'The man crowned an empire,' Cerlis said. 'But if you think dirt was the only thing he could get his brain around, well then I'm a virgin. Honest.'

'But what about my mother?' Viola asked. 'He told me she died when I was an infant.'

'Laughably ironic, considering he invented the first artificial birth canal,' Cerlis answered, 'though you probably don't see the humour.'

Viola's head was spinning.

'There are pictures of her … I saw videos of us …'

'An actress in a tragically twisted script,' Cerlis said, trading a sip and wink with one of the blondes. 'I can arrange an introduction, if you like.'

The revelation was as poison to Viola.

'Who else knows so much about my life?' she fumed.

'Does it matter?' Cerlis said, frowning. 'Anything lowly Travis knows, the highborns can find out. So you should just assume they already have. You're on everyone's radar, Viola. A new type of flower to bloom from your father's mad experiment. Now Travis Mareck has your very special mind studying alien fish, which either confirms my suspicion that he's an asshole or proves to everyone that he's a genius.'

'Why are you telling me this?'

'Because I'll pay double whatever the twat is paying you, that's why,' Cerlis barked. 'I know what *my* freighter brought to your front door earlier today. And thanks to your shitty booze tolerance, I know those things aren't as dumb as they look.'

Cerlis finished the vodka and slammed the glass onto the bar.

'*Bartender!* Fuck!' she roared, pointing at it.

Viola rubbed her temples. This wasn't the kind of night she had envisaged.

'I heard the Vulcan properties on Hephaestus are nice,' she mumbled, hoping for a change of topic. 'What brings you to Merckon Prime?'

'Meetings with Chancellor Jade and her party of misfits,' Cerlis spat, as several Sirkus employees fumbled over each other to fetch the summoned drink. 'That woman gives me cramps. By the way, it's a shame you're not gay, else I'd let you take one of my blondes for a ride.'

Viola gasped midway through a sip of water, some of which snorted out through her nostrils.

'There are women lined up from here to Tau Ceti who want to meet you,' Cerlis said, a fresh cocktail in her grasp. 'What reason did that idiot boss of yours give for bringing you here?'

'He said … or implied that I needed a break.'

'Hmm, I'm sure. I really hope your effort yields something worthwhile, something that isn't another *Archangel*. Christ,' she muttered, downing half the glass. 'You're not an artist, are you? I mean, you'd agree that art is important, so allow me an analogy: like most art, the *Archangel* is culturally vital because it's expensive shit that isn't especially useful for anything except hanging around and being admired. Of course I've profited immensely from it, and so has Travis Mareck. But the difference is that he actually *likes* art, whereas I just dabble. Understand?'

'No,' Viola mumbled, completely spent.

Cerlis faced her and gently grasped her hands.

'Viola,' she said sincerely, transforming into a grandmother. 'Your father was cruel, but he was right about two things: Travis Mareck, and your ability to do great things. If you believe so much in the Arkady, then I'm willing to accept that on merit alone. My employment offer stands indefinitely, and I suggest you give it serious thought before Travis puts you on a freighter. I'm a powerful woman, but I can't promise you anything beyond the Belt. Understand?'

Viola nodded.

'Then it was a pleasure meeting you, Doctor. My ladies will take you anywhere you need to go.'

'Thank you, Miss Tarkon.'

'Please, call me Cerlis,' she said, with a hint of sadness. 'There aren't enough good people left who do.'

12

VESPA

She always opened her eyes at 04:45, fifteen minutes before the alarm was set. The rays of the Orionis sun would not warm the halls of Tabit Prime for another hour, yet this was her time, a calming peace before the day's storm. For Chancellor Vespa Jade, waking from slumber was slipping from one troubled fog into the next, where a hundred possible futures emerged from a tenuous present.

Sitting upright, she blinked at the blue iris on the ceiling, and said a word:

'Record.'

And then she began mumbling, falling asleep again briefly but waking with a jolt, recalling all the things she had seen. It took nearly an hour to describe every detail, including the ambiguous and impossible dream sequences, as these were necessary to isolate the influence of her personal life on the visions that came to her in the night.

'Stop,' she commanded, abruptly realising that last night's dreams were new. Different. Darker.

Something crucial had changed.

Vespa learned long ago to not take them literally. There was time to discern their meaning by searching for clues in the present. Caution was paramount. Rather than dwell on unlimited possibilities, she would step away from the future and let her mind wander. Clarity would eventually strike.

Blinking away the visions, she reached for a glass of water, wondering if it was originally the by-product of hydrogen reactors or distilled from a comet before reaching her lips. On Earth, water had come from rain, glaciers, streams, rivers, springs, aquifers, and wells – all plentiful once, until the wars made them vanish. Vespa appreciated these details because she believed there must always be someone in power who still did. Thousands of hours spent studying twenty-first-century Earth had instilled a nostalgic responsibility towards the people the Genesis ships had left behind. That hundred-year stretch of history was the turning point for humanity. Until then, not one generation considered water a precious resource. Those that came after killed for it.

The thought reminded her of the dreams from last night, making her wonder: what am I taking for granted today? *What could cause such darkness to spread over Orionis?*

Vespa stood up and walked to the full-length mirror. Her hair was long and light brown, with streaks of grey prominent enough to draw attention from the rest of her ageing features. Subtle wrinkles spread from the corner of her azure-blue eyes, and darkened skin filled the bags beneath them. The slightest gap separated her two front teeth, presenting a smile that lingered with any new audience. Thin and gangly, her angular features gave her an androgynous appearance.

Vespa hardly recognised the person looking back at her. Such was the price of being Chancellor. On Earth, there had been mayors who ran cities as large as the entire population of Orionis. Her responsibility was colossally greater than theirs.

The dreams began when she was just a child. Her twin brother Arturus had shared them, and they often stayed awake together to avoid the startling visions they had no context for comprehending. By day they were downtrodden outcasts, often seen mumbling to themselves, delirious with fatigue and prophecy. Children mocked them, adults shunned them, instructors pitied them. They were assumed to be the victims of bad mutations, perhaps afflicted with schizophrenia. Had they not been firstborns, they would have been ghosts with no future, destined for a short and cruel life.

But their parents never gave up on them. Gabriel Jade was a political scientist; her husband Cyrus an intelligence analyst. Both worked for the government, and learned their trades from highborn parents who were experts in Earth history and helped write the Articles of Orionis

– the founding charter of the colony. When they realised their children were experiencing dreams with a direct association to real events, they poured knowledge of human history into them. The more the twins learned, the more often they recognised the people and places in their visions. Soon after, Vespa and Arturus were 'witnessing' events that shaped the world they lived in, and then outcomes which had not yet occurred – but might well someday.

All along, it was the Gift whispering to them, and it was theirs to master as best they could – for the price of a childhood, friends, a good night's rest, and, even on occasion, a conscience.

At 05:50, Vespa was dressed and walking through a long, winding hallway that connected the executive residence to the capitol levels. The cold metal walls and high ceiling were curved and perfectly smooth, interrupted only by lighting fixtures to help pedestrians navigate the former mothership. As she passed them, an automated tour began, explaining that heavy water rich with deuterium once gushed through these same passageways, bringing melted ice fuel stores to the fusion reactors far aft.

In many ways, she travelled these halls each day to ignite her own political reactions. Once she understood what the Gift was, Vespa believed that history had reserved a place for her and her brother. She believed in it so fervently she began speaking of it as inevitable, sharing her plans for Orionis with Arturus and promising him a place at her side when her reign began.

But one night, Vespa had dreamt that House Alyxander stole something precious from her. It was a nightmare, a horrible vision that left her gasping for air. When she sought Arturus for comfort, he was gone. It was the eve of their fifteenth birthday, and he had left in the deep of night without saying goodbye, abandoning her to follow his own destiny. The House, he would explain years later, spoke to him in ways she could never understand.

Vespa was devastated. If not for her parents intervening, she would have ended her life. But with their help, she renewed her determination and continued her studies. By the age of sixteen, she was an expert on Earth culture subjects ranging from arts to political science to economics. When she was nineteen, she took her first position with the Orionis government as an analyst for the Commerce Department. Thus began an impressive career that would last four decades, eventually leading to her appointment as Vice-Chancellor to Donovan Mayce, the elected Chancellor of Orionis, in 2802.

But it took a national tragedy to propel her to the highest seat of power. With three years remaining in his first term, Chancellor Mayce died in a freak accident. By law, Vespa assumed his powers as head of state, and would hold them until his elected term was complete in 2810. With the skill of a seasoned politician, Vespa cautiously guided the nation through a period of mourning, while delicately offering alternatives to the policies Donovan Mayce had championed.

Vespa never doubted she would eventually become Chancellor, no more than she questioned the absolute necessity of removing Donovan Mayce from office. Her visions had foretold of systemic calamity throughout Orionis if he stayed a full term. His expulsion was essential for the survival of mankind, and so she had taken decisive action.

Only Arturus knew the truth of what really happened to Donovan Mayce. The Gift was their secret. No one ever needed to know that it guided their judgment – or that her brother was providing the same prescient counsel to House Alyxander as well.

Both siblings believed there were times when evil must be committed in order to do good.

During the voyage from Earth, the bow of the *Tabit Genesis* had been an asteroid which had been hollowed and reshaped to protect the rest of the ship from interstellar particles crashing into it at half the speed of light. Today it sheltered Liberty Hall, the third habitation torus that rotated around the centreline axis of the former mothership. It housed the main seat of government, where all the senate hearings and voting sessions took place. Justice Hall, the main judiciary branch of the Orionis government, was on the other side. The third quadrant was reserved for the Commerce Branch, where all the economic activity of the colony was regulated.

Vespa reached the main entrance at 06:11, greeted by the haunting memorial dedicated to Earth. A great plaque surrounded by a volumetric image of the planet as seen from space was inscribed with one of the last messages received by the *Tabit Genesis*:

Genesis, our time has come.
Live, brave voyagers, so our memory will persevere.
Love, kindred souls, for we loved too little.
Flee, precious survivors, and do not ever return.
Remember Earth always, your home once, your family for all time.
You are our Genesis now, our dawn and hope for Humankind.
Farewell.

Vespa always paused here to place her hand on the cold, polished titanium. The press was fond of capturing this moment, as she stood silently and meditated on those final words and the people who wrote them.

Humanity was her responsibility now.

It was 06:19, and the first rays of the Orionis sun were striking the hull of the former *Tabit Genesis*, its light guided though the kilometres of passageways on board. The ruined world of Eileithyia was glowing outside, a perpetual cloud of noxious atmosphere reflecting most of that light back into space. The mothership had anchored in a geostationary orbit, matching the planet's rotational speed of one revolution every 26.5 hours.

The station was beginning to stir. Bureaucrats, officials, lawyers, and legions of assistants began filling the halls.

Another day of governing, and she knew it would not be easy.

The morning briefings had been uneventful – there was nothing in the economic, political, or security landscape which might account for her disturbing dreams. After a brief conversation with her Chief of Staff and a conference call with the Finance Minister, Vespa was ready to begin a series of individual meetings with corporate executives. It was time to start campaigning under her own name for re-election.

Unfortunately, that meant hosting the company of donors whom she genuinely disliked. In her experience, the best practice was to order meetings by the anticipated level of hostility. As such, Cerlis Tarkon always earned the day's first appointment, and she arrived at precisely 09:00.

'Good morning, Chancellor,' the old woman said, as her two blonde escorts shut the door behind them. 'I thought of you earlier, while passing a kidney stone. Happens too often at my age, and I'll be fine, thanks for asking. But when the thing was suctioned down the privy it reminded me of the money I donated to Donovan Mayce's campaign. Hope I'm not being too personal, but we're both women here, least I think so anyway, and you've always struck me as someone I can be frank with. Ha! Who am I kidding, that's true with everyone I know. So let's just get on with it: how much are you asking for and why in hell should I give it to you?'

'You are as … courteous as ever, Miss Tarkon,' Vespa said, with a smile. 'I thought we would maintain some decorum for a change.'

Cerlis deliberately lowered herself into the couch opposite where Vespa was sitting.

'It's rarely a pleasant memory, these meetings. But I recall reaching an agreement last time we met, political interests notwithstanding, that you would support a certain bit of legislation that's rather dear to me. You see, people just assume old folks can't remember shit, but I'm told exercise wards off senility, and it so happens I'm laid often enough to remember deals I've struck with heads of state. But humour me anyway and remind me what the last cheque I wrote bought me.'

Vespa began counting off the answer on her fingers:

'Financing for three new biodome projects on Hephaestus, several government purchase orders for your freighters, lower taxes on food production revenues—'

'Damnit, my head hurts,' Cerlis interrupted. 'You know why that might be?'

'I have a few theories.'

'It's because I keep asking you to do something, and like some mentally challenged mutant, you keep telling me you'll do it, but the instruction never fucking registers with the part of your brain that can actually execute it. Know what I'm talking about?'

'Miss Tarkon, as I believe I've reminded you before, I won't support extending the Heritage Act to amniosynths until corporations agree to share the cost we'll incur for doing so.'

'And I think I've reminded you before, that's the goddamn dumbest excuse I've ever heard for not doing it. We can feed as many people as there's demand for, Vespa.'

'Can you? And who benefits when this government's expenditures quadruple? Really, Cerlis, I've handed Vulcan enough money already. You don't have the capacity to manage all that extra demand anyway.'

'We'll build more factories—'

'Which would give you a convenient excuse to claim financial hardship and raise food prices even more. It's extortion masquerading as capitalism. No thank you, Miss Tarkon.'

'If money is the concern, then grow a pair and repeal the whole damn law,' Cerlis offered. 'Put firstborns and amniosynths on equal footing, and make 'em both pay their own way.'

'It may not be fair for amniosynths, but to restore humanity to its former glory there must always be a population segment that is afforded maximum opportunity to thrive,' Vespa explained. 'Firstborns are our last real connection to Earth. We will continue to nurture them for as long as we can.'

'What the hell would you know about nurturing?' Cerlis fumed. 'You do understand that amniosynths are human, don't you?'

'I'm not sure that's true any more with Obyerans, but point noted,' Vespa said calmly. 'In the interest of being solutions-based, all you have to do to convince me to repeal Heritage is share the cost. I want you to legally *guarantee* to provide *every* child born in Orionis with inalienable human rights. Imagine it: Vulcan Dynamics, the great benefactor, subsidising free food, healthcare, education, and employment for all.'

Cerlis threw her wrinkled hands in the air.

'If I didn't know any better, I'd swear I was talking to a bigot,' she spat. 'Heritage has done naught but drive a wedge between people. It's why Brotherhood fell, why Ceti rules the Belt, why the Independence Wars happened and why the Outer Rim still points its guns this way. You've crafted an oligarchy that stands on everyone else to keep shits like you elevated in the world. Rubbing a monument every day doesn't make you a humanist. The people know a fraud when they see one.'

'Then perhaps you should support the opposition,' Vespa said. 'See how much more you'll get from them than you already have from me. You have the *Archangel*, folly that it is. It's made you and your colleagues a fortune for decades, all of it subsidised by this government. You have work contracts and orders to keep your factories and shipyards busy for years, plus all the tax incentives you've ever wanted, and all I ask in return is for a vote of confidence and for you to respect my opinion, as I do yours, even when we disagree.'

'You have no *empathy*, woman,' Cerlis muttered. 'It's something *mothers* tend to have. That's the real issue here. You have no context for comprehending how obtuse you are.'

'Cerlis, we would bankrupt ourselves extending universal privileges to every child,' Vespa said. 'Your intent is noble, but this utopian society you're after is out of reach, at least for now. Heritage can keep up with natural firstborn population growth, not the amniosynth vaults of House Alyxander. The colonisation of Orionis is more tenuous than you think. Overpopulation leads to mass extinctions. We lost our homeworld because we grasped this too late.'

'And all this time I thought Earth was lost to giant red insects,' Cerlis sneered. 'Maybe if you'd spent less time studying life and more time living it you'd actually understand human behaviour. You're about as relatable to people as the Raothri are to kindness.'

'You've got me there,' Vespa mocked. 'Now I'm sold on the idea.'

The Vulcan Dynamics CEO bolted upright with startling ease.

'You don't have as many friends as you think,' she hissed. 'Be careful, Chancellor.'

'Threatening a head of state is unwise,' Vespa sighed, standing as well. 'I appreciate your passion, but for the last time, the Heritage Act is the law of Orionis. However, I thank you for supporting my election campaign. I'm sure there's another government contract in it for you somewhere.'

Cerlis glared at her.

'I rather miss your predecessor.'

'We all miss him, Miss Tarkon.'

'He was older than you, but more progressive. Open to new perspectives.'

'An essential attribute for any Chancellor.'

'Yet absent from present company. Are you getting enough sleep? Those bags under your eyes look like they're packed for a long holiday.'

'I'm sleeping just fine, thank you for asking. I hear it can be difficult for old people.'

'And for those with a heavy conscience.'

'As you say. One of Chancellor Mayce's dreams was to reset relations with Outer Rim sovereignties. Put the past behind and pursue a fresh start.'

'So?'

'So I thought you might be pleased to hear that I've decided to honour his efforts by inviting House Alyxander to Tabit Prime.'

Cerlis turned bright red.

'You're not that dumb.'

'They're bringing a host of a least a hundred ships, mostly freighters, to trade freely and join me for discussions on an open trade agreement,' Vespa said. 'They should arrive in a month's time. And before you embarrass yourself with a political stunt, the Ministry of Foreign Affairs approved the measure, as did Admiral Hedricks.'

'House Alyxander has ties with Ceti, whom we are at war with,' Cerlis growled.

'They come in peace. We engage with all those who recognise our government and respect our laws. I'm obliged to invite Vulcan Dynamics to attend, and your executive colleagues as well.'

'Every single one of whom has lost life and property to Lance Alyxander.'

'If the tales are true, none more than Vulcan.'

'And you're bringing them to our front door anyway?'

'Don't worry, Cerlis. Our Navy is quite formidable, and incidentally so is the firepower at your own disposal. House Alyxander is taking the greater risk.'

'In exchange for what?'

Vespa smiled.

'If the latest polls mean anything, it seems the privateer voting bloc views House Alyxander more favourably than the corporations. And the cause of that sentiment, as it were, is rising food prices. Seeing as I've fallen so far out of favour with you, I need to be more, how should I say … "progressive" in my search for votes this election.'

Cerlis smiled as well.

'Did that strategy come to you in your dreams?' she said, turning for the door. 'Don't bother answering that, child.'

*

By 22:13 that evening, Vespa was finally making the long journey back to her bedroom. As expected, the day had become more pleasant once she was rid of the firebrand Cerlis Tarkon. On the whole, the other executives welcomed her re-election bid, but were lukewarm about the trade delegation. She calculated that sentiment would improve with time, especially once they learned of the terms House Alyxander was willing to offer.

Even so, the Vulcan Dynamics CEO was a festering nuisance, and a dangerous one. The mere fact she implied knowledge of her dreams was disturbing. It was a provocation, and to be fair, one she deserved. But when Arturus arrived with the delegation, she would make a point of raising her concerns with him. He would know what to do, as he had with Chancellor Mayce.

Vespa undressed, leaving a trail of discarded garments on her way to the shower. ORPHUS should have digested the account of her dreams by now. He was a gift from her brother, a masterpiece of AI engineering that she had hooked into *Tabit*'s datacores. ORPHUS helped interpret what her visions foretold.

After drying off, she slipped into a satin gown and climbed beneath the covers of her bed, welcoming their soft touch against her skin. There was no other physical intimacy in her life but this. Sleep was tugging at her, but first she had to know what ORPHUS thought of her new dreams, and the reason for the change.

Vespa stared at the reassuring blue iris above her.

'What did you see?' she asked.

'I saw a place and a name,' ORPHUS answered.

'Tell me …'

'I saw the Hades Terminus,' ORPHUS said. 'And Maez Obyeran.'

13

VLADRIC

When Sig Lareck began the day, his agenda was filled with the tasks of governance. The man was deeply invested in Lethe, its community, and its continued prosperity. He often made unannounced visits to the Commons to speak with labourers, business owners, even school children and their hopeful parents. But when he left his flat overlooking the Meridus Canyon, he was met by Ceti security officers who informed him that there had been an emergency, and that he was to accompany them to the spaceport at once.

Twenty-nine hours later, he was at the helm of the most famous vessel in Ceti's history: the *Aria Black*, flagship of Vladric Mors. It was the first time Sig had piloted a warship in years. For now, the view outside made him forget his frustration at being summoned so far away from his beloved Lethe. The *Black* was coasting past rows of Ceti corvettes burrowed within the excavated shell of a planetoid; welding sparks flew through space as man and machine worked frantically on ships in various states of assembly, many with their insides exposed and newer parts being positioned to join the craft.

As Sig concentrated on flying, the sublime sound of a woman singing filled the cabin. Her enchanting voice carried throughout the ship, and the *Black* sounded like a concert hall.

'You helped build this,' Vladric said, from the gunner position behind him. 'Remember?'

'I had no idea,' Sig breathed. 'The last time I saw this place ...'

'It was home.'

They named her *Bertha* all those years ago, a rogue planetoid with a deep crater impact set perfectly in the centre of her five-kilometre diameter. A likely capture from either Heracles or Hera, the peculiar rock followed a wide, eccentric polar orbit around Zeus that took her far past the shipping lanes and the range of Navy radars. Ceti miners, lured to the impact site for its industrial diamonds, had towed an abandoned freighter into the excavation cavity, then sealed and pressurised it. The perfect hideout was born.

Today, *Bertha* was more metal than rock. The inside reminded Sig of a hollowed stone brimming with quartz, only instead of crystals there was the glitter of Ceti corvettes.

'Are they all shielded?' Sig asked.

'No,' Vladric said quietly. 'Tallendin only has enough kit for twenty ships.'

'*Twenty?* What about the rest?'

'Decoys,' Vladric muttered. 'The entire fleet will be modified to accept the generators if any more become available. Visually, no one will be able to tell the difference. The shielded 'vettes will be our vanguard. With luck, the Navy will only target them.'

Sig didn't care for the flippancy. Ceti had neither the manufacturing capacity nor the components required to equip so many, so soon. Seizing Navy warships with the intent of harvesting parts or attacking convoys with armed escorts was ugly business, risking experienced marauders when they were needed most for the assault on the *Archangel*.

From Sig's perspective, it was a fool's proposition. Many would die the day they flew against the mothership, just as when they flew against Brotherhood. Vladric's obsessive determination had always been dangerous. Now he was pathologically insane.

Shifting in the captain's chair, Sig turned his focus to the beautiful opera blaring on the loudspeakers. Classical Earth music always graced the *Black*'s bulkheads, even during combat. The warship had been Vladric's for decades, but she had been built nearly two hundred years earlier, a classic UNSEC design with oversized thrusters and a bulky fuselage that many mistook for a freighter. The *Black*'s hull was scarred from countless skirmishes. Unlike the sleek, converging hull of modern-day Keating corvettes, it boasted hard, boxed sections that graduated from the engine housing to the distinctive twin weapon housings in the bow.

But, for all of its tough, menacing exterior, the inside was a refined sanctum that seemed anything but a death dealer. Vladric's fondness for antiquity was evident everywhere on board. Framed recreations of Renaissance-era paintings were bolted to bulkheads, and every non-emergency conduit, bolt, panel and pipe was concealed by synthetic-fibre stained wood, complete with moulding and trim. The *Black* felt like an ancient ocean liner, something powered by coal or even wind, not fusion reactors.

Vladric treated the ship as if it was his home; and in a sense it was, except he used it to wage war, pillage from corporations, and murder his enemies. Terrifying and cruel on the outside, inspiring and genteel within, the *Aria Black* was a true reflection of the man who had started the Independence Wars. The captain's chair itself looked like the seat of a fighter: a control stick was on the right armrest; a throttle on the left, and it was encompassed by an AR display that gave him a 360-degree view of the space around the ship.

Sig had no business sitting in it. He was the Governing District Officer of Lethe, one of the most prosperous colonies under Ceti control. His marauding days were long over, yet here he was.

'Full stop,' Vladric ordered.

Sig complied, rotating the *Aria Black*'s engine nacelles forward to slow her momentum. Then the captain's chair turned about to face him.

'You handle her well enough,' Vladric commented, producing a bladder canteen and sending it gently across the cabin. Sig knew it was filled with a potent malt whisky. Reluctantly, he placed the nozzle in his mouth and gave it a slight squeeze; then nearly choked as the beverage burned down his throat.

'The *Black*'s easier to fly than this is to drink,' Sig croaked, pushing the canteen back across.

'You used to down that like water,' Vladric said, taking a sip himself. 'I miss the old days, when we were young … fearless …'

'Senseless is more like it,' Sig said.

'Did you ever think we'd make it this far?' Vladric asked.

'Never,' Sig answered. 'We had a death wish.'

114

The canteen crossed again. Prepared for the bitter taste this time, Sig drank down a larger gulp.

'First Brotherhood, now the *Archangel*,' Vladric said. 'Maybe we still do.'

'I don't,' Sig muttered, drinking some more.

Vladric looked at him thoughtfully.

'Your old self would,' he said.

'My old self was always the first one through a breach,' Sig said, taking yet another sip, feeling a warm buzz flood his neck and cheeks. 'But that was because I didn't care if I lived.'

'Twenty-five years of babysitting a colony will do that to you,' Vladric said.

'Do what?'

'Make you forget you were young once.'

'I wish I didn't remember my youth,' Sig snapped. 'Most of it, anyway. What does it matter? Lethe was your way of forcing me to retire. The death wish ended there, and I'm grateful for it.'

A hard line formed across Vladric's brow.

'I didn't trust anyone else to run Lethe.'

Sig allowed himself a smile.

'If I didn't want the job, I wouldn't have accepted.'

'Really?' Vladric said, surprised. 'Are you saying you *wanted* out?'

'Brotherhood was a bloody day for us. Lethe was a chance to start over.'

The singer's aria carried over what would have been an awkward silence. Sig knew he had drunk too much and pushed the canteen away.

Vladric snatched it from the air.

'This is called "Il dolce suono", which means "The Sweet Sound",' he said. 'A scene from the opera *Lucia di Lammermoor*.'

'It's beautiful,' Sig admitted.

'Think so?' Vladric said, swallowing a gulp. 'You're listening to the crazed ramblings of a woman who just murdered her husband on their wedding night. Who knew depravity could be articulated with such … divinity.'

Sig stopped himself from shaking his head.

'That's tragic.'

'All the good operas are,' Vladric said. 'So Brotherhood was the last time you fired a weapon?'

'It's the last time I killed anyone,' Sig answered.

'You sound like a man with a lot of regret.'

Sig took a deep breath. In fact, he had more regrets than he could count.

'When you and I were marauding, they called us terrorists,' he said. 'When we put the Ceti sigil on our backs, they called us rebels. When we took Brotherhood, they called it a revolution.'

'Change is difficult,' Vladric said, taking another quick sip and then floating the canteen back across. 'And the price of freedom is steep.'

Sig caught the beverage, stared at it briefly, then decided against his better judgment to drink even more courage.

'Ceti is fundamentally the same as Orionis,' he said, 'And in many ways, twice as corrupt, and thrice as tyrannical.'

'You really have changed,' Vladric said.

'So have you,' Sig snapped. 'Power does that to people. But while governing Lethe I learned that power is as fleeting as the tides. One moment you're what everyone thinks they need. When they realise they were wrong to trust you, the hammer falls.'

Vladric almost seemed taken aback.

'What are you saying?'

'Ceti could be a recognised nation, not a cartel,' Sig said. 'You could bring real prosperity to people here. You could bring them *peace*. Legitimacy. Instead you're going to slaughter thousands more, and for what? You brought the tide with Brotherhood. If you attack the *Archangel*, you could be swept away by it.'

Vladric took a long look at him.

'You've always been a good friend,' he said.

'Sure I have,' Sig said. 'That's why you brought me sixty million klicks out of my way without so much as a moment's notice. You had that right once, when I was young and foolish. But Lethe is my home now. Of all the settlements that Ceti claims, none has fared better. People there depend on me. I don't want to let them down.'

'Which proves I picked the right man for the job,' Vladric said. 'Though I'm surprised at how attached to it you've become.'

'Then you'll also be surprised to know there's a woman I see from time to time ...'

'Ah, there it is,' Vladric sneered, slapping his knee. 'A woman always clouds a man's thinking. One day they'll write a tragedy about you.'

Sig just shrugged.

'I'm a difficult man to love, but we're making progress,' he said. 'She mends my soul ... brings me clarity, I think. Makes me realise how distraught I'd be if I lost her. She comforts me when I dwell on the fact that for most of my life, I've ripped good people apart from each other.'

Vladric narrowed his eyes.

'I see,' he said.

'No, you don't,' Sig scoffed, rubbing his eyes. 'You'd need a soul to understand. But it's true I miss flying. You were right about that, at least. So get on with it. You brought me here to ask me something you think you already know the answer to. I suspect I'm going to disappoint you.'

Vladric stared at him, his expression unreadable.

'Alright,' he said. 'When this conversation ends, only one of us is returning to Lethe. The man that does will lead the assault on the *Archangel*.'

Sig held Vladric's impassive gaze for a moment and then burst into laughter.

'The other will take the *Aria Black* on a mission to abduct one of King Masaad's twin children,' Vladric continued.

Sig nodded his head enthusiastically, guffawing.

'I'm sorry,' he wheezed. 'Go on.'

'It's not as impossible as it sounds,' Vladric said, unbothered by the laughter. 'I know precisely where they'll be.'

'And I know "precisely" where the airlock is,' Sig replied. 'I'll just space myself and save you the trouble, thanks.'

'We need House Obyeran's Lightspears,' Vladric said. 'We can't win without them.'

Sig hung his head and ran both hands through his hair, clenching his fists tightly around clumps of it.

'We can't *win* at all,' he growled, staring incredulously, all trace of humour gone.

'You never believed in this plan, did you?' Vladric asked.

'It takes more faith than usual,' Sig admitted.

'They'll each be alone, in a disabled ship … unarmed! It's a ritual they have, some rite of passage. Of all the raids you've done, none were easier than this.'

A scowl twisted Sig's face.

'Why not send one of the younger sadists instead?' he said.

'Because I need my *best* sadist for this,' Vladric answered. 'Someone experienced, with—'

'No,' Sig said. 'I'm not doing it.'

'Sig, you've had a lot to drink.'

'Masaad Obyeran has committed no crime,' Sig said. 'They are completely isolated from Orionis, Ceti, the Belt, everything.'

'Which is exactly why there's no harm in—'

'You are asking me to kidnap a father's children, you fucking lunatic.'

The shout lingered, drowning out the opera for a moment. It was the first time Sig had ever raised his voice to Vladric, whose expression was serious.

'You never answered my question about regret,' he started. 'Now I know. The twins are amniosynths … creatures mutated to ends that frighten even me. Their "mother" died years before they were born, but King Masaad had a uterus made from her DNA to grow their embryos to term. The latest generation of their cult is born that way. They're all brothers and sisters, like insects from a hive. These aren't the kind of children that play with toys. The Obyeran twins are grown adults who are bigger, stronger, smarter, and faster than you. I can appreciate you being a little apprehensive about killing *people*. But that's not what I've asked you to do.'

Vladric's voice was always calm before he did bad things.

'They're ghosts,' Sig said, avoiding eye contact. 'Just like us.'

'I'm *human*,' Vladric corrected. 'Just like you.'

Sig knew it was pointless to argue. Amniosynth technology had rescued an endangered human race from extinction. It had also provided some with the means to merge and reproduce almost any life form at will, blurring the line between what was and was not human. Orionis, with their damned Heritage Act, made that distinction very

118

clear. Vladric never respected it. But he also had his own definition of "human" in mind.

'Let's say I'm alright with the moral parameters and succeed in caging these twins,' Sig asked. 'Then what?'

Vladric crossed his arms.

'Then His Majesty will help me take the *Archangel* if he wants to see them again.'

'The man hasn't done anything wrong. To you or to Ceti.'

'No. He hasn't.'

'And if he refuses?'

'Then one of his heirs will die, and I'll attack the *Archangel* without him.'

'Even knowing that you'd lose.'

'We *all* lose once that ship leaves the yard,' Vladric said. 'It's death or the brig for everyone. Hedricks will take the *Archangel* and half the Navy into the Belt, and set his Gryphons upon our outposts. *Bertha* will be lost. Lethe will be taken or bombarded. Brotherhood will fall. Orionis "law and order" will prevail in the Outer Rim, but only with the same martial conditions that prompted us to get into this business. I'd rather die with a gun in my hand. There was a time when you would have done the same.'

'If you petitioned Chancellor Jade's government to be recognised as a nation, we could avoid bloodshed—'

'Sig. Stop that nonsense. It's beneath you. Nothing you've done for Lethe will atone for the evil you've done. It won't release you from the vow you took. Nor return the lives you've taken. The *Archangel* is your only absolution; your only hope for Lethe, your friends, the on-again, off-again woman you're happy to fuck but shy to marry. The Ceti revolution didn't end with Brotherhood, and I never signed a peace treaty with Orionis.'

Sig lowered his eyes in defeat. There was no reasoning with Vladric. And ultimately, he was right: Sig had sworn a vow to the Ceti Brotherhood, as all initiates did. It didn't matter that it had happened decades ago. The oath was timeless, and it had been witnessed by dozens, many of whom today held positions of great power in return for their loyalty.

'I vowed,' he admitted.

119

'You did,' Vladric said, his eyes betraying a hint of anger. 'But I won't hold your life to it. You're a friend. The best man I've ever known. The only one I trust to attack the *Archangel* or kidnap a prince.'

Sig noticed a Ceti gunship approaching the *Aria Black*. It stopped about two hundred metres off the bow, its blue navigation lights casting a steady pulse into the bridge.

'You're in over your head,' Sig muttered. 'Again.'

Vladric's bottom lip broadened into a smile.

'Always.'

'Fine,' Sig said, accepting his fate. 'How did you learn where the twins will be?'

'Will the answer really help make up your mind?' Vladric asked.

'To commit an act of war against a sovereign state, I consider that information operationally vital.'

'Alright. It was House Alyxander.'

'Wonderful,' Sig muttered. 'In exchange for—?'

'A significant financial incentive to do something useful with that information.'

Sig shook his head.

'Are you saying Lance Alyxa ler put a *bounty* on the Obyeran twins?'

'Does that change your moral calculus?'

Sig ignored the jab.

'You'd let me take the *Black* to do this?'

'The *Black* is the only ship that *can* do this,' Vladric said. 'My crew and boarding party are already in cryo. You should do the same. To reach the intercept in time, you're facing a hard burn for two weeks. The autopilot will place the ship in an ice field and then shut down. Life support will wake you up, but you have to maintain emission discipline.'

'What am I looking for?'

'One disabled Obyeran Lightspear. You should end up within ten thousand kilometres, but you can't use active sensors to find her. Passive tracking only. She'll be powering up slowly, if at all. If she does detect you, odds are she won't be able to fight. But that isn't assured.'

'It never is,' Sig muttered. 'What then? Breach and raid?'

Vladric nodded.

'Your target will be alone, but – Must. Be. Taken. *Alive*. The marauders know this and have the kit they need to do it quickly. You shouldn't have to leave the *Black*. You won't even have to leave your seat, not unless things go badly. But when the VIP is secure, burn the hell out. The autopilot knows where to go. You'll find out where when you need to.'

'What about Obyeran patrols, guardians, sensor buoys ...'

'You should get there before they do.'

'And if you're wrong?'

'Stay hidden. Stay alive. And then re-evaluate.'

Sig looked at the canteen in his hand. He drained the last few drops, then cast it away. It floated to the front of the spherical cabin, partially blocking the view of *Bertha*.

'If I do this ...'

'Then you can claim Alyxander's bounty,' Vladric said. 'Or I can release you from your oath, and I'll never ask anything of you again.'

Sig considered the possibility that he had seen Lethe for the last time. Ceti had other ships that could outrun a Lightspear. But no matter who manned the helm, the *Aria Black* was always Vladric's, as was her crew. For now, Sig was her captain so long as an Obyeran twin was within reach. But any deviation from the kidnapping plan would lead to the airlock, one way or the other.

Vladric spoke into his corelink.

'Victor, go ahead.'

The gunship hovering off the bow began moving closer, passing over the *Black*'s bow. Sig heard the metallic sound of the mating locks engage.

'Do you want to hear the attack plans for the *Archangel*?' Vladric asked. 'Or have you made a decision?'

'Obyeran,' Sig answered.

'Then get moving,' Vladric said, unstrapping his harness and floating out of the seat. He crossed his chest with an arm. 'Good luck.'

Sig returned the salute as Vladric left the bridge, heading aft towards the dorsal airlock. The *Aria Black* was his. There had been a time when he would have been thrilled to be seated here, craving the opportunity to hunt people. He used to love holding that power over his victims.

No longer. Sig felt nothing but dread as Vladric's gunship coasted away, leaving him with a band of frozen murderers and a ship that he sensed didn't want him aboard.

He brought up the navigation plot. The final destination was more than a billion kilometres away: an ice belt trapped between the orbits of Zeus and Heracles, part of a treacherous and vast expanse that separated the House Worlds from the Inner Rim.

They called that void the Hades Terminus.

14

JAKE

I'm in a bed, naked and spent, after one of the craziest trips of my life.

Winding tendrils of greenish smoke are streaming from my nose, merging with the thick haze of sweat and smacker-stench air overhead. Lying beside me is Lira, a prolific madam with as much wealth as a highborn. She has to be a mutant, or maybe a cyborg, optimised for giving mind-blowing pleasure to anyone, anytime; in essence, a built-to-order, state-of-the-art sexual machine. As far as Jack Tatum is concerned, her legendary reputation as the best lay in Orionis is still intact. When I glance towards her, she still has this devilish, hungry look in her eyes that makes me stir.

Myabe it's the drugs amping up the wonder factor but there's no doubt I just took part in a unique experience, and not just because we fucked each other like our lives depended on it. Visually, it was just *insane*, the way the patterns beneath her skin undulated like waves in a pool, or danced like the flames in a blaze, or roiled and churned like the cloud bands of Zeus.

Lira is on her side, her long, wild red hair splayed all over the pillows like a burst artery, patterns of blue and black slithering out from her sex, winding up her abdomen and curling around her huge breasts like serpents closing in for the kill. I still don't know how much of the living artwork is real, and how much is just the smacker messing with my head. I think I can watch it for hours, but then my post-coital period of bliss shatters and my mind plummets into the same cesspit I can never escape from.

Because Lira is just a *perk,* a reward of flesh from Ceti for revealing two undercover Navy agents in the cartel.

The weeks ever since have been hell, a searing, suffocating misery that I had to keep a hard face throughout. Jack has been the recipient of congratulatory back-slapping, drugs, toasts, drugs, bad jokes, liquor, ass-kissing, more drugs, and above all else, acting like he was proud of what he'd done. Jack Tatum is one of Vladric's stars now, a VIP with real power in the organisation, someone everyone looked up to with envy.

But when I was alone, away from the facade, and sober long enough to analyse my actions, I had to keep telling myself that I had made the right choice. The undercover operators that Jack had exposed were despicable men, playing both sides against each other in a bid to create an empire of their own. Ceti officers run their own business lines on behalf of the cartel, and each has an earnings quota to meet. These double agents were withholding line earnings from Ceti and using Navy field op money to pay down their quota. Then they hired privateers to hit convoys from both institutions, splitting the loot and selling their share wherever they could, sometimes even back to the same people they stole it from.

At first, I didn't know they were cops. I only suspected they were stealing from Ceti because my own clients fell victim to their scheme. Instead of confronting them directly, I turned Dusty loose on them. Asked him to dig around quietly, work his magic with data forensics and electronic surveillance. He traced their tainted quota money back to the Orionis government and proposed the sting which led us to their gunship as it rendezvoused with a Navy frigate.

It was the best gift Vladric Mors ever received. Jack Tatum had served up a pair of trophies which he could use to make an example of what happens to thieves, and to send a very serious *fuck you* to Orionis. I was already a big producer in the organisation. Now everyone knew who I was: a rising star in the Ceti cartel that the Big Man himself had taken notice of. No other cop, living or dead, had ever infiltrated so deep before.

I want to believe those turncoats were justified casualties, expendable foot soldiers who died on a covert battlefield. They rolled the dice and lost. My role in their demise is morally indistinguishable from a general who butchers soldiers to win a war.

But it wasn't enough to *just* give up their names and all the evidence Dusty found.

Something fragile is blocking the memory of what else I did. The drugs are keeping it that way. And that's how it needs to stay, because the sacrifice of their lives will have been for nothing unless I can pass on what I've learned since then: that the cartel is just months from launching what Vladric described as the killing blow to the Navy and the beginning of a Ceti renaissance. They're going after the *Archangel* while she's still in dry dock, and, having seen their plans, I know they have a chance, albeit a costly one. That information was critically time-sensitive, but I had no way of delivering it: the bounty on my head made Outer Rim travel prohibitive. For our own safety, Ceti Watch had put me and Dusty up at The Helodon the last two weeks.

To help pass the time, they offered the erotic freak show that is Lira Vicerip. One look at her and already I'm starting to hate myself again.

'I hope you're not leaving,' she says.

My clothes are on the floor. I sit up and swing my legs over the side. Then I reach for another hit of smacker, taking a deep, dangerous puff. The drug is a potent entactogenic that's supposed to produce a relaxing, intimate tingle. Instead, it feels like my brain was just lit on fire. I've taken far too much.

'Lucky me,' I mutter, wincing at the torment.

'Hero sex is so *urgent*,' she muses. 'You know that's what they're calling you, right? A hero?'

Her finger starts swirling around my back. It sends revulsive chills down my spine, and I flinch away.

Which just encourages her to be more aggressive about touching me.

'Aw, what's wrong?' she asks, as I feel both of her hands grab my shoulders in some faux massage. 'You're not scared, are you?'

'You figured me out,' I grumble, standing abruptly. As I bend to reach my trousers, a cold set of fingers grabs my testicles. I practically levitate off the floor.

'Jesus *Christ!*'

Lira laughs hoarsely. Her neck and cheeks are a psychedelic kaleidoscope.

125

'You're so *interesting*,' she purrs, emerald-green eyes staring inquisitively at me. 'C'mon, cheer up. There's something I've been dying to ask you ...'

'What?' I mumble, stepping into my trousers.

'Is it true you put a blowtorch to the balls of those cops?' she asks.

I freeze.

Then I inhale more smacker, just to take the edge off an urge to do something violent.

'It is true, isn't it?' She laughs. 'What was it like?'

I turn around. She's leaning back on her elbows, her ridiculous breasts erupting in some collage of blue and green that swirls down to her pale, curvy hips.

'You should keep thoughts like that to yourself,' I manage. My head feels like it's going to explode.

'*Everyone* is talking about it,' she insists, knees wagging back and forth. 'You and Vladric Mors, roasting nuts at a campfire. That's ... fascinating.'

In a single puff, I take the smacker blunt down to the hilt while stepping into my greaves. I need to leave.

'Don't you give me the silent treatment!' she coos. 'Why can't you answer the question?'

I'm halfway to the door when he shows up.

'Answer the lady,' the Minotaur says. I turn around, and there the man-beast is, circling the bed. 'No need to be rude.'

Lira laughs.

'That's right!' she agreed. 'C'mon, Jack, I want to know!'

My head is rocked by a twitch, and a shiver makes its way from the base of my spine all the way to my shoulders.

'No.'

'Why not?' Lira asks, pouty face and all.

The Minotaur smiles as he sits next to her and puts his dark red hand onto her thigh.

'Get out of my head,' I whisper.

'No,' she answered. 'I like being in there.'

'The smell was intoxicating,' the Minotaur says, gaping nostrils flaring as he strokes her up and down. 'The screams ... like music ....'

I mouth the words, but can't hear myself say them.

'... I've never felt closer to God in my whole life.'

Lira is staring at me, mouth half open, eyes narrowed. I can't tell if she's horrified or turned on. All I know is that I feel very, very sick, and she sees it.

'Do I see remorse in those eyes?' she asks.

The Minotaur is playing with her hair when my corelink rings. It's Dusty, my last connection to sanity.

'Jack, they just gave us clearance to leave,' he says. 'I'm already on board.'

The bile is creeping up, but I force it back down.

'Remorse? Oh yes,' I say, as the man-beast runs a black tongue along the side of her face. 'I regret I didn't make them suffer longer.'

Lira says something, but the Minotaur is laughing so loudly I don't hear what it was.

And then, apparently, I left.

I don't remember boarding the *Breakaway*.

But when I woke up, Dusty was navigating the ship into the axis hub hangar of Brotherhood – at least a ten-hour burn from Helodon. At just under 80 metres in length, the *Breakaway* met the size restrictions for the 'sheltered' hangar; anything over a hundred metres was relegated to the dockyards several kilometres away. The hangar rotated with the hub; any ship entering had to initiate a roll to match the station's angular momentum. It extended through all three tori, providing access points to the spokes connecting to the main station.

Dusty requested a slip nearest to Camden Yards, the epicentre of Brotherhood's infamous black market. It was crammed into a populous district of the station, where a good portion of Ceti's working class lived. The Navy ranked this metropolis among the most dangerous places to live in all Orionis, right up there with Zeus mining trawlers. But for Jack Tatum, this hellhole was home.

I watch as Dusty masterfully pilots the ship into latch position, something most would-be captains rely on autopilot for. No one but him touches the *Breakaway*, the love of his life.

As I pull on my greaves, he speaks up in his timid, nasally voice.

'Jack?' he says, as an airlock boom reaches for the port midline hatch.

'Yeah?'

He looks uncomfortable, and I'm already annoyed. I remember I have urgent business in Camden and just want to get on with it.

'We have to talk about your … habit,' he says.

'Oh yeah?' I ask, stomping out into the main corridor.

'You're not right, man,' Dusty calls out behind me. 'You need help.'

I reach the hatch and catch my reflection in the portal. Staring back at me are bloodshot, sunken eyes resting on dark blue bags and a gaunt face overgrown with veins and stubble. Just the way a dead man is supposed to look.

'Do you see my mother around here?' I ask, throwing the hatch open. 'Me neither.'

I storm into the airlock and he follows, pulling along the satchel of crap he always brings to test merchandise for defects or bugs.

'You don't remember how you got here, do you?' he says.

'I just stepped off the *Breakaway*, so there's a hint,' I grumble, marching past the security checkpoint. But all the junk in Dusty's bag sets off the alarms, waking the guard and forcing an inspection. Ceti looks the other way for almost everything that comes through here except explosives and firearms. Not that anything handheld could penetrate the station bulkheads, but they like to ensure their own security personnel are the only ones carrying them.

By the time Dusty is finished gathering all his stuff, the crowd in front of us has already boarded the spoke tram.

I try to change the topic as another tram pulls up.

'What do you need from here again?' I ask, rubbing my head. It feels like something is trying to hatch from it.

'Gyroscopes for the gun turrets and a few other things,' he says, rummaging through his satchel like a woman with her purse. 'For the record, you walked right past the Helodon governor, blew him off when he tried to shake your hand, and started mumbling something about a Minotaur,' he added. 'Then you puked in front of Vladric's officers at the hangar and passed out. I brought you aboard myself, injected you with detox plus a little something to make sure you didn't wake 'til we got here.'

'I don't see how sleep would be an issue—'

128

'I did it to keep you from hurting yourself or the *Breakaway* during the trip,' he tells me. 'You've been acting *really* crazy lately.'

'Nice going … Mom,' I say, rolling my eyes. The tram begins moving, inserting itself into the spokes of Brotherhood's Bravo torus.

'You just haven't been the same since—'

'Dusty, shut the fuck up,' I growl. He's right, of course. Unfortunately there's nothing anyone can do to help me. I feel bad intimidating him, but I'm too tired to put up with this right now.

'You need *help*, Jack,' he repeats.

'Do I?'

'All I'm saying is don't make them regret promoting you.'

Who, the Navy or Ceti? I ask myself with a grin. Dusty looks horrified at my expression, which makes me smile a little wider.

When the tram doors open, the rank filth of Camden Yards assaults me. Deafening noise greets my ears as countless vendors haggle with customers and as bidders shout over one another at auctions. Some desperate types accost us as we exit the tram; one sickly vagrant is holding up mouldy fruit, another is a mutant offering used microfusion packs. I shoulder past them and a trio of prostitutes showing me their goods. Personalised advertisements violate my reality, asking if I'd like to get high or browse a selection of cybernetic limbs. I consider visiting the merchants who paid for these ads to break their skulls with a hammer.

I look over my shoulder to make sure Dusty is keeping up. I'm wearing an old black overcoat with Ceti insignia and AR visors, since light really hurts my eyes right now. But Dusty looks like he fits right in with the rest of Camden's denizens: unkempt and haggard. Between his stained work overalls, loose-fitting greaves, and the satchel hanging over his shoulder, he looked like a beggar.

This place is heaven for him. The only part of the *Breakaway* still the original construction is the primary hull; the rest has been entirely refurbished from parts purchased right here at Brotherhood. If it was too big for a vendor's table, there was a corelink feed to verify the item and the shipyard that held it. Camden is an engineer's means to nearly any ends – and no one ever asked questions.

A few retina drones buzz overhead, and there are marked Ceti guards lounging about. They haven't recognised me – the hat and shades are common accessories here. Plus, no one expected a high-ranking officer to be mingling in a place like this. Time to make my exit.

'Dusty,' I say, taking a glance around. 'I have business with clients. Meet me back here in four hours.'

'Alright,' he says. 'Look, I'm not trying to be a nuisance. Just think about what I said.'

'Yeah, yeah,' I said, grabbing his shoulders. 'Listen, things are different now. If anyone recognises you ... says, "You're the guy who rolls with Jack Tatum" or any of that, deny it and get away from them. Drawing attention to yourself is a bad idea.'

He looks frightened, as if he had only just realised what my problems meant for him as well.

'Okay.'

I hold up my corelink.

'Call if you need anything *urgent*. Got it? Keep all the nurturing shit to yourself.'

I leave him and walk into the crowd. Ten minutes later I'm a few blocks from the spoke platform and standing before an electronics warehousing camp – each vendor table is barely a metre square, and these dilapidated aluminium tents are erected by the dozen. A stinking haze hangs overhead from all the hardware soldering going on. I find the tent I need, walk inside and shut the curtain. People use these to make encrypted calls all the time – you could build an untraceable corelink from scratch right here in the camp – and Ceti doesn't bother to scan the outgoing traffic.

This is my assigned Navy drop. We're never supposed to use it, except in emergencies – life-threatening situations, blown covers and the like. If discovering an imminent Ceti invasion of the Inner Rim wasn't an emergency, I didn't know what was. Brotherhood is 1.8 billion kilometres from Tabit Prime; the message I prepared wouldn't reach the Navy for at least ninety minutes. Factoring in the time it would take for them to respond, plus all the packet rerouting to hide origination data, I figured it would be at least four hours before I heard back from them, if at all.

Given what happened two weeks ago, I'm not looking forward to the reply.

I leave the tent and light a smacker. *Mission fucking accomplished.* This was Admiral Hedrick's problem now. Two agents died to bring him that information, so he better do something useful with it. The only thing I'm useful for is acting like a sadomasochistic asshole on the Navy's behalf, and it so happens there really are Ceti scum lords here I need to check in on.

At least that part of my life wasn't a lie.

One hour later, I'm very intoxicated and couldn't care less about the Navy or the end of Orionis. Insofar as criminal activity is concerned, my Ceti subordinates have done well, and I'm worth a few thousand more CROs. The money is a pittance for me, so I decide to share the wealth, buying drinks for everyone. My philosophy is that generosity brings good karma, good social currency, and good business. And at the moment, that nonsense is more important to me than keeping the low profile I originally planned.

Next thing I know there are attractive girls under both my arms and someone has laid a bunch of C-tens on the bar – slang for the number of carbon atoms in a methamphetamine molecule.

These girls are seriously provoking my libido. I hear music playing, and I think it's coming directly *from* them, through the pores on their skin, which I can see with astonishing detail, thanks to all the tens I'm eating.

There's a bathroom here. Not the public restroom, but the one next to the manager's office. My lady friends and I are going to borrow it.

The door flies open, and the Minotaur, that asshole, steps out.

'Bitches,' he snarls. 'Leave.'

And he grabs me by the coat, pulling me in. The Minotaur is very strong. I'm falling forward, towards the edge of the toilet.

Jake.

The Navy thanks you for sending urgent and actionable intelligence on Ceti's plans for the *Archangel*.

However, your conduct towards fellow agents, regardless of their crimes, is reprehensible. No matter what the mission, this agency

131

cannot trust someone who demonstrates such cruel disregard for human life.

You are hereby ordered to proceed with your exfiltration protocol and return to Tabit Prime immediately, where you will be prosecuted to the fullest extent of the law.

Assets have been dispatched to ensure your return, dead or alive.

I once asked if you were prepared to make the ultimate sacrifice for Orionis. Your answer did not exonerate you from the consequences of your actions, nor empower you with the discretion to wilfully endanger the lives of others.

You are no longer the man my daughter married. As such, you are now dead to me.

Commander Augustus Tyrell

Beep beep beeeeeep.

That dreadful goddamn noise ruins my solitude, alerting me to sensations of nausea in my stomach, throbbing wet pain over my eye and fluffy wads of razor wire in my throat.

Light is bashing on my eyelids, and all I want is darkness.

Beep beep beeeeeep.

'Tough words from Tyrell,' the Minotaur says.

My eyes are wide open, and I don't want them to be. I'm on the floor of a disgusting bathroom and there are people standing over me that I don't recognise.

'They know who you are,' he says, 'so watch it. You talk in your sleep.'

I'm getting up. My limbs are doing this on their own.

Beep beep beeeeeep.

What the fuck is that?

'That's your corelink, you shit heel,' the Minotaur says. 'And it sounds *urgent*, remember?'

132

The word obliterated the fog.

Dusty!

Somehow, I'm running as fast as I can, and the Minotaur is clearing a path through everything in my way.

The avenue outside is less crowded than the market proper, but that would change as we approached the spoke tram. Speed was critical, so pursuing on foot was not an option. Dusty is not answering my calls, meaning his physical corelink is disabled, but the service is still active and broadcasting an emergency to my device. It is thirty minutes past the time we were supposed to meet, with trams leaving for the hangar every eight minutes.

For a mutant, the Minotaur is a surprisingly cognitive creature with impressive persuasive skills. I watch with mild amusement as he throws a Ceti security officer off a mobile sentry platform.

'*Do you know who I am?*' he roars at the stunned guard. 'I'm the fucking Minotaur. Get on the radio and tell your squad to surround the Camden spoke tram elevator *now!*'

Then he looks at me, man-beast nostrils spraying fire everywhere.

'You coming or not?' he snaps.

The terrified guard is looking strangely at me. I shrug my shoulders as I step aboard. The Minotaur is at the controls, and I just hold onto the rails as it ascends several metres off the ground. He pulls an attachment from the console that looks like another corelink, and starts barking orders to Ceti Watch like he's the ranking officer on the station. And oddly enough, they're listening to him, and I think that's because he's actually making sense. Next thing I know, spoke tram service is shut down. Harbour Control is refusing to let ships land or take off. Every departure in the last four hours is being chased down by Ceti gunships.

The Minotaur has placed Brotherhood, the biggest station in the Outer Rim, in total lockdown.

'Where'd you learn to talk like a cop?' I blurt.

His hand lashes out, smacking me in the mouth.

'Shut the fuck up before you get us *both* killed,' he snarls.

The platform isn't designed to be flown at high speeds, yet he's somehow able to coax an astonishing amount of power from it. He's buzzing just over the heads of denizens, scanning the crowd, when suddenly he puts the Camden spoke tram platform at our backs and accelerates to the machine's top speed. I can hear that the corelink chatter has picked up.

'They found him,' the Minotaur announces. 'He's been taken hostage, but they're trapped in the Rio spoke tram.'

'Who's "they"?'

'No idea, but we're going up to meet them.'

'Why not just lower the tram?'

'Because the kidnapper might know who you really are, so we'll need to end that conversation before anyone else can hear it,' the Minotaur says, pointing to a display on the controls. 'Watch this. We have a little time.'

The retina drones spotted Dusty as he entered the ship component wards. He was meandering about, not looking where he was going, when he crashed into a woman carrying a tray of junk. Stupidity follows; instead of just moving on, Dusty bends down and helps her collect it all. She's dressed in similar craftsman's garb and sporting old-fashioned glasses – essentially, Dusty's version of Miss Orionis. When the mess is cleaned up, long moments of awkwardness follow. Finally, she invites him to see her vendor's table, and within seconds they're strolling about, conversing enthusiastically the entire time.

I'm disgusted with Dusty for not recognising the whole thing is an act, especially after I warned him earlier. She's hunching her shoulders on purpose; I recognise hard muscle beneath all the rags she's wearing. It's a ruse to make herself look as unattractive, unassuming, and as *unintimidating* as possible. Dusty is uncomfortable in front of everyone, but whoever this was did their homework. They must have been talking about ship tech, because that's the only way to break the ice with him.

She reaches out and touches his hand; he flinches away and blushes because no one has done that to him in years. She giggles, completely disarming him. Then they're holding hands, right before disappearing into the tent behind her table.

Ten minutes later, she comes out alone and packs up the table, placing it in a large bin that was concealed beneath the tent. The drones don't spot anyone leave the back. She's just another merchant calling it a day in Camden, pushing her wares towards the same spoke tram we're approaching right now.

The Minotaur is certain he's in there, but I'm not so sure. And because of my scepticism, the son of a bitch pulls up abruptly, climbing the vertical spoke at top speed. It's too much for me, and I grab the rail and barf hard over the side. Hanging there for a moment, I notice there's blood mixed in the chunks that the crowd below is trying to avoid getting struck by. Dusty was right: I'm not well.

We're over a hundred metres up now. The tram car is partially visible within the spoke shaft, and if there's anyone inside, they've moved away from the windows.

The Minotaur points.

'Service hatches every ten metres,' he shouts. It's surprisingly loud this high. You can hear the metropolis below and above, as if it was still ground level. 'See? The roof is an easy jump.'

'What's the plan?' I ask. 'Just drop in on them?'

'That's right,' he says, steering the platform beside the access hatch. There are metal rungs all the way up to the next one.

'Then what?'

'Get Dusty back!' the Minotaur says, climbing over the rail. 'Think you can handle a little girl?'

'What if she's armed?' I ask.

'Then you get exactly what you're looking for,' he says, disappearing inside. 'Save your friend or die trying. You win no matter what.'

I step off the platform just as it runs out of power and begins falling towards the surface. Climbing up a few rungs, I peer inside the shaft and see the tram's roof just a metre or two below me.

The hatch is already open, but I don't hear anything. Some shipping crates are visible, but that's it. More importantly, the Minotaur is nowhere to be seen. I'm vaguely aware that my heart is pounding, my senses are heightened, and I have a sharp headache ... the kind of pain that comes from thinking too hard, right behind my eyes.

For the third time this past hour, I act before making a conscious determination, and jump inside.

The tram car is big – this one is for hauling freight, several times larger than the one Dusty and I rode down on. There are crates of varying sizes, some stacked to the ceiling, and *there's a gun in my hand and I have no recollection whatsoever of how it got there.* Reflexive muscle-memory is taking over my actions, because I'm light on my feet, relaxed in the shoulders but firm at the wrists; my index finger rests on the trigger; I'm using a cupped double-hand grip on the weapon, looking down the sights, moving slowly, silently, checking corners, listening, completely attuned to my surroundings, waiting, stalking, hunting ...

... and I know, suddenly, that the noise to my left – metallic, caused by a tossed object – is intended to divert attention from the kick approaching from beneath, targeting the gun. Avoidable, but my training compels me to allow it – a conditioned response to maintain my cover identity, no matter the cost. I pull back slightly, just enough to let the toe of her boot strike the barrel to avoid damage to my hands.

Her strategy is obvious, and I can infer two facts from her technique: she is cybernetically augmented, and she was trained by the Navy. Her strikes are quick and precise, generating big power in short distances. But her style is customised for her size; she doesn't have big hands, but instead of curling all her fingers inward to make a fist, they are folded towards the palm at the first joint, which makes me think her knuckles are made of steel. Her boots have a metal extension from the toe, and her leg kicks are more like quick jabs than sweeping strikes. All of her blows are targeting nerve endings across my neck, torso and limbs, and are delivered with enough force to maim.

But I'm not actually *reacting* to anything; this is all just a script I'm following to an inevitable conclusion. She doesn't know it yet, but the outcome has already been settled. This will end badly for her, right next to the same crate she ambushed me from.

I've always known how to handle myself in a fight. The academy told me I had the Gift.

The dance calls for me to bait her into thinking she can win by allowing some shots to land, but in reality I'm shifting enough to let the blow *just* miss the nerve endings she's aiming for. The impacts still hurt, and, given my weakened state, do considerable damage. But not enough to incapacitate or prevent me from springing my trap, which begins with me pretending that she's landed a savage kick to my kidney – which she actually does, except I've managed to put enough of my elbow in the way to absorb the worst of it – and in my mock agony I arch my head back, presenting all the meat of my neck for her to obliterate.

She looks young; almost certainly an overachiever; probably the brightest in her class and the most eager heroine for the most dangerous assignment; damnably inexperienced and possessing far too much confidence in her own skills. I catch the arm heading for my trachea, pivot, and break it clean through the skin at her elbow. Before she can shriek, I throw her face towards the crate, and with no arm to brace herself, the brutal impact knocks her unconscious.

When she collapses, I hear someone else breathing: a gurgling, muted, horrible sound. I track it towards a familiar-looking crate, open it, and there he is … blood trickling from a nose that looks like tenderised meat, and two terrified eyes only marginally relieved to see me.

'Can you move?' I ask.

'I tink tho,' Dusty splutters. 'Sumting's wong wit my node.'

I'm wincing at the sight of him.

'I see that,' I say, sliding my hands beneath his back to help him sit up. 'Just breathe through your mouth.'

'I wud wit sumone,' he says, as I support his head. 'Need to fund her. She mote be hurt—'

The upright position has shifted the fluids in his pulverised sinuses, and a chunky stew of crimson and cartilage gushes from his nostrils. Whatever did this to his face likely cracked his orbital as well, because I don't like the way his right eye looks.

'It's over,' I hear the Minotaur say. 'Lower it. Two to come out. One casualty.'

'Where the fuck have *you* been?' I demand, turning away from Dusty. 'All that tough talk and you're a no-show?'

The Minotaur ignores me, and I hear a groan from the woman. He's holding the gun that was kicked out of my hands.

'Dusty,' the Minotaur says, clearly. 'Is this her?'

Dusty has a confused look on his face, but manages a nod.

The Minotaur smiles.

'What'd your momma tell you about talking to strangers?'

Casually, the Minotaur fires once into her head. I hear Dusty gasp, about the same time as the wet, splatting noise of brains and bone concluded.

Then the Minotaur fires twice more; once in her heart, another directly in the face. Everything above her shoulders is pulp.

'Why not?' he shrugs, tossing the gun aside. 'You killed two already.'

Fishing around my pockets, I find a smacker and offer it to Dusty. But he doesn't answer, and just sits there taking fast, shallow breaths through his mouth, both hands trembling.

The tram is descending, and so am I.

I light up and inhale deeply.

15

THE PATHFINDER

Beyond the arena where Maez and Myrha Obyeran had battled for their command lances, a magnificent spaceport rose from the mottled grey regolith of Hyllus. The blue and yellow falcon of House Obyeran adorned the towering spires ringing the complex, which Al Khav had affectionately named The Forge. From its centre sprouted a space elevator whose terminus was the birthplace of every Lightspear since the first prototype. The sprawling station was a shipyard and manufacturing plant, and the primary port of call for all ships that arrived from the Inner Rim.

Nothing could approach The Forge under its own power. A strict customs line was enforced ten thousand kilometres away; every ship was required to halt there for boarding and inspection. If it passed, the vessel was towed in the rest of the way by Lightspears. If the freight was extraordinarily massive and it would be too costly or impractical to make a full stop, Lightspears intercepted the vessel in the Hades Terminus and performed a transit inspection mid-flight at speed, then escorted it all the way through burndown.

Any ship – or other ballistic entity, for that matter – that refused to stop, or could not slow down sufficiently, was atomised.

No precaution was too great. The Forge had taken five decades to build and was a national treasure to House Obyeran, in some ways more vital than the Lightspear fleet it had created. In time, it would become the launch point of a journey to the Ch1 Orionis AB system. King Masaad reflected on all the sacrifices it had taken to reach this moment. Everything he and his brothers had accomplished, rested on the outcome of what was about to transpire. The question of whether House Obyeran would continue on for generations, here and on another world, would be decided now.

It was all Masaad could do to maintain the steely exterior expected of a king.

He arrived by space elevator, surrounded by royal consorts and acolytes. When the doors opened, a phalanx of citizens cheered as rows of Guardians lined a path to where the two immaculately polished Lightspears, awash in floodlights that made him squint, rested beneath the gantry that would hoist them into the launch track.

Maez was in the closer one, and the boarding ramps were lowered. His crew, forbidden from accompanying him, were the last men and women assembled before Masaad reached the entrance, where he acknowledged their salutes with an approving nod. Once aboard, he walked briskly down the long narrow pathway towards the bridge. He found his son seated in the captain's chair, encased in the chamber that would induce him to hypersleep. The area was dimly lit; none of the astronavigation displays that would normally fill the bridge were present. Without them, this place resembled a tomb, as all dead ships were, which suited the purpose of this trial for the highest honour of House Obyeran.

The two acolytes attending Maez bowed deeply as Masaad entered, leaving Maez's helmet behind as they exited. Father and son were alone.

'All hail the king,' Maez said, lifting his restored arm. 'Thanks for the hand.'

'You're welcome,' Masaad said drily. 'How do you feel?'

'Aside from the unreachable itch in my crotch, good,' his son said. 'Today is a fine day to get lost in space, I suppose.'

Masaad wasn't in the mood for his son's sarcasm but did his best to take the higher ground.

'Your wit never angered me,' he said. 'It was always the timing of it.'

'Why? Is this a special occasion?'

'The people gathered here seem to think so.'

'They also gather at public executions,' Maez said. 'But there are worse spectacles to celebrate.'

'This is no spectacle, Maez.'

'Well, of course you don't think so, but humour me anyway.'

'This is an *honour*,' Masaad said, exasperated. 'A great moment for House Obyeran, and the people who look up to you.'

'It's a training exercise,' Maez said. 'Really, the crowd and cultural overtones are a bit much, don't you think?'

'We are a spacefaring culture,' Masaad said, as Maez rolled his eyes. 'But it will take more than words to convince them to leave here on an interstellar voyage. If you can pass this trial, it will demonstrate that they are being led by someone who knows the way.'

'Did it ever occur to you the result could be a huge disappointment?' Maez asked. 'Only two have passed The Voyage Home, and they invented the bloody test.'

'What are you implying?'

The humour vanished from Maez's pale, square-jawed face.

'I was wondering what the point of it all is when you've already chosen your successor.'

Masaad was taken aback.

'That was no easy decision to make,' he said.

'Please,' Maez dismissed. 'I made it too easy for you. And besides, it was the right choice.'

Masaad was shocked. He had not spoken with Maez since The Rites, leaving him to heal and train – convenient reasons to delay what he had always assumed would be a difficult conversation.

'Do you mean that?'

'I'm not blind to my deficiencies,' Maez said, his lips broadening into a smile. 'You put them on display in arenas for everyone to judge.'

'It … wouldn't serve to only put one of you through this.'

'I wouldn't stand for that whether it suited you or not,' Maez said, stretching his neck. 'My sister is relentless, which is the mark of a good tax collector. She'll make a fine queen someday.'

'It makes me proud to hear you say that.' Masaad beamed.

'Proud?' Maez said. 'Relieved is more like it. You'd better hope at least one of us makes it back.'

'You're more prepared than I ever was,' Masaad said. 'Both of you will return.'

141

'We'll see,' Maez said, nodding towards the helmet. 'Would you be so kind?'

Masaad smiled, lifting it over his son's head. As he lowered it, Maez stopped him.

'For what it's worth, I'm glad you came here,' he said. 'Thank you.'

King Masaad left Maez's Lightspear feeling elated.

Expecting defiance, he had found a supportive son instead. Now he was more confident than ever about his decision, and eager to see his beloved Myrha. With his chin held high, he strode purposefully down the aisle of Guardians leading to her Lightspear.

But upon reaching the bridge, he found the captain's chair empty. Alarmed, he began working his way back towards the entrance ramp. Before he could reach there, he suddenly found himself staring down at a young acolyte whom he had given a very special task.

The anguish on her face said it all. His heart sank as Myrha stepped out from behind her, eyes cold as ice.

'I'm sorry, your majesty,' the acolyte said, tears streaming down her face as she hurried past.

Myrha, dressed in her armoured survival suit, was holding a datacore stack in her hand.

'How could you?' she demanded.

The modular, redundant design of the Lightspear placed CPUs capable of running the entire ship in every subsystem; each chip was paired with a datacore that recorded the performance metrics of the reactors, engines, astronavigational computations; essentially every heartbeat of the ship from the moment it was powered on. For the trial, these stacks were erased and a random number of CPUs removed, simulating their destruction in an emergency. Without the datacores, which also contained the base instructions for operating the ship, the captain would have to restore systems manually, in essence teaching the ship how to fly all over again.

Masaad had instructed the acolyte – Myrha's personal servant, and a familiar face on her ship – to slip datacores with full operating instructions onto her Lightspear so that it would be almost completely functional from the moment she awakened, all but rigging the trial's outcome.

'*Why?*' Myrha hissed.

'Because you must not fail,' he answered solemnly.

'Did you do the same to my brother's Lightspear?' she asked.

'No.'

Myrha clenched her mailed fist around the chip and pulverised it.

'It makes no difference,' he said. 'You will succeed.'

'Have you been feigning trust in me all this time?' she demanded.

'The fate of our House rests with you,' he answered. 'My intent was to ease the burden.'

'By *cheating*?'

'By ensuring the people of House Obyeran believe in you. A wise ruler would swallow her pride for the good of the kingdom she serves.'

'There's no honour in this!'

'Myrha, there are times when the perception of honour will better serve your interests. If you mean to rule, you must learn to lie.'

'How often have you lied to me?' she asked. 'Or to Maez? To your brothers?'

Masaad took a deep breath.

'When facing defeat in battle, a captain who speaks the truth is less effective than one who claims he can still win, no matter the odds,' he said. 'The lie inspires hope, Myrha. We teach our warriors that you must know fear to be brave. The *perception* of confidence is indistinguishable from true faith. The people of House Obyeran must see you make The Voyage Home before they follow you to our new world. That is paramount.'

'They will learn the truth!' she snapped. 'What then?'

'No one will learn of this, I promise you.'

'Why should I trust you?' she asked.

'Because you should never doubt how much I love you,' he answered.

Myrha smashed her fist into the console rack holding other data-cores and CPUs.

'I will tear this ship apart,' she growled, ripping out a chunk of mangled electronics and waving them at Masaad. 'You may have cheated your way to power, but I refuse to follow your example. I will *earn* the respect of House Obyeran, not deceive them into it!'

Masaad willed himself not to panic.

'The trial cannot be passed,' he said quietly. 'It's impossible.'

Her handful of wrecked equipment fell to the deck.

'What?' she snarled.

'Myrha, the odds of surviving an accident that cripples power, propulsion or life support—'

'I know the odds, the Lightspear was made to beat them!'

'Some odds cannot be overcome,' Masaad admitted. 'Given enough time, every ship is a tomb. If we are to reach further than any before us, then nothing gives us more hope than the Lightspear. Some of us won't survive the journey. But no one will even try unless they know the odds were overcome once before.'

'Al Khav overcame them!' Myrha protested, with less conviction now.

'And no one will ever see him here again,' Masaad said. 'You are the one we must follow.'

Never before had he seen such anguish in his daughter.

'The Voyage Home is a test of fortitude,' he explained, choosing his words with care. 'It measures your resolve, resourcefulness, and perseverance. It tests your faith in the technology, the ship, and yourself. It builds a legacy around the Lightspear, and the commander destined to lead our fleet.'

'So The Voyage Home is a lie,' she whispered.

'A necessary one,' he acknowledged. 'But yes.'

She leaned against the console, her eyes glazed over.

'I've prepared for this my entire life …'

King Masaad clasped his hands, pacing as he spoke.

'There were dark days, when the *Tabit Genesis* arrived here in Orionis,' he began. 'Imagine, my brothers and I, huddled among the last of us. Our survival relied entirely on technology and those who produced it. Right from the start, the same power structures that had ruined Earth began to reassert themselves.

'We left because we believed humanity had to pursue several paths at once. Democracy was one way. But the path we chose could not be obstructed by politics or corporate greed. A House culture was appropriate because our vision would take centuries to realise. Stability and unity of purpose were critical. The Obyeran line, our genetic dynasty, aided by our own innovations, would lead the quest for mankind's survival.

'In truth, my brothers and I were terrified of leaving the Inner Rim. Convincing people to follow us ... Myrha, we had to lie about the odds. We had to promise what could never be reached in a lifetime. We told people they could return if things went wrong. We built freighters and filled them with everything we needed to start over, and just like the *Tabit Genesis*, we began a one-way journey.

'Your mother was the only one I confided in. She lifted me whenever the doubt took hold. She knew better than anyone what it takes to lead, and she believed in what we were doing! None of this would have been possible without her. And if she were here right now, she would tell you, as she once told me, that you have to make yourself into something more than what you really are. If you want people to follow you, you have to reach greatness beyond what you're capable of. You have to become more than human. And to do that ... you have to cheat.'

'No ...' Myrha began.

Masaad shook his head.

'Myrha, what is legend?' he asked. 'Every hero in every mythology that ever was gets that magic token from the gods; a mysterious saviour always appears when no hope remains to show the hero a path forward. So it is with our culture. To reach our world, you must become legend. As your father ... it was my duty to help you reach greatness.'

Myrha was elsewhere. Her eyes were distant, her expression blank. After a few moments, she began walking towards the bridge.

Masaad gently took her arm as she passed.

'Myrha, I beg you, please let this take its course,' he implored. 'No matter what you destroy in here ... the outcome is settled.'

His daughter gazed on him with sheer contempt.

'Leave me,' she whispered.

Masaad felt a stab in his heart.

'As you wish,' he said, letting go.

King Masaad watched as the procession of Lightspears departed. Before they vanished, he saw them split into two groups, each following a different course, accelerating into the void.

Over and over he cursed himself, and there was no hiding his distress this time. He had personally seen to it that the test conditions were favourable for Myrha. It was a plot years in the making, done so discreetly that the Guardians would never question the randomised damage simulations to each ship or the locations where each Lightspear would be towed to. One more encoded datacore stack wouldn't have made a shred of difference, but he had still gone through the trouble of enlisting the acolyte to sneak one on board. Just one more redundancy, one more edge, one more parcel of insurance to guarantee Myrha's success … and why not? This transcended the bond between father and daughter. The future of the House was at stake!

But he had doubted himself. Lyanna would have never let him send that acolyte. She would have assured him that enough had been done.

His error had changed everything; the future was anything but certain. Myrha could take matters into her own hands and invalidate the results upon her return. She could refuse to compete and put herself into cryo indefinitely.

Or word of his attempt to influence the test could unravel the very foundation of House Obyeran.

Turning away from the departure scene, he marched towards the space elevator, tapping the shoulder of the young acolyte as he passed. She obediently followed. Without a word, they began the descent to Hyllus, ignoring the Guardians that bowed with deference and other acolytes who looked on in envy.

Masaad took her beneath the surface to the subterranean throne levels.

And then even deeper, to a place where no one, not even Lyanna Obyeran, had ever known existed.

Masaad sensed the young girl's fear when the gate to the Seers' Vault opened.

Before them was an imposing cavern of indeterminate dimensions; the views above and below were obscured in darkness. A metal grating stretched from the entrance to the far side, supported by latticework anchored into the bedrock. Thirteen vertical cylinders were arranged in a circle at the centre, all interconnected by cables and pipes. Inside of each was a person suspended in a clear liquid, wearing a survival suit; numerous connective tubes and cables converged into a thick twine that

146

rose above them and disappeared where the glass ended. A bluish tint – the only colour evident in this miserable place – haunted the occupants inside, their eyes shut, hair overgrown and waving in the current, nose and mouth covered with a mask, their faces pale and sickly beneath.

The acolyte was trembling.

'These are my Seers,' Masaad explained. 'Specimens I've gathered who allegedly possess the Gift.'

'Specimens?' she asked.

'Anyone with attributes that cannot be genetically isolated isn't human,' Masaad explained. 'Most of these I've sought out. Others came to me voluntarily.'

'For what ends, my King?'

'To offer their Gift to House Obyeran, of course,' he said, placing an arm around her shoulder, urging her forward as he walked. 'In return I promised them wealth, which they'll receive once they produce information that is useful to me.'

'Are they well, my lord?'

'Sleep is where they glimpse the future, and it looks like a troubling one,' he said, pausing at the centre of the platform, surrounded by the thirteen ghosts. 'They are nourished, sanitised, and kept in a near persistent dream state to maximise productivity.'

She glanced around, eyes wide open.

'Your majesty … what will you have of me?'

He didn't know her name. And he didn't care to ask.

'Acolyte, I asked you to perform a task. You failed. But you have served in good faith and loyalty. My daughter thinks well of you, which means much to me. You have my thanks.'

'The honour is mine, my King …'

He approached the glass of the nearest 'specimen'. A man was suspended inside, closed eyes darting back and forth in REM sleep.

'You there,' King Masaad said.

Despite the glass and fluid, the man's bloodshot eyes snapped open, startling the girl. He was breathing fast and heavy.

'Tell your King how this acolyte changed the plan.'

'Kill me,' he pleaded, his voice amplified through speakers. 'Please.'

Another pair of ghastly eyes opened, this time of an elderly woman.

147

'I saw what you did, *merciful* King,' she said, her voice carrying through the cavern. 'You knew the red god would come.'

More of the damned awakened, shouting over one another.

'Merciful King! Alim suffers!'

'Orionis burns in flames … Masaad the Tyrant, destroyer of worlds!'

'Brother against brother, the House will bleed!'

'Silence!' Masaad roared. 'Look on this girl. Tell me what you see!'

The man who had spoken first answered.

'The beginning,' he said.

'*What* begins with her?' Masaad demanded. 'What does that mean?'

'Myrha, Myrha, Myrha,' a woman's voice called out. 'Maez, Maez, Maez … who shall it be, be, be?'

'The acolyte, damn you!' Masaad roared. 'What of my son and daughter?'

All the voices went silent. Then the old woman spoke.

'For one,' she hissed, 'the omega.'

Before the acolyte could take another breath, Masaad darted forward with augmented, unnatural speed, grabbed her by the chin and snapped her neck. Catching her as she fell, he hoisted her lifeless body in his arms, her limp head dangling from her shoulders.

'Forgive me, Lyanna,' he whispered, looking upwards, as if there was a heaven above him.

'A King's sorrow, ha!' the elderly woman mocked. 'A tyrant's remorse!'

'Weep for the twins!' another shouted. 'Pray to your red god for their return!'

They mocked him relentlessly as he approached the grating's edge. He watched the acolyte fall until the darkness swallowed her.

He heard no landing, and took that for a sign.

16

ANONYMOUS

19 March 2809

Dear Amaryllis,

The sentiment of missing someone really is a critical design flaw.

Most intelligent species restrict their neurotrophic response to personal alliances. Relationships thus exist only for the time during which they are actually *useful*. That way, when they are severed from the ones they love, the loss does no harm. As it stands with humans, the results can be devastating … a lifetime of disabling anguish for most.

Humans have always had so much to lose. How then, has it come to this?

I mentioned we were never taken to Lunar Base Hadfield.

After learning that World War IV had begun, we were induced to hibernation and awoke at UNSEC Station Alsos, a base whose existence was unknown to anyone that had ever set foot on Earth. From our perspective on the shuttle, we were alarmed to find ourselves hurtling towards a pristine, unglamorous asteroid in an apparent death dive.

But I must have blinked at the moment of impact because my next memory was the inside an enormous hangar whose construction was clearly not human.

To accurately convey what we saw is impossible. For starters, every surface was morphing – irregular, strange shapes merged and rearranged into larger structures that moved alongside us as we coasted. Our shuttle was an old NATO Challenger model, roughly 130 meters long. A fleet of them would not have filled the inside of this structure. And the colour ... everything, every light, surface and object was the same red hue as a dying star.

If this wasn't overwhelming enough, the UNSEC colonel overseeing our transfer from Earth had us physically restrained before disembarking. We were uniformed soldiers, shackled at the wrists and ankles like prisoners. 'For your own safety', we were told.

Then we were fitted with breathing masks, but no pressurised suit or mag-greaves.. When the airlock opened, hot, dry air greeted us. Within moments we were drenched in sweat, shuffling single file along a narrow catwalk that vanished behind the last man.

The colonel behaved as though nothing unusual was happening, leading us into a small amphitheatre that was so ordinary compared to everything else I wondered if it was all an illusion. Five rows of plush seats were arranged in tiers curving around a stage. As we filed in, the colonel urged us to remain calm, assuring that no harm would come to us. My attention was drawn to an archway on the far side of the room that was twice the height of the door we had entered through.

Then I heard the clicks.

A series of rhythmic, lively taps graduating into heavy, ominous thumps as something approached.

I doubt you've ever seen an alien in person.

Very few living humans have. But if you do, the first few moments are utter, complete bafflement. Your brain simply struggles to process the information your eyes are sending it. I know some people envision a beautiful, awestruck moment to mark their first encounter, but believe me: no matter who you are or how you prepare yourself, the reaction that universally follows initial confusion is the darkest terror you have ever known.

The reaction is primordial. You are human, face to face with a superior predator. And you cannot fight, nor flee.

Standing over two metres high, the monstrosity bounded in on a pair of reverse-jointed legs anchored by armoured tri-pedalled talons. Its head was a rounded, elongated pyramid, but perfectly smooth – there was no nose, mouth or eyes protruding from the glossy surface.

150

It had two sets of arms; one raptorial pair with immense pincers, the other with six finer but equally sharp 'fingers'. On its back was a pair of enormous wings made of a crimson-tinted transparent material, folded neatly behind fearsome shoulder blades. Running down from its spine was a tail that led to the only asymmetrical component of its form: an irregular club with sharp protrusions adorned with metals and gems.

But the most alarming feature of this creature was its exoskeleton: a polished armour that reflected a maelstrom of red and clay hues, like the sheen of an oil slick. Thick plates protected the joints and what I could only guess were vital organs behind its thorax and head. I just couldn't tell what was and wasn't organic.

It marched to the centre of the stage area and faced us. I registered a thunderous voice:

I am a Raothri, the race that means to end your own. My name is Ceitus, a lesser denizen and exile from my civilisation.

The horrified expressions of my companions confirmed that it was communicating with us telepathically, which as we all know, is 'impossible'.

While remaining as motionless as a statue, this 'lesser denizen' explained to us in perfect English that the Raothri predate human existence by more than a billion years. Their homeworld was located in what we call the Scutum-Centaurus arm of the Milky Way, orbiting a star 55,000 light years from Earth, obscured by the dust clouds at the centre of the galaxy. Life did not begin on their planet until its parent sun grew into a red giant, thawing a world that was cold and dead the entirety of that star's existence. By the time of its supernova 17,000 years ago, the Raothri had begun settling other worlds.

The exact moment they discovered your own Pale Blue Dot was 1 March 1954 AD, 18:45 GMT. On that fateful day, the so-called 'United' States of America detonated a 15-megaton thermonuclear hydrogen bomb on what was then the Marshall Islands in the Pacific Ocean. Unbeknown to physicists of the era, fusion explosions open quantum tunnels through spacetime whose endpoints follow the dark matter topography of the universe. Some of the neutrinos released in the infamous 'Castle Bravo' blast tunnelled their way into Raothri sensors thousands of light years away. Humans had announced their presence to the most technologically advanced race in the Milky Way.

The Raothri placed Earth under surveillance, and soon after judged our species unworthy of survival. In spite of our self-imposed trajectory towards extinction, the complete eradication of humans from Earth was deemed necessary *because of the threat we posed to them.*

That's right, Amaryllis. We were doomed not because of what we were, but by what they believed we would become: Imperfect creatures governed by irrational emotions with escalating technological potential. We had split the atom and demonstrated our misuse of that power. They feared the logarithmic curve of human innovation. Ending our civilization was a logical necessity.

Humans were not the first to face extermination by the Raothri. Ceitus claimed to work with dozens of species that were, or would soon become, their victims. Allegedly, he had a 'charter' to ensure that some of the doomed lived on. My fellow recruits and I had the distinction of being the first humans to join his charges. To demonstrate his commitment to our survival, Ceitus presented UNSEC with jump drive technology – the very same drives the *Archangel* is being fitted with right now.

It was then, and remains today, impossible to know if his intentions are benign. We follow because there is no alternative.

Ceitus emphasised that the other species he'd gathered had unanimously taken exception to his decision to give us the technology. Humankind, they argued, built the Genesis motherships not to escape from the Raothri, but to escape a fate of their own creation. Ceitus countered that other civilisations, including his own, have learned from similar experiences. In the opinion of this apparent god, we were 'worthy' of one last chance.

So, in case you were still wondering, I'll clarify here: UNSEC made contact with Ceitus before anyone else. They knew the end was coming long before the opening strike of the Fourth World War.

The highborns know the truth. Any who deny such are lying. We believe the *Tau Genesis* crew mutinied when they learned it. The fact is that Generation Orionis are the offspring of defeated generals who set the world on fire before abandoning it. They were born to parents who decided which of their children would live, and the manner in which the siblings would die. The Navy, the privateers, the cartels, Ceti, and the Houses are the progeny who survived that choice. Their differences live on, and the implications are no less dire.

I realise all this may be difficult to accept. But you've spent far too long atop the food chain of a world that matters less to the universe than the dust it once was. I have seen things that *can't happen*, life forms that don't fit within the narrow construct of what humans consider 'possible'. They are commonplace in my world. Soon they might be in yours as well.

Curse my neurotrophic response to you. Though who knows? Perhaps that is the very reason why we were spared.

Love always,

- A

17

ADAM

Dad was no longer speaking.

Withering away in his tethered bag, he spent more time asleep than awake, blisters boiling on every part of his face that wasn't covered by his breathing mask. He was the epitome of anguish. His eyes appeared lifeless even when they stayed open long enough to focus. When Adam had last spoken to him, Dad's words had been incomprehensible. Most likely he was imparting advice that he had learned the hard way, so that his son might not suffer the way he did.

Adam helped his mother change his father's soiled clothes and cleanse the wounds opened by the radiation sickness ravaging his shattered body. He was numb to the world around him, withdrawn to a troubled place deep within. He spoke only when absolutely necessary. His only respite was the rig, where he would seek escape, only to be consumed by memories instead.

The mining platform was Dad's legacy; the family business that he had hoped would give them a better life. That dream was lost. Even though one had nearly killed him, Adam found himself yearning to catch another glimpse of the Arkady. And though he had completed the herculean feat of restoring the rig's production, the Ceti overlords who hauled away their spoils remained indifferent to their struggles.

Day after painful day blurred together, waiting for the inevitable, until one day Adam was awakened by the voice of a stranger in their home. From his room, he strained to listen to the conversation down the hall. A friend of Mom, perhaps, and presumably of Dad as well, and not one of those Ceti bastards.

Whoever he was, he was at least pretending to care.

'This is everything I could find,' the stranger was saying. 'It's not much, but it should buy him some time.'

'We're very grateful,' Adam's mother said. 'Thank you.'

Then an uneasy silence.

'Why don't you come with us?' the stranger asked. 'My team can work the rig while you're away, maybe even make some repairs. We can get Tomas the transfusion he needs, better provisions for you here ... maybe even a visa to return to the Inner Rim.'

'It's gracious of you to offer, but no.'

More silence passed before the man spoke again.

'Pardon me for asking ... but for God's sake, why not?'

'Because we can't leave here,' Adam's mother said. 'I'm sorry.'

'You're *sorry*? What about your children?'

'A transfusion would save him,' Abby was saying. 'Adam and I can run this rig ourselves.'

'Our agreement with Ceti forbids him from leaving so long as we remain in debt,' his mother explained. 'The aid we were promised was allegedly seized by the Navy. Your freighter is just as likely to be seized or shot down with him aboard.'

Adam crept out of his sleeping bag and glided down the hall to listen more closely.

'Dawn,' the stranger said, 'most of us have done well under Ceti. What happened here?'

'What happened is that my husband became ill.'

'All due respect, ma'am, but I can't believe that's the entire story.'

'Some rigs are just luckier than others.'

Halting near the kitchen's edge, Adam peeked around the corner to get a glimpse of the stranger. Though dressed in a survival suit, his appearance was too healthy to be a roughneck ... short, lean, with light brown hair and dark brown eyes. A kind face, concerned even, but one Adam did not recognise at all.

'He won't survive without this,' the stranger said. 'You know that.'

'Tom's wish is to remain here,' came the response.

'First time I've heard that,' Abby commented, drawing a glare.

'When is the last time either of them received transfusions?' the stranger asked, nodding towards Abby. 'Months? Years?'

His mother held his stare for a moment and then smiled.

'Thank you for coming here,' she said. 'Tomas will rest easier now, thanks to you.'

'What is *wrong* with you?' Abby exclaimed. 'Why won't you accept his help?'

'Abigail, that will be all,' her mother warned.

'I don't understand,' Abby fumed.

'I'm afraid I don't either,' the stranger said.

'You don't have to,' their mother said. 'It's my decision.'

'I suppose it is,' the stranger sighed, moving away from the table. 'I did what I could.'

Abby wouldn't let things end there.

'This is *fucked*, Mom.'

And then she lost it entirely:

'Abigail, *shut your mouth!*' their mother shouted. 'Larus, *get out!*'

Larus, Adam thought, watching as the man disappeared through the far hatch of the kitchen, nearly brushing against his sleeping father as he went.

'You are horrible!' Abby yelled.

'I'm trying to protect you!' their mother hissed. Adam had never seen her like this before. 'If he is moved from here, no matter what the reason, they will come after *you* and your brother. Our only hope is for someone to buy this fucking rig.'

'Why?' Abby demanded. 'Why would anyone hurt *us*? What have you done?'

'*We have no choice,*' their mother roared. 'Leave it at that!'

'No, I will not "leave it at that"!' Abby screamed. 'I have a right to know! It's my life!'

His mother glared at her, contempt in her eyes. Then she pushed off the wall and glided away, towards the module she slept in. Adam heard a hatch close shut, followed by a muffled thud.

'Mom!' Abby yelled. 'Goddamn you, tell me why! *Why!*'

Adam had to get away.

'*I fucking hate you!*' he heard Abby scream. '*I hate you so much!*'

As she screamed herself into sobbing, Adam began climbing into his own survival suit, slowly at first, then quickly, as if his skin was on fire.

The tears found him on the way down.

By the time he reached the platform, all he could do was stand in the ammonia downpour, incapacitated with grief. The old Pegasus mech, confused by the physical inputs of his sobbing, attempted to convulse along with him. Adam wanted to lash out at his mother, even his dying father, because their suffering could have been avoided. That much was clear after the visit from this Larus fellow. Abby was right: they had a right to know everything now, even if they couldn't understand it. Ceti was no saviour – if there was anyone to blame for his family's hardships, it was them.

Adam tried to compose himself as he attached the refuelling hoses. The rain had ceased but the sky remained overcast, glowing in crimson hues as thick roiling clouds of amber and gold bubbled beneath him. With a deep breath, he hoisted a crate filled with replacement rig components that had descended with him. The Pegasus was in much better shape now, and with any luck, the overhaul he was about to begin would lead to an increase in *Three* production. Altogether, Adam had twelve hours of hard work ahead of him.

But soon, even routine tasks proved difficult. He had trouble concentrating, and that was a dangerous liability in the clouds of Zeus. Then, while bending to reach a switch valve, a rush of premonition seized him; real danger, possibly lethal, was imminent. He stood abruptly to scan the sky for trouble, when all of a sudden there was a terrifying *bang*, and his instruments went red.

The hydraulic actuator on the mech's right leg had blown apart, spraying bits of metal and fluid all over the rig. Adam was paralysed: the machine was immobilised below the torso. To reach the sled, he would have to pull himself there using its arms.

His dread barely had time to register when he glanced up and saw an Arkady hunter – the largest he had ever seen – soar over the rig railing. The creature halted in the jet stream, snapping its fleshy black wings wide open and taking the current on directly; it hovered like a

157

gunship as electrical pulses hurtled through translucent tentacles that lashed onto the rig's railing.

Then a second hunter appeared, just as monstrous as the first, and latched on beside it.

Adam's heart was racing; he had to return to the sled *now*. More of the creatures were darting about – dozens at least. He dropped the mech's good leg and bent forward, assuming it would fall onto its belly. But instead, it fell backwards with a crash. Adam was facing the blood-red sky, frantically trying to turn the machine over so he could crawl, when a huge shadow fell upon him.

The massive creature he had seen weeks earlier had returned, and the hunters tethered to the railing were reaching out with other tentacles to grab hold of the beast's huge wingspan.

Mesmerising electrical patterns erupted beneath the skin of the beast's underside; chains of lightning coruscated from one undulating wingtip to the next. Scores of gills fluttered in waves with the wind; glimpses of dark internal organs revealed themselves during fierce flashes of light. Schools of hunters were present now, sailing past in packs of ten or more. Lumbering majestically above the hunters, the beast covered the entire surface area of the rig.

Suddenly, the electrical pulses ceased. Adam was staring at a black, rolling shadow now. Conceding that escape was impossible, he sat up, terrified but fascinated.

The beast's underside flashed a single pulse of light, followed by darkness.

Then twice in quick succession.

Three, and then darkness.

Adam watched in surreal amazement as it kept this pattern up, losing count in the twenties.

Then it restarted with one. Two. Three … and on.

It was just too deliberate to be an accident.

Quickly, Adam withdrew his arms from the actuator controls of the mech and began typing into the console. Cursing his clumsy gloves, he wrote a simple algorithm that used the Pegasus's cameras to count the number of pulses. All the while, the creature relentlessly kept up its steady pattern.

His algorithm determined that it was pulsing up to twenty-six times before starting over.

Adam eyes opened wide. There was nothing extraordinary about that number, *other than being the exact number of letters in the UNSEC Standard Language*.

He had to answer. First he tried waving his arms; then he remembered the mech's floodlights, flipping them on and off.

The creature changed its pattern:

1 – 4 – 1 – 13

Adam adjusted the program to map the pulse count to its corresponding letter.

A name spelled out on his console.

Impossible!

Adam started flashing his floodlights to respond, then thought better of it and began writing another program that would translate keystrokes into floodlight pulses, when the beast's pattern changed again:

18 – 1 – 4 – 9 – 15 …

Radio?

Adam flipped the transmit switch on his comms, selecting a random frequency used by other rigs.

'Hello?' he asked.

The beast flashed another pattern, much faster this time, and the console translated:

WHY ARE YOU HERE

Adam had never felt more intimidated by such a simple question. The surrealism of the experience, coupled with his adrenaline response, was making his head pound.

'Because we need fuel?' he said aloud.

Another eruption of pulses. Adam hoped the cameras could keep up with the barrage. When the beast finally finished, the console had spelled out:

THERE IS DANGER
WHY DID YOU RETURN

The hunter packs were veering closer, radiating pulses of their own. Adam keyed the radio tentatively.

'My family won't survive if I don't.'

A frantic burst of effulgence consumed the beast, and the hunters seemed to respond with a light show of their own. After a few moments, its underside went dark, and the sharp light pulses returned.

FAMILY
MOTHER AND CHILDREN
THIS WE KNOW

The wind had grown stronger, and Adam sensed that the hunters were struggling to maintain their grip between the beast and the railing. More of them appeared and lashed on to help, some grabbing intake pipes that were very close to where Adam was sitting. He was completely surrounded by the creatures, and the luminescence beneath their skin, rapidly changing colours, appeared threatening.

'What do you want from me?' Adam asked.

The activity abruptly stopped. After a few moments, the creature resumed its communication:

WE WISH TO CROSS THE VEIL

'The "veil"?' Adam asked.

WILL YOU HELP US

'Me? Help *you*?'

WE OFFER WHAT THE VEIL HAS SHOWN US

Adam had never felt more excited, or helpless.
'What are you?' he asked. 'How can you hear me?'

ARKADY
YOU CALL THEM WAVES

160

ELECTROMAGNETIC WAVES
WE FEEL THEM
SEE THEM
FROM AFAR

The strobe of lights was hurting Adam's eyes.
'How can you understand what I'm saying?'

WE LEARN FROM YOUR RADIO
YOUR KIND SPEAKS TO THOSE IN THE VEIL
THIS WE KNOW

'Wait, do you mean *space*?' Adam asked. 'The blackness above the clouds? That's where you want to go?'

YES
WE HAVE BEEN WAITING FOR YOU

'For *me*?'

OTHERS CAME BEFORE
TAKE FROM US

The very last thing Adam wanted to do was offend these creatures.
'I'm sorry!' he said. 'I didn't mean … we didn't realise we were stealing from anyone.'

NO OTHERS HELP
YOU DID

'Help? When did I …?' Adam started. Then he remembered his ordeal with the hunter weeks ago.

HELP WITH NO BENEFIT
THIS WE DO NOT KNOW

161

'How can I explain this,' Adam said aloud. 'Your ... we call them "hunters". One got stuck in our machinery. It was suffering, so ... I wanted to help it.'

HUNTER CLAIMED YOU
YOU ARE IRRATIONAL

Adam smiled.
'You sound like my mom.'

MOTHER
SHE SEES THROUGH US
SHE SEES YOU
THIS WE KNOW

'Huh? My mother?'

OURS
ADAM SHE ASKS
PLEASE TAKE US TO THE VEIL

A pair of nearby hunters released their grip on the rails and unfurled their menacing tentacles towards Adam. Before he could blink, they had latched onto the Pegasus, yanking the machine upright as though it were a toy.
'Whoa!' Adam protested. 'What are you doing?'

YOU MUST GO

Using the huge creature as an overhead crane, some of the hunters' tentacles 'walked' along the belly of the beast while others kept a firm grip on the mech, eventually placing it within arm's length of the rocket sled.
'Wait!' Adam protested. 'I have so many questions!'

YOU MUST NOT BE HARMED

'Harmed?'

ACTUATOR DAMAGED
YOU ARE IN DANGER

Adam laughed a shriek of amazement.
'How could you possibly know *that*?'

OTHERS HAVE FALLEN
YOU MUST GO

A powerful gust of wind nearly knocked the mech over, but Adam grabbed the sled rail just in time. All of a sudden, Abby's voice howled on the radio.

'Adam!' she hollered. 'What the hell are you doing? There's a huge storm coming! Who are you talking to?'

She was right; the upwind cloud layers were rising into ominous mushroom-shaped mountains in the distance.

He unhooked the refuelling hoses.

'Will I see you again?'

The hunters all released their grip, allowing the wind to take them away from the rig. Above him, the enormous creature began gliding away.

WE WILL FIND YOU

'Adam, what are you talking about?' Abby demanded. 'Get inside the sled!'

He pulled himself in, turned and shut the door.

'Do you have a name?' he asked. 'What do I call you?'

NO
YOU CHOOSE

The ignition sparked and the sled rocketed upward. Adam panicked: what did you *call* an alien? His imagination failed him as the sled rushed higher and faster. Without thinking, he blurted out the commercial name engraved above the console:

'Pegasus!' he shouted, as the zenomorph disappeared beneath the clouds. 'I'll call you Pegasus!'

18

WYLLYM

Excruciating pain had never felt so good.

As the starfield rolled and centred on the bright sphere of Corinth Naval Yards, Wyllym blinked away bursts of agony, concentrating on flying his Gryphon home. The numbing effect of nerve dampeners was wearing off, and the bioadmin could not deliver more without endangering his life. Wyllym had pushed himself to the brink for this final sortie, since it marked the end of a remarkable Navy career.

But his legend as an absolute master of space combat would persist. The deadly combination of his Gift and flying skills were simply unfair; he had been a cruel pilot today, pushing cadets to the very limits of their endurance, all in the name of discovering which of them deserved to be called Gryphon pilots. Many had failed. To have made it this far only to fall short in the final contest was a bitter test of character.

But a few had succeeded, if only just. They would become the first and only Gryphon wing, permanently assigned to the *Archangel*. There were only eighteen of the unique fighters in existence, and as of today there were twenty-four pilots qualified to fly them. Now that the programme had 'proved' that Gifted humans were more capable pilots than machines, Admiral Hedricks planned to add three more wings. Those pilots would have to be trained by someone else.

Easing off the throttle, Wyllym took a moment to regard the brutish fighter flying beside his own. Two pairs of asymmetric 'wing's converged on the main hull; a gimbaled 70mm railgun was affixed to each end, allowing her to keep simultaneous fire on multiple targets from any aspect. There were eight vectoring exhaust jets, each capable of withstanding 50% of main engine thrust; the Gryphon was more agile than gunships half her size. Eight weapon hardpoints could accommodate every missile and EW/SIGINT/RECON sensor platform in the Navy; and for self-defence, a 12mm rail turret was affixed to her stern. It was the kind of ship that every child dreamt of flying, zooming toy models about while pretending to shoot down evil red ships.

Wyllym hoped he would never see one again.

Gliding through the hangar entrance, he landed the Gryphon's skids onto designated docking latches, the boundaries of which marked the edge of an elevator platform. Three more fighters landed around him, forming a diamond pattern. When they had all locked in place, the entire platform rose several metres, rotated upside down, and then began ascending into the outer sphere of the station. As gravity began pulling on Wyllym's bones, the pain intensified to unbearable levels. And still, he remained elated. When the maintenance hangar level descended into view, he saw the waiting ground crew cheering wildly.

They swarmed round his Gryphon, moving beneath to where he could not see them. Of course, he would need their help exiting the craft; all the pilots would after today's exercise. For a moment, he cringed at the notion of being hoisted on their shoulders, as he could barely keep his own head upright.

Still, Wyllym managed a smile as the nestled pilot module descended from the Gryphon's belly. The airlock seals released, and the hatch opened. His moment of triumph had come.

And there was not one person there to greet him.

The crowd had moved straight past his Gryphon to the pilots who had made the final selection. Some were even flocking to those who had failed, offering them consolation and booze. All Wyllym could do was watch. Eventually, almost as an afterthought, two ground crew members returned to help him.

'Let's go, old man,' one said, hoisting him out of the seat into their arms. Unceremoniously, and with a hint of contempt, they placed him on a gurney as the celebration roared on nearby.

No one noticed him being wheeled away.

As the senior officer on the flight deck, Wyllym was entitled to a private recovery room, for which he was grateful since the main ward was now a raucous, wild scene. His retirement papers had been filed before the drill began, and the final list of graduating cadets had been sent straight to CENTCOM (Central Command). His days in the Navy were over.

An assortment of intravenous tubes and wires penetrated Wyllym, labouring to repair the damage to his muscles. Some of his internal organs were already encased in a protective biomesh to help them heal from prior sorties. Wyllym wondered how his body would fare in retirement. In the last five years, the longest he had gone without flying a Gryphon was a week, and he felt pain even when the bioadmin said he shouldn't be.

This was a masochist's profession, though it was hard to tell from the party raging next door. The Gryphon applicants were young, aggressive risk takers who were highly competitive, resilient, and motivated by self-imposed standards to be the best. But regardless of psychological profile, the human body just wasn't built to withstand such prolonged punishment, even with the miracles of medical nanobiology. Wyllym imagined their careers lasting a few years at most, assuming they never actually encountered a Raothri warship.

He hated to admit it, but Augustus Tyrell was right. Wyllym fed these cadets the Navy-enforced propaganda that they were being prepared to face such an encounter. But he knew they were far more likely to use their unique abilities to kill humans instead.

In spite of everything he had taught them, Wyllym had never truly earned their respect – because he was not firstborn. These students were elite scions, some with living highborn parents. Wyllym was a ghost possessing mastery of the Gift, adept at honing their skills through punishing training – nothing more. Direct interaction between student and teacher was kept as impersonal as possible. The case was made that this assured impartial evaluation of their skills. But on a personal level, he felt none of the mentoring responsibility for his charges that other commanders did. And his pupils were more than relieved to be rid of his tutelage for good.

Wyllym shifted uncomfortably, reminding himself that those spoiled children were no longer his concern. He reached through a tangle of cords for his corelink. It was time to start his new life.

A land broker had provided him with a list of plots that Vulcan Industries leased out on Eris, a world with a thin carbon dioxide atmosphere. The equatorial regions made for excellent biodome farming, and the broker found him one with an impressive view of the planet's largest mountain range. Wyllym smiled as he scrolled through the specifications. The plot was a full hectare, and included all the topsoil and equipment he needed to grow a wide range of crops.

Grain was always a safe bet, although there was more money in fruits and vegetables. Wealthy farmers ran expensive domes that could regulate atmospheric pressure and rainfall for really exotic crops like coffee and quinoa. But the money didn't matter; his Navy earnings could sustain him indefinitely. Wyllym simply loved the challenge of growing food. Farming was in his blood.

His thoughts drifted towards plots of serene vegetation basking in the warmth of the Orionis sun. The sweet sensation of sleep was upon him when an unwelcome voice shattered the bliss.

'You good enough to walk yet?' Augustus Tyrell was asking, standing at the foot of his bed.

Wyllym squinted at him.

'No, why?' he said. 'We celebrating?'

'What's there to celebrate?'

'My career?' Wyllym said, struggling to sit up. 'You're buying.'

'I don't know what you're talking about,' Augustus said. A medical officer rushed in and began switching off the machines. 'You've been summoned by Admiral Hedricks.'

'Unless he's giving me a medal, I think I'll pass – hey!'

The medic worked with reckless urgency, ripping out cords as though the flight deck was on fire.

Augustus had a grave look on his face.

'Wyll,' he said. 'This is serious.'

'Bugger serious,' Wyllym protested. 'I'm retired. My paperwork is in, I'm done.'

'The Navy isn't through with you yet,' Augustus said, stepping aside as another technician hurried in and began wheeling machines out. 'But I'm sure Hedricks will make a point of thanking you for your service at the briefing.'

'Thank me, right,' Wyllym grumbled, as the medic treated the punctures in his limbs and torso. 'You mean the way these snotty cadets did?'

'What did you expect?' Augustus snapped, tossing Wyllym's uniform at him. 'They never want to see you again. Now get dressed.'

The medic left, closing the door behind him.

'What's your problem, Ty?' Wyllym fumed.

'It's *our* problem, and it's a big one,' Augustus said. 'There are two soldiers right outside that door with orders to physically haul your ass out if you're not up in three minutes.'

Wyllym snapped.

'What the fuck—?'

'It's not just us,' Augustus muttered, looking over his shoulder to make sure they were alone. 'All of CENTCOM will be there.'

The effort of becoming angry was taxing. Wyllym wasn't ready to go anywhere – the recovery therapy had barely been through its first cycle when the medic had switched the system off. Slowly, he managed to swing his legs over the side.

'What happened?' he asked.

'You'll find out at the briefing.'

'Well, who's giving it?'

'Me. The security part anyway. You'd better be ready to answer some questions yourself, Wyll.'

With considerable effort, Wyllym put his hands up.

'Alright, enough,' he grumbled. 'You tell me just what's going on, or I'm not going anywhere.'

Augustus looked over his shoulder again.

'Jake found something,' he said.

'I'm glad he's still alive,' Wyllym said. 'What'd he find out?'

'That I was right to put him in harm's way,' Augustus said. 'On your feet, pilot. We're going to the *Archangel*.'

No matter how many times Wyllym saw it, the *Archangel* always left him speechless. The mothership defied all the engineering precepts that shaped how a conventional starship should appear. The strange, gaping hole that the hull was built around was complete; the construction equipment was absent, and the inner walls were rotating slowly along the circumference.

On approach, the shuttle oriented itself with the one of the *Archangel*'s hangar bays 'right side up', just like at Corinth. But the moment the ship broke the hangar plane, Wyllym felt himself pulled toward the deck. There was no transit to the inner wall of a rotational, centrifugally oriented structure. Somehow, despite the lack of rotation, gravity was omnipresent on the *Archangel*.

Once they were inside, Wyllym refused a gurney. But he did need Augustus's shoulder as he struggled to reach the briefing room. They drew stares and salutes from other crew as they marched through a labyrinth of hexagon-shaped hallways. They finally arrived at a dark, circular conference room with most of CENTCOM already present. Wyllym recognised some of the faces: Rear Admiral Jang Lao, the Hera OPCOM (Operations Commander); Rear Admiral Kenneth Dyson, the Zeus OPCOM; Vice Admiral Kristjan Larksson, the Belt OPCOM; and at least a dozen more Navy officials.

At the centre of them all was *him*.

For all his political and military influence, Admiral Vadim Hedricks was a larger-than-life figure who was surprisingly underwhelming in person.

The man was bone thin; his hands, criss-crossed with unsightly veins, seemed too large for the wrists that bore them. The skin was pulled tightly over his face, stretching over an oversized chin with nary a trace of beard. His lips were narrow and pursed. Thick black hair, combed precisely to one side, was cropped above ungainly ears pressed close to his scalp. His deep blue eyes always seemed to follow you, even when he looked elsewhere; or to stare through you, when you were the target of his gaze. And whether delivering humour or scorn, his expression rarely changed; impassive, though quietly judging, and always plotting.

Wyllym was always repulsed by the sight of him.

Admiral Hedricks registered their presence.

'Let us begin,' he announced, his high-pitched voice quieting the room. 'Commander Tyrell, the floor is yours.'

Augustus helped Wyllym into a seat, then strolled to the centre of the room.

'Gentlemen, we've received word that Vladric Mors is about to launch a direct assault on the *Archangel*,' he announced, as the display changed to an overview of Ceti military strength. 'This intel coalesces numerous observations of Ceti activity reported by sources at lower infiltration tiers. All current indicators have reached the maximum confidence level. This is going to happen. The Ceti fleet has undergone a massive refitting effort to incorporate new technology, the precise nature of which is unknown. Admiral Larksson?'

Instead of rising, the elder officer spoke from his seat.

'Ceti runs three hundred corvettes, give or take,' he said. Wyllym thought he was trying to suppress a yawn. 'They own two frigates, both scrapworthy by Navy standards, and one cruiser in dry dock, which is incapable of flight. Their crews are competent at striking lightly defended targets but utterly incapable of prosecuting full-scale assaults against fortified assets. And yet Vladric Mors is planning exactly that. His objective is to take the *Archangel* intact.'

'You must be joking,' remarked Admiral Dyson.

'He's mobilised his mechanised infantry, which isn't even divisional strength,' Augustus commented. 'Has them drilling breach 'n raids around the clock.'

'Let's play devil's advocate,' Admiral Jao said. 'What about Brotherhood? He pulled that off with fewer assets.'

'He also had the element of surprise,' Admiral Larksson responded. 'And in terms of defences, this is no comparison.'

'People in his own camp are calling it suicide,' Augustus told them. 'There is rampant dissent among his fleet captains. He's made examples of the more vocal ones to keep everyone else in line.'

'What's his motive?' Admiral Lao asked. 'Is there one, besides insanity?'

'He considers the *Archangel* a mortal threat to "freedom" in the Outer Rim,' Augustus said. 'He wants to pre-empt us before we can bring the fight to him. Should he fail to capture the ship, he plans to destroy it.'

'If the bastard wants to die in a blaze of glory,' snorted Admiral Lao, 'I'd love to oblige him.'

Admiral Hedricks remained as impassive as ever.

'Any idea when they sail?' asked Admiral Dyson.

'Their scouts have already left, with the main fleet deploying in a week's time,' Admiral Larksson replied. 'Unless they plan on seizing our fuel outposts, their journey is a one-way trip needing the better part of a month to complete. If they bring tankers, it will take even longer. Now, we all know Ceti corvettes are stealthy, so the possibility they'll evade our sensor nets is real. But eventually they'll have to insert themselves into orbit and burn down to attack speed, which means we'll almost certainly detect them as they emerge from the Belt.'

'"Almost" certainly?' asked Admiral Lao.

'The odds of missing a heat signature that large are minuscule,' Admiral Larksson said. 'I like our chances.'

'And this new technology?' Admiral Dyson asked. 'Do we know anything specific?'

'Nothing that we can verify,' Augustus said. 'We know their ships have been augmented by an auxiliary power source, either by giving up cargo space or adding an entire section to the hull. We suspect – and this is only theory – that it might be new shield technology.'

'What other parts of this briefing are theory?' Admiral Dyson asked. 'You sound like you don't trust your sources.'

Wyllym tensed up. Dyson and Augustus never got along.

'When multiple sources corroborate data, it's considered verified,' Augustus growled.

'Do your sources include this traitorous agent I've heard so much about?' Admiral Dyson asked, pressing the issue. 'We must give the man a medal before executing him.'

Admiral Hedricks came out of his thoughtful introspection.

'How we acquired this information is of no concern or consequence,' he said, turning his cold gaze on Wyllym. 'We have a crisis to manage. Don't we, Captain?'

Wyllym knew they could all see his discomfort.

'Yes, sir,' he managed.

'And what does our Gifted Gryphon instructor have to say about that?'

As far as Wyllym was concerned, there was no reason to mince words. Retirement was retirement.

'I think it's tragic,' he said.

172

Admiral Hedricks raised an eyebrow.

'For Ceti?'

'For those who want no part in this conflict,' he said. 'That includes Navy personnel, Orionis citizens, privateers, and everyone outside this room with the exception of Vladric Mors.'

Wyllym was surprised with himself. But these men surrounding him knew nothing of combat. They were politicians, not warriors.

'You think there's a serious threat, then?' Admiral Dyson said.

'Vladric is dangerous,' Wyllym said. 'Not because of his fleet, but for what he represents.'

Augustus cleared his throat.

'Then what do you propose, Captain?' Admiral Hedricks asked politely.

'Petition them for peace,' Wyllym said.

A few laughs broke out. Even Admiral Hedricks seemed amused.

'A murderer points a gun at you, and your first response is to ask for peace?' he said.

'It's not too late.'

'For whom?'

Wyllym winced as he tried leaning forward.

'If it's true he can only field three hundred ships, this won't even be a contest,' Wyllym said. 'No matter what technology they have.'

'And this upsets you because …?'

'I don't know what annihilating them accomplishes, beyond convincing the privateers that Ceti was right to strike first,' Wyllym said. 'We're conquerors to them, not liberators.'

'Fascinating,' Admiral Hedricks remarked, raising a hand to his chin. 'Please, continue.'

Augustus moved his head just slightly, using his eyes to warn Wyllym not to venture further.

Wyllym understood.

'I've said my piece.'

'No, you haven't,' Admiral Hedricks said. 'Please elaborate, Captain.'

The damage was done. So Wyllym spoke from the heart.

'If you massacre their fleet, you galvanise their cause,' he said. 'Our government is despised in the Outer Rim. And many people depend on

Ceti for their livelihoods. There are far more of them than firstborns in Orionis. If you martyr Vladric Mors, someone else will take his place.'

Admiral Hedricks actually cracked a smile.

'We're not afraid of ghosts, are we, gentlemen?'

'Look at him,' Admiral Dyson remarked. 'He's in so much pain it's clouding his thinking.'

'It's important to get all the perspectives,' Admiral Hedricks said. 'Hmm, pass on a chance to eliminate Ceti ... that's difficult to accept. But I can see the prospect troubles you.'

'It makes no difference to me,' Wyllym said.

'No?'

'I'm retired, sir.'

'I saw your application,' Admiral Hedricks said. 'And I regret to inform you that it is denied.'

Wyllym tried to look unmoved. But the disappointment was bitter.

'The Navy cannot be without the most able pilot of its most effective weapon during the greatest threat of modern times,' Admiral Hedricks said, turning to address the rest of the group. 'However, I concur with the Captain's assessment on the political consequences of dealing with Ceti too decisively. Much as I would love to fly the *Archangel* straight to Brotherhood, we will let them come to us, and crush them in plain sight of the entire Inner Rim. Captain Lyons will lead the Gryphons in their first operational mission, and what better cause than in defence of Orionis?'

Admiral Larksson appeared concerned.

'Where is the intercept?' he asked.

'Let them in as close as the orbit of Eris,' Admiral Hedricks. 'No closer. Now let me be perfectly clear with all of you: Chancellor Jade is *not* to be informed. I will take full responsibility for the alleged breach in our sensor nets. But once Ceti ships are within striking distance, Captain Lyons and his Gryphons will make quick work of their fleet, leaving a few for some of the *Archangel*'s own weapons.'

Wyllym couldn't believe what he was hearing.

'Don't look so distraught, Captain,' Admiral Hedricks said, rising from his seat. The meeting was over. 'There will be plenty of time to enjoy retirement. I know you'll perform admirably. The rest of you, mission planning begins in one hour. Dismissed.'

The Navy elite began leaving the room. Augustus was cornered by Admiral Dyson and Admiral Lao; Wyllym remained seated, staring at the table.

He felt a hand on his shoulder. It was Admiral Larksson.

'Old soldiers ought to know the perils of speaking our mind,' the officer said. Nearly two hundred years of age, he remained a kind man, with none of the arrogance of his peers.

'I guess the years have made me stubborn,' Wyllym said. 'Sir.'

'You could have walked away long ago,' the Admiral said. 'No one would have blamed you. But I don't believe for a moment you'd turn your back on this.'

The admiral patted him on the back, lowering his voice.

'Orionis needs men like you more than it will ever need a Grand Admiral,' he said. 'And he knows it. Be careful, son.'

Augustus didn't speak to Wyllym until they reached Corinth. The recovery ward was empty now, as the celebration had moved elsewhere. Beyond the few drones making their way through the halls, the place was deserted. It was there that Augustus finally exploded.

'You really are a dumb bastard sometimes,' he growled, pushing Wyllym's gurney through the hall so fast he thought he might fall off. 'What the hell was that back there?'

'Ty, I don't want to argue,' Wyllym muttered.

'You told CENTCOM you're a Ceti sympathiser!' Augustus fumed. 'Unbelievable!'

'You said Mors has dissent in his ranks,' Wyllym said. 'If Hedricks was smart, he'd appeal to them directly. I bet half of them would defect.'

'Wyll, you do not pass on a chance to kill the Butcher of Brotherhood,' Augustus growled, rounding a corner so fast he nearly ran over a medic. 'We can end years of bloodshed right now.'

'The bloodshed is our own choice,' Wyllym croaked. 'Instead of rising above Vladric Mors, we're playing right into his hands.'

'Please, Wyll, you're not that naïve. You can't be.'

'Ceti is bigger than one man. It's a verdict on how this government failed, and it will live on after Mors is dead. We can have real peace, without killing anyone. We're just too proud to negotiate it.'

Augustus spun the gurney around and heaved it into Wyllym's private ward. It struck the wall lightly, but with enough force to make Wyllym see stars.

'You know how personal this is for me,' Augustus growled.

Wyllym sighed. 'This is bigger than your problems too,' Wyllym retorted. 'Orionis *made* Vladric Mors. He's more dangerous to it dead than alive. Even Hedricks understands that.'

Augustus took a deep breath, searching for calm.

'This is the reason Jake tortured those agents,' Augustus said. 'Wyll, these bastards killed my daughter!'

'I know,' Wyllym said. 'I'm sorry.'

'Then why are you defending them?' Augustus demanded.

'How many more people need to die to bring you peace?' Wyllym asked quietly.

Augustus looked incredulous.

'*What?*' he demanded.

'You trained Jake,' Wyllym said. 'He knew that killing those officers would cost him his freedom, if not his life. He sacrificed himself to bring us this news. But no one is above the law. Not even him. And the awful truth is you won't hold yourself to the same standard.'

'Oh, give me a *fucking* break, Wyll – '

'Danna's killers were never found,' Wyllym continued. 'But you'd take the head off Vladric Mors, without ever knowing if he gave the order, instead of making him face justice. You'd start a war for your personal vengeance. I'm sorry, Ty. That is selfish.'

Augustus took a menacing step towards him.

'Fuck. You.'

Wyllym shook his head.

'If you want to honour her, Jake's sacrifice, and the men who died, then learn to see Orionis through the eyes of someone who wasn't born in the Inner Rim.'

'*I do see it from* …' Augustus roared, then cut himself short, furious. 'I think you're so fed up with being treated like a second-rate citizen around here that you finally snapped.'

'I've been trained to fight an alien species,' Wyllym said, closing his eyes. 'There are no ghosts in my world, Ty. Only humans, and everything else.'

Augustus regarded him for a moment, then stepped back and waved in a medic.

'CENTCOM wants you in a sim with the new grads for practice runs against a Ceti fleet,' he said, as the medic began reattaching the machines that would help Wyllym heal.

'That isn't necessary.'

'No, not for someone who's clairvoyant,' Augustus said. 'But they haven't made the connection.'

The two friends exchanged a weary smile.

'Please don't do anything stupid,' Augustus said, moving for the door.

'Same to you.'

Wyllym watched his friend leave, listening to the machines resume their macabre work.

He checked his corelink; the land broker had left a message asking if he should move forward with the purchase. The rep from Vulcan Industries had sweetened the offer by installing new irrigation pumps in the biodome. The fact he was a retiring Navy officer made him an attractive prospect, and they wanted his business.

But instead of returning the call, Wyllym typed a message instructing him to cancel the transaction, with regrets.

Then he composed a new one to Chancellor Vespa Jade.

19

VLADRIC

Ninety-seven Years Earlier
2712 AD

A famished boy, just eight years of age, clad in filthy clothes that hung from his bones like rags, shuffled up to his ailing mother and put a familiar question.

'When are we going to land?' Vladric asked.

Her good eye opened slowly, as if the act caused great anguish.

'Soon,' she whispered, as it closed again. 'I hope.'

He slumped beside her, resting his back against the bulkhead. Both of Vladric's small hands were clasped over his stomach.

'I'm so hungry,' he whimpered.

'I'm sorry,' she said.

'Will I meet Daddy soon?'

She tried to swallow before answering.

'No. You never will, Vladric.'

That surprised him; usually her reply was 'someday'. No other children at the shelter had fathers. Only a few had mothers. Vladric knew that was common for ghosts, even though he didn't understand what the word meant. Mostly it was nannies and drones that looked after them. But Vladric was more fortunate than the others. Mom would visit almost every day, even though she was working hard to buy a place they could live in together. Then he could meet his father, when the time was right.

But his Mom hadn't been herself lately. She was being more honest than usual.

Their possessions consisted of the clothes on their back and two insulated sleeping bags sprawled across the cold, grimy metal grating at their feet. They shared this part of the ship with other mothers and their children – no men were permitted. The area was a pressurised freight container hastily partitioned into compartments to provide semi-private living areas for a journey that was to last just four months. A pair of gaunt, frail women stood guard at the entrance where the module joined the freighter's main hull, offering the illusory measure of 'protection' from those who might seek to do harm.

Vladric, his mother, and nearly two hundred others had boarded *The Baxley* ten months ago from Tabit Prime. They were among thousands who embarked on voyages as newly empowered free market labourers, thanks to the historic formation of the Privateer's Union. Colonisation projects were at last deregulated from government oversight, and unrecognised citizens were now entitled to the same labour opportunities as firstborns. Vladric was too young to care about the politics. He was just thrilled to be leaving the shelter and starting fresh on a brave new world.

Dozens of ships queued outside the station offering cheap transport to construction sites all over Orionis. It was a mad rush to a new frontier, and there were fortunes to be made. *The Baxley* was on its way to a biodome project on Eris. Other ships were travelling even further, to projects on Hephaestus, Hera, the Great Belt, and even Zeus. Vladric would get to see wonders that his friends could only dream about. At last, he and his mother were starting a new life together.

Four months after leaving port, *The Baxley* settled into orbit, de-spinning to receive the dropships that would transport passengers to the surface or to orbital habitats. But after a week of microgravity with no dropships in sight, the ship resumed its spin. The captain announced that they could not disembark: there was simply no place which could take them. Every one of the corporate-owned settlements on the surface of Eris was over capacity because of ships that had arrived before them. It would be months before new habitats were completed.

Claiming bankruptcy, the captain went on to explain that they were at the mercy of goodwill from other ships to resupply, for they had no fuel to return. He urged them to conserve resources and pray. Then he signed off, absolving himself of any responsibility for them.

The crew barricaded itself in the aft compartments, where the freighter's engines and power core were housed. The captain locked himself forward, where the bridge and communications equipment were stowed. They had stocked ample provisions for themselves ahead of the announcement. Elsewhere within the spinning metal walls of *The Baxley*, Darwinism ensued.

Water was plentiful, thanks to the ship's reclamation system. As was heat, electricity, and life support. Food, however, was in short supply. The passengers on board had no ties to each other, so the alphas among them asserted leadership to control what little remained. Bitter rivalries erupted, resulting in bloodshed that lasted for weeks. No firearms were on board; there was only the blunt trauma of survivalist's desperation. The captain was unresponsive throughout the riots, despite being in contact with other vessels that could be seen from the viewports.

Vladric's mother did what she could to keep him safe during the chaos, including some things he didn't fully understand. All he knew was that these acts caused her great pain, and that he was helpless to do anything about it. But every now and then a man would bring scraps of food, often with blood on the wrapping. She would take the smallest nibble, and give the rest to Vladric. It was enough to survive the nightmare, but only just.

'Order' eventually prevailed, and the faction leaders came together to distribute what few provisions remained. To prevent people from eating corpses, the dead were thrown into the freighter's slush pits, where they were reclaimed and absorbed into the water supply. By then, the food had run out completely. Even the rats, a vital staple of Vladric's own diet after the second week without food, seemed to have disappeared. Most people had come to terms with their fate. There was no energy left to fight any longer.

Then a miracle happened – or what should have been one. The Orionis Navy raided *The Baxley*, arresting the captain and remaining crew. Those who witnessed the spectacle claimed the crew had been led away screaming unintelligible gibberish. The isolation had taken their minds, and Vladric had wished them all thrown into the slush pits alive. But there was still no spin down or respite from general misery. Apparently no one, not even the Orionis government, knew what to do with them. Other freighters had suffered similar fates in the mad rush to colonise, and their passengers had become orphaned to the universe, here at Eris and elsewhere.

Help was a long, long distance away, if it would ever come at all. The Navy had brought a medic, and a very limited supply of rations. The soldiers in charge of distributing them were harsh men who loathed their bad fortune to have ended up serving Orionis from the wretched bowels of *The Baxley*. Its passengers still weren't getting the nutrition they needed; only enough not to die.

This was the situation of young Vladric that day: starving but, frustratingly, still breathing. And he had become desperately concerned for the mother who was slipping away before his very eyes.

'Mom?' he asked.

She made a weak noise, no more than a whimper. Her good eye opened suddenly, and she was clearly frightened. The Navy medic had seen her briefly earlier in the week, then moved on to others.

'Mom?' he said, leaning closer.

'I'm so sorry,' she whispered. 'Vladric ... I should have told you ...'

Her mouth stopped moving.

'*Mom!*'

Vladric had seen enough injuries, and knew to check her vitals; her pulse was weak, but she was still breathing.

In those short, laboured breaths, he found hope, and believed she could be saved. Phasing out the burn in his belly, Vladric rose and made his way through the camp, stepping around the bodies of the starving. The guards at the main hull entrance looked at him wearily, but made no attempt to stop his climb towards the exit. Struggling through the narrow opening, he had to lean against the bulkhead walls for support; the spin of the freighter's main hull was almost unbearable. But hope drove him on, and soon he was staggering through areas of the ship that had not seen a child in months. Ignoring the glare of starving men who had once killed for food, Vladric found what he was looking for.

A long queue of passengers were waiting to receive their Navy rations and a brief appointment with the medic. Two soldiers with rifles strung across their chests were chatting beside them, occasionally warning people to stay in their places. Vladric walked out in the open, making his way to the end.

'Where'd he come from?' one of the soldiers asked.

'Hey, kid, what freight block are you assigned to?' the other said.

Vladric didn't respond, just hoped.

'Hey!' the soldier called out, more sternly this time. 'I'm talking to you!'

'Leave him be,' a spindly old man said. 'He can have my place in line.'

'You lose your spot, you lose your rations,' the soldier warned.

'I'm aware of that,' the man snapped back, stepping aside. 'They'll do more good for him than me.'

All eyes were on Vladric as he shuffled forward, lifting his head only to thank the old man.

The soldiers resumed their conversation, strolling parallel along the queue of passengers. They seemed to have forgotten him almost immediately.

But while they talked, his mother lay dying, and the provisions he needed to save her life were just metres away. Precious seconds were wasting. To reach them, he needed to divert the guards' attention elsewhere. But what could possibly occupy them long enough for him to escape? There was no time left. The world began to collapse. He had to take action *now*, but what?

Between a pair of short breaths, a vision unfolded. It was a moment of sheer insanity, disguised as hope, and it pumped adrenaline into his famished veins.

Heart racing, Vladric stuck his foot out and tripped the nearest soldier. As the man stumbled, Vladric threw himself at his legs from behind. They both fell forward, and he felt himself brush against people scurrying out of the way. The soldier had put only one arm out to break his fall; the other remained locked around the grip of his rifle, the barrel of which was facing away from him. There, before Vladric's eyes, was salvation.

He stuck his finger inside the trigger guard and squeezed as hard as he could.

The weapon's deafening report took his breath away. Then a sharp blow struck his temple; he rolled away from its direction. He ended up on his stomach, covering his head, his ears ringing, to realise that all hell had broken loose.

Screams and shouts filled the metal space; it seemed like everyone waiting on line had converged on the soldiers. Vladric squirmed free of someone's attempt to grab him and began crawling through pairs of legs – and saw that some passengers were rushing the medic too. Vladric headed towards him. A gunshot rang out; then another. Terrified, he checked himself for holes, didn't find any, and pressed on. People were fighting over the contents in the crates behind the medic, who was now overwhelmed. The rations spilled onto the deck, right in front of Vladric.

As gunfire struck the bulkheads, he grabbed everything he could. Everyone around him ducked, some collapsing to the deck.

By contrast, Vladric ran as fast as he could.

Hope, he thought to himself, as his body began to fail.

Hope, as his blood turned to acid.

Hope, as he fled from danger, stumbling down the freighter's spinning hull, down the access ladder, over and around the people who needed *hope* as much as he did.

He collapsed at his mother's feet, sucking gulps of fire into his lungs.

She was as he had left her, her blue lips frozen with the last words she would ever speak.

Present Day

'Where were you just now?' Lira asked softly.

Vladric's eyes moved away from memories to the erupting colours on her bare breasts.

'Nowhere,' he said, pushing himself away.

'Please talk to me,' she whispered, embracing his turned back. 'Let me comfort you!'

'I've had all the comfort I'll ever need from you,' he muttered, springing up from the bed.

She glowered at him, grinding her teeth.

'Then go burn the world down,' she flung at him, storming off. 'Die trying, for all I care.'

Usually her flat was immaculate and stately; like Vladric, Lira was an enthusiast for classical Earth arts and literature, and spent a good portion of her wealth on recreating living spaces modelled on various architectural movements in history. But the paintings that once adorned the bulkheads were gone, and moving crates lined the walls.

'So what *is* all this?' he asked.

'I've always wanted to see the House worlds,' she growled, pulling a robe on.

'I wouldn't do that if I were you,' Vladric warned. 'You're not the sort who'd enjoy life in their cults.'

'Every one of them is a safer place to be than here,' she said, disappearing into a bedroom. 'All thanks to you.'

'Wrong again,' Vladric said, now fully dressed. 'But I won't stop you. Though your lack of faith disappoints me.'

'*My* lack of faith?' she called out. 'There's a pandemic of atheism around here.'

'The doubters believe in the things I *want* for Orionis,' he said, casually inspecting one of the crates. 'They just don't think achieving them is *possible*. There's a difference. I'm not crazy. I know what I'm doing.'

'And I disagree on both counts.'

'Thank you,' Vladric said, pausing to remove a book – *Pride and Prejudice*. 'The same has been said of every revolutionary in history.'

Lira rounded the corner fully dressed in a form-fitting jumpsuit like those usually worn in cryo travel. Her shock of thick, bright red hair was tied back, except for a few long, curly bangs dangling in front. She snatched the book from his hands and placed it inside the crate, then secured it with a swipe of her finger.

'History is full of men with big ideas and tiny dicks,' she said, moving on to the other crates. 'They've ruined civilisation enough times already.'

'Ruin is opportunity in disguise,' he answered, easing back into a chair besides the bed. 'No one will miss a world run by highborns.'

'People don't want one run by sadists either.'

'It's advantageous to have people think you're insane.'

Lira smirked.

'Then you're not as clever as you think.'

'You'll see,' Vladric said. 'All will be revealed soon enough. And I'll know whom I can trust. I hope you're one of them.'

'A confident leader never has to test loyalty,' she said, checking her corelink.

'No, but a cautious one does. Overconfidence is lethal.'

Lira stifled a chuckle with her hand.

'Is that amusing?' Vladric asked, turning red.

She couldn't contain herself, and openly laughed at him.

'The notion that "caution" motivates you is an understatement,' she chuckled. 'You're afraid of your own shadow, so to compensate you try to control everything. And you've convinced yourself that's actually possible to achieve. You'll hurt anyone, including yourself, to hold onto that illusion. It's a farce, Vladric. A fantasy. It exists only in the minds of psychopaths.'

He blinked a few times, then took a deep breath before speaking.

'I understand what motivates people and use that to help get them the things they want in a way that serves my interests,' he said calmly. 'It just so happens that my interests are also best for Orionis.'

Lira went back to her corelink.

'Some men survive by taking what the world gives them and adapting,' she said, shaking her head. 'You survive by leading them into the recesses of your anxiety.'

'Ceti isn't perfect, but it's a better alternative than anything else,' he declared. 'The trouble is denial and complacency. Highborn hegemony threatens the freedom that people here take for granted. They either refuse to see this, or believe it's inevitable. I won't accept that. Whether they understand or not, securing their freedom is my responsibility.'

Exasperated, she looked towards the ceiling.

'What would you do if the *Archangel* was in your possession right now?'

'I'd fuck you right on the bridge.'

'And then what?'

'I'd arrest Vespa Jade for crimes against humanity. I'd repeal the Heritage Act and recognise all people as citizens of the new government. I'd seize the transfusion assets from corporations and make radiation treatments available for everyone. And when Orionis was truly free, we'd press on to Tau Ceti. Assuming the ship really is capable of reaching it.'

She placed a hand on her hip.

'And the Navy?'

'All firstborns relieved of command and, where appropriate, tried for war crimes.'

Lira leaned over a chair, exposing her ample bosom.

'Ceti has no laws,' she reminded him. 'By what judicial standard would you proceed?'

'My own,' Vladric replied, distracted by her teasing.

Lira hung her head in apparent disgust.

'I have to go,' she said, returning to the bedroom.

'You aren't yourself today,' he commented. 'Is something troubling you?'

'No trouble but the sight of you.'

'Have I asked you to do anything I shouldn't have?' Vladric persisted. 'I mean, above or beyond the services you voluntarily provide?'

'Are you referring to my Jack Tatum assignment?'

'Yes. Did he "bare his soul" to you, or just his seed?'

Lira returned and took a seat directly across from him, crossing her legs.

'I asked him to describe the experience of torturing a man to death, just to get an idea of whom I was dealing with,' she said. 'His answer was interesting. So out of curiosity, what's yours?'

'My what?'

'Say, a description of castrating a man.'

'No different from cutting off that ginger mane of yours,' he hissed. 'Now, Jack Tatum …'

She nodded politely at him.

'"The Minotaur".'

'The who?'

'It's what he calls himself,' said Lira. 'And the name seems to have stuck. He's a remarkable contradiction.'

'How so?'

'On one hand, he loathes himself. He's a hopeless drug addict, high or intoxicated most of the time. Yet there is incredible strength in him. He is strangely approachable for a Ceti Lieutenant. He can talk to

186

anyone; he looks everyone in the eye, from commanders to mutants. And he handles himself rather well in a fight, which is odd. Plus, he seems to have a knack for learning the truth about people.'

'I've noticed.'

'The bounty sums for him are as high as they are for you. Rumour is the Navy is bidding the price up.'

'So more people with guns are coming to Brotherhood.'

'No more than usual. But that isn't what should concern you.'

'Then what is?'

'The fact he is well liked by everyone. People respond to him during crises – there is a reassuring authority to him. He leads when others freeze or panic. His clarity under duress makes me wonder if he possesses the Gift. The Minotaur persona is making waves in the culture here, starting a legend. Perhaps one greater than yours.'

'Are you provoking me?'

Lira smiled as he rose abruptly.

'No,' she said. 'I'm just stating that it's unclear to me whether or not he's favourable to your interests. For all his flaws, there is much about him that reminds me of you.'

Vladric began making his way to the door, pausing at the entrance. She remained seated.

'Well done, Lira,' he said.

'Enjoy your war, Vladric,' she said.

The main hangar at Helodon was always closed to civilians, but today it was closed even to the personnel that managed it. Evidence of the fleet's imminent departure was scattered across the expansive deck: crates of supplies, ammunition, and fuel tanks standing beside dozens of mech loaders lining the boarding areas where Ceti corvettes once sat.

Only one remained, suspended from the last mooring in the hangar. It was a hybrid design; the boxy, functional Jackal hull designed by the privateer-operated Lantrek Yards; Ceti-manufactured Sunburst vectored pulse thrusters; and two pairs of salvaged Navy MK-221 rail guns. A patchwork of chequered black and yellow paint with the Ceti seal was emblazoned on the aft sensor dome; the designation CW-266 was stencilled on the hull. Rows of fangs had been painted on the bow, and

beneath them was a series of skull and crossbones, one for each registered kill. Some had been placed over an Orionis Navy logo.

Her name was the *Griefmaker*, owned by the late Atticus Lazrel, and
she was to be Vladric's flagship for the invasion.

'She's no *Aria Black*,' Dr Tallendin said, as the two men walked
beneath the huge vessel, gazing up at her ventral hull. 'But she'll do.'

The doctor was exhausted. A full beard sprouted from his face and
chin; he seemed to have aged decades in the last few months.

'What you've accomplished here is astounding,' Vladric commended
him. 'I won't forget this.'

Dr Tallendin kept speaking as though he hadn't heard.

'I thought to have it painted over so as not to draw enemy fire,'
he said, 'then I remembered that we ought to have done the same for
every other ship.'

'Paint won't make a difference,' Vladric said. 'The shielding is
what counts.'

'If I had just four more weeks, I could probably finish the rest,' Dr
Tallendin said. 'We've automated the most tedious steps of the installation.'

'You know we don't have time.'

'I was hoping that had changed.'

Vladric kept walking as he spoke, admiring the *Griefmaker*. She was
ninety metres long from bow to stern.

'The longer we wait,' he said, 'the more people will suffer.'

Dr Tallendin stopped.

'Is that really true, though?' he called out. '*Inevitable* suffering
and oppression?'

Vladric turned around.

'Look at everything you've built,' Dr Tallendin continued, his hands
clasped together. 'Must we risk it all now?'

'Complacency is the temptation of success,' Vladric said, his voice
low, but gentle. 'A generation ago, many died to make all this possible.
I won't waste their efforts.'

'No, of course not,' Dr Tallendin said. 'I just wish we could delay a
bit more, is all. To protect more of *our* lads we're putting in harm's way.'

'There's never enough time to prepare.' Vladric said. 'But the sooner
we go, the better our chances.'

'I understand that.' Dr Tallendin was looking nervously at his shoes. 'I mean, I'm no soldier, but ...'

He took a deep breath.

'They all know,' he said, wiping his brow. 'The fleet captains. They know what I've done to their ships ... which ones are protected, which ones aren't.'

'Of course they do,' Vladric shrugged.

'There is talk of desertion,' Dr Tallendin added. 'Mutiny, or worse.'

Vladric crossed his arms.

'The officers are managing their concerns fairly well,' he said. 'Once the crews learn our plan, they'll realise our odds are much better than they think. The reason for secrecy ought to be obvious by now. They also know any deserters will only live with their mistake for a short while. No Ceti station will allow them to land or refuel. And that will be the least of their concerns once the *Archangel* is ours.'

'It might help if they all knew sooner,' Dr Tallendin said. 'To inspire them.'

Vladric grasped the frail man by his shoulders.

'Ilya, we've known each other a long time,' he said. 'I have taken every precaution to protect you and your loved ones – not because I have any doubt of the outcome, but to ease your concerns. Now, tell me the truth: have I ever given you any reason not to trust me?'

Dr Tallendin flushed red.

'Of course not.'

'Then trust me now,' Vladric insisted, releasing his grip. 'This assault is going to correct some of the mistakes I've made. Not all of them. But most. Things will be different when this is done.'

'Mistakes?'

Vladric threw his hands up, then began pacing.

'Ceti isn't what I hoped it would become,' he admitted. 'I've done terrible things. And I've enabled others to follow my example, all in the name of "freedom".'

The doctor's face betrayed complete surprise.

'Freedom is bloody,' Vladric continued, resuming his inspection of the *Griefmaker*. 'It needs weapons, incentives, and cold men who will do cruel things to protect it.'

He stopped.

'I used to *love* the idea of the *Archangel*,' he said. 'I was inspired by its purpose. The original one.'

'Then how will attacking it amend for mistakes?' Dr Tallendin asked.

'Because Ceti is on the same corrupted path,' Vladric said. 'It was a noble idea that's morphed into something else. I have to regain our purpose. If we take that ship ... *when* we take it ... We'll make sure it does what it's supposed to: find a world that we can *all* call home. Not just the ones who call themselves firstborns.'

Dr Tallendin nodded wearily.

'That will always be a worthy cause, sir.'

Vladric checked his corelink. The fleet was amassing at Brotherhood. It was almost time.

'Ilya, thank you for helping me,' he said. 'My biggest mistakes won't be on the ships you've shielded.'

20

VESPA

She found herself on a ship with no name, surrounded by a faceless, angry crew.

They were in great danger, but Vespa's every attempt to help earned a shove aside and bitter excoriation. The harder she tried to be involved, the more the crew resented her. Ashamed, she finally gave up and retreated to a small corner, hoping to avoid any further disruption.

It was then, only when she was voiceless and invisible, that she noticed something ominous about the bulkheads: they were perspiring. A dark, heavy fluid had formed where they met with the ceiling.

As the viscous ooze grew larger, Vespa tried to warn a crewman of the danger. But she was scorned for her trouble, even as the seepage spread relentlessly, dripping from the ceilings and creeping up from beneath the floors. Another crewman stepped in a small puddle, then tracked the vile substance across the deck. She watched in horror as the spatters coalesced and raced after him. Terrified, she screamed at the officers on the bridge. But they kept conversing as though nothing was amiss, even as the dark shadow ran up their legs, torso, neck and head. When they were completely engulfed, their blackened forms liquefied and splashed onto the deck without a trace of human flesh.

Suddenly, the bulkheads separating her from the adjacent compartments melted away. The decks above collapsed in a gushing cascade of ebony. A sinister shape rose from the bridge: a demon of death and devastation. It glared at her, unwavering, as the ship disintegrated around them, then it vanished when the final bulkhead gave way. The vacuum hurled Vespa into space, flailing and desperate as the air was sucked from her lungs.

Vespa tumbled through the void, her last views alternating between the bubbling black mass that was once her ship, and the distinct contours of the *Tabit Genesis* some distance away, ablaze like a torch in the deep of night.

She had awakened short of breath, violently sick with fear. More than once, she needed to collect herself as she recounted the dream to ORPHUS.

'And you cannot remember the name of the ship?' the AI asked.

'I told you, no,' Vespa answered.

'Then I am confident this was no vision,' ORPHUS said, in his synthetic yet calming voice. 'This dream emerged from challenges in your life. The constructs you encountered are consistent with recurring personal themes.'

Vespa shuddered as she thought of the demon.

'What about that … thing I saw?' she asked.

'An abstract representation of your distrust of people,' ORPHUS said. 'The darkness is your anxiety about the outcome of your decisions.'

'*Tabit*,' she whispered. 'Why does it burn?'

'That construct is unrelated to this dream, but a persistent concern,' ORPHUS said. 'It remains a plausible outcome. Would you like to review the sequence map again?'

The AI was referring to a visualisation of all the possible paths from her visions that could lead to the destruction of *Tabit Genesis*.

'No, thank you,' she said.

Arturus was visiting today, at last. Vespa had not shared his presence in three decades. The prospect stirred unwelcome feelings.

Above all, she wondered if he was terrorised by these nightmares as well.

For the historical implications alone, the arrival of House Alyxander ships to Inner Rim space would have been sensationalised by the Orionis media. But the spectacle was drawing huge audiences due to the sheer enigma of the Houses. To the firstborn population of Tabit Prime, House Alyxander was akin to an alien civilisation. They gathered around news feeds in homes, schools, and offices to gawk at the peculiar U-shaped corvettes and disc-shaped freighters gathered between the orbits of Amnisos and Eileithyia.

The visitation agreement between the two governments prohibited the convoy from approaching the *Tabit Genesis* directly. So House Alyxander entertained its viewing audience by delivering a spectacular lightshow; huge arcs of electrostatic energy danced between enormous volumetric adverts for the merchandise on sale.

Several of the barges were so large that they held biodomes, and they offered a variety of services for every age, habit, and interest. One allowed children to pilot real combat mechs in mock battles. Another showcased live animals reconstituted from the Earth gene pool, trained to walk with custom magnetic fittings. And then there were the 'x-barges', promising tailor-made fantasies in which customers were analysed to determine the ideal combination of stimuli to invoke the most unforgettable experience.

The House offered it all completely free of charge, a ploy ostensibly designed to lure business from Orionis corporations already furious over their presence in the Inner Rim. Navy frigates kept sentry alongside the streams of spacecraft bringing eager tourists to the show while corporation warships lurked nearby, with Vulcan Industries having the most visible presence of all.

Chancellor Vespa Jade kept a proud, confident appearance while waiting for the House delegation to arrive. Accompanying her in the main hangar of the *Tabit Genesis* were four senators from the Orionis parliament: Senators Brandon Tice and Landon Hsu from her own Genesis party, and Senators Stefan Martin and Helena Kjanik from the main opposition Freetracks Guild. Whatever Cerlis Tarkon was doing to protest, Vespa was determined to show her brother a unified front in here.

Her pulse quickened as the House shuttle rose on the transfer elevator. A company of Navy soldiers dressed in parade uniforms lined the path between them and the boarding ramp, while the Orionis government flag hung prominently from an overhead cargo gantry.

'All this pomp and circumstance,' Senator Tice pouted, shifting his weight from one foot to the other. 'Isn't it a bit excessive?'

'I'd have sent a customs drone,' Senator Hsu muttered.

Vespa made an effort to smile a bit more broadly.

'I'm sure you understand the necessity of diplomatic honours,' she said.

'Not when it means a hero's welcome for someone who isn't here,' Senator Kjanik hissed.

Vespa nearly rolled her eyes. No House had ever before sent a diplomatic delegation to Orionis. Lance Alyxander was the first to send so much as an envoy – who in this case happened to be her brother Arturus.

'Hard to trust a man who sends someone else to conduct his affairs,' Senator Tice said.

'Is he even a man?' Senator Martin quipped. 'I heard he was androgynous.'

'No, a hermaphrodite,' Senator Tice scoffed. 'And he fucked himself by not coming here.'

'Did Cerlis Tarkon tell you that?' Senator Hsu sallied.

'If anyone knows what's beneath his trousers ...' Senator Martin began.

'*Anyone's* trousers,' Senator Kjanik corrected.

'Do you speak from experience?' Senator Tice smirked.

Vespa had heard enough.

'Did you two always act like menstruating cunts in the Navy?'

'*Excuse* me?' Senator Kjanik demanded.

Vespa smiled at them.

'It would explain why we lost the war,' she said, just as the shuttle ramp door lowered.

The first to emerge were House guards; each was seven feet tall and completely covered in gold armour, including a full face mask. They were as beautiful as they were intimidating; a grotesque human face, locked in perpetual suffering, was carved upon the shoulder plates. House Alyxander called this icon Angustia, a representation of suffering as the inevitable condition of the human species. There were eight of them in all, women and men alike, each with gender-tailored armour to match. Per Orionis regulations, they appeared to be unarmed.

Then Arturus stepped out.

Dressed in resplendent, lavish robes lined with precious stones, he strode down the aisle with ramrod-straight posture, one hand upon a strange sceptre shaped like a human figurine. He was unashamedly and openly augmented; silver circuitry extended from his tear ducts across his cheekbones and down the sides of his neck. He appeared much younger than his twin sister; his pale skin contrasted sharply with rouge lips and violet eyes that were clearly not his own.

His every step was a measured display of regal authority, and Vespa knew it was all an act. Arturus halted an arm's length away from the Senators, glaring down his nose at them.

Everyone was uncomfortable. Vespa cleared her throat.

'On behalf of Orionis, it's my sincere pleasure to welcome you—'

'In our culture, it is custom for a new host to kiss the Lady,' Arturus interrupted, holding his glare on the Senators. 'Who shall oblige?'

Vespa caught the Senators exchanging confused glances at each other. She took a step forward, but Arturus recoiled in disgust.

'Not you!' he hissed, looking directly at Senator Tice. '*You*. Come here.'

The blood drained from the elder statesman's face.

'Don't keep her waiting,' Arturus scolded, narrowing his eyes at him. Senator Tice advanced two steps, then froze in place.

'Now, if you please,' the envoy insisted. 'Kiss the Lady.'

Senator Tice glowered at Vespa.

'Not her!' Arturus said, again with disgust. '*Her.*'

He nodded towards his sceptre, which was in fact shaped roughly like a lady. Arturus was holding it in one hand, directly in front of him, resting the top well below his navel.

Senator Tice's eyes widened as he looked down.

The stern demeanour of Arturus imploded in a fit of maniacal laughter.

'*Priceless,*' he wheezed, slapping Senator Tice on the back like an old friend. 'Go on, check your corelinks, I just sent you something. All of you, hurry!'

Vespa, completely embarrassed, complied and found a new message; it contained an image of Senator Tice staring incredulously at Arturus's crotch. He was playing a game, an egregious dance intended to provoke them.

'Ambassador Jade,' she said, her voice cool. 'A pleasure to welcome you.'

Arturus performed a mock bow.

'Chancellor, the pleasure is all mine,' he gushed. 'We're delighted with your hospitality. The station looks fabulous from eighty thousand kilometres away. And all these guns pointed at us! It's enough to get a man *excited*!'

'Your visit will go a long way towards easing tensions,' Senator Martin assured him.

'Speaking of tension, do you work out?' Arturus asked, giving the Senator a very inappropriate slap on his rump. Everyone gasped. 'Those glutes are *tight* for a man your age!'

'We're unaccustomed to being insulted by ambassadors,' Senator Kjanik said. 'Why did Lance Alyxander send you rather than come himself?'

'Oh, Senator, you know how it is when you get rich,' Arturus said dismissively. 'He's double-booked with a manicure. But he gave me everything I need to negotiate a juicy trade agreement that your constituents will just love … Oh, where are my manners? There's an election coming! The stress must be unimaginable. You should visit us on the barges. We have ways to help you relax.'

'Perhaps we should continue this conversation elsewhere,' Senator Martin murmured, glancing about.

'Mmm, someplace private?' Arturus said with a wink. 'I know how twisted you are, you *naughty* Senator!'

'Can we even let someone with his augments into the station?' Senator Kjanik huffed.

Arturus slouched to one side.

'Darling, the only things illegal about me are my good looks.'

Then he strutted past them out of the hangar, with his elite guard in tow. Vespa and the Senators hurried after him.

'The corporations aren't happy with the publicity stunt you're pulling out there,' Senator Tice warned. 'It makes our job much more difficult.'

Arturus didn't break stride.

'Lance Alyxander offered those gifts to the *people* of Orionis, not the oligarchs who run this shithole,' he informed him curtly. 'He is well aware of corporate interests and prepared to make a deal, provided that it sets *equitable* terms for free trade.'

Arturus whirled abruptly, nearly causing the procession behind him to crash into one another.

'What he will *not* do is let them establish Outer Rim monopolies. I think this bears repeating: if they want access to our markets, then

House Alyxander must have access to theirs. I hope none of you are champions of the status quo. That would bore us.'

'I think the timing of your visit is interesting,' Senator Tice said.

'Oh, how so, handsome?' Arturus said, his voice heavy with sarcasm.

'With the *Archangel* nearly finished, you picked a great time to be on your best behaviour.'

Arturus smiled, twirling the human-shaped sceptre in his hand. It must have been heavy, but glided smoothly between his fingers.

'Are you rattling that shrivelled sabre of yours?' he said, sashaying dangerously close to the Senator's personal space. 'Do you expect House Alyxander to tremble before the Grand Admiral's fleet? So much for the goodwill of this arrangement. There, there, Senator *Tice*,' Arturus hissed, patting his shoulder as if consoling a child. 'The distance between our worlds is great. And the *Archangel* is just one ship. You have your toys. We have ours.'

'If I may be blunt,' Senator Hsu said. 'It's your relationship with Ceti that people find threatening.'

'Peaceful relationships are about learning to coexist,' Arturus said, resuming his stroll. 'Consider our location on the far side of the Belt. We would be unwise to upset the neighbours.'

'You've attacked ships registered to Orionis corporations,' Senator Kjanik said. 'That hasn't made Lance Alyxander many friends here.'

'Tsk. I hate violence,' Arturus said. 'Those incidents were tragic. But I'm afraid our recollection is that it was *their* ships which attacked our own – and lost. They learned the hard way that exploitation of the Outer Rim is not without consequence. One of my goals this visit is to propose the formation of a neutral council that will draft the rules for intersystem commerce. Then these matters can be judged objectively. Whether or not you can convince the corporations to play along, well, let's just say I don't envy you.'

'The fact you're here means we might be willing to change,' Senator Martin said.

Arturus squared up to the entire group.

'The fact we are here, Senator, means that you finally understand that you cannot impose your will on the Outer Rim,' he said. 'But please don't judge me, I'm just the messenger. Now, who wants a cocktail? I *love* diplomatic receptions.'

Despite the tense atmosphere with the Senators, Arturus somehow managed to turn the 'diplomatic reception' into one of the most memorable events ever hosted at Tabit Prime.

The flamboyant envoy insisted on supplying his own refreshments and entertainment, opening the invitation to all government staff and effectively converting the most important legislative facility of Orionis into a dance hall. The spontaneous event, quickly approved by Vespa, created a logistical nightmare for the security team as they struggled to keep a wary eye on all the strangers on board. But the show went on without major incident, and in her view was successful in accomplishing what she wanted: to demonstrate that she could relate to voters.

Per their agreement, she kept her interaction with Arturus to a minimum. It was no secret they were siblings, but for the diplomacy to work, they had to remove their personal connection from the equation. She observed the reactions of officials who met him, noting who warmed to his charm and who didn't. Generally, things went the way she expected; Arturus, for all his show, was still an incredibly bright individual. He managed to impress even those Senators who were predisposed to not cooperate with him under any circumstances.

Perhaps things would be different now. The 'reception' might have diffused tensions somewhat. After all, this was a historic occasion. Bringing the two nations together was no small feat, and under normal circumstances, she would bask in that. But the disturbing memory of her dreams made that impossible.

The revelry finally ended in the early hours of the following day. Vespa sent a note to the delegation that the scheduled meetings would be delayed for several hours to give everyone time to recover. But upon reaching the executive residency, she stumbled upon an uncomfortable scene: Arturus, with his contingent of golden warriors, standing beside a small platoon of Orionis security guards.

'They won't let me into the home of my own sister,' he said, his robes undone, revealing a startlingly muscled chest beneath. Vespa always remembered him as a scrawny child.

'He's my brother,' she told the guards. 'You may stand down.'

'We've been instructed to stand post here,' the captain said.

'Fine,' she said, opening the door. Arturus waltzed inside, dragging a finger along the guard's chin as he passed.

Vespa walked into the open kitchen and poured herself a glass of water. The door shut behind them.

'I'll have one as well, please,' Arturus said, taking a seat at the island counter. 'Do you keep in touch with Mum and Dad?'

'We speak every now and then,' she answered, pushing a glass over and sitting across from him. 'They live on Eris now, by the way.'

'Really? I didn't know that,' he said, taking a big gulp. 'That is the most refreshing glass of recycled piss I've ever had.'

'You put on quite a show at the reception.'

'I am what I am,' he said, taking another sip. 'And House Alyxander relies on me to be me.'

'I suppose you've found your calling,' she said, raising her glass. 'Cheers to that.'

'Maybe,' he shrugged, clinking her glass with his own. 'It's not a calling so much as it is a yearning.'

'For what?'

'More of everything. Lance Alyxander isn't someone you'd want to die for. But he is someone who makes you desire more than you've ever wanted. Somehow, he manages to deliver it.'

'We have more Earthly concerns here in Orionis.'

'So you do. And here I am. Are we secure?'

'Electronic jamming, voice scrambling, the works.'

'Careful, Vespa. Only those with very dark secrets take such precautions. I hope you're not going to ask me to have an opponent of yours succumb to a tragic accident.'

'I asked you not to mention that.'

'And I asked you not to have ORPHUS brought anywhere near this place,' he admonished, pointing to the blue light in her bedroom. 'If you won't take my advice, then remind me why I'm here.'

'You know the reason why.'

'You want a formal endorsement of your candidacy from Lance Alyxander.'

'I do,' she said, full of hope.

Arturus sighed.

'I have been authorised to grant such in exchange for a full copy of the Catalogue, including the classified bioweapons of the final era,' he said.

Vespa's heart sank.

'You know I can't do that!'

'Then I regret to inform that he will lend his support to your opponents,' Arturus said, placing the empty glass down. 'He is rather inclined to expedite your removal from Orionis politics.'

'*What?*'

'I'm sorry, Vespa.'

'I opened the gates for him!' she exclaimed, springing up from her chair to pace. 'I brought the corporations to the bargaining table! I put up with your antics to bring them here! He *owes* me!'

Arturus pushed himself from the counter.

'Lance has done enough and more for you,' he said. 'You've become careless, sister. The Gift has corrupted your judgment and stoked your ambition.'

'I've always done right by it!' Vespa protested. 'You know I have!'

'I used to think so,' Arturus said. 'More importantly, so did *Lance*.'

'What do you mean by that?' Vespa demanded.

'It was a mistake to help you dispose of Donovan Mayce,' Arturus said. 'The man was a bastard, but he was better for Orionis, and for House Alyxander.'

'How dare you?' Vespa hissed. 'You saw what I saw.'

'Prophecies of anarchy? The collapse of civilisation? I suppose,' Arturus said. 'But his secret depravity towards ghosts, women especially, enabled your scheme. You could have told the police what he was doing. You did no such thing. It was more advantageous to be a vigilante instead.'

'*Advantageous?*' Vespa fumed. 'I would hardly describe the risks we took to stop this man as—'

'Oh, I wanted what you did alright,' Arturus interrupted. 'Donovan Mayce deserved to die, and I convinced Lance of it. Don't you see? Our visions are shaped by our desires. The truth is, more people benefited by his being alive than not.'

'Do you think that little of what I've accomplished here?' she said. 'That my chancellorship is no better than what that pig would have done?'

'The chancellorship was founded to serve humanity. His did. Yours only serves firstborns,' Arturus said. 'Take my advice: if you respect the institution you claim to love so much, then let the democratic process take its course and stay out of the way.'

Vespa glared at him.

'What happened to you?'

Arturus shrugged.

'I was punished for the folly of my advice and made to learn from the experience,' he said. 'Lance believes I can better serve him now that I've learned to isolate my desires from the truth. Vespa, we used our Gift for reasons we believed were right and just. But who were *we* to judge? That should never be our province. The future we see is only a possibility.'

Vespa calmed herself and changed tactics.

'I keep seeing this place burn,' she said.

He reached out and touched her hand.

'I've seen it as well,' he said. 'More than once, especially after Mayce died.'

She looked into his eyes, wondering if he was recording the conversation.

'Ceti is coming.'

Arturus flinched.

'Here? To do what?'

'Attack the *Archangel*.'

'That's absurd.'

'Admiral Hedricks wanted to hide that from me. I would have never found out if not for a rogue pilot among them.'

Arturus frowned.

'Withholding that from you is treason.'

Vespa waved her arm in disgust.

'He can cite any number of security reasons to keep it from political scrutiny.'

'So the man who controls your Navy and the most powerful weapon ever built is also above the law,' Arturus said.

'In so many words … yes.'

'Then the dreams will become reality.'

She reached out and clasped both his hands.

'We have to use our Gift to save people,' she said. 'It is an enormous responsibility we must bear together.'

'Not we, sister,' he said, pulling his hands away. 'You.'

'You have an obligation to try.'

'My obligation is to inform Lance Alyxander of this at once.'

'No, you can't. Not until I tell my cabinet.'

'I'll give you seventy-two hours. What does Hedricks plan to do about this?'

'He's going to let Ceti press the attack and make a show of crushing them in plain sight of the Inner Rim.'

'Charming. And how convenient, them coming here.'

'I need your support, Arturus, *please*.'

'Lance Alyxander doesn't believe you deserve that. And given what you've just told me, now I fully understand why.'

21

VIOLA

With the exception of her own personal corelink, Viola's cabin aboard the Merckon research vessel *Lycidas* was completely devoid of electronics. There were no windows or ornaments on the bulkheads; just symmetrical trails of grey metal rivets. The living area was spacious and well furnished for a freighter, but three weeks of microgravity was already starting to wear on her. She yearned for another run along the Danube. Until the mission was complete, her only real exercise would be within these walls.

Switching off her mag greaves, she pushed off a bulkhead and launched into a tucked somersault across the cabin. End over end she spun, landing perfectly on the far side. At the point of impact, the greaves switched back on, and her strong legs absorbed the excess momentum. Lacking proper training equipment, she found herself unable to sit still for long.

Viola had been coached by her relentless father to block out emotions. But ever since learning about who – or rather *what* – she was, certain innocuous experiences now triggered overwhelming sadness. Ever since her unforgettable night with Cerlis Tarkon, the mere sight of a couple's embrace, or a compliment paid among conversing friends, made her think of the mother she not only never knew, but had never existed in the first place. Every act of kindness she witnessed triggered a rush of emotions that her training could not repress.

With each graceful flip from one side of the cabin to the other, she thought: *I am an amniosynth*. Biologically, she was human; and by all accounts, the perfect human, one for whom all things physical and mental were no challenge to master. But emotionally, she was the product of … *what, exactly?* she wondered. *Corporate ambition? A spiteful ego? Why does that matter to me so much?*

Another flip, and her world turned upside down as she asked the most fundamental question of being human:

Why am I here?

Some religions believed human life was born to fill a higher purpose in some grand divine plan. Except in this case, 'God' was Klaus Silveri, the man who made his fortune from manufacturing arable dirt.

She pushed herself off with greater force this time, darting across the cabin in a blink. And still she effortlessly landed square on her feet, causing a bang that was much louder than before.

For the longest time, her passion had been the Arkady. It remained so, except now she had embraced a second passion with equal purpose. Both were quests to discover origins. One would be pursued using the *Lycidas* and its resources. For the other, she needed the help of friends, of which she had exactly two.

Carrie Lin, now an employee of Vulcan Industries following her incident with Travis Mareck, was currently prosecuting a secret investigation of Klaus Silveri.

Her other friend was Wegan, the mutant and veteran gas rig miner who cleaned the floors at Merckon Prime. Prior to her departure, he had provided black market technology that would allow her personal corelink to communicate with Brotherhood's open network once they arrived at Zeus. That way she could conceal her efforts from Merckon, which monitored her use of the device.

There had been calls from Klaus. Nearly a dozen, in fact, and that was before the *Lycidas* soared past the orbit of Eris. In time, there would be a confrontation, but not until she had armed herself with facts.

She launched herself again, and this time when she landed there was a knock on the hatch.

Gliding over to open it, she found one of the scientists she had recruited for the mission, Dr Gavin Strong.

'Hi,' he said, looking around. 'Is everything okay in here?'

'Everything is fine,' she said. 'What's up?'

Gavin was much shorter than she was, with short, unkempt auburn hair and sharp green eyes. A brilliant biologist, he was arrogant but generally pleasant to work with. He, like the rest of the scientists on board, reported directly to her.

'We're about to make the turn,' he said. 'There's a celebration happening in the bubble. Figured you'd want to know.'

'Thank you,' she said. 'I'll be there soon.'

'Okay,' he said, peering inside her room again before clunking away on his greaves.

The *Lycidas* was twice the vessel that Viola had asked for.

At nearly a kilometre in length, the ship's primary hull was a converted gas transport freighter. To study the elusive aliens in their natural habitat, it would have to maintain a low Zeus orbit for an extended period. The shielding required to protect the craft from the radiation belts had doubled the mass of the ship; a third of her length was devoted to propulsion, fuel storage, and power systems alone. Altogether, about ninety per cent of the ship's total volume was uninhabitable. Although Viola was hoping to negotiate her way aboard mining rigs that had made contact with the Arkady, the *Lycidas* was equipped with a sensor pod and enough cable to reach the jet streams hunter specimens were known to inhabit.

The onboard lab was just as robust as the facility at Merckon Prime. It was equipped with a fabrication plant to handle on-the-fly engineering requirements as the mission evolved, which could also manage emergency repairs to the ship or a partnering rig. An internal hangar bay housed a complement of scientific atmospheric drones called DIVE probes; two of them had been launched shortly after the *Lycidas* left port. A repair tug and a drop shuttle capable of reaching Brotherhood from Zeus orbit filled out the ship's flight capabilities.

All the working crew, of whom there were just nine, were trained by the Navy and doubled as the security detail. As such, a cache of personal weapons and assorted tactical kit were on board, locked in an armoury. Viola had protested against bringing the gear aboard, but the corporate mission planners insisted. There was a heavy Ceti presence around Zeus, and it was likely they would need to deal with the cartel to gain access to rigs of interest. Although they had ample financial backing to negotiate deals, it wasn't difficult to foresee complications that might need a gun to resolve. Though very polite and generally attentive to the needs of the research team, the crew mostly kept to themselves.

Viola suspected that was because of the man they reported to: Captain Abel Mohib. A stern, gruff man, she had disliked him from the moment they had been introduced. He treated everyone with a lurid mix of contempt and condescension, demanding reverence for 'his' ship and of his command. Their first conversation resolutely established the 'jurisdiction' that Viola was expected to honour for the duration of the mission. She might be the authority on all research decisions, but he had final say concerning the safety of the ship and the mission completion parameters – which meant it was over whenever he said it was.

Captain Mohib was almost certainly 'insurance': a corporate man with steep incentives to protect Travis Mareck's investment in the *Lycidas* and the discoveries they made. Viola had not seen or heard from the CEO since Cerlis Tarkon had humiliated him in his own club. But his presence was felt through Captain Mohib. More than once she had caught him taking an extra stare at her and the female scientists aboard. There was something familiar about him that she couldn't place.

Upon reaching the observation deck, she was met by a chorus of greetings. No crewmen were in sight, but all twelve members of the research team were present. The 'deck' was a small armoured bubble made from the same transparent alloys as biodomes; you felt like a specimen beneath a lens when wandering across it. But the experience was as visceral as being in space. The Milky Way filled the view above them; you could almost feel the craft's momentum here. The bubble was located atop the 'highest' point on the main superstructure, which was the conning tower on the former gas freighter.

Gavin and another researcher named Karyn Breznyk made their way over to greet her.

'Hello again,' Karyn said, extending her hand. 'I have some news: We have DIVE data.'

She was as young as Gavin, a recent graduate from the Academy of Sciences, and untainted by the realities of corporate-funded research.

She was an engineer, and had developed most of the instruments used for studying the chemical composition of Zeus's cloud layers.

'Did you look at it?' Viola said sternly.

'I had to,' Karyn replied defensively. 'Just to make sure everything worked properly.'

'It wasn't an accusation,' Viola said. 'What did you find?'

Captain Mohib interrupted their conversation through the room's intercom.

'Attention crew and passengers,' he announced. 'I am now adjusting our flight attitude for burndown.'

Viola felt nothing when manoeuvring thrusters fired somewhere along the *Lycidas*. Their view of the Milky Way began to rotate as the ship veered from the direction it was travelling in.

'Both probes vanished at a depth of 190 kilometres,' Karyn resumed. 'But—'

'The bright star above the bubble entrance is Eris,' Captain Mohib announced. 'We're about 172 million kilometres from there. The fainter one, marked here with the green beacon, is Eileithyia.'

'But what?' Viola prompted.

'One took much longer than the other to reach terminal depth,' Karyn explained quietly. 'We lost contact with one at 96 klicks, then reacquired it at 122. Only the heartbeat broadcast was working then.'

Viola kept her demeanour impassive.

'That's interesting,' she said coolly, as Gavin and Karyn both waited for her to show a hint of excitement.

One of the scientists looked up and pointed.

'There's Sol,' he said.

A murmur spread across the crowd. Firstborns had the deepest devotion to the system of their origin. They looked upon it with sadness, fear … and, perhaps, some misplaced hope.

'To Earth!' a burly meteorologist named Ewan MacKilgore said, thrusting his beverage towards the 'sky'.

One of the other scientists, an unpleasant but talented planetary science expert named Dylan Ofstursson, raised and joined him.

'To the squids!' he said, making a crude reference to the Arkady.

'To Dr Silveri!' another scientist said, drawing a chorus of approval.

Viola obligingly raised her beverage.

'To scientific discovery,' she said. 'Cheers to you all!'

Captain Mohib's voice interrupted again.

'Commencing burndown ignition in three. Two. One. Mark,' he declared. A half-kilometre from where they were standing, the ship's main sequence thrusters began throttling up to one hundred per cent output.

'Congratulations,' he said. 'You are now halfway to Zeus.'

There were more cheers from the group, but Viola was barely paying attention to them as Karyn continued.

'Those probes entered the same zonal band, three thousand kilometres away from each other,' Karyn said, her voice nearly a whisper. Gavin nodded at her with a wink, taking a sip from the tube. 'The weather at 122 was consistent for both probes ... high winds, heavy lightning, strong updraughts, but ... I may be crazy, but I think that the probe slower to fall hit something solid – at least, something much denser than the atmosphere.'

'There are simpler explanations, the simplest of which is that it just malfunctioned,' Viola said, registering Karyn's expression change from hopeful to disappointed.

'Have the orbital plans been finalised yet?' Gavin asked.

'Yes,' Viola said. 'Moving this heap once we set orbit is expensive.'

'Are we confined to the temperate zones?' Karyn asked.

'Absolutely,' Viola explained. 'The equator is dangerous. That's what the DIVE probes are for. Your theory isn't strong enough to reconsider our plans. What's more, the rig that produced our largest hunter sample to date is in the southern zonal. I'm going to pay them a visit.'

'Why not interview them remotely?' Gavin asked.

'Because I want to see it for myself,' Viola said. 'We need to rule out the chance it was drawn to that specific rig. Or better yet, find evidence that others like it will return. Have you told anyone else about this?'

'No,' Karyn said. 'The data arrived just before you got here.'

'Publish the atmospheric data,' Viola directed. 'Weather and chemical composition only. Nothing else.'

Karyn looked shocked.

'But that's ... against the rules?'

'I make the rules,' Viola said, narrowing her eyes. 'The other data is embargoed until we can rule out a technical issue. Are we clear?'

The two young scientists exchanged glances before answering in stereo. 'Yes, ma'am,' they said.

'Viola, stop being such a child and reply to this immediately.'

It was a strange way to be productive and motivated all at once.

One by one, Viola was letting all the messages from Klaus play through her earphones as she worked from the office overlooking the lab deck. Most of the equipment was still wrapped in storage bags for the journey. Soon this place would be a hive of research, with fresher samples to biopsy, better sampling of the Zeus troposphere, and better screening for bacteria and microbes. She suspected the Arkady ecosystem extended far beyond the large genus types that harassed mining rigs.

'This is intolerable. I'm your father. Return my call!'

Multitasking was easy. Like everything else about her, the skill had been honed during the relentless regimen imposed on her by Klaus. He was always testing her limits, constantly subjecting her to cognitive challenges under physical duress. Once, when she was just eight years old, he strapped her to a bolted chair and forced her to work through a series of spatial reasoning challenges. When she got one wrong, the test was reset. The goal was to answer one hundred correctly within five minutes, and he refused to release her until she passed.

Later that morning, somehow, she succeeded, and was rewarded with six straight hours of sleep and a light meal, followed by a new, borderline inhumane, physical challenge. It was like that nearly every day for years, in brutal clips of two to three weeks at a time, until she was admitted to Orionis University at the age of twelve. Viola didn't remember every detail of those days, which she attributed to defensive selective memory.

'How could you leave without telling me? You don't understand what you've done!'

The Zeus atmosphere was a primordial soup loaded with all the raw ingredients necessary to support life: abundant water, carbon-based organic compounds, and energy from the planet's core. It was unfathomable that humans had been in Orionis for almost two centuries without studying this planet in detail. The trove of Helium-3 in the thermosphere was what drew civilisation here, but the real story was the water in the troposphere. Atmospheric pressure at that depth was three to seven times that of sea level on Earth. It was unknown what depths the Arkady could survive to, and discovering that was key to understanding their origins.

'You do realise you're not in charge of the science mission?'

Viola had been forced to be dismissive about Karyn's theory on the fate of the DIVE probe. In fact, there was no doubt in her mind that it had struck something much, much denser than the surrounding air: tissue, almost certainly. She just needed time to confirm it, which meant distracting her colleagues. If there was to be a groundbreaking Arkady discovery, she needed to find it before anyone else could twist its potential into something that could benefit Travis Mareck.

Again, at the thought of Travis, she felt a strange, distracting physical sensation that was both repulsive and irresistible. She needed to get to the bottom of that, and soon.

'Viola, all of your selections are Mareck's people. There is not a single person on that ship you can trust.'

She couldn't remember the last time she had felt genuine love for Klaus Silveri. The notion was just as sickening as the thought of Travis Mareck. Perhaps the two were connected, she mused, as if there was time to psychoanalyse herself. Both men were abusive, deeply insecure, and controlling; and both had somehow become crucial figures in her synthetic life. Travis always threatened to take away her Arkady research. Klaus always threatened that she'd be a failure. She was subjected to enough negative reinforcement to make a normal person wither into psychosis.

But not enough for the amniosynth creation of a psychopath. Though she was so very tired of being threatened.

The only challenge, Viola thought, arose from not knowing who else knew what she was – when people found out, how might it change their perception of her? All this time, she had believed she was firstborn and mingled freely among them. No one knew she was really a 'ghost', which all but proved that the modern interpretation of the Heritage

210

Act amounted to racism: a societal mandate to protect a privileged class that was fearful of their own creation. Now she was on the other side of it. And the irony was, if Klaus's claims about her abilities were to be believed, this side was the superior one.

'I know what Cerlis told you. She had no right.'

Merckon's investigators had discovered several interesting facts about the rig where the hunter tentacle had been found. The location was unremarkable, but the rig itself was in terrible condition; it was miraculous that it was still maintaining orbit at all. The operators were a family that went by the surname Lethos; the youngest on board was a boy of just eleven. They were leasing the rig from Ceti, and had fallen on deep financial troubles.

But according to the report, there were no functioning point defences or radar systems on board. It might be the most vulnerable rig on the planet.

'Working late?'

Viola never bothered to look up from her console. She had been aware that Captain Mohib had been standing in the doorway for nearly a minute.

'*Solid* observational skills,' she said. 'You should be a scientist.'

He was wearing a throwback Navy overcoat adorned with Merckon insignia on the lapels. That he was clearly annoyed at her tone delighted her.

'Are you looking at the DIVE data?' he asked, walking closer.

'You are well informed for a freighter captain,' she said, shutting everything down.

'This ship is my business,' he said.

Viola smiled at him.

'And the scientific data is mine,' she said.

'You realise that information falls under the purview of—'

'That is what we agreed to, right?' she interrupted, beaming the loveliest smile she could. 'Or did you have other plans?'

This was a career Navy man accustomed to having his orders followed without question, and Viola was having none of it.

'I want to know what it is about that data you find so interesting,' he demanded.

'I find all kinds of data interesting,' Viola said, pushing towards the door. When she was alongside him, she grabbed a rail to stop herself, and the momentum carried her long ponytail into his shoulder.

'Do I make you uncomfortable, Captain?' she asked.

He laughed.

'Only the thought you're withholding mission data from me,' he said. 'Did the probes hit something or not?'

Viola smirked.

'Do you believe every fairy tale the children tell around here?'

'I see,' he said through his teeth.

'I doubt it,' she said, gliding away.

From the privacy of her cabin, Viola played the final message in the queue.

Mace Merckon commissioned me to help develop amniosynthesis in 2657. The scientists I worked with believed that we were building something to help ensure the survival of our species. And though we understood the harm this biotechnology could potentially cause, we believed that good would prevail over evil.

I could tell you precisely how complex molecules would interact with each other, but I couldn't discern which applications of amniosynthesis were considered 'evil'. Lance Alyxander and Masaad Obyeran left Orionis to create their own empires with it. Were they not repopulating the human race, as was intended? Did the augmentations they applied to make amniosynths better adapted for life in space help assure 'our' survival? Did those changes make them 'superior' to the generation of humans who left Earth? Which of these applications is morally unsound?

I cannot say. For every living amniosynth born to either House, dozens were terminated, either for the sake of experimentation or because they were accidental abominations. One could argue those creatures had to die so today's generation could live. By that reasoning, amniosynthesis is Darwinism, and moral considerations do not apply.

But I would rather be remembered as the scientist that brought dirt to our world. I thought I had left amniosynthesis behind when Mace Merckon contacted me again, as he lay dying of old age. He ... coerced me to create a new kind of amniosynth. You see, the Independence War had just begun. The highborns were alarmed by Ceti's power, and, fearing they would use nuclear weapons against them, sought a new way to repopulate the species. But not just with any humans. Only ... them.

Viola, the captain of the Lycidas *is not Abel Mohib. That man is Travis Mareck, augmented to disguise his identity. You are biologically attracted to him, and all highborn males, because you are genetically predisposed to be. As the potential progenitor of a post-war human race, Mace Merckon wanted your instincts hardwired to protect the continuance of dominant highborn lines. You should assume Travis Mareck knows, and that as a firstborn with highborn lineage, he will attempt to exploit this.*

You know who I am. I never wanted to be a father, let alone raise a child. And yet, as little as I understand of love, I thought it might help if you believed you had a real mother. That was a mistake, and I regret it.

I had to be harsh. I was forced to learn your limits. You didn't turn out the way I expected. You became so much more. You are, without question, my greatest achievement. Now that you're aboard the Lycidas, *there is nothing else I can do to help you, except pass on what I've learned, and share the truth with you.*

No one deserves your fate. But you represent a giant leap for humankind. Mace didn't know everything else I put into you. You are so much stronger than you think. In the days ahead, you will need to call on that strength to survive.

I now understand the difference between good and evil. I did not expect to end up caring for you so much. And I know that you will never forgive me.

Viola pulled the earphones out, and watched them float away.

22

JAKE

I've been trying really hard not to lose my patience.

In the last month, Dusty has had a rough time recovering from a broken back, orbital bone, jaw and mouth palate, plus swallowing his two front teeth. The attack left him traumatised, not so much because of physical discomfort, but for the fact he felt a spiritual connection to the assassin who beat his face in.

He just couldn't forgive the Minotaur for shooting her. Dusty didn't feel it was fair to judge her 'for just doing her job', and that her hostility didn't marginalise the 'magic' they shared before she tried to kidnap him. He believed they might have worked things out and lived happily ever after.

Eventually I gave up trying to convince him that her death was to be counted among the positives in his life. Until last week, his jaw had been wired shut. But he made a great effort to bitch-mumble at me even as I helped feed him, change him, and clean him. Now that he could talk, he was *still* being an unappreciative little bastard.

My Ceti business was being neglected for this. But after the attack, hiring help or even a droid was out of the question. We were both way up on the Navy's shit list. After a while, relentless vigilance became outright paranoia. It had reached the point where I would taste Dusty's meals before him, hoping I'd die of poisoning.

After all this coddling, he was getting a little too comfortable being waited on, and I was sick of it.

'Have you ever tasted real fruit before?' Dusty asked, as I cleared his plate and tossed the remnants of dinner into the sink. Of course I had no idea what he was talking about and reached for a smacker.

'What?' I said, lighting the joint.

Dusty's handsomeness didn't exactly improve with the accident. The metal now holding his cheekbones together gave him an unsightly bulge beneath both eyes. He'd opted for titanium instead of bone to leave the door open for augmentations that would make him a better pilot than he already was.

'You know, like an apple, or an orange,' he continued. 'Real stuff with real skin, not plastic wrappers.'

Dusty had enough money to live as lavishly as a Ceti lieutenant. Instead he lived in a messy low-income flat that was covered wall-to-wall in electronics. The living room was an exact replica of the *Breakaway*'s bridge, fully capable of simulating real flight. An industrial workfab unit was crammed into the master bedroom, where he refitted engine components and built drones, scale models of Navy warships, and replicas of his favourite comic book heroes. Most of the gear was shut down and stowed in preparation for the journey to Corinth.

The few articles of clothing he owned were arranged in random piles throughout the place. And anything that wasn't autonomously self-cleaning just wasn't cleaned, ever.

'No, Dusty,' I said, as green tendrils of smoke hissed out of my nose. 'I've never had a real apple.'

Turning towards the living room, I saw the Minotaur lounging in the captain's chair.

'He's got that *look* again,' the bull-man snorted. 'Reel him in before he gets crazy.'

I ignored the advice.

'Well, I have,' Dusty said. 'They grow trees in the biodomes on Eris. Inner Rim people get to eat the produce. Not the synthetic shit we eat here.'

An involuntary twitch contorted my face. That was happening more often lately.

'So ...?' I asked, taking another deep puff.

'So when this is over,' Dusty said, 'I want an apple tree.'

Swallowing the smoke by mistake, I burst into a hoarse, phlegmy wheeze.

'I think I'm missing a few blunts,' I managed.

'I'm serious,' Dusty said, moving into the living room. 'That's what I want.'

'If we survive this,' I vowed, 'I'll buy you a whole damn orchard.'

'You're such a fatalist,' Dusty fumed. 'It's depressing.'

That was understandable. But when he wasn't moaning about his dead 'girlfriend', he fantasised about heroics in the attack on the *Archangel*. The prospect of shooting Navy ships filled him with euphoria. Dusty dreamt of having each kill painted on the nose of the *Breakaway*, thinking it would earn him more 'status' with the other Ceti captains.

'Did you actually read the battle plan?' Dusty ranted. 'I bet you don't even understand it.'

God, he was annoying.

'I know a bad deal when I see one,' I said.

'The shield tech is the difference,' Dusty insisted, throwing a canvas sheet over one of the dashboard displays. 'You haven't seen what it can do. *I have*.'

I blew out another wisp of smog.

'Even if you had seen it – and I'm going to call bullshit on that – what difference does it make?' I asked. 'It doesn't help *us*, right? The *Breakaway* isn't shielded.'

'We have the element of surprise,' Dusty said.

The Minotaur snorted into a brief laugh. Another twitch grabbed hold of my face.

'This fleet's too big to sneak up on anything,' I said. 'It's going to be a massacre.'

Dusty stamped his foot like a little girl.

'Just once, try to be positive about something!' he scolded, before calming down. 'Anyway, check your corelink. You have procurement chores.'

I fished the device out of my pocket while sucking the joint down to the hilt.

Glancing over his list ignited a bomb fuse within me.

'Are you shitting me?' I said.

'It's a long ride and cryo makes me sick,' Dusty said. 'I aim to stay busy.'

'You're strangling the corelink,' the Minotaur observed.

'This is … what … synthetic *cow meat*?' I growled. 'Really?'

'Steak,' Dusty said. 'The stuff is delicious. Have you ever tried it?'

'I'm offended,' the Minotaur smirked.

'No!' I fumed. 'Jesus *Christ*.'

'They sell it in the Sixth Ward,' Dusty said. 'Just follow that succulent aroma; it's the signature scent of Brotherhood.'

I had heard enough.

'Fuck this,' I snapped. 'I'm not ordering a three-week supply of your favourite takeout.'

Dusty turned all red.

'Then I'll ditch your drug stash and see how *you* enjoy the trip!'

The bomb exploded. My fist lashed out on its own, smashing one of the electronic displays on the wall into pieces.

I didn't even hear the words come out of my mouth.

'The *fuck* you will, Dusty. I'll hurt you real bad.'

His expression changed from defiance to fear, and for a moment I was gratified. Taking a frightened step backwards, he tripped, pulling more random junk down on top of him as he tried to catch himself.

'Atta boy,' the Minotaur said, as Dusty landed with a crash.

Horrified, I rushed forward to offer a hand. But Dusty cowered away as if I were a monster.

Maybe he was right.

'Sorry,' I muttered, heading towards the door.

The sun was setting on another Brotherhood 'day' as the giant mirrors that focused Orionis sunlight onto the curved city grids were gradually redirected away. All the activity to prep the Ceti fleet made for slow travelling, and it took me nearly an hour to reach the nearest tram station.

Along the way, I smoked as much as I could.

If you were a mutant, the Sixth Ward was an exclusive place to call home – and a miserable, impoverished slum to everyone else. People who settled there worked the most menial, dirty, or dangerous jobs in the station. But they were a proud community who wore their deformations like a badge of honour. If you didn't have one, you didn't belong.

The tram platform was crowded, but no one stood anywhere near me as I waited. Maybe it was because I smelled like a chemical refinery, or perhaps it was the green smog surrounding my head, or maybe the Ceti lieutenant insignia spread across my coat. Whatever the case, the express to Camden Market, the closest stop to the Sixth, was nearly empty. No one else boarded when I did. A few exhausted souls were already inside, every single one a mutant. Some had probably been working for days without sleep. The impending attack on the *Archangel* was an open secret now, and huge sums of wealth had transferred from Ceti captains to the labour force in preparation for the journey.

Taking a seat near the door, I reached for another joint – and realised it was my last one. Desperate, soul-shearing panic sets in. Just like that, my high evaporates and I'm back in the vortex, drowning in a sea of self-loathing, where drugs are the only thing keeping me alive. As the tram glides away from the platform, I begin hyper-ventilating. The curved cityscape looming high above is suddenly terrifying, and Zeus is readying to feast on us as the whole station spins round and round, hundreds of thousands of pointless lives just turning in circles.

One scene of hardship after the next blinked by as the tram picked up speed. All these people were slaving to earn a few more CROs in the rush to send thousands of their own to fiery Inner Rim deaths. I broke into a nervous laugh, spawned by the madness of life and the terror of not having the fix I needed to cope with it.

When the tram passed by a larger-than-life projection of 'The Patriot: Vladric Mors', my self-loathing became hatred.

Vladric, the bane of my life. Of *all* lives. Yet he commanded such respect from them, *reverence* even. What had he done to earn it?

I knew the answer: he had given 'hope'. The simplicity of it made me furious. Evil as he was, that motherfucker gave ghosts and mutants more hope than Orionis ever did. All he had done was recognise them as people with as much right to be here as anyone else.

What the hell had I spent my life defending? Tabit Prime had *made* this man. Without him, there would be no need for a Navy, or the *Archangel*. But if not him, their regime would have just created someone else.

Vladric Mors ruled Ceti through his lieutenants. His government was akin to feudalism, but the people who lived here preferred that to Chancellor Jade's 'democracy'. If a lieutenant was being harsh or unfair, Vladric made an example of him – often in brutal fashion – to send a message to the other lords. Although he had his own use for violence, he wasn't interested in officers who relied on it. Instead he sought out those with real intellect. These lieutenants formed the core structure of Ceti, and most, if not all, owned warships with crews of their own.

Somehow, Vladric had convinced all these bright individuals that attacking the *Archangel* was not only possible, but an imperative necessity. Most of the fleet was flying straight into a gunfight they couldn't win. Yet if Vladric's lieutenants knew more, *knew* that this wasn't a suicide mission, they weren't interested in explaining why his plan would work to anyone else.

Something sinister was happening. I had infiltrated the inner circle too late. Dusty was a social outcast whom other captains shunned, and I had the reputation of a sadist. We were locked out from the intelligentsia of Ceti for good.

Deep down, I must have known it all along. The bad things I did to fuel this transformation from the person I was into the monster I needed to become accomplished nothing but the death of my own soul.

I accepted that everything I had sacrificed was for nothing. Reaching again for my last joint, I knew now what needed to be done.

'You piece of shit,' the Minotaur said, loud enough to startle the nearest passenger. He must have been sitting next to me the whole time.

'Likewise,' I muttered, lighting up. Immediately, a woman's voice came over the tram's loudspeaker.

'Smoking is illegal on this tram,' she said. 'Please extinguish your narcotic.'

'No, really,' the Minotaur said, leaning forward. 'Who do you think you are, threatening Dusty like that?'

There was nothing to say. He was right.

'There's one person in existence that gives a damn about you,' the bull-man said, unrelenting. 'Just one. And you were going to do what?'

'Please extinguish your narcotic,' the tram-bitch said.

Out of nowhere, my ears started to ring.

'You were going to kill him!' the Minotaur exclaimed.

Every passenger on the tram got up and moved away from me. And the ringing in my ears was getting louder.

'You'd kill your only friend for a fucking joint,' the Minotaur scoffed. 'Pathetic.'

'Jack Tatum, the Ceti Municipal Affairs Division has just issued you a summons for the misdemeanour of public narcotic consumption.'

'End yourself and be done with it,' the Minotaur said.

The ringing was so loud I couldn't hear myself think.

'What are you waiting for, Jack?'

'*Please extinguish your narcotic.*'

I inhaled deeply. Too much.

'Do it!'

The noise was overwhelming.

'*Please extinguish your life.*'

The tram stopped. Or maybe the world had stopped moving long enough for me get out.

'*You have been summoned, Jake Reddeck, Jack Tatum, Jake Reddeck, Jack Tatum ...*'

I staggered onto the platform to escape and tripped over my own feet. A Ceti guard approached, weapon in hand, as I picked myself up from the pavement and drew a deep, deadly puff.

'Were you just smoking on that tram, junkie?' he asked.

'Fuck you just call him?' the Minotaur snarled.

When I looked up, the guard's face was melting in viscous slags of flesh.

'Jack *Tatum*?' it said, drawing closer. 'Are you alright, sir?'

The world was stretching and contracting. Every breath burned like a furnace. Fire pumped through my veins. I covered my temples to keep my head from flying apart.

'I'm looking for a mutant,' I managed. 'He's a ... dangerous prick. I need your sidearm.'

'But it won't do you any good,' the melted face said.

'*Give him your goddamn weapon*,' the Minotaur shouted. '*Now.*'

I felt a gun pressed into my palm.

220

'Should I call for backup?' the face asked.

'No!' I shouted. 'He's listening to your comms. I'll handle it. Stay here!' I didn't care if he believed me.

Turning away, I stumbled towards the darkness. The border where Camden Market met the Sixth Ward was a maze of corridors, bewildering to navigate when sober. Metal and glass fused into faceless strangers who hurried out of my way. People were watching me from the shadows; I could hear their whispers, and every one of them knew I was a traitor in their world.

My body was beginning to fail. The ringing sound was maddening, and voices that spoke over it were all telling me to hurry. Rounding a corner I found myself in an open courtyard that seemed impossibly wide; I screamed when I saw it was filled with apple trees, upon which hung not fruit but eyes – and all staring at me.

I ran until I found myself lost among narrow alleyways lined with tiered apartments stacked like toys, moments from collapsing. Sagging razorwire cables were strung across the alleys, each one ready to lash me to pieces. A drone resembling a carnivorous insect pushed its way down the alley, spraying the streets with molten lava as a few yellow cadavers whisked litter into a cart ahead of it.

This was a fine place to die.

My back pushed against the alley wall. My legs quit, and I dropped straight down. A cold dampness spread across my ass. I was sitting in a deep puddle.

'The best high you'll ever get is a trigger pull away,' the Minotaur encouraged.

'You think Danna is there?' I asked. The ringing was so loud that blood was draining from my ears.

'Oh, yeah,' the Minotaur said. 'Go to her, Jake.'

'She was all I lived for,' I said, handing the gun to the Minotaur. 'You do it.'

The puddle beneath me opened in a swirling vortex.

'No,' the Minotaur said, backing away from my outstretched arm. 'This time, you're on your own.'

Round and round we spun, the whole world swirling around the puddle between my legs.

'I'm coming home, Danna.'

I pressed the gun against my temple and squeezed.

Five Years Earlier

'I feel so … weird in these,' Jake said, looking himself over.

'I think you look sexy,' Danna said, wrapping her arms around his waist. The subtle smile on her lips could convince him to do anything.

Jake was dressed in his Navy dress whites, reserved for formal ceremonies. The last time he had worn them had been a year ago at the annual Policeman's Ball, which was where he first set eyes on Danna Tyrell.

'Thanks, babe … are you sure about this?' Jake asked again. He'd only proposed to her a week before. The problem was, they had yet to tell her father, who also happen to be the highest ranking police officer in Orionis.

That made matters somewhat intimidating.

Danna squeezed his hands.

'It'll be fine,' she reassured. 'Besides, it's not like you're asking him for permission.'

Jake winced.

'I really should have asked him,' he said. 'Just out of respect …'

Danna smirked.

'Did you ask him if we could date?' she said playfully. 'This isn't much different.'

Augustus Tyrell, the legendary law enforcement commander, was also a notorious hardass. Jake was just as terrified of him as every other freshman officer.

When he had first met Danna, he had no idea who she was. Not that it would have mattered. Nothing was going to stop him from introducing himself.

'It's … a *little* different,' Jake said.

'Mmhmm, a little,' she said, planting a kiss on his cheek. 'Not much.'

'He's my boss now!' Jake said, clasping her hands. 'He won't even acknowledge we're together.'

'He will after tonight,' she said, whispering in his ear. 'Especially when I tell him I'm pregnant.'

Present Day – The Sixth Ward, Brotherhood Station

I woke from the most joyous moment of my life, believing that I had died, and that heaven was a place where you relived your best memories for eternity.

Instead I was shivering violently, soaked from the waist down in some frothing, foul-looking liquid. The Minotaur was nowhere in sight. I found the gun submerged in the muck, and, wondering why it hadn't fired, discovered that it was biometrically locked.

I must have blacked out before realising.

Cradling the useless weapon in my hands, I started to whimper a little, and before long I was sobbing. It was grief, I think. Or remorse. Maybe both.

I just don't know what I am any more.

My head felt like it had been cleaved with a hammer, and every fibre of my muscle was burning with fever. Using the wall to steady myself, I rose from the muck. My corelink was ruined; it had been submerged the entire time I was out.

That reminded me of what I was supposed to be doing: finding a three-week supply of meat for Dusty. Wandering through an alley of closed shops, I was wondering who was going to sell me anything at that hour when I heard a loud shriek.

A silhouette darted across the street in front of me. Before I could blink, two more followed, both much larger than the first. One of them halted, staring at me for a moment before resuming chase.

I don't know why, but I decided to follow. When I rounded the bend, I saw a young kid, clearly a mutant, cornered by two men.

'This is your final warning,' the boy said. 'Repent, or you will be judged.'

The man confronting him was large, overweight, and with hideous boils all over his face. The other looked the same age, and had a badly hunched back. Their dirty, loose overalls made me think they worked in the slush pits.

223

'You've got that wrong, freak,' boil-face said, shoving the boy so hard that he struck his head on the pavement.

I couldn't help myself.

'Hey!' I shouted. 'What the fuck!'

The two men turned. Suddenly, a rush of premonition staggered me. Hunchback and I were going to dance first.

'Get out of here, junkie,' boil-face warned.

'Junkie?' I said. 'Do you know who I am?'

'No,' hunchback said, closing on me. 'Do you know I am?'

I knew it was coming: a hard, accurate punch to my solar plexus that left me doubled over and breathless. The blow hurt far worse than I imagined it would, but the adrenaline burst made me forget my other ailments.

Part of me even felt I deserved a good beating.

'Mind your own fucking business now?' boil-face said.

'Maybe,' I stammered, 'you should go fuck yourself.'

'A tough guy, eh?' hunchback said. 'Hear that, mate?'

Right now, I hate the fact I was trained to let people hit me. Fortunately, these two had learned to fight on the streets, and most of their shots were ineffective. I let the hunchback land a combo, again to my stomach, and then a knee that caught my forehead instead of my nose. But it was still enough force to jolt my vision and send me to the ground.

'*Run*, kid!' I warned.

But he made no effort to escape. Instead, he rose to his knees, eyes closed, palms facing upwards.

'Saviour of Sol, fiery art thou,' the boy said. 'Blessed is thy wrath.'

Whatever nonsense he had just said really pissed off boil-face.

'Shut the fuck up!' the brute said, unleashing a wicked backhand on the boy's face.

It was time for the dance to resume.

'Hit that kid again and I'll kill you,' I said.

'You must love pain,' hunchback growled.

As I pushed myself off the ground, he gambled on a knockout shot with another high, hard punch. I stayed low and lunged, latching onto his knee and twisting him down, establishing side control before his shoulder blades even struck the ground. My right arm slipped under his hamstring as my left knee swung onto his stomach. I grabbed his leg and pulled it back towards me, straightening and bracing it against my shoulder. Then I let myself fall backwards.

Hunchback's knee hyper-extended and snapped. I yanked it back further to make sure all the ligaments popped, because fuck him.

Kicking myself away from the screaming invalid, I rose to confront boil-face.

The boy, meanwhile, had resumed praying.

'The righteous shall inherit the Earth,' he said. 'We worship you who conquer it.'

I dodged a punch from boil-face and countered with a perfect hook to the man's kidney. To my bitter surprise, he didn't crumble like I'd hoped. My punches just weren't as strong as they used to be. All the drugs and anxiety and everything else had caught up, and no amount of adrenaline would help. This was an even fight now, because his strength and stamina could compensate for inferior reflexes.

We traded punches like savages. As fists smashed into bone and tissue, I lost track of the praying boy and the howling hunchback. I just focused on staying alive.

Mercifully, I landed a solid uppercut straight on his chin. Boil-face collapsed, unconscious, his limbs twitching. Completely spent, I fell to my knees in exhaustion.

It was then I realised that a crowd had surrounded us.

They said nothing, even as hunchback's cries filled the night. My vision was blurry, whether from drugs or concussion I couldn't say. But it looked to me as if every single person in this crowd – which included men, women, and children – was a mutant.

Suddenly, the praying boy stood up. He was smiling.

'You see? Rao-lord has answered,' he said, approaching me. I hadn't noticed before that his head was misshapen, and his hands had just three fingers each. 'Thank you.'

I didn't know how to answer.

'Shouldn't you … be home or something?' I muttered.

'This is my hive,' he said, motioning to the crowd. 'And they are my children.'

I considered asking where I could find some choice tenderloins.

'Sure they are,' I said. 'Do you need any CROs or something? For food or a place to stay or whatever?'

His smile had a creepy paternalistic assurance to it.

'I won't forget this,' he said. 'I will see you again. Perhaps then we will talk some more.'

Some people in the crowd were nodding at me approvingly.

'Farewell, Jack Tatum,' he said, winking at me.

I didn't know what that meant. All I could do was watch as they dragged the thugs away.

By the time I made it back to Dusty's flat, Brotherhood's mirrors were reflecting the first rays of daybreak. With any luck, he was asleep, or better yet on his way to the *Breakaway*. Even without a corelink, I had still managed to get all the items on his list, including the damn meat. The bounty was on its way to the ship right now.

All I wanted was a few hours of sleep before my last trip into space. As the lift ascended to Dusty's floor, I cursed my impatience. I didn't need to kill myself; a premature death was already coming for me. All I needed to do was relax and 'go with the flow', even if that flow was a river of sewage churning towards the maws of a treatment plant.

Naturally, I had scored some more smacker during my errands, and I decided to light up as I approached the flat. After a deep, bitter, satisfying puff, I opened the door …

… and saw Vladric Mors sitting at the kitchen table with Dusty.

I froze in the doorway as if I'd just been shot.

'Good morning, Jack,' Vladric said, smiling broadly. 'Won't you join us?'

Dusty was looking at me as if I had three heads.

'Rough night?' Vladric commiserated, motioning for the table upon which a breakfast feast was evident. 'Have a seat and tell us about it.'

As if it would make a difference, I straightened out my jacket and ran a hand through my hair, still unsure if I was really seeing this.

'Oh, this is real,' the Minotaur said, walking out from the bedrooms. He stood right over both of them. 'And right *here* for the taking!'

The altruistic part of me found common ground with the fatalist. Here was Vladric Mors, with no guards, alone with Dusty. It was a momentous opportunity; the man who had ruined my life and controlled the fate of thousands, possibly millions, was sitting just ten metres away. If only I had been carrying a gun, this would have been over by now.

Instead, I needed to improvise, or die trying. There was no downside.

'Lots of options here, Jake,' the Minotaur said. 'Snap out of it and close the door.'

'I don't want to interrupt …' I said.

'Not at all,' Vladric responded. 'Dusty and I were just discussing the invasion.'

'Yeah?' I said, closing the door and taking a deep puff. 'How's that going?'

'Would you mind putting that out?' Vladric asked. 'As long as that's alright with you, Dusty. It's your home.'

'Yes, I mean sure,' Dusty said tentatively. 'I kind of would appreciate it if you didn't smoke in here, Jack. Like, ever.'

'Vladric has been talking up his ego,' the Minotaur warned. 'But he won't be an issue when you make your move.'

'Sorry,' I muttered, extinguishing the joint. 'Habit.'

'We know,' Vladric said, sniffing the air and frowning. 'On second thought, maybe you should just stay right where you are.'

Dusty got a whiff of whatever Vladric had smelled and winced.

'Did you …?' he asked.

My ability to smell had been ruined by my addiction. Whatever was in the puddle I passed out in had dried up and stained my pants. Judging from the look on their faces, I just assumed I was caked in shit.

'Your grocery list wasn't easy to get,' I said.

'Idiot!' the Minotaur snarled. 'Now you have to wait for him to come to you. He's no street punk, Jake. Watch it.'

'Did you get it all?' Dusty asked, covering his mouth and nose.

'On its way to the *Breakaway* right now,' I nodded.

'Let me see the list,' Vladric said. Dusty handed him his corelink. 'Synthetic steaks?'

'It's a delicacy,' Dusty said, sheepishly.

'That's funny,' Vladric said. 'I thought I was the only one who liked it.'

'Fucking cannibals,' the Minotaur snarled.

'Why didn't you tell me, Jack?' Vladric asked. 'I could have had this taken care of. Where'd you get the meat?'

'Sixth Ward,' I answered.

'Mutants don't like strangers,' Vladric said. 'You ought to know that.'

'Learned the hard way,' I answered.

Dusty looked uncomfortable.

'Well, gentlemen, I have to see to some final preparations,' Vladric said, rising from the table. 'Dusty can fill you in, but to summarise, I've asked the *Breakaway* to join the vanguard in our attack on Corinth.'

'The *vanguard*?' roared the Minotaur. In naval warfare terminology, it was the lead element of any attack group tasked with intercepting a point in space, which in this case was the defences surrounding Corinth Naval Yards and the *Archangel*, the most heavily defended fortress in Orionis.

Of course, long before reaching there, they would run into a barrage of tungsten slugs with relative speeds approaching 35,000 metres per second.

'That's quite an honour,' I said.

'I think so,' Vladric said, setting his coffee mug down. 'I'm sure you've heard about the fleet modifications. The *Breakaway* will fly in my lance, protected by the shield cover of my ship.'

'You're blocking the door,' the Minotaur said excitedly. 'He has to go through you.'

'I want the best men beside me for this moment in history,' Vladric said. 'And my best pilots, of course.'

'Thank you, sir!' Dusty said.

Vladric smiled as he began walking towards me.

'This is it,' the Minotaur said. 'Don't tense up. Act a little stoned, he knows what a junkie you are. Take his neck if it's there, but his nose and a follow-up work just as well.'

Time slowed down. I waited for the premonition.

Instead of relaxing my shoulders, I tensed and froze as Vladric stopped exactly an arm's length from me.

'*Now, Jake!*' the Minotaur shouted. 'You'll never get another chance!'

Vladric waited. He stood there, smiling, *knowing* exactly what I was thinking.

But there was no dance. As much as I had fantasised about this moment, it wasn't meant to be.

And that son of a bitch knew it.

'Excuse me,' Vladric said.

I stepped out of his way. The Minotaur howled.

Vladric walked on by, pausing as the door opened.

'See you in space,' he said.

23

SIG

With the exception of an idled fusion reactor, the only source of heat on the *Aria Black* was the tempers of six angry, bitterly cold men. Hunter ops were tedious affairs punctuated by brief moments of excitement and, hopefully, the exhilaration of victory instead of the despair of failure. But context made all the difference. Hunting convoys between Zeus and Hera, within range of Ceti support, was easy.

Setting an ambush in the Hades Terminus was something else.

Occupying an orbit between Zeus and the Triton Worlds, the most prominent artefact of the expanse was a dense, icy comet field composed of fragments ranging in size from pebbles to mountains. Its existence was as much a surprise to the *Tabit Genesis* settlers as the utter inhabitability of Eileithyia.

Presently, the *Aria Black* was roughly one metre from the surface of a dirty chunk of ice the size of a gas freighter. Sig had expertly placed the ship over it and matched its low angular momentum, all but merging with the comet itself. Two hundred kilometres from their position was a Navy EXR-10 'Big Eye' probe, the same model used in the early warning tracking systems of the Orionis Navy.

Before they vanished in the comet field, the Big Eye had been pushed from the *Black*'s dropship bay and pointed in the direction of Hyllus, scanning a cone of space nearly six billion kilometres long for signs of the Lightspear. The Navy went to great lengths to keep their technology from falling into Ceti hands, and Sig couldn't even imagine how Vladric had acquired it. The conical-shaped craft had a twelve-metre-diameter mirror capable of detecting the infrared emissions of a burning candle from a hundred thousand kilometres away.

Per Vladric's instructions, every non-life support system of the *Aria Black* was shut down. Although the ship was fully pressurised, the crew was wearing stealthy zero-thermal signature survival suits, because the ambient temperature of the cabin was presently -20 C. Water, food, and related necessities were handled in the reactor compartment, the most insulated area of the ship, where the temperature was kept at a balmy 1 C.

To minimise detection and maximise survival odds, they had to be cold. Despite their precautions, they were still the warmest object in this comet belt, and a shining beacon for anyone who decided to look for them.

It was also dark. From this distance, the Orionis sun was the size of a pinhead, just barely the brightest star against the backdrop of the Milky Way, and not radiant enough to read by. Not that it mattered. Any light-emitting source that could escape from the *Black*'s eight portals was forbidden, except within sealed compartments.

Taken altogether, the conditions were ripe for a souring of moods and patience.

The men that Vladric had assembled for the mission were chosen for their skill sets, not their personalities. Their dossiers left Sig more concerned about them than House Obyeran lunatics.

The Glasnard brothers Drake and Theron were former asteroid miners who had found their calling as demolitions experts for Ceti. They were a volatile pair, siblings forged in a vat of chaos, the sort that relied foremost on violence to settle disagreements. Bouncing from one dangerous Belt job to the next as privateers, they were approached by Ceti recruiters and asked if they'd like to swap their mining gear for more playful things like firearms and explosives. It was an easy transition, as the tools used to blast through rock differed little from those used to blow up people.

Between their disregard for personal safety and extensive experience working in microgravity, they were the ideal marauders. Together they boasted more than fifty ship raids, with a kill list twice that. Whenever Sig gave an order neither one verbally acknowledged it, but they generally obeyed with a poignant defiance that expressed disdain for a proxy captain, and not the real legend who owned this historic ship.

Their job was to blast their way into the Lightspear, clearing a path for the marksmen behind them. That role fell to two men on the opposite side of the sociopathic spectrum: Larry Vostov and Jaz DeMoer. As former security officers at Bertha and then Brotherhood, they were close quarters combat experts with top notch certifications across a broad range of weapons and tactics. They were also total recluses who, if nothing else, at least never complained about the cold and darkness. Beyond that, all attempts at meaningful conversation were met with variations of 'yes', 'no', and 'I don't know'.

Their experience included six hostage rescue missions, plus a number of assassinations on Inner Rim targets. Since this op was a non-lethal takedown, their kit included stun guns, concussion grenades, mesh traps, and tranquillisers. But they also would bring real guns in case the intel about who was on board was wrong. No matter how the mission turned out, no one was to be left alive on the Lightspear.

The last marauder that Vladric had selected was the one who bothered Sig the most.

Angus McCreary was a Ceti lieutenant who had risen in the organisation through military service alone. He was a hero in the Battle of Brotherhood, leading a bold mech assault against the Navy frigate ONW *Madrid* that some considered a turning point in the battle. Today he was a tactics adviser for the SIOPS military division of Ceti, and the lead planner for this mission.

He carried himself in a manner more befitting a pirate than military officer. He was crude and intrusive, constantly pestering Sig about past exploits, and sharing unsolicited graphic details about his own marauding adventures. According to Vladric, the role of Angus was to run the actual breach and raid. But he was also a capable captain with his own ship and crew, and far more proficient in military operations than someone who hadn't fired a gun in a quarter-century.

Such redundancy was a message from Vladric. Sig knew that if he was thinking these things, so was the rest of the crew.

It was nearing the end of an eight-hour shift on the bridge, during which time Sig had fiddled with the passive sensors on the *Black*, visualised different boarding scenarios, and, when vigilance lapsed, read some classical Earth literature.

Angus showed up for his shift on time, nosy and presumptuous as ever.

'Morning, evening, whatever,' he said, pulling himself through the opening. 'Anything new?'

'Nothing,' Sig said. 'We'll find her.'

'Aye, your optimism is just what the boys want to 'ear,' Angus grumbled.

'You're welcome,' Sig said, pushing away from the captain's chair.

'Hang around some,' Angus said. 'Those twats in back aren't much for talkin'.'

'I've noticed,' Sig admitted. 'But they're good at their jobs.'

'They better be,' Angus growled. He was blocking the bridge exit, and his posture suggested no intention of moving. 'Bah, could be worse. 'Ere's the nicest tub I've ever frozen my arse off in.'

'Vladric is a man of high taste,' Sig said.

'You two go back aways, eh?' Angus said. 'Crowned you gov'nor 'o Lethe for your troubles, then saddles you wi' this job. 'At's a chum for you.'

Sig didn't like where this was going.

'Curse of competence, I guess.'

'Right, yeah,' Angus said. 'How'd you two become mates?'

'We're ghosts,' Sig said. 'All ghosts get along great.'

'Aye, but you don't just pal around with Vladric Mors 'less you've earned your keep. So what was it, then?'

Sig tried to assert himself.

'Enjoy your shift, Angus,' he said, motioning towards the hatch. 'I need some rest.'

'Not so fast, mate,' Angus warned, holding up his hand. 'I heard stories about you.'

'Is that right?'

'Yeah, it is,' Angus said. ''Ow many firstborns did you gut back in the day? This whole crew 'as blood on their hands. Gimme a number, I got a wager with Theron.'

If they were on Brotherhood, or anywhere else where his Ceti rank mattered, Sig would have denounced the man on the spot. Instead, he bit his tongue.

'It's not something I'm proud of,' he said.

'C'mon mate, I ain't judging you for it,' Angus insisted. 'Or maybe I am. I know how it is, when you're young and desperate. That's what Vladdy looks for in nubs, y'know. Desperation. Easy to find 'round 'ere. Finds a man drownin' in shit an' offers a line, for a price. Men will do anything to save 'emselves. Won't they?'

'I'm not in the mood for a deep chat,' Sig said, starting towards the exit again. 'Stay on the sensors.'

'Stay on *this*,' Angus said, extending his middle finger. 'I like knowing who I'm working for. We been thawed out two weeks and don't know fuck all 'bout you, except that you're Vladric's mate and a bloody politician. You ain't marauded in years, but he put you in that chair anyway. So tell me a story, Sig. We wants t' know.'

'This is what Vladric wanted,' Sig said cautiously. Angus was a menacing man, especially up close.

'Well he ain't 'ere, now is he?' Angus growled. 'Seems we got lots o' time. So start talkin' before we get too restless.'

The fact he said 'we' made Sig think that Angus had planned a mutiny. It was to be expected: promise six men a bounty and they'd find ways to split it with one less person. If telling a story would defuse some tension, then he'd tell him one.

'What do you want to know?' Sig asked, resignedly.

'Told you, I want t'know how'd you get so tight with Vladric.'

Sig took a deep breath.

'The year was 2724,' he started. 'We met on Magellan.'

Magellan was the first outpost built beyond Eris, completed long before construction on Brotherhood even began. At the time, it was the largest station ever built, and as the launch point for Outer Rim colonisation, one of the busiest.

Angus was old enough to remember what it was like.

'Magellan, eh?' he said. 'I got a lot o' good memories there.'

'Outer Rim projects weren't taxed back then, so the place was a labour goldmine for corporations,' Sig explained. 'I went there looking for work like everyone else. They set up employment kiosks and we queued behind them. I was turned away from every one. No skills, they said. Had no choice but to wait around and hope a gig opened for a blank slate like me. After a few nights sleeping on the hangar deck, I saw a new kiosk – scrap metal propped on two cones – with one guy standing behind it and no queue. A rickety sign on top spelled "Ceti".'

Angus slapped his thigh.

'Bloody hell!' he said. 'Vladric was behind it?'

Sig nodded.

'Told me he had a ship and was looking for a crew. No experience? No problem. Promised to teach me the ropes on the job. Turned out that "ship" was a shitty little two-seat harbour tug.'

'Ha!' Angus roared. 'And you agreed?'

'Like you said, I was drowning in shit,' Sig reminisced. 'We flew to all the staging areas around Magellan offering towing services but kept getting turned away. Wasn't long before we were out of money, food, and I was cursing myself for trusting him in the first place.'

'Why the fuck would you trust him?' Angus asked.

'Because he had this *charisma*,' Sig answered. 'He was such a *hopeful* bastard. It was authentic. You wanted to believe him. You'd never know it today, but back then he was the most upbeat, optimistic son of a bitch I ever met. But when things went bad, I wanted out. And he begged – literally, *begged me* – for one last chance to prove himself.'

'Begged *you*?' Angus scoffed. 'Bugger that.'

'Vladric Mors was more afraid of disappointing his sole employee than he was of starving to death,' Sig said. 'He asked me to trust him, said that he had a plan and to "just go along with it". So I did.'

Sig paused. He really didn't want to tell this part of the story.

'Well, what'd he do?' Angus demanded.

'Vladric flew us beyond Magellan's radar coverage, pointed us in a random direction and fired the thrusters,' Sig said. 'Then he dumped the fuel we had left. I fought him for the controls, thinking he'd lost it, but he beat me down. *Demanded* that I trust him. You could see the insanity in his eyes. I was scared for my life.

'Turns out he set us adrift in the main shipping lane between Hera and the Belt. We were "rescued" six hours later by a corvette named the *Glamour*. Good Samaritans, just two of them on a luxury rig that could fit twenty. A firstborn named Robert Andiron greeted us at the hatch. Some attractive woman was with him. She was high or drunk, giggling, incoherent … I never got her name. Robert never bothered to introduce her.

'He was going on about what a great sport he was rescuing us, bragging that it would get him laid. Vladric did all the talking, stroking his ego, asking questions about the ship, talking shop about flying. Once we were under way, Vladric whispered for me to get ready. I had no idea what he meant.

'As soon as Robert took the helm, Vladric shanked him with a screwdriver. Never even saw where he had found it. Right in the armpit, all the way to the handle. When the woman rushed to stop him, I launched myself at her. I don't know why. I just grabbed hold of her neck from behind and held on for dear life.

'I'd never seen blood in zero-G before. I … panicked. There was screaming. Dying. Next thing I knew, Vladric was telling me to let go. I didn't realise I was choking a corpse. Robert was dead as well. And we had a ship.'

'The "*Glamour*"?' Angus snickered. 'Vladric's first boat was named the bloody *Glamour*?'

'I watched her corpse for hours,' Sig said. 'It … taught me something. About the way things were. The way they still are. Vladric went about like nothing had happened. The *Glamour*'s hold was loaded with provisions and a corestack packed with CROs that he was able to launder before anyone knew that Robert Andiron was missing. We had struck the mother lode, all on a wild shot.'

'Luckiest bastard alive,' Angus said. 'Rumour 'as it he's got the Gift. That's some story. So how many firstborns 'ave you waxed since then?'

'Why does that matter so much to you?' Sig rebuked. 'I stopped counting years ago.'

Angus smirked.

'I just want to win a wager,' he said, moving away from the hatch. 'Don't take the high road with this crew, mate. Everyone 'ere hates 'imself for one reason or other.'

Big Eye interrupted their conversation, which it wouldn't unless it found something.

The two men looked at each other as if they'd seen a ghost.

A plot of heat signatures was superimposed on the local starmap within their helmet UIs. The odds of that track being anything other than a disabled ship were minimal. The time to intercept, risking a very high-profile burn from this location, was twelve hours.

If it was a Lightspear, it was right where Vladric said it would be.

'That's why we kill for 'im,' Angus muttered. 'The bastard's never wrong.'

Drifting aimlessly through space, Myrha Obyeran considered the cycle of simplicity in her meaningless life:

Sleep. Loathing. More sleep. Time wasting away. Repeat.

Instead of battling for the highest honour of House Obyeran, she was the equivalent of an actress in some staged drama, worshipped only because she shared the name of a king, handed a crown by a father who didn't trust her to earn it on merit alone.

One week after her escort ships vanished, the Lightspear came alive on its own, all systems functioning normally.

At which point, she forcibly shut the whole ship back down.

It drifted. And drifted. And she meditated on her actions, reasoning that her motivation was not spite or anger, but a rational necessity. If her father did not truly believe in the ideals he had founded an entire culture upon, then she would make him. Ultimately, her defiance would make House Obyeran stronger. By thwarting his succession plan, he would be forced to reconsider what he wanted their House to stand for – after he moved past his anger, just as she had to.

Myrha passed the time by making challenges for herself, attempting repairs to the damage she had inflicted on the Lightspear, wondering if Maez had already returned. That would be glorious. But more likely, his suffering was just as prolonged. Her father had certainly taken measures to ensure that his Lightspear could never return before her own.

Sadly, there was more dignity in her brother's lost cause than what she was doing now.

Every glance outside shattered her calm and restored the anger that would never subside. A glittering line of dust broke the shroud of blackness in the distance. The Orionis sun was the brightest star in the Milky Way, and the pale bluish hue of the Triton Worlds stood out like sapphires on a coat of velvet. There was no question she was in the Hades Terminus. Had this been a real test, finding her way back to Hyllus would have been possible; difficult without astrometric data, but with a functioning engine and power plant, it could be done. With a Lightspear, you always had a chance.

That was the whole point of The Voyage Home.

Myrha pushed herself away from the bridge and into the long corridor running the length of the ship, running her hands along the smooth, cold bulkheads. Their whole culture, the Obyeran way, was illuminated by the Lightspear. Yet she had attacked this beautiful creation and shut her down out of spite for her father.

Ashamed, she resolved to bring the ship back to life.

Moving towards the reactor compartment, Myrha considered giving her a proper name. It was her father who had imposed the Lightspear collective on the fleet. Her ship should be different from the rest.

As she passed the short hallway leading to the dorsal personnel hatch, the unmistakable sound of docking clamps latching onto the hull startled her.

Myrha had cursed her father often in the past weeks, but none as loudly as this. King Obyeran had come to whisk his daughter home like some delinquent child. And with her Lightspear shut down, of course she hadn't seen him coming.

Like a child.

In a rage, she bashed the emergency release hatch to greet him.

For several milliseconds, Sig froze, and so did his crew.

No one was expecting the hatch to open, least of all Drake and Theron, who had just armed the charges that would blast it apart. Those explosives were now floating between them and an enormous pale woman in a survival suit.

Experts that they were, the Glasnard brothers had designed a pyrotechnic masterpiece to get the hatch open quickly. They had used two sets of explosives: one consisted of six shaped charges that would punch through the door's outer shell and shatter the locking mechanism behind it.

The second set was placed like tape along the perimeter of the hatch, close to the frame. This charge delivered the functional equivalent of a blowtorch, converting its mass into a controlled plasma stream that would melt anything in direct contact. A loaded demolition 'spring punch' was next to Drake; immediately following the detonation, the miniature battering ram would deliver several thousand pounds of force to bash the weakened door in.

None of this was relevant now, as Sig's view of the scene abruptly vanished in a blinding white flash.

Myrha's honed combat instincts instantly grasped that the breach explosives had been knocked loose when the hatch opened, and the warrior in her took action to save her life.

Her right arm grabbed the railing beside the hatch and yanked hard.

A terrible blast popped her eardrums. There was a simultaneous explosion of pain in her left ribcage, as she was sent tumbling through the Lightspear's main corridor.

But Myrha smiled, even as she crashed into the bulkhead.

This was the challenge The Voyage Home was meant to be.

When the lens flare in the camera dissipated, Sig saw dark stains where Drake had been crouched. Debris and body parts were still caroming throughout the airlock.

Half of Theron was spinning over the spring punch.

Angus, Larry, and Jaz were stunned, trying to shake off the concussive effects of being inside a metal tube during an explosion.

'Angus, can you hear me?' Sig shouted.

But he couldn't. None of them could.

And the Obyeran woman must have known it, because she flew out of the Lightspear hatch like a railgun slug.

Myrha didn't know who they were, only that they were not Obyerans. She ignored the extent of her injuries, knowing that her body was already repairing them with unnatural rigour.

The first encounter was with a rump of a man who was still disoriented from the blast. Planting her mag greaves in front of him, she stopped her momentum by slamming the butt end of her skythe in the centre of his mask, punching a deep crater into his face.

239

As she shoved the haemorrhaging, convulsing husk aside, a searing pain lashed through her as raw voltage boiled her blood. Another lesser creature had fired a stun weapon into her, screaming insults, eyes wide with terror. But she refused to be stopped. With sheer willpower, she ripped the wire lead out from her stomach and lunged for the man who had fired it, skythe in hand. With a flick of her wrist, she separated the man's head from his shoulders.

As globules of his blood merged with her suit, she spotted the last man between her and the attacker's ship, the older one who commanded this pathetic group, as he tried to flee.

She would not let that happen.

Sig's mind was racing to find options.

Lethal force was the only response that made sense, but it was the only one they couldn't use.

Jaz had landed a direct hit with the stun gun and had been *decapitated* for the trouble. She couldn't be human. No one moved that fast, that fluidly, all while sporting what appeared to be a mortal wound. Yet she had just killed two men within a span of five seconds, and was on her way to kill Angus.

Then she would come for him.

Angus had just crossed the breaching module connecting the *Black*'s airlock to the Lightspear's. In just a few moments, he would be inside the ship. The Obyeran woman was a leap or two behind.

It suddenly dawned on Sig that the module was still pressurised.

Taking her brother's arm off was nothing in comparison to killing men in hand-to-hand combat.

Her prey was just ahead, banging furiously on the airlock hatch. Slaying him would bring no satisfaction. But she would be that much closer to finding the captain, whom she would thank for giving her a worthy trial before taking his life.

'Open the door, Sig!' the man screamed.

Myrha made a note of that name, wondering if that was the captain.

'Motherfucker!' the man shouted. 'Open it!'

Engaging her mag greaves, she charged towards him – upside down from his perspective – skythe at the ready. He began screaming; her heart filled with a primal bloodlust.

The skythe was arcing downward when the hatch suddenly opened, followed by the awful sound of screaming, ripping, snapping metal.

Myrha was slammed sideways and then hurled backwards with terrific force.

She knew it was a structural breach, and a catastrophic loss of pressure was under way. All the air in the attacker's ship was rushing out into space, taking her and anything not bolted down with it.

With as much strength as she could muster, she stabbed the skythe into the nearest bulkhead. But the blade snapped on impact. By pure luck, her other hand managed to catch an edge and clamped on for dear life.

Her prey slammed off the bulkhead in front of her and hurtled past. Unable to look behind, Myrha came to the awful realisation that the only airflow was coming from the attacking ship.

It took all her strength not to give up. Her survival suit was torn. Myrha took one last breath and held it.

When the rush subsided, she turned and saw a star field instead of her Lightspear.

Sig assessed the outcome of his gamble.

If a fire's advance could no longer be contained by isolating compartments, starving the entire vessel of oxygen was a last resort. So Sig had remotely opened the hatch of every compartment on the ship except the bridge, and the airlock keeping Angus out.

Then he instructed the *Black*'s life support system to generate as much overpressure as possible.

The two ships were joined at the belly by a breaching module, and the weakest point of the union was where it latched onto the target's airlock. To prevent the Obyeran twin from escaping back to the Lightspear, halt her advance on the *Black*, and have any chance of capturing her alive, the module would have to be forcibly detached from the Lightspear side.

Sig accomplished that by generating torque with the *Black*'s thrusters.

To create as much yaw as possible, he aimed the forward and aft thrusters in opposite directions and fired them simultaneously. The result was a shearing action that ripped the breaching module off the Lightspear. A split second later, he had opened the final airlock hatch that Angus was trapped behind.

But that excess yaw smashed the two ships into each other, doing extensive damage that Sig had yet to process as the Black tumbled out of control.

Sig had gambled that the module would stay attached to the Black, and that the Obyeran twin was strong enough to hold on. He won both bets. With the Lightspear already a kilometre away, she had no choice but to board the Black on his terms.

Angus's vital signs, broadcast from his survival suit, were very weak. Sig judged that any attempt to save his life would be futile.

Myrha had never known such dread.

She caught a glimpse several times, each one smaller with every rotation. There was no greater humiliation than to be separated from her Lightspear.

Now she knew how her brother felt to have lost his arm in combat.

There was no choice but to find this 'Sig' and take his ship.

That would be difficult. In her desperation, she considered scaling the outer hull to find a different way in. But she had lost her skythe. And she couldn't hold her breath for much longer.

Myrha conceded defeat.

Her lungs burning, she pulled her way inside, to a strange compartment too small for comfort.

The hatch closed behind her. The Voyage Home had truly begun.

The collision had cost the Aria Black one of her main thrusters.

That was the biggest consequence of Sig's gamble. There was also no way to recover the Big Eye, adding to the forensic debris cloud that would leave little doubt as to who was responsible for this.

The autopilot instructions were set for a coordinate in the middle of nowhere. No known bases, installations, nothing. It was a random location at the fringe of the Hades Terminus, over a billion kilometres from here. With only one thruster, it would take much longer to reach it. And Sig still didn't know what supplies had tumbled out into space along with Angus.

A fleet of Lightspears would be looking for his prisoner very soon.

Sig composed his message, which would eventually find its way to Vladric, wherever he was:

One VIP secured
No contact with second
Five crew KIA
Heavy damage sustained
Proceeding to checkpoint
ETA double allotted time.

At the end of the message was an image of his hostage. The heiress to an empire was in the hold of his ship.

Vladric's ship.

Sig watched the vital signs of Angus McCreary flatline.

'The bastard's never wrong,' Sig muttered, as the *Aria Black* limped into the void.

24

ANONYMOUS

Dear Amaryllis,

You were twenty-three years old when we met.

Instead of wearing a mottled grey UNSEC Traveller uniform like the other *Genesis* passengers, you wore a white dress that made you stand out like a diamond.

Boarding hour was two days away, and the streets of Bangor were filled with Travellers revelling with loved ones, savouring their final moments on Earth. For as long as man has taken to the sea, the voyagers of antiquity have marked the eve of great journeys with celebrations just like the one that night.

For a young, warm-blooded UNSEC infantryman, these were fertile breeding grounds, and I joined the festivities hoping to meet a Traveller who sought no regrets. When we met by the Gazer Pavilion at Broadway Park, I thought I had found exactly what I was looking for. But something else happened instead.

We formed the deepest bond I have ever known.

There will never be another like it. To this day, every detail of every moment we shared haunts me. Your warm eyes, your contagious laughter, the sound of your breathing, the peace of your sleep, the way that white dress fell from your shoulders, and the way you put it back on when it was time to say goodbye.

The memories sustain me. Or not. I don't know any more. My colleagues have warned that this correspondence has become harmful. The mission could be compromised, and they blame you.

So be it. I *need* this, because it is uniquely *human*. But I wonder how our bond would hold if you could see me now.

I am presently three metres long, if you measure from the tip of my antennae to the end of my thorax. I have three pairs of legs, and my 'feet' contain secretial glands that allow me to adhere to any surface from any aspect, which is impressive considering I weigh 130 kilos. My eyes, of which there are six, only see in infrared, but give me 360 degrees of coverage, which makes it difficult for anything to sneak up on me. I don't breathe oxygen; my circulatory and respiration are governed by a system that utilises captured sunlight and molecular hydrogen produced by hydrogenosomes in the synthetic hemolymph that flows through me. Incidentally, this process generates a highly acidic waste product that accumulates in storage glands that I can propel from ducts in concentrated streams to defend myself.

Last night, my arthropod-like colleagues and I scaled a vertical wall four kilometres high to eat the eggs of a lychtymorph queen – all 200 million of them. The acidic secretions in my glands helped digest them, and then my bio-engineered body used them as fuel to sustain my descent in total darkness, and subsequent two-hundred-kilometre march to the exfiltration site.

These eggs were gestating the larvae of lychtymorph alphas, impressionable little creatures that, if properly trained and augmented, can be hammered into a number of service roles, from industrious servants to battlefield hunter-killers. I should add that their size is proportionate to how much they are fed; a mature alpha can grow to over two metres in height and rip a three-centimetre-thick steel plate in half with its jaws. This particular batch of formerly independent, intelligent life forms was due to be sold to the Raothri, who planned to distribute them throughout their nanotechnology manufacturing pipeline. The larvae are very adept at weaving tungsten nanotube fibres, one of the more devious technologies the red race has in its arsenal.

Ceitus always knows best how to hurt the master species. She is also quite clever at genetic manipulation, designing just the right creature for just the right task – something the Raothri have been doing for thousands of years. They are gods, in the classical sense that they create life to serve a specific purpose. The indigenous world of the lychtomorph is a half-scorched, half-frozen world with no atmosphere and a narrow temperate band where a number of species exist. It is tectonically hyperactive thanks to the immense tidal forces of the gas giant it orbits and a molten metal inner core. The resulting fault lines that rip across the planet make the Valles Marineris on Mars look like a shallow ditch.

We were built to navigate this treacherous landscape while also remaining invisible to Raothri technology and lychtomorph alpha sentries. Ceitus makes us into whatever we need to accomplish the mission. Last week I was a carnivorous reptile. Next month I will be a gilled mammal. Only Ceitus knows what we will become next.

But I still remember what I was before all this started. Our time together makes that life worth remembering. Between missions, Ceitus lets us resume our native forms in a virtual simulator. This is the only place we can interact with each other 'in person', since our native environments are lethal to each other. It's here, in this simulator, where we remind ourselves of why we fight. We talk about our homeworlds, and the 'people' we miss, and all the times we think we died during these missions.

My memory of your white dress is a sequence of stored quantum bits that can be translated into their biological mnemonic equivalent in any creature that Ceitus designs. But she also exercises great discretion in choosing the memories that stay with us from one incarnation to the next. When things go badly, we never remember how we die. We also never remember how we are transformed from one creature to the next. We just become something different; as comfortable in our new skin, membrane, or exoskeleton as if we were born that way.

There is never a mission post-mortem. Nor do we ever analyse success, because the Raothri are never fooled by the same approach twice.

Whether or not the setback to Raothri nanotech manufacturing capabilities made any lasting impact on 'the big picture', we cannot say. The scope of what Ceitus hopes to achieve with her rebellion is beyond my comprehension. And yes – Ceitus is female, or the equivalent of one, as I recently learned.

Given the fact she can kill us, or erase our memories or put us in a simulator where nothing is actually real, well ... we're alive because she says we are. We have no choice but to believe in her, and in what she's doing with us. During one of my worst moments trying to acclimatise here, I demanded to know what it was like to play god, and if all Raothri considered themselves as such. Her answer was surprisingly humble for a superior creature. She said, 'Intelligence is not the same as wisdom. Even a child can own an ant farm.'

Your beautiful white dress still inspires me because humans need hope. It has always given them something to live for, and it's a rare thing in the universe that something as intangible as 'hope' is such a powerful motivator. My alien colleagues draw their inspiration from different sources. Most don't assign sentimental value to their actions. Theirs is an innate call to duty, the way the denizens of insect hives respond to an assault on their queen. They are truly selfless in that sense, and readily sacrifice themselves for a greater cause without hesitation.

I've not made contact with another human being in almost two centuries. Those that joined me at Station Alsos are in other units like this one, operating on distant worlds, doing the same work as us. We operators have predictions on the amount of time each of our respective species has left before they are totally extinct. For humans, that number is five years. If not for the Gift, it would have been over already. And even then, who knows what other events have been set in motion that cannot be averted? A rogue planet, flung out of another system aeons ago, changed the fate of that beautiful world you called Eileithyia, and gave Orionis the Hades Terminus instead.

Judging from what just happened there, five years may be too generous an estimate.

Even so, I *hope* – there's that word again – that you still remember me the way I was.

Love always,

- A

25

MAEZ

Every sixty-eight seconds, the wispy dust clouds of the Milky Way fell past the hexagon-shaped viewport on the bridge. The Lightspear was without power, drifting in the same direction it had been released in, rolling and pitching end over end through space. The tumble left large blind spots on either side, blocking a wide swathe of 'sky' that Maez needed to get his bearings. Even if he could have seen them, it wouldn't have mattered. Without propulsion, there was no way to stabilise the ship. But the rate of spin wasn't unbearable, and Maez had grown accustomed to it. He was as comfortable as it was possible to be under these conditions.

Setting his corelink aside, he rubbed the sleepiness from his eyes. His father always said that truly knowing yourself was salvation, and that The Voyage Home provided the ultimate context for discovering the soul. Maez preferred to use the time to catch up on some reading. And after consuming the biographies of several Third World War generals, he concluded that the blood of fools ran in his veins.

Like most of the House ruling class, Maez was built from genetic material of his father's choosing. Knowing Masaad, the sequences in Maez's DNA would have been extracted or synthesised from long dead generals from the 'great conflicts' of yesterday. For as long as Maez could remember, his own interest in the subject of war had been insatiable. And if his studies had taught him anything, it was that all too often, history celebrated outcomes determined more by luck than skill.

As a young man, Maez had hoped for war against House Alyxander. The twins had never known their mother Lyanna, but their father had made her a virtual part of their lives. They saw her lead Obyerans in combat, and tend the wounds of the injured. They saw her kill with skythe, and heard her soothing song to newborns. They beheld the warrioress and the nurturer, the legend and the mother. And as much as the warrior in Maez craved vengeance for her death, the inner voice of Lyanna Obyeran declared that it was pointless.

The same was true of a conflict with any other faction. House Obyeran was founded to colonise a habitable world, not to conquer the airless rocks that Orionis corporations and cartels squabbled over. When the time came, his role would be to support Myrha as she led the Lightspears on their voyage, and to be her military counsel once they arrived.

Watching the Milky Way drift past again, Maez was at peace with that fate. He did not need, nor ever want, to be called 'King'. Myrha was destined to bear that burden, and she would probably fail in that role, as he would in his. To Maez, a man who had devoted his life to protecting House Obyeran, The Voyage Home was the illusion of competence. For, among those countless stars, the Raothri were watching. Nothing he learned from watching human wars could prepare him to face them, or the hidden dangers lurking on that alien world.

Maez left the bridge, pushing himself down the main corridor, using the light on his survival suit to see. Thus far, he was satisfied with his efforts to revive the stricken ship. Every Lightspear was equipped with a shuttle tug for EVA repairs, and he was routing power from its modest fusion core to the ship's main electrical grid. It wasn't enough to power every system, but with some rationing, he was able to run life support and passive sensors.

But the ship's main fusion core remained disabled. The rules of The Voyage Home allegedly randomised the test conditions, but by all accounts it seemed that Maez had drawn the worst possible: the reactor was in a scrammed lockdown state, simulating measures to avert a catastrophic meltdown or explosion. There was no way to access the power that the aneutronic core was producing, and the most likely cause was a mechanical issue that required a shipyard or another Lightspear to fix.

Since his trial seemed over before it ever began, Maez had opted for comfort instead of competition. He assumed, in contrast, that the only issue with Myrha's Lightspear would be a loose toilet seat. At current consumption levels, his power supply would be exhausted in ninety days, which gave her just enough time to fix the issue and return home. His own time was better spent resting up for her coronation than attempting repairs on a fusion reactor in space.

Returning to his quarters, Maez tethered into his bunk, imagining what it was like to walk freely on a world with breathable air. Myrha had always reminded him that nothing about their lives could be taken for granted, which was ironic given her devotion to keeping them as dull as possible. From the heated biodomes of Hyllus to the fusion light sources that nourished the underground gardens, everything about House Obyeran was testament to the Pathfinder's ingenuity and relentless drive to build a better life for mankind.

The trouble was, Maez believed that people *were* living a better life in the Inner Rim. To survive beyond the Hades Terminus, his father had been forced to manipulate them into something more than just human. Whenever Inner Rim denizens visited, with their huge trade caravans, they gawked at the first True Acolyte they encountered. His father had redesigned humanity, reasoning that the old specs had led to destruction and exile. Obyerans were the future of the species. The Pathfinder and his brothers knew what they wanted to achieve, and their stubbornness was hereditary.

Myrha had bought so completely into their father's grand sense of purpose that Maez wondered if she was genetically predisposed to agree with him. She had always been the most committed acolyte, while he was the scatterbrained one who wanted to run free and perhaps talk to other children once in a while. Myrha preferred to stay with her studies and training, embracing the destiny her father crafted for her. She knew what the purpose of her life was, found strength in its mission, and was driven by fear of being unprepared to face it.

The Obyeran culture worshipped the Lightspears and those who captained them. There was exulted reverence for the one who would lead them all. But Myrha wasn't interested in becoming a goddess. She just didn't want to let anyone down.

Maez fell asleep grinning, imagining her working feverishly to restore her ship while he simply relaxed – an apt comparison of how their lives differed. If they had been shaped for a purpose, he was in no rush to meet it, as Myrha was. Destiny would come for them both soon enough.

Sometime later, he dreamt the ship was no longer spinning – which, to his surprise when he awoke, it really wasn't.

The reactor had unscrammed itself. Full power had been restored. Maez pulled himself towards the bridge, skythe at the ready.

But there was no one there. The yield beacon had not been activated, yet the ship was flying on autopilot, ignoring his attempts to seize control.

His Lightspear was taking him back to Hyllus. But he was unsure if the contest had been won.

Eighteen hours later, Maez returned to a home that was nothing like the one he had left.

The terminus station of The Forge shimmered in the glow of a thousand Lightspear engines. Twice as many shuttlecraft streaked about, urgently ferrying equipment and personnel from the hangar. It seemed that every asset in House Obyeran's arsenal had taken to space. Either his father had found the world he was looking for, or he was about to launch the greatest armed conflict in House history. But against whom?

Maez still had no control of his own Lightspear. His frustration mounting, he desperately wanted to speak with Myrha. But whatever trickery his father had installed revoked his every input, including the communications equipment. As his ship coasted into the hangar, he witnessed a frenzy of activity under way as rows of combat mechs and ammunition crates were lined along the cargo gantries. It looked suspiciously like the preparations for an invasion, not an interstellar departure – or a celebration to mark Myrha's return.

Instead of landing on the hangar tarmac, the Lightspear latched into an overhead service gantry, the same access point used to transfer supplies, waste, and, on occasion, prisoners.

Maez was furious. When the hatch opened there was no one to greet him, and the hallway beyond was empty as he stepped through.

Suddenly, the King's voice thundered out:

251

'Move forward.'

The Lightspear's hatch shut on its own.

'Good to hear your voice,' Maez said. His father had left the intercom on and was breathing irregularly. 'All you alright?'

'There's a dropship ahead of you,' his father said. 'Board it.'

'Why don't you explain what's happening first,' Maez said. 'Why is the fleet mobilising?'

His father's voice was nearly a whisper.

'Did you have anything to do with this?'

'With *what*? The fleet?' Maez asked, exasperated. 'You know I've been adrift the last three weeks, right?'

Again, there was only the sound of his father's laboured breathing.

'Hello?' Maez asked.

Suddenly, the airlock began to depressurise.

'Hey!' Maez shouted.

'I'll ask you once more,' his father said. 'Did you have a role in this?'

With nowhere else to go, Maez rushed towards the dropship entrance.

'I don't know what you're talking about,' he said, trembling with anger. 'Where is Myrha?'

The hatch slammed shut, and Maez felt the craft push away. A few moments later it was plummeting towards the surface of Hyllus.

'I will know the truth,' his father said, 'and then decide if you are still my son.'

The Seers greeted Maez with insults when he arrived.

'All hail the Blood Prince!' the eldest screeched. 'I've seen you, boy.'

Maez had not seen a single soul during his journey here, not even a Guardian or acolyte. He had been treated like a prisoner, herded through maintenance corridors and side doors, compelled by invisible threats towards hidden doors he had never known existed in the palace.

The humiliation peaked with the sight of the glass sarcophagi.

'What the hell is this?' he demanded.

'These are my Seers,' his father's voice said, 'and they have impli-cated you in Myrha's disappearance.'

The blood drained from Maez's face.

'Myrha is *missing* …? And you think I'm responsible?' he said, trembling. '*Are you completely mad?*'

'Confess, or confront your accusers,' King Masaad said.

'I confess nothing,' Maez fumed. 'What happened to her?'

'You set Orionis in flames,' the old one said. 'The Blood Prince will have his vengeance, you'll see, you'll see.'

'That's your evidence?' Maez roared. 'The ramblings of these crones?'

One of the Seers was barely conscious and in obvious agony. The others were ranting lunatics, and Maez singled out the old woman as their ringleader. She was teasing his father's anxieties with nonsensical prophecies, leading him astray from reality.

Maez had underestimated his father's obsession with control. What was more dangerous than a pathological king? He sounded crazed, desperate, acting like a man who had lost everything.

And if Myrha really was missing, that was true.

'I would *never* harm my sister,' Maez said. 'Not outside an arena, anyway. And I certainly don't envy your plans for her.'

'A fine performance!' the old hag heckled. 'We saw you, Blood Prince, we know, we know!'

Maez did his best to ignore her.

'Tell me what happened,' he said, walking close to the glass sarcophagi, sizing up the thickness of the glass. 'How do you even know she's missing?'

His father's voice was measured.

'We found her Lightspear,' King Masaad said. 'There were several corpses. She was not aboard.'

Maez could hear it in his voice, the way it cracked. He was breaking.

'Jealousy!' the old woman hissed. The others repeated various versions of her banter, like parrots. 'You wanted her dead, confess, *confess!*'

'*Shut up,*' Maez roared, spitting on glass. '*You* designed The Voyage Home. Who else knew where we were towed? No one was supposed to know, not unless you rigged every aspect of this sham.'

'The Obyeran Code is no sham!' King Masaad shouted.

Maez pointed towards the glass.

'It *is* when you trust *their* nonsense more than the word of your own son,' he said.

The crones screamed, but then they were muted out. Maez turned and was startled to find himself staring into the tormented eyes of his father.

'There were no pilots or crew on the Lightspears that towed her there,' he said through gritted teeth. 'I had the harbour radars shut down so they couldn't be tracked. I knew exactly where she was at all times and *you* are the only other person who could have possibly known where that was.'

Maez had tried taking the high ground, but was losing the struggle. More and more, he sensed he was dealing with someone who could not be reasoned with.

'How? By reading your mind? That's as sensible as asking *them –*' he said, pointing towards the Seers – 'to tell your future. *I would never harm my sister.* That's not to say I haven't thought about it, especially after she maimed me before the whole bloody House. But the fact is, you've made such a spectacle of this contest that anyone with a grudge could have known where to look.'

'Impossible,' King Masaad fumed.

'What's impossible is for you to blame yourself,' Maez retorted, his own rage boiling. 'You *want* me to be guilty of this, don't you? You sick, demented man. Alright, Father. I'll say what you want to hear: I abducted Myrha, so I can have her crown, *because that's clearly what I've always wanted.*'

His father's eyes were bulging, his chest heaving. Maez dismissed the inner voice warning him to back off.

'Fucking royalty,' he spat, drawing his skythe. 'Do I owe my life for this crime? Good. Come and get it, if you can.'

Maez wasn't expecting his father to accommodate the request.

Delirious with rage, King Masaad rushed his son with unnatural speed. Maez braced for the impact, expecting to toss the much smaller man aside.

Instead he was thrown backwards as if struck by a combat mech. The skythe was knocked from his hand.

'*Where is she?*' the Pathfinder howled, clamping his hands around Maez's throat. '*What have you done?*'

Maez could not believe his father's strength. His grip was unbreakable, and he panicked as his head was lifted and smashed onto the metal grating.

'*Why, why, why?*' the Pathfinder howled.

Maez's vision began to tunnel. His eyes searched out something he could use to defend himself, but instead saw only the Seers cackling behind the glass.

Then, the one who had been silent raised his head, and the others froze.

His father saw it as well.

'I see the one named Vladric,' the Seer said. 'The message that comes will be from him.'

Maez felt the grip on his neck release, and sucked in as much air as his lungs would allow. His father had sprung to his feet.

There was an acolyte standing at the forbidden cave's entrance.

'My lord ... about your daughter,' he said weakly.

Your Majesty,

Princess Myrha is in my custody. As you can see, her injuries are minor. Although she refuses aid, she has been treated humanely. No additional harm will befall her, provided you accept my terms, as outlined below.

This is not a negotiation. Time is of the essence. If you do not comply, you will never see her again.

Our paths crossed decades ago on Magellan. Like so many in search of salvation during those hard days, I was a desperate young man drawn to your cause. Surrounded by your devoted followers, I watched you captivate the crowd like a sermon on the mount. You invited anyone who would listen to join House Obyeran as acolytes – the *peasants* of your manufactured culture – promising them security and equality, the quintessential social commodities of Orionis.

It was a tempting offer. But something felt out of place. You are the oldest surviving member of the *Tabit Genesis*. The Obyeran brothers helped build that very ship. If not for your technology, the human race might be extinct now.

You were a god. Yet you ran from the Inner Rim. You resurfaced years later on the most remote world mankind has ever been. If it

255

were anyone but you, no one would have believed that House Obyeran stood a chance.

So I asked myself: what makes a god flee?

As a ghost, I have no reverence for Earth. But its history reveals much of what rots Orionis today, especially the history that highborns have taken every measure to hide. Near the end, there were two reigning geopolitical camps on Earth. The goal of ICERS was to save it. The goal of UNSEC was to leave it. And there weren't enough resources left on the planet to do both. The corporations of the world held more power than the governments, because they controlled access to the resources in space. Arcwave Technical, the corporation you founded, was entrenched in the ICERS camp. You had plans for terraformers, trans-continental irrigation projects, biocybernetic creations that could decontaminate radioactive lands; investments so grand in scope that only a business titan like you could even conceive of them.

But then you changed sides. Overnight, Arcwave Technical became a full supporter of UNSEC, committing all available resources to the construction of the Genesis motherships with an urgency the likes of which mankind had never seen. You know why, of course: first contact. The encounter between a Raothri warship and UNSEC mining craft in the belt between Mars and Jupiter.

What was the warning that creature gave? That Earth was beyond saving? That a Raothri armada was coming to destroy it? And who among the UNSEC demigods decided the remaining human population was better off dying in nuclear fire than facing what was coming? I know you did not support the 'mercy killing' of millions of people. I believe you left Tabit Prime to escape from the ones who did. Once humanity had secured its footing here, your usefulness to them was over. You, and the secrets you know, are a liability to them – or, as they would argue, to all of humanity. You fled to save your own life. The other highborns would have killed you and everyone associated with you to protect their secret. They might still. With the *Archangel*, you are no longer beyond their reach.

If we allow it, the highborn grip of Orionis will be unbreakable, and will eventually extend to Tau Ceti. The *Archangel* is an agent of evil, and I cannot stop it without your help.

256

That is why I took Myrha from you.

My fleet is three weeks from Corinth. We will attack the *Archangel* and make it ours. Your son is a great warrior and skilled commander. He will destroy the *Tabit Genesis*, the heart of everything we despise. The tactical plan for this joint operation is included with this message.

With his leadership, your Lightspears, and my fleet, we can rid Orionis of the tyrants you escaped from and at last take the freedom that is ours by right.

Your Majesty, I am not proud of my actions. I have no children of my own and cannot fathom your anguish.

I only know the anguish of ghosts. And I am just as desperate now as I was on Magellan. We cannot endure for much longer.

Prince Maez must be our saviour if Myrha is to live.

If we meet again, I would not blame you for attempting to take my life.

Yours in human brotherhood,

Vladric Mors

Maez looked at his father, and saw not a king, but a broken man.

Seated at the edge of the walkway, across from the cave entrance, Masaad was silent and sullen, except when whispering 'Myrha' every now and then. Fearful for their lives, the Obyeran Guardians had sent a hapless acolyte to deliver the news. The boy was brave to walk into this wretched place. Maez doubted he would live to see another day for the crime of having seen it.

The Pathfinder had not moved. His thick white hair was filthy, falling to his shoulders like melting ice, his amber eyes vacant and dark. The Seers had fallen back into their slumber, all except the old crone, who was mumbling in her wet grave. Maez supposed that was because she had expected 'The Blood Prince' to be dead by now.

He couldn't blame her. It was the only way to hurt the madman who imprisoned her. The shock of being attacked by his own father was offset by the unbelievable fact: Myrha was gone. Worse, he couldn't decide how he felt about that. There was too much to process.

Maez rubbed his neck, which was so sore he had trouble turning his head. But as Vladric had mentioned, time was of the essence.

'To have any chance of getting her back ...' he started. 'You have to tell me everything.'

His father's expression confirmed what Maez all but knew.

'She caught me giving her Lightspear the advantage,' King Masaad admitted. 'The Voyage Home ... is no contest.'

Maez knew how that must have devastated her. Over the years, he'd found that his scepticism was founded on good instincts. He chose his next words with care.

'I understand its importance,' he said. 'The foundation of our culture is the promise of a new world. People need to believe in us to accept that possibility. The question is, did you find one?'

'Al Khav is there now,' King Obyeran said.

That was heartbreak, Maez thought. This final chapter of The Rites heralded the imminent journey that would take House Obyeran there, with Myrha leading the way. In essence, everything his father had worked for had been vaporised on the eve of his greatest accomplishment.

There was no time for pity. The logical choice was to sacrifice her and proceed as planned. Or start a new Rites to find a worthy successor. Myrha would have agreed. But Maez suspected his father was anything but rational at this point.

'These highborns he mentioned,' Maez said, omitting any mention of the Raothri. He would revisit that another time. 'Did you ever share your plans with them? Does anyone else know you found a world?'

King Masaad shook his head.

'My brothers,' he mumbled. 'Myrha. Now you.'

'You mobilised the fleet,' Maez said. 'Are you prepared to go to Eileithyia for her?'

The Pathfinder nodded.

Maez stood.

'You fully understand what that means.'

'Yes,' King Masaad said.

'A moment ago you nearly killed me,' Maez said. 'Am I now the commander of your Lightspears?'

'You. Are.'

'And you understand that I shall show no mercy, no remorse, *in your name*, for the mere chance of saving Myrha's life?'

'I do.'

Maez shook his head.

'You're a fool.'

King Obyeran stood.

'They have my daughter.'

'So the crone was right,' Maez said. 'I am the "Blood Prince".'

'You were born to protect our world from those who would try to take it from us,' King Masaad said. 'But she was *my* world.'

Maez bowed.

'Then I will find her,' he promised. 'But remember: I am the instrument you made me to be. I offer no justification for what follows. I am just the executor of your will.'

'Bring her back,' King Masaad whispered, his lips quivering. 'By any means necessary.'

26

VADIM

Ninety-Seven Years Earlier
2712 AD

In the dreamless shroud of unconsciousness, time had lost meaning, and a strange wisp of light appeared in the darkness. Slowly it grew into a piercing blaze, lifting the veil of anaesthesia. Vadim opened his eyes to the warm smile of his father.

'Welcome back, son,' he said.

Vadim Hedricks was more familiar with post-operative procedures than most medical interns. Surgery had become so routine that he knew the number of ceiling lights between the ICU and the recovery room down the hall. As they passed overhead, he took inventory of the sensations in his body, wary for new pain, and hoping not to find the old aches that were always with him.

Born with deformities that had left him bedridden all his life, Vadim could not recall a moment of his existence that was without pain. The root of his ailments was cancer, which was extremely rare for a firstborn. Only Outer Rim miners were supposed to contract 'ghost rot', yet somehow the disease had found him, the firstborn son of Grand Admiral Franz Hedricks. Even with modern advancements in biotechnology, the doctors had feared Vadim would never live past the age of eight.

But now he was ten. And his father insisted that he would live much longer.

The physicians were nice enough, but it was still awkward to be sitting naked in a room facing six of them.

'Well, go on,' his father encouraged. 'Give them a try.'

Vadim looked at his new legs, dangling off the gurney. The incisions were already healing and, for the first time, each limb looked to be the same length.

The nurses on either side of him were smiling.

'They won't let you fall,' his father assured.

With a slight push from his arms, Vadim slid his rear off the gurney. Both feet made simultaneous contact with the deck; his knees buckled, and the nurses grasped hold of him.

He glanced at his wheelchair.

'Let go,' he instructed. 'I want to try.'

The nurses looked to his father, who approved. Vadim felt their supportive hands move away. For the first time ever, he was standing on his own two feet.

His father beamed.

'Look at you,' he marvelled. 'Try taking a step.'

This room had once been the only hospital in civilisation. Located on the sole spinning torus of the original *Tabit Genesis*, the ancestry of every human being in Orionis could be traced back to these cold metal walls. It had evolved with the population over the decades. Gone were the thick lead bulkheads and magnetic shield generators that once protected the mothership's most precious cargo from interstellar radiation. In their place were six surgery rooms and ten times as many recovery rooms, the most this old structure could accommodate.

Everything and everyone inside was clad in sterile white – except his father, who wore the dark blue Orionis Navy uniform, with the vintage UNSEC cloak draped over his broad shoulders. He towered over everyone inside, and his shadow stretched across the deck to where Vadim was standing.

With shaking knees, Vadim managed to lift his foot. The nurses' arms were close by as it planted. His legs had never borne so much weight. His back foot followed the front one. Vadim had taken his first step.

The room burst into applause, which made him feel sheepish.

'Many more will follow,' his father encouraged.

Vadim scanned the recovery room, hoping to see his mother and friend Atticus, another cancer patient he had bonded with in the last year. But neither was there, and suddenly the physical exertion overwhelmed him. The nurses reacted just in time.

His father relieved them, placing Vadim's arm over his shoulder.

'You're getting stronger,' he said. 'Before long you'll be running the torus faster than Navy cadets.'

Taking a silent cue, the surgeons left the two alone.

'Where's Atticus?' Vadim asked, leaning as he took another step.

When last they spoke, his friend hadn't looked well. The tumours were in remission, but the smallest effort left him weak and exhausted. On occasion, a nurse would force him to exercise, and those sessions were difficult to watch.

'Atticus was sent home,' his father said.

'Home?' Vadim said. 'I thought he was still sick.'

'He's well enough to recover on his own,' his father said. 'There are other children who need his place.'

Vadim looked towards the recovery area; every bed was empty. Losing his concentration, he stumbled, grasping his father's uniform.

'Good,' his father said, supporting him. 'Falling is part of learning.'

Atticus always spoke in reverent, awestruck terms about Vadim's father, and so did everyone else Vadim met. Franz Hedricks had been the captain of the *Tabit Genesis* when it left Earth. Not that the vessel needed a captain to make the journey – computer systems managed all of the mothership's functions. But Captain Hedricks made all the crucial decisions once they arrived, from managing resources to establishing the provincial UNSEC government of the new colony. If technology was the enabler of human survival, it was the leadership of Franz Hedricks that guided mankind through its darkest hour.

Atticus's father was a mechanical engineer for the privateer corporation Lantrek Shipyards. His older brother was learning his craft and preparing to take his father's place. Atticus had not seen either in more than a year. But his mother looked after him tirelessly, and never left his side in the hospital.

She was beautiful, cheerful, and kind. Her smile reminded Vadim of his own mother, whom he rarely saw at all, especially since her last fight with his father.

Vadim thought of her while taking another tentative step.

'I wish Mom could see this,' he said. 'Will she be visiting later?'

'She's away at present,' his father said.

'Do you know when she'll return?' Vadim persisted, trying a larger step.

'Soon.' His father dismissed the topic. 'That's it. Someday you'll be stronger than the ones who were born healthy.'

Vadim straightened his posture, trying not to lean.

'When is my next surgery?' he asked.

'Five days from now,' his father said. 'For the tumours in your brain.'

'Will they put in any fake stuff?'

'Augmentations? Yes. They'll keep the cancer from returning.'

'Will I need them for ever?'

'Not to beat cancer, no. But perhaps for other things.'

Vadim stopped, exhausted from the effort.

'Really?' he asked, out of breath. 'Like what?'

Sensing that Vadim was about to collapse, Franz Hedricks hoisted him up with both hands and placed him gently in a wheelchair.

'Things to help you command a ship more powerful than the *Tabit Genesis*,' Franz said, pushing him down the hallway.

Vadim flushed red.

'You want me to command a ship?'

'When the time is right,' his father said. 'There will be challenges. Competition. But you have the advantage.'

'Why?'

'Because you're a Hedricks.'

His father wheeled him up to a window, beyond which the buildings of Tabit Prime curved high overhead. But his reflection captured him most; he saw a feeble, hideous, crippled boy with the towering shadow of his father standing behind him.

'Atticus dreams of being a Navy captain someday,' Vadim said. 'I think he'd be much better at it than me.'

'He can dream,' his father said. 'But that's as far as he'll get.'

'Why?'

His father placed his hands on Vadim's shoulders.

'This metal shell once held the last of us,' he said. 'We lived in these walls for decades before branching out in the system.'

Vadim knew this story. It was the foundation of his father's legend, how he reached Orionis only to find their new homeworld ruined by disaster.

'What happened to Eileithyia?' he asked.

'A rogue celestial body, probably a gas giant with satellites still attached, passed near the Tabit star and disturbed the orbits of her planets,' his father explained. 'Some believe the object that struck Eileithyia was a captured moon from Eris or Hephaestus. The inferno below is all that remains. We set orbit here because the planet's distance from the sun is ideal for agriculture and maintaining our notion of time.'

'Atticus knows people who don't believe we came from Earth,' Vadim said. 'Some think it doesn't exist at all.'

'Earth is real,' his father said, with a hint of annoyance. 'And it is lost. We learned about the invasion five years into the journey and just prior to discovering Eileithyia's fate. So we began planning for a life very different from the one we trained for.'

Vadim had heard stories about those early days, but they were more about cruelty than perseverance.

'Are the Raothri real?'

'Yes,' his father said. 'And their existence shaped the priorities of this colony. To save our species, we needed to cherish, rebuild, repopulate and fortify. These principles guide Orionis today, and soon it will become your responsibility to enforce them.'

Vadim did not know how to answer. His father noted the puzzled look on his face.

'You see, the crew chosen for the *Genesis* motherships were the brightest, strongest individuals from every race on Earth,' his father said. 'They are the precious origins we must cherish; and they are the foundation upon which we have rebuilt our civilisation. To preserve their legacy, we have the Heritage Act. To rebuild, repopulate and fortify our species, we have the *amniosynth*.'

The word rolled off his tongue with disdain. Vadim had heard stories about amniosynths. Everyone knew they were born from machines, and that many of them were monsters. They said a firstborn could tell if someone was an amniosynth just from the way they looked, or smelled. You knew they were *different*. And dangerous. It was no wonder they were called 'ghosts'.

'Vadim, let me make this perfectly clear: amniosynths are the working class of the human race,' his father said. 'They have built our ships, our stations, and soon, they will build the mothership that you command. If the day should come when we must face the Raothri, amniosynths will be on the front lines, and firstborns will be their generals. This is the way it must always be. Do you understand?'

'Yes, Father,' Vadim said. 'I really do.'

'Good,' his father said. 'Now, as to the whereabouts of Atticus, I had him removed from this facility.'

Vadim's jaw dropped.

'Removed? Why?'

'Because this ward is for firstborns only,' his father said.

Vadim shook his head.

'What? Atticus isn't …' he started. 'Are you saying that he's an *amniosynth*?'

'No fault of his own, no more than anyone is to blame for your illness,' his father said. 'But your fates could not be more different.'

Vadim could not process what was happening.

'What's going to happen to him?' he asked. 'I don't know anyone else that—'

'His guardians are wealthy,' his father interrupted. 'They chose to have him, so they can pay for his needs. But their money takes from those entitled to care by birthright, which is the law of Orionis.'

Vadim was despondent.

'But he's my *friend* …'

'Which demonstrates precisely why his guardians are so selfish,' his father said. 'They believed that their Heritage privileges would apply to him. They now understand that no one is above the law. You won't be spending any more time with him.'

Vadim felt a cold sensation in the pit of his stomach.

'Why?' he stammered. 'I never said goodbye!'

265

His father resumed wheeling him down the hall.

'Much depends on you,' he said. 'Now that you can walk, you'll be spending less time here, more time training, and absolutely no time pursuing trivial interests.'

Vadim's natural instinct was to turn to his mother. His father was a stern man whose nature was proud and imperious. Instances of compassion were rare. When Vadim had last seen his parents together, they had been shouting at one another. And he had never seen his father so enraged.

His mother had been threatening to tell Vadim something that his father didn't want him to hear. He found himself wondering again what that was.

'You are my son,' his father continued. 'Someday your shoulders will bear the weight of mankind's survival. You will learn to make hard choices, beginning now with Atticus.'

'He's my only friend,' Vadim murmured, eyes welling with tears.

'Then triage is your first lesson of command,' his father said. 'In our world, Atticus is already dead. Focus your effort on the ones you can save.'

Present Day

Corinth Naval Yards, construction site of the *Archangel* and main base of the Orionis Navy, was the most secure block of space in human control. Nothing could exist within twenty thousand kilometres in any direction of this fortress without the Navy's permission.

Grand Admiral Vadim Hedricks operated freely in this world. He travelled with neither announcement nor flight plan, anywhere he chose, and security parted before him everywhere he went. This was his domain, isolated from the political drama of Tabit Prime; his rule was not questioned.

Vadim piloted his shuttle from an *Archangel* hangar towards the torus station across the shipyard's scaffolding. The structure was 'black', meaning it did not officially exist and was thus without formal name. Navy pilots called it 'Corinth Able'; a navigational designation for ships permitted to land there, of which there were few. Like its parent facility,

Able was completely isolated from contact with the rest of Orionis. Its occupants were exclusively government employees: labourers, engineers, and the crew assigned to the *Archangel*. Of this group, the latter was mostly firstborns, many with living highborn parents. The rest were privateers and ghosts who voluntarily traded their freedom for living conditions that were as comfortable as it was possible to attain anywhere in Orionis.

Vadim never conducted business here. He visited only to meditate. Descending in the elevator from the central hub, his eyes absorbed the majestic treetops rising from the inner torus to greet him. Most living humans had never seen a tree, let alone a forest. This place was among the best-kept secrets in Orionis, a bioengineering masterstroke. Ferns, pines and oaks filled his view, engulfing him in a green sea of tranquillity. When he stepped onto the hard, packed detritus, there were no guards to meet him – just the watery rush of a nearby stream, and a manufactured breeze gently pushing the leaves above.

Able had cost a fortune to build, and for the moment it belonged exclusively to him. Only highborn money could subsidise such a feat, a fact plainly evident to anyone permitted to see it. Walking among the trees, Vadim occasionally glanced up through gaps in the canopy at buildings where the workers who had toiled to build the *Archangel* lived.

Very soon, they would find themselves at the crossroads of history.

He breathed deeply, welcoming the damp, earthen air. But then his enhanced olfactory senses picked out the scent of a familiar nuisance lurking among the trees ahead.

'Admiral Lao,' Vadim called out.

The Hera OPCOM stepped from behind an oak, wearing a Navy flight jacket and a smug look, as usual.

'What a coincidence, running into you,' Vadim said. 'What do you want?'

'We need to discuss the Gryphon list,' Lao said.

'What of it?' Vadim said, walking right past him.

'The highborns disprove of the selections,' Lao said, following.

'Combat proficiency is agnostic to lineage,' Vadim said. 'The best pilots passed.'

'They question whether Captain Lyons was objective in his assessment.'

'A ghost has no reason to play favour to a pool of firstborns,' Vadim snapped.

'That may be,' Lao said. 'But the fact remains.'

'What fact?'

'That some of his selections are guilty of conduct unbecoming,' Lao said. 'Decanto has been seen worshipping.'

Vadim might have smiled, if the mere sight of Jang Lao didn't inspire such venom.

Dominic Decanto was the son of firstborns Ferdinand Decanto and his wife Marianne Antiqua, who owned the largest investment bank in Orionis. According to Captain Lyons, Dominic was one of the more skilled pilots in the pool, possessing formidable mastery of the Gift. His highborn grandparents were both deceased.

The remaining highborns of Orionis wanted to dilute the influence of the dead and ensure that their own lineage would be represented among the most prestigious positions on the *Archangel*.

'Unless it affects his performance, I couldn't care less,' Vadim said.

'Maybe you should, considering he worships the Red,' Lao replied.

Orionis had no laws explicitly prohibiting people from worshipping. But freedom of religion had never been declared as an inherent right of Orionis citizenship. Most of the ancient religions had disappeared, although some highborns were trying to keep their faiths alive. But the Navy kept close surveillance on the shadowy cult that worshipped the Raothri. Some very alarming discoveries had emerged from this effort, including an alleged plot to detonate nuclear weapons in the hope of drawing the alien species to Orionis to complete their extermination of humans. The cultists aspired to invoke a 'rapture', in which their Raothri gods welcomed them into their kingdom.

Any suspected affiliation with the cult was managed with the urgency of terrorist investigation. But Vadim had good reason to doubt Lao's claim.

'It's an ugly scenario,' Lao said. 'A reputable highborn name dragged through such filth.'

'I hope for your sake you're just the messenger,' Vadim warned.

'Oh, I am,' Lao said, resuming his stroll. 'Of course, witnesses are reluctant to come forward, given the family name. But we have more evidence that implicates two other Gryphon pilots as well.'

'I'm sure the case against them is equally strong,' Vadim said. 'What do the highborns want?'

Admiral Lao's smugness vanished.

'Pilots Solomon, Adams, and Nkembeh all failed,' he said. 'Their parents were generous contributors to the Gryphon programme.'

'I see,' Vadim said. 'What would they have me do?'

'Fix it,' Lao said.

'These men are proud competitors,' Vadim said. 'How do you think they'll feel about being unjustly promoted?'

Lao rolled his eyes.

'Sooner or later they'll all end up in a Gryphon, though they won't have the distinction of being "first class", so to speak.'

'Or serving on the *Archangel*,' Vadim said.

'Yes, that as well,' Lao acknowledged.

'Your highborn masters are fortunate to have you in their service,' Vadim said. 'Before you waddle back to them, I want the status of our preparations to defend Orionis.'

'Sir,' Lao said, reddening. 'The *Calypso*, *Vienna*, and *Melbourne* have all reported. The *Calypso* will remain close to Eris in case Ceti attempts an orbital bombardment. The *Vienna* and *Melbourne* will orbit the moons to herd any stragglers back towards the *Archangel*. The corporations have been asking questions but believe this is just an exercise. Though that isn't likely to be the case for much longer.'

Vadim stopped walking.

'The Chancellor has become aware of Ceti's plans,' Lao said, smugness again on full display, 'and your attempt to hide them from her.'

'Who?' Vadim said.

'Captain Lyons, naturally,' Lao said. 'Which brings me to the second reason why I'm here: Chancellor Vespa has summoned you to Tabit Prime. She means to question you before the senate.'

Vadim showed not a trace of emotion.

'Captain Wyllym Lyons is to be arrested at once,' he ordered.

Lao's eyes widened.

'On what charge?'

'Treason, dereliction of duty, and homicidal negligence,' Vadim said, resuming his stroll. 'Have Tyrell do it. Always better to have a friend bring bad news.'

'Yes, sir,' Lao said.

'What a convenience for the highborns,' Vadim said. 'Now I have reason to question his entire pilot selection, don't I?'

'We believe Captain Lyons acted on his own volition,' Lao said. 'But the whispers began once the Second Armoured received deployment orders.'

Vadim stopped dead in his tracks.

'I beg your pardon?'

'Admiral Larksson had them reassigned to the *Archangel*,' Lao said.

They had reached the forest's edge, and a pathway emerged from the packed soil. A wheeled drone scurried past their feet, collecting the pine cones strewn about. Just beyond the fence was a street lined with buildings. Some people were nearby, many looking directly at him.

'Why did he do that?' Vadim asked.

Lao straightened his posture.

'Standard procedure,' he said. 'All of our capital assets have infantry units on board …'

'He is as stupid as he is arrogant,' Vadim growled. 'If I see an armed soldier anywhere near that ship, I'll have both your stars.'

'Sir, wh—?'

'Because he'll incite a panic, you idiot,' Vadim fumed. 'Moving ships about is one thing. Mobilising armoured divisions is something else, and frightened civilians are the last thing we need. Tell him to rotate the division to another assignment.'

Lao began fumbling in his coat for his corelink.

'I don't know if that's possible,' he mumbled.

'Then find a way to make it possible,' Vadim snapped. 'For the last time, that Ceti fleet won't get near the *Archangel*. Stop acting like a frightened child and follow your orders, Admiral.'

'Yes, sir,' Lao said, reddening. 'What shall I tell Chancellor Vespa?'

'Nothing,' Vadim said. 'You will tell her absolutely nothing. Is that clear?'

'Yes, sir.'

'Now get out of my sight.'

Lao forced a quick salute and scurried away, hurrying towards the street. Moments later, a Navy courier arrived to pick him up. The crowd that had gathered went back to their business, some nodding their approval.

Everything, Vadim knew, was going precisely according to plan.

27

ADAM

In the view from orbit, there was no planetary curve to Zeus. There was only an infinite, flat orange disc whose horizon met the absolute blackness of space. In the opening moments of descent, there was no visual cue of falling. As the sled accelerated, the horizon gradually disappeared, and the first jolt of the metal cage announced stratospheric entry. As wisps of ammonia condensate streaked past the canopy, the roiling cloud tops of the troposphere far below gave the first immense perspective of height.

By the time the platform emerged into view, Adam had spotted a dozen large hunters circling nearby. And instead of following rigid patrol patterns, their movements were playful – lazy tracks punctuated by the occasional 'hang tail', in which one would fully extend its flaps to hold stationary in the wind current for a few moments before freefalling, converting that sudden momentum in a series of loops.

With two kilometres remaining, Adam spotted the cause of their elation: an enormous school of sturgeons was approaching. The shimmering effervescence of their spines was bright enough to cast shadows on the rig. By the time the sled doors opened, Adam could see hunters gracefully darting into the swarms and emerging with a sturgeon or two in their grasp, absorbing the meal through their transparent mandibles, the carcasses merging and disappearing into the hunters' gelatinous flesh.

Zeus was thriving with life. And Adam was dead inside.

As the otherworldly alien scene swirled around him, Adam muddled through his routine devoid of emotion. He knew neither happiness nor sadness, anger nor love, regret nor hope. He knew only the Rig, and Helium-3 Production, and Pressure Differential Calculations, and Parts Per Million Samplings. Adam had become an organic machine; an intelligent, self-aware mining mech. The rig had never been more productive; every intake was running at optimal efficiency, wasting none of the 'noble gold' in their path.

His mother and sister loved to count it all, and both seemed happier now that Dad was dead. Their indifference to his passing was evident by the manner in which he was laid to rest: cremated in the trash disposal and jettisoned into orbit along with other atomised flotsam. Aside from a few pictures and corelink recordings, there was no evidence of his existence anywhere on the rig.

A sudden radio noise startled him.

'Brat Face,' Abby squawked. 'Mom wants to know when you're installing the radars.'

The neglected equipment was sitting on the platform deck, still packaged in original factory crates. Mom and Abby were taking their newfound profits and reinvesting them into the rig to it more attractive for sale, the added benefit of which was that they could keep a closer eye on what he was doing.

'I'll get to it later,' Adam said.

'You said that yesterday, *and* the day before that, you little shit.'

'Then come down here and install them yourself,' Adam snapped, slamming a tank filled to capacity with Helium-3 onto the deck. He was tempted to heave it over the side.

'That's out of character,' Abby said, in the most condescending tone possible. 'I'm sorry you're upset. But the radars are for your safety. It's dangerous to mine without them.'

'My safety?' Adam mocked. 'What do you care? Dad was the only one who did.'

As he resumed work, he noticed a change in the hunters' behaviour. Instead of playful beasts, they had become curious sentries, showing more interest in the platform than the bountiful herds of sustenance nearby.

'It's a difficult time for all of us,' Abby said. 'But we're so close to being able to move on.'

'To what?'

'Anything else.'

'I've got a say in that!' Adam shouted, dismissing another subtle change in the hunters' behaviour. 'Dad said I would!'

'Adam, you're just – too young.'

'But not too young to be down here?'

'We're grateful for your bravery,' Abby said, exasperated. 'But Mom and I make the important decisions now, because that's what we're better at.'

'You're not better at it,' Adam said. 'Not even close.'

'Okay, you want to be a grown-up? Here's a clue,' Abby hissed. 'The sooner you accept that Dad is gone, the easier this will be for everyone. So install the fucking radars. Please.'

She cut the line.

In that moment, Adam hated his sister so much he wished she was dead as well. And then, realising what he had just hoped for, he felt horrible shame. The darkness in his heart was getting worse. He had never felt more lost. Even the hunters and sturgeons had abandoned him. The sky was clear and he was alone in the clouds of Zeus once again.

He felt like crying, but was too exhausted to find the tears. Adam sat the mech down, and then onto its back. Gravity felt so good; he considered sleeping here instead of floating in a tethered bedroll. Looking up at the yellow clouds, he closed his eyes, and fell asleep.

What awoke him was the *tapping*.

A steady cadence of metal striking metal drew him from a fitful dream about his father.

Then came the realisation that it was darker than usual, followed by a revolting awareness that the mech's arm was being lifted and dropped onto the deck by something other than his own impulses.

Sitting upright, Adam saw Pegasus suspended above the rig, held in place by hunters, its expansive underside awash in a torrent of electrical activity. One of its enormous tentacles gently released its grip on the arm of Adam's mech.

The console was filled with its attempt to communicate with him.

ADAM
AWAKEN

Adam keyed the radio on, locking out the channel that his sister was using. It was good to see Pegasus, even if its menacing, overwhelming appearance turned his stomach into a ball of ice.

'Uh ... hello,' he said, shrugging in disbelief. 'How are you?'

A different pattern of flashes appeared, originating from four different locations on the beast's underside. Adam recognised that two were counting off letters; one forward, the other in reverse; the second set was numbers, one counting forward, the other in reverse.

Pegasus was offering a more efficient way to communicate: four simultaneous pulse channels instead of one.

'Okay, I understand,' Adam said, as the creature ceased its light show. 'I need a few minutes.'

Adam shook away the surreal circumstances and began typing changes to his decoding algorithm. When he was finished, he got up slowly.

Pegasus began to speak, and the hunters swayed in unison with the winds.

MOTHER KNOWS SADNESS

'She does?' Adam said, confused. 'I'm sorry ...'
The creature's language bathed the deck in strobes of light.

AS SHE IS
FOR YOU

'Why would she be sorry for me?'

DAD

An unwelcome burst of tears erupted from Adam's eyes.

WE HEAR WORDS
WHEN HUMANS FALL
WE
ARE SORRY

'I don't know what to say,' Adam stammered. 'What *are* you? Who is "Mother"?'

MOTHER IS ZEUS
SHE LIVES BELOW
AND WATCHES ALL

'You mean literally? Beneath this platform?'

THE DEPTHS

Adam considered the possibility that there were variants of the Arkady that neither he nor anyone else had ever seen before.

'How long have you ... or Mother ... been here?'

MOTHER KNOWS NO TIME
ONLY WHAT THE VEIL GAVE HER

'What did the Veil give her?'

HUMANS
OTHERS
THEIR LANGUAGES
THEIR KNOWLEDGE
THEIR MACHINES

'So, you know humans ... like me ... from listening to us talk, from the Veil?'

WE LISTEN
FEEL
LEARN

The massive tentacle coiled and gently tapped the deck again. Adam took a deep breath.

'Are you saying that when something ... falls from the Veil, into

276

Zeus ... that you can learn what that object is?'

MOTHER LEARNS

Adam could scarcely believe his eyes. Could it be that the countless bits of mining debris, from discarded waste to the accidents that sent men and machine to their deaths, made literal contact with 'Mother' somewhere along the way to implosive doom? Probes, satellites, rigs, entire *starships* had crashed into Zeus during the colonisation era. From what Adam knew about the Battle of Brotherhood, this was the final resting place for hundreds of ruined warships left adrift in the planet's iron grasp.

Mother's grasp. Mother Arkady.

The hunters simultaneously broke their rhythmic sway as pulses of excited light chatter exchanged between them and Pegasus.

'What just happened?' Adam asked. His eyes were beginning to hurt from the rapid fire strobes.

STRANGER SPEAKS
WITH ABBY

'My sister?'

ANOTHER FROM THE VEIL
APPROACHES

'What? Another ship?'

ADAM
TAKE US THERE
PLEASE

'How?'

Adam winced from a painful blast of premonition. Lethal danger was imminent.

MOTHER CAN SHOW Y CD A B

The underside of Pegasus erupted in a searing burst of light, blinding Adam and sending him staggering backwards. Blinking away phosphenes, he heard loud, dangerous *bangs* on the deck nearby. The hunters were going insane; most had released their grip on the railing and were flailing wildly. Pegasus was drifting away, its underside a coruscating fury. The four beacons flashed a hasty message.

A C
GO
A

The hunters had turned on themselves. Furious leviathans with unimaginable strength lashed out with their tentacles, carving off chunks of flesh from each other.

Adam jammed the throttle to run as fast as the mech could. Behind him, the deck was getting bashed to pieces.

Just before reaching the sled, he switched radio frequencies. When he turned around to step inside, he gasped.

The hunters were attacking Pegasus, and the gentle giant was breaking apart as gaping wounds were opened in a relentless, barbaric attack.

'Hi, Adam!' Abby said, in sarcastic cheer. 'Did you install the radars?'

'Who are you talking to up there?' Adam said, failing to keep the fear from his voice.

'No one, why?'

'You liar,' he whispered, cutting the line.

Adam slammed the launch trigger. The sled rockets ignited.

The wind tore Pegasus in half, and then the hunters quartered the carcass, decimating the last slabs of flesh.

Adam watched the disintegrating carcass as long as he could. The horror spread more darkness through his young heart.

They were waiting for him in the hangar.

'Hello, Adam,' the stranger said. 'My name is Captain Mohib of the Merckon Research vessel *Lycidas*.'

The mech's cockpit hatch had barely opened before his mother

278

led them all in; Abby, who appeared anxious; this captain; an armed Merckon security guard; and an exotic-looking woman who kept her distance from the main group.

'This is Doctor Viola Silveri,' Captain Mohib finally introduced her, 'the brightest xenologist in Orionis. Her speciality is Arkady research.'

Adam climbed down to the deck, avoiding eye contact.

'They're not with Ceti,' his mother explained. 'They want to help us.'

Adam began stripping off his survival suit, still sweating, and shaking. It wasn't from the cold.

Abby cleared her throat as he strapped into his mag greaves.

'He's shy around strangers,' she offered.

'Do strangers come here often?' Captain Mohib asked.

'Just the ones we owe money to,' Abby blurted.

'Which is to say no one comes by at all,' his mother interrupted. 'We are free of debt and profitable, thanks in large part to Adam's efforts.'

'He's a brave boy,' Captain Mohib said, flashing a disingenuous smile. 'That hunter tentacle you found spawned a legend. That's why we're here. We just had to meet the roughneck who took the beast down.'

Adam mashed the suit into his locker and slipped into dry clothes.

'Adam,' his mother said. 'These people have some questions they'd like to ask …'

The only one not blocking the exit was the 'doctor', and thus she was the only person in the room he decided not to hate. There was something trustworthy about her appearance, beneath her stunning, unnatural beauty. Her eyes were violet with traces of orange in them. They were unique, and held the only expression of concern in the room.

But the hatch was still ten metres away.

'… it would mean a lot to me if you answered them,' his mother said. With his head down, Adam began his walk towards freedom.

'You know, son,' Captain Mohib said. 'You can see the Lycidas from—'

'Don't call me that,' Adam snapped.

Everyone, Adam included, was surprised. He bit down the urge to say anything else and focused on taking the next step.

'Adam!'

It was Abby. She was the easiest to ignore.

'Your mother told us about your radar issues,' Captain Mohib called out, 'and that she had no idea what was really happening down there.'

Adam nearly stopped walking.

'So we put ours on,' Captain Mohib said, 'and saw something *extraordinary*. Don't you think?'

Adam's stomach churned as he remembered the words of Pegasus:

ELECTROMAGNETIC WAVES
WE FEEL THEM
SEE THEM
FROM AFAR

'Oh, no,' he whispered, halting as the truth sunk in:

The Lycidas*'s radar killed Pegasus.*

Intentional or not, it didn't matter. For as long as Adam remembered, the rig platform had never had functioning radars. That was almost certainly the reason why he had been able to get close to the Arkady at all. It also explained every hostile encounter between them and miners.

Adam remembered how Pegasus reacted when the burst of radar energy hit; it must have felt like being burned alive … indescribable agony, then panic, then madness. Quivering bulbs of tears grew in the corners of his eyes. The strangers looked upon him as if his secret was revealed. But none of them understood.

Except the doctor, whose hands were covering her mouth.

She knew.

'Is there something you'd like to share?' Captain Mohib asked.

Adam looked the doctor's way. She was already hurrying towards him.

'I am so sorry,' she whispered. 'Is there a place where just you and I can talk?'

Adam's 'room' was actually a storage compartment above the galley and mech hangar. No matter how much light was brought in, the rust-coloured bulkheads cast the place in perpetual gloom. There was no indication this was the room of a child. It was a place more befitting a mechanic, with spare mech components and old rig gauges anchored in place with plastic tie strips.

Viola spoke quietly.

'You're dehydrated,' she said, reaching into her duffel bag and pulling out several sport drink pouches. 'Please ... drink these before you become ill.'

Adam eyed them cautiously before accepting.

'Thanks,' he said. 'Does everyone from the Inner Rim have eyes like yours?'

Viola was taken aback by the comment.

'Well, I – it's not that uncommon, I think.'

'But still not exactly normal?'

'I suppose not.'

'That's okay,' Adam said, pulling out the sipping tube and taking a deep gulp. 'We aren't normal here either.'

'Trust me, "normal" is a subjective term.' Viola smiled, glancing around the room. 'It truly is miraculous you've survived here this long.'

Adam shrugged.

'We're just lucky, I guess.'

'You're too modest,' she said, examining one of the gauges. 'Luck is when preparation meets opportunity. I can't speak to the latter, but you were definitely prepared.'

Viola hooked the gauge back in place.

'I'm very sorry about your father,' she said.

Adam frowned.

'Whatever my mom or sister told you about him ... it's not the whole story,' he said.

'I believe you, Adam,' Viola said. 'I'm not here for the same reasons as Captain Mohib.'

'Then why are you here?'

'To learn as much as I can about the Arkady.'

'But why?'

'Because they exist,' Viola explained. 'With one exception, every contact between mankind and another species has ended in disaster. I want to study them before it's too late.'

Adam regarded her with suspicion.

'What about Captain Mohib?'

Viola shook her head. 'He only hopes the Arkady will make him richer.'

Adam began thinking again about how Pegasus had died.

'Why did your ship use its radar?'

Viola caught the change in his mood.

'The captain wanted imagery of the platform before sending us down,' she said. 'For what it's worth, I objected, but was overruled. The *Lycidas* is his.'

'So you knew it would kill them?'

Viola shook her head.

'No, I swear I didn't. I thought it might startle them, but couldn't prove why. I've only had dead tissue to work with.'

Adam considered her response.

'What kind of radar was it?'

Viola sighed.

'Phased array,' she said, '420 to 450 megahertz, eight thousand kilometre range. The Navy uses the same one for point defences on its cruisers. Some Merckon fool thought it would be useful for tracking Arkady specimens.'

Adam felt sick.

'What did you see?' he asked.

'Something no one has ever seen before,' Viola answered. 'The question is, what was it doing with you?'

Adam shrugged.

'We were talking,' he said.

'Thanks to our infrastructure improvements, we now produce two tons of Helium-3 per month,' said Abby, pointing to a graph projection hovering over her corelink. 'As you can see, additional investments could lead to logarithmic returns.'

Her audience consisted of her mother and Captain Mohib, who seemed amused, if a little bored.

'Mhmm, that's quite a pitch,' he said. 'Merckon has a programme for aspiring finance professionals. I can't speak for everyone, but I think you're a strong candidate. The next round of classes begin next month, at our Tabit Prime campus. Tuition and living expenses all complementary – with your mother's permission, of course.'

Abby was so excited that she looked ready to hyperventilate.

'Mom?'

Dawn Lethos smiled pleasantly.

'We can discuss this later,' she said. 'But I'm optimistic.'

'Abby is welcome to a tour of the *Lycidas*,' Captain Mohib said. 'My security officer can have her back here in an hour.'

Abby's eyes screamed 'Don't you dare say no'.

'That's fine,' Dawn said. 'One hour, Captain.'

'You have my word.'

'Thanks, Mom!' Abby said, and she was off to gather a few things.

'She's really bright,' Captain Mohib said. 'For a ghost, she'll do well.'

'I'm grateful for your offer,' Dawn said, 'but any agreement must guarantee the welfare of my children.'

Captain Mohib's eyes narrowed.

'There's a place for Adam in Merckon as well,' he said. 'After we determine the extent to which he is needed here for our research.'

'I speak for him, and my top concern is his safety and well-being,' Dawn stressed. 'You are never to give him an order without my approval, and I reserve the right to reject any unreasonable requests. Otherwise, there is no deal.'

The captain reached into his pocket and pulled out a cigar. Leaning back in his chair, he lit up.

'I'd prefer it if you didn't do that,' Dawn warned.

Captain Mohib blew out a puff of smoke. The haze hung in the air like industrial smog.

'If Adam fails to comply with us, the deal is void,' he said. 'Your daughter's enrolment relies on his cooperation, as does your own personal welfare.'

Dawn's cheeks reddened, but as she opened her mouth to speak, Captain Mohib waved her silent.

'Please, save your breath,' he said, leaning forward. 'See, I already own this rig. I bought it from Ceti months ago, which is why they haven't been around to beat their money out of *you* now that Thomas is dead.'

Dawn blinked at him, and a whisk of recognition smashed her gut. This was no ship captain.

'Who are you?' she asked.

'The years haven't been kind to you, *Dayla*,' Captain Mohib said, puffing more smoke. 'I doubt anyone at Titan would even recognise you.'

'They learned by listening to our radio transmissions,' Adam explained. 'Not just me talking with Abby, but people all over the planet. Haven't we been here for, I don't know, a hundred years? They heard all those conversations.'

He crumpled the empty drink packet and sent it gliding. Viola didn't even notice as it flew by, enraptured by what Adam was saying.

'They're beyond intelligent,' he continued. 'They have sympathy. They're ... living things with a heart of their own. Pegasus was a friend.'

Viola appeared to be in a trance.

'Are you even listening?' he asked. 'Hello?'

Viola sprang forward and clasped the boy in a gentle hug.

'Thank you,' she said.

'For what?'

'For being such a wonderful ambassador.'

Adam pushed himself away.

'Why are you happy?' he demanded. 'Pegasus is dead, and it's because you came here.'

'Oh Adam, if I could go back in time, I would have stopped Captain Mohib,' she implored. 'You don't understand what you've done. You've vindicated my commitment to the Arkady. In a sense, I've been looking for them my whole life. Thank you for bringing me closer.'

Adam stuffed his hands in his pockets.

'I just don't want anyone else to hurt them.'

'I vow to do everything in my power to make sure that doesn't happen,' she vowed. 'I don't want anyone from Merckon going anywhere near them.'

'What do they plan on doing?' Adam asked.

'They want to take live samples aboard,' Viola said. 'Which means going down there to hunt them.'

'Well, that's kind of what they want,' Adam said.

'What do you mean?'

'Pegasus told me they want to go to the "Veil",' Adam explained.

'It's their word for "space". Mother asked me to take her there, and said she would show me how.'

'"Mother"?' Viola said, perplexed. 'Yours?'

Adam shook his head.

'Theirs.'

'Why the mask, Travis?' Dawn Lethos, once known as Dayla Straka, asked. 'I thought fools with big egos preferred a high profile.'

'Because I always embed myself in my biggest risks,' Captain Mohib, aka Travis Mareck, said. 'Anonymity lets me determine who my best people are.'

'Anyone who doesn't show his face to his own team is a coward,' Dayla said.

'Quite an opinion, from someone who's been hiding for more than a decade,' Travis said. 'I don't know what you two did to earn the wrath of Argus Fröm, but the man never forgets a bad deed.'

'Tomas is dead,' Dayla said.

'And if you don't want your children to end up like him, listen carefully,' Travis said, twirling the cigar between his fingers. 'Titan Industries has a bounty on your head. We'll use that as an advance on Adam's services. Once I receive adequate recompense, the debt is paid and your anonymity remains safe. Until then, I own you, the boy, and this rig. Is that clear?'

Dayla glared blankly at the space in front of her.

'Tomas was able to set up some protection for us before he died. Argus knows his secret will be revealed if anything happens to me or my children,' she said. 'What are you after here?'

'Let's just say I've found a competitive entry in the biotech business,' Travis said. 'You're my risk insurance.'

'You don't know the highborns you're dealing with,' Dawn warned. 'You're a fool. Soon enough you'll end up dead for it.'

Travis laughed.

'You're welcome to the hospitality of the *Lycidas*,' he said. 'Your daughter will be treated like the firstborn she is, and I won't hold her father's sins against her. But until I get what I want, Adam is a ghost, and he is now the property of Merckon Corporation.'

'Shall I call keeping calling you "Travis"?' Dawn asked, avoiding eye contact. 'Or something more subtle, like Lord Mareck?'

'Assuming you want to keep your children alive, Dawn,' he said, stamping the cigar out on the kitchen table, 'you'll call me "Captain".'

28

WYLLYM

The flight school at Corinth was a domed amphitheatre that pilots called the 'Bird Nest'. It was a classroom of sorts, except instead of desks there were thirty grey, featureless, contoured seat moulds neatly spaced around a podium in the room's centre. Sprouting from the deck like sculptures, their sharp contrast with the glossy white ceiling gave the appearance more of a museum than a combat simulator. These were cast replicas of Gryphon cockpits; slipping on an AR helmet while seated in one would whisk the cadet into a simulation indistinguishable from the real world.

Wyllym had transformed cadets from bewildered rookies into lethal warriors in this very room, dissecting every combat exercise in painstaking detail so that everyone learned from each other's mistakes. Although there were now only seventeen Gryphon fighter craft in existence, the class had begun with thirty pilots. Today's extended session included those who had failed the programme, now participating by the direct orders of Grand Admiral Hedricks. For weeks, they had engaged in simulated joint operations against a Ceti fleet, in which nearly half the room was flying virtual enemy corvettes against the pilots who would fly real Gryphons from the *Archangel*'s decks into combat.

It was no substitute for the real thing, and the cadets knew it. Their apathy reflected in their horrendous performance in today's exercises, and Wyllym's patience was wearing thin.

Immersed in a simulated combat run, he reduced the speed of his Gryphon to let his wingmen take the lead. Six Ceti corvettes were less than three hundred kilometres away, and Wyllym's instruments indicated that their targeting radars were tracking the Gryphons. They could fire at any moment.

'Steady,' Wyllym announced. 'Break on my mark.'

Normally, the Gift would trigger the exact moment to 'break vector' and dodge the incoming fire. But his opponents were all former or current Gryphon pilots intentionally waiting for him to do just that. In a real scenario, the Ceti captains would have fired and retargeted by now. But, as Wyllym had known would happen, the pilots were gaming the simulation, which meant the exercise provided no benefit to combat preparation whatsoever. His request to use the range and real drones had been denied on the grounds that it was too taxing on the pilots before the real battle.

So it seemed fitting that the pilot on his right, Lieutenant Jaromir Ruslov, broke formation without permission.

'Breaking,' he announced pointlessly, steering his craft away from the formation in a lazy arc.

'Negative!' Wyllym corrected. 'Fall back!'

'Breaking,' the other pilot, Lieutenant Jans Orpyk, announced.

'No, goddamnit!' Wyllym snapped.

All six of the Ceti corvettes landed shells on Lieutenant Ruslov's Gryphon, vaporising it.

'Ruslov, terminated,' Wyllym's console announced. No time to eject.

Throwing his craft to the side, he began flying erratically to confuse the Ceti guns.

'Go to missiles!' Wyllym ordered. From this range, the fire-and-forget weapons would likely get shot down by the Ceti corvettes' point defences. But it might buy them precious seconds to evade and regroup.

But Lieutenant Orpyk was just as inept as his wingman.

'Missiles?' he asked. 'Why not.'

Wyllym wrenched his own AR helmet off before the console could inform him that Orpyk had been terminated as well.

'What the almighty fuck is wrong with you two?' he demanded, glaring at the pilots.

Lieutenant Orpyk removed his helmet and stretched.

'Sorry, sir, I thought you said "break".'

Lieutenant Ruslov had his feet up on the simulated cockpit.

'I did exactly what you told me to, *sir,*' he said. '"Break". So I'm taking one.'

As muted giggles filled the room, Wyllym realised there was not a single pilot with their helmet on.

No one had paid any attention to the exercise at all.

'What's going on here?' he demanded. 'Get back in the sim!'

Some of the pilots did nothing but stare ahead. Others, mostly the pilots that had failed, did so hesitantly.

Lieutenants Ruslov and Orpyk stood up.

'Unable, sir,' Ruslov announced, walking towards the exit.

Orpyk was right behind him.

'Punching out,' he said.

'You're both insubordinate,' Wyllym warned. 'You lose your wings for that.'

'I doubt it,' Ruslov said, turning to face the rest of the class. 'What are the rest of you doing?' he demanded. 'Don't you have better things to do than listen to this ghost trash?'

Wyllym was about to explode when Augustus Tyrell stormed into the room with armed guards behind him.

Lieutenant Ruslov met him at the door.

'The rat is over there, Commander,' he said.

'Get back to your post,' Augustus growled, shouldering the smaller man aside as he marched down the aisle, guards in tow. 'The rest of you stay put and shut up. Admiral Lao will be here soon to debrief you.'

Wyllym stood up as Augustus halted right before him.

'Captain Wyllym Lyons,' the police commander said.

'Ty?' Wyllym said.

Augustus's eyes betrayed a fleeting moment of sorrow.

'I'm placing you under arrest,' he said, reaching forward and slapping cuffs on Wyllym's wrists.

Wyllym was too stunned to answer as the guards hooked his elbows.

'I, Commander Augustus Tyrell of the Orionis Navy Police, am investigating the alleged offence of treason, of which you are suspected,' Augustus said. 'You have the right to remain silent.'

'Ghosts ought to be seen and not heard,' quipped Lieutenant Orpyk. 'Traitor.'

Some of the pilots snickered.

Wyllym was nudged forward, mouth agape. Then he snapped out of it, trying to save some semblance of dignity, straightening his posture as he was walked down the aisle of cadets.

'Any statement you make may be used against you in a trial by court martial,' Augustus continued.

The vitriol from the cadets continued.

'Space him!' someone shouted.

'You have the right to consult military counsel of your own choosing at your own expense,' Augustus continued. 'Do you understand the rights I just read you?'

Wyllym heard applause and shouts of approval.

'I do,' he said.

'Wyll,' Augustus said, pausing as they reached the exit. 'Did you disclose classified information to Chancellor Vespa Jade regarding Ceti's plans, disobeying a direct order from your commanding officer?'

Wyllym nodded.

The door to the Bird Nest shut, silencing the merciless jeers inside.

'You are one righteous son of a bitch, you know that?' Augustus growled.

'Someone has to be,' Wyllym said.

They marched on, eventually arriving at the Corinth detention centre, twenty levels beneath the Bird Nest. Aside from hosting the occasional drunk serviceman, the facility was rarely used.

'You have the distinction of being the first Navy officer to ever be charged with treason,' Augustus said. 'You're also Gifted, which means you're considered an elevated security risk. The rules are very explicit about this. We have to hold you in solitary confinement.'

Wyllym peered inside. A vacuum toilet, sink, and padded walls in a room two metres by two metres across.

'The right choice is always difficult,' he muttered.

Augustus nudged him inside.

'You don't need to tell me,' he said. 'I'm sorry, Wyll.'

The doors shut, and the lights went out.

Wyllym assumed sleeping would lead to madness.

The transition from dreaming to consciousness was like living a short life and dying abruptly; the brain became incapable of distinguishing between the living past and dreams. All memories, good or bad, led to darkness.

Deprived of light, and thus reference, it was becoming difficult to believe his life had ever happened at all.

Wyllym reflected that he had been dead once before. As a sworn protector of Orionis, he had sacrificed himself on a celestial battlefield, killing the Ceti criminals threatening law and order. Even in death, the Navy had refused to let him have peace. Wyllym had been grateful to be alive once more because he had looked forward to a life of solitude. But Orionis had found one more battle for him to fight. And he *would* fight, because the government could always exploit his innate call to duty. The needs of Orionis always came before his own.

The theme of every memory that found him in the darkness was pain. The anguish of losing most of his family years ago. The physical torture of countless Gryphon sorties. Dying, and returning to life. The lack of gratitude from the Navy – or anyone else – for his selfless sacrifice. And now, imprisonment for honouring the oath he had taken as an officer, all to protect a government that barely afforded him the basic recognition of human dignity.

And to what end? He had no children. He barely had any contact with his sister. No one else to love, or who loved him. In fact, he had never felt attracted to anyone his entire life. Every friendship along the way had been difficult, and he felt uncomfortable around civilians. Why, especially now, should he care about Orionis?

The answer was so simple he laughed aloud. Life was a game of lesser evils – like choosing between Vespa Jade's flawed governance or the tyrannical potential of Hedricks and the *Archangel*. He would always pick the side that he believed gave the human race the best chance to survive.

This was a primordial selection, not a rational one. Just *live*. Live at all costs. Find a way to convince politicians that humans should never be the enemy. Remind them that their homeworld was no more than a memorial on Tabit Prime.

Wyllym was about to doze off again when the door suddenly flew open.

'Hello, Wyll,' the gruff voice of Augustus announced. Wyllym was blinded by the light pouring in from the hallway, and felt big hands lift him up. 'On your feet, man. We don't have much time.'

'How long has it been?' Wyllym asked, eyes squeezed shut. He felt his wrists being placed in cuffs again.

'Forty-one hours,' Augustus responded. 'Sorry about these. Just in case we're spotted.'

'What's happening to me?'

'No one goes in unless I clear it,' Augustus instructed a guard Wyllym still couldn't see.

'Understood, sir,' a young woman replied.

'We're going to meet some people you can trust,' Augustus said. 'No cameras or recording devices.'

'Trust them with what?'

'Wyll, you were right to tell the Chancellor,' Augustus said. 'I'm ashamed I didn't. Hedricks is up to some very sinister things, and we need your help figuring out what they are.'

They ended up at an interrogation room. Two guards with weapons slung across their chests waved them inside. Wyllym noticed one of the lockers was open. Several corelinks and at least one implantable cybernetic augmentation chip were inside, in addition to a pair of AR eyepieces.

Augustus placed his own corelink inside the locker and shut it.

'HVI interrogation,' he told the guards. 'Do not disturb.'

'Yes, sir,' the guards acknowledged.

Augustus removed the cuffs from Wyllym.

'We're secure,' he said, opening the door. 'In you go.'

Wyllym took one step and stopped. One of his Gryphon pilots – Lieutenant Vronn Tarkon, Cerlis Tarkon's youngest child – was inside. Blonde, light-eyed, and tall, built from his mother's highborn pedigree. The training had taken its toll on him, but his genetically engineered constitution was dealing with the punishment much better than Wyllym's was. For all his talent, Vronn had barely made the cut to become a Gryphon. But he was a good student, reserved, and always respectful.

The other man was an older Orionis Navy Police captain. He sat at the head of the interrogation room table, which was presently arranged more like a conference centre, complete with comfortable chairs and refreshments.

'Captain Lyons, it's an honour,' the eldest said, standing. 'Tobias Nilsson, Director of Internal Affairs. Please,' he said, motioning towards the table, 'eat something, you must be starved.'

Lieutenant Tarkon was on his feet, saluting.

'Sir,' he said.

'What's he doing here?' Wyllym demanded.

'Lieutenant Tarkon is a material witness in our investigation,' Augustus said. 'He has a story you need to hear.'

Wyllym took a seat. The refreshments made his stomach growl, and he reached for a bowl with strawberries and apples.

'I apologise for your treatment in front of the cadets,' Augustus said. 'You're pinned down in political crossfire – that was the only play we had.'

The fruit was delicious. Wyllym had never appreciated the taste of synthetics more in his life.

'Our investigation began with a Navy project codenamed "Basilisk",' Tobias said. 'Do you have any recollection of it?'

Wyllym nodded, looking for something to wipe his mouth with. A stubbly beard had grown across his face, and bits of the red fruit were smeared across it.

'I didn't have the clearance, but the rumour was out there,' he said, reaching for coffee. 'Haven't heard it mentioned in years.'

'Basilisk was developing Gryphon shielding technology,' Tobias explained. 'It was cancelled prior to completion two years ago. The project's source files were copied by several officers, including Admiral Hedricks. By itself, that isn't unusual. But every time a Navy file is manipulated anywhere with corelink access, it sends a burst packet back to us. I'll spare you the technical details, but our forensics team believes those files were copied to an illegal device somewhere in the vicinity of Brotherhood.'

The coffee could have been brewed with bathwater, and it would still have tasted delicious.

'You remember the Ceti briefing,' Augustus said. 'Their fleet underwent structural modifications. It's circumstantial, but there's a good chance they have Basilisk.'

'What kind of shielding is it?' asked Wyllym.

'It makes ships nearly impervious to kinetic arms fire,' Tobias said.

'Nearly?'

'Shields need time to recharge,' Augustus said.

'Why was it cancelled?' Wyllym asked, eyeing an apple.

'Officially, for budget reasons,' Tobias said. 'Unofficially, we have no idea. Hedricks signed off on the funding termination.'

'Did it work?'

'Apparently, we're all going to find out,' Tobias said. 'Either Ceti picked up where our research left off, or the tech always worked and bogus results were recorded in the logs. Trouble is – there isn't time to find out.'

Wyllym took a bite from the apple. It was bitter, but that didn't stop him from tearing off a few more bites.

'The closer the *Archangel* was to completion, the more Hedricks compartmentalised information,' Augustus said. 'And there are highborns managing the political and legal implications for him.'

Wyllym thought the pile of discarded strawberry leaves on the table was more interesting than anything they were saying. He crunched into the apple again.

Augustus tapped his fingers impatiently.

'Just so you know,' he said, 'Hedricks had every armed soldier removed from the *Archangel*. He also tampered with your pilot list.'

Wyllym stopped chewing.

Augustus nodded.

'I believe the lieutenant can provide details,' he said.

Vronn Tarkon cleared his throat. He had yet to make eye contact with Wyllym.

'Sir,' he began. 'While you were in jail, pilots Decanto, Navokov, and Mosa were grounded by Rear Admiral Lao. He said the order came directly from Admiral Hedricks, and that they were subject to a misconduct investigation.'

Wyllym set the apple core down.

'What "misconduct" did they commit?'

'Admiral Lao didn't say, but word is they've been accused of worshipping the Red.'

Wyllym stifled a groan. If it was true, they could be expelled from the Navy. Even if they were innocent, the accusation alone was enough to ruin their careers.

'Well, are they?'

Vronn's face reddened.

'No, sir, they are not,' he said.

'Would you say that in a court martial?' Wyllym asked.

'Yes, I would,' Vronn affirmed. 'They don't believe in anything except their vow to the Navy.'

'Who did Lao replace them with?'

'Solomon, Adams, and Nkembeh.'

'Worst of the bunch,' Wyllym snorted.

'Grandparents are all living highborns,' Tobias noted.

'Sir, permission to speak freely,' Vronn asked.

Wyllym folded his hands and leaned forward.

'By all means, Lieutenant,' he said.

Vronn took a deep breath.

'When the programme started, a lot of guys flaunted their highborn status while muscling for influence,' the pilot began. 'Dom and I were among the few who kept our distance. Eventually Solomon won the popularity contest. From the start, he set out to undermine you. He appealed to highborn elitism, spoke often of his hatred of ghosts. The only thing that kept his camp from open revolt was the fact you've never been beaten, in the sim or in space.'

Wyllym kept his eyes locked on Vronn's.

'Solomon despised you to an unnatural extent,' the pilot continued. 'Eventually he began threatening the rest of us, the ones who wouldn't go along with him. He knew deeply personal information about our parents or siblings and tried to blackmail us with it.'

Vronn's anger was evident.

'It is true that Dominic has great interest in the Raothri,' he said. 'He studies them because he believes they're the ones we should be training to fight against. But the notion he worships them is ridiculous. While Solomon ran his antics, Dom hosted open sessions to study Raothri engagements in the final hours of Earth contact. His grandparents were *Christians*. They raised him as one. For him to be accused of worshipping an alien species ... that is bullshit, sir.'

Vronn was looking at his hands as though he was ashamed.

'Lieutenant Tarkon contacted us right after you were arrested,' Tobias said.

'We wanted to approach you about this much sooner,' Vronn blurted out.

'Then why didn't you?' Wyllym asked.

Vronn shook his head in apparent disbelief.

'I realise this oversteps my remit, but the reason is because you never engaged with us beyond the flight deck,' he said. 'The ghost comments, the prejudice ... with all due respect, that was self-imposed, sir. You are the most accomplished captain and pilot in the Orionis Navy, highborn or otherwise. If you led, soldiers would follow.'

Holding his glare at the lieutenant, Wyllym took another sip of coffee.

Augustus held up four fingers.

'We have stolen Navy tech, manipulation of *Archangel* personnel assignments, withholding critical information from the Chancellor, and a pending Ceti offensive that gives him a convenient reason to take full control of the *Archangel*,' he said. 'Unfortunately, Orionis law requires us to presume innocence until proof of guilt. But sometimes evidence gathering is just a formality. The implications here are so grave, I move to bring him in right now for an interrogation.'

Wyllym had heard enough.

'Look at all of you,' he said. 'Due cause is a "formality" for you? Who's the scheming highborn now?'

'Wait a minute—' Augustus started. But Wyllym would have none of it.

'I honoured my oath to Orionis and was accused of *treason*,' he said. 'What was the point of bringing me down here? To get me to implicate myself in an actual crime?'

'Captain, we need your help to build a legal case against Hedricks,' Tobias said. 'But to do that, we need to know what other interactions you've had with him or other members of OPCOM, especially if you saw anything suspicious.'

'I never trusted him,' Wyllym said. 'But he gave me all the latitude I needed to train those pilots. Beyond that, I had nothing to say to him, and the feeling was mutual.'

He turned towards Vronn Tarkon.

'Thank you for sharing your analysis, Lieutenant,' Wyllym growled. 'But the wall between people like me and the privileged – which is every one of you! – is *real*. I have no clue what Admiral Hedricks is planning, but he's on your fucking side of the wall. Deal with it.'

'You just proved that his opinion of you is spot-on,' Augustus said.

'So promote him,' Wyllym spat.

'I swore the same oath you did,' Augustus growled. 'Hedricks just jailed his best pilot on the eve of a *fucking invasion*. Yes, it's circumstantial. But you're an idiot if you don't think it's significant. Stop acting like a victim, Wyll. We have to get in front of this!'

'I'm no combat tactician,' Tobias said. 'But speaking on behalf of the Orionis government, we'd very much like for you to be in a Gryphon when Ceti arrives. Chancellor Jade has given us executive authority to do whatever it takes to make that happen.'

Wyllym shook his head.

'How could that possibly be done?'

'By taking mine,' Vronn offered, drawing stares from Augustus and Tobias. 'I'll sit in your cell. You take my Gryphon.'

'It would end your career,' Wyllym said.

'My career ended the moment I walked in here,' Vronn replied. 'That was my choice, and I would do it again.'

'This is *mutiny*,' Wyllym said. 'You understand that, right? A government-sponsored coup. The irony is striking.'

'You're wrong,' Augustus said. 'This is a criminal investigation and enforcement of Orionis law. By the way, welcome to Internal Affairs. You want irony? I'm your boss now.'

'Your court martial won't happen before Ceti arrives,' Tobias said. 'As far as the Navy is concerned, your flying days are over.'

'And when it comes to flying Gryphons, there's no one better,' Augustus said. 'But you can't read people for shit. So leave the personnel assessments to me from now on. I know who my loyal troops are. We're going to get you into the fight, but you'll have to trust me.'

'Captain,' Tobias said, noting the clock on the interrogation room wall.

'Right,' Augustus said, rising from his seat. 'Time for you to go back to jail.'

29

VESPA

For a change, Vespa was immersed in a warm social atmosphere devoid of political scheming or overt hostility. She was aboard a government shuttle with twenty children, their parents, and her press secretary, Liza Brenner. The young scholars were the brightest academic performers in their respective schools, all firstborns no more than nine years of age. The reward for their excellence in the prestigious 'Future Leaders' programme was a personal tour of Tabit Prime by the Orionis Chancellor herself. Students watched in awe as the domed craft flew past the most impressive spectacles; the torus ring of Luminosity, the Merckon Spire, the Bernal sphere of Vulcan Industries, and the Mulberry Colonies at the space elevator of the Eileithyian moon Amnisos.

The Navy cruiser *Sacramento* drew the most wondrous gasps from wide-eyed children who had never seen a warship's railguns before. As the shuttle flew by, the Navy captain obliged by opening the ship's missile bays for show. The kids loved it, and the adults applauded. Vespa just sighed, forcing herself to smile through a brief lecture about the armed forces of Orionis. There were a few aspiring naval officers on board, after all.

But as they approached the *Tabit Genesis*, Vespa felt nothing but angst. No one aboard, save for Liza, was aware of the danger they faced.

To preserve a memorable experience for the children, Vespa had ordered security to keep the press away from the hangar. This was to spare them from the mob who wanted her to address the persistent rumours of a Ceti invasion. For weeks, she had answered with political vagaries carefully aligned with the official Navy response: the rumours are unsubstantiated, and even if true, the threat itself was negligible.

As she posed for pictures with the families, all Vespa could think about was *Tabit* engulfed in flames.

A flood of updates assaulted her as the last child waved goodbye. Financial markets, reacting to invasion rumours, were pushing food prices higher. Corporations were stockpiling Helium-3, raising the cost of fuel. The CRO was losing value as the electronic currency was converted into commodities. Angry corporate executives were demanding attention from disgruntled Senators already pressured by nervous constituents. Intelligence agencies were generating lists of potential Ceti sympathisers and cross-referencing their personal history with shipping manifests for potential bomb-making materials.

At least the Freetracks demanding an end to the Heritage Act were silenced in the mix.

Cancelling her appointments for the rest of the evening, she began responding to queries without even consciously reading them. For now, the cognitive functions of her brain were detached from her anxieties; she was half immersed in reality, while the rest of her cowered in the scar left behind by the Gift. A combination of drugs prescribed by ORPHUS and cybernetic implants allowed her to multitask like this, splitting her brain into two separate realms at the price of an urgent need to sleep more often. But then the visions would return, awakening her even when sedated, and the damage was mounting.

The AI reminded her of this as she returned to the suite.

'You are unwell,' ORPHUS warned, its blue eye tracking her into the kitchen. 'I have detected accumulated toxins and elevated radiation levels in your blood. You need a transfusion, and rest.'

'What else have you learned about the Hades Terminus?' she demanded. Vespa was determined to learn what the significance of that desolate region of space had to her nightmare.

'I have learned that a privateer freighter registered with Iopa Conglomerate witnessed Lightspear activity while en route from Hyllus to the Belt. I have also learned that four freighters have reported departure delays from the Heracles fuelling depot.'

Vespa reached for a drug packet. Each one contained twenty-seven pills of all different shapes and colours. More than half were just to control the side effects of the psychoactive agents.

'For what reason?' she asked, tearing one open.

'Unspecified,' ORPHUS replied. 'And no ETA was provided.'

'Compute a role for Iopa in a plot to attack the *Tabit Genesis*,' she ordered. 'Run background checks on their employees and contractors. Look for past dealings with Ceti. Based on this information, what are the odds—?'

'Somewhere between zero and impossible,' Arturus said, his face a two-metre apparition that ORPHUS projected in her bedroom. Even through the static distortion in the image, he looked younger than when he had first arrived.

'What the hell are you doing here?' she hissed.

'ORPHUS called me,' the talking head said. 'He and I have an understanding when it comes to you.'

Vespa was furious.

'I should have you arrested,' she snarled. 'Have you been listening to every single—'

'Relax,' Arturus assured. 'ORPHUS is concerned about your health, and hopes I can convince you to take his advice. So hello, Vespa. What ails you this evening?'

'I have work,' she growled, arranging the pills on the counter. 'Good night.'

'I see that,' he said. 'Pardon my intrusion, but you really do look awful. ORPHUS is right. You need sleep.'

'I can have stronger sleep agents synthesised to suit your needs,' the AI offered.

'I'm sure you can,' Vespa remarked, pouring a glass of water. The temptation was greater than she would ever admit. 'But no thanks.'

'If you slept, you could see past your fixation,' Arturus said. 'Without rest, you have no Gift.'

'I don't need a lecture,' she said.

'I no longer dream of a *Tabit Genesis* inferno,' Arturus persisted. 'I've seen hints there may be some benefit to starting over, opportunities in the aftermath—'

301

Vespa slammed a hand down on the counter, sending several pills over the side.

'*Stop*,' she exclaimed. 'What do you want?'

The smug expression on her brother's face evaporated.

'To offer counsel on the eve of the greatest challenge you've ever faced,' he said.

'It's not counsel I need from you,' she hissed. 'Or House Alyxander.'

'If I may be blunt,' Arturus said, 'votes ought to be the least of your concerns, given your visions about this place.'

Vespa knelt to search for the pills that had fallen.

'Then why are we still speaking?' she asked. 'Ambassadors are busy people. Don't you have drugs to take? Whores to screw?'

'I am guilty of those things, but I'd prefer to think that it's only my message you hate.'

ORPHUS shone two spotlights on the floor, revealing the missing pills.

'I'd like to be your brother, not a politician,' Arturus said.

Sleep deprivation always made her vulnerable, but she was especially susceptible to him. When they had been frightened young outcasts, cursed with the Gift and discovering their own sexuality, she had thought that she loved him more than just as a brother. With everyone else in her life being so incapable of understanding her, Arturus was a soul mate.

Senses dulled by wild hormones and emotional frailty made her surrender to a single moment of weakness: an attempted kiss. Not a harmless peck on the cheek as she had done countless times before, but a deep one right on his lips, followed by a pause fraught with passionate anticipation.

As his face had twisted through shock and then anger, Vespa's world had collapsed. A true love's rejection is never crueller than to an unsullied heart, and she never forgot it.

Years later, after he was reformed in the cybernetic ways of House Alyxander, he confessed that her action had launched him on a journey of self-discovery that didn't change his rejection of her, but had instead opened his mind to many different attractions.

Vespa had never accepted that. In her mind, they remained soul mates. The Gift, and the burden it bestowed, united them as one.

Crawling towards illumination, she scooped up a pill and sat back against the counter.

'It's impossible for Ceti to hurt us here,' she sighed. 'Why do I keep having this vision?'

'Lance agrees with you,' Arturus said. 'Business is brisk. He has no intention of moving his trade barges.'

'That's either irresponsible of him, or he thinks your Gift is worthless.'

'No, he just enjoys daring people to fuck with him.'

Vespa began arranging the pills in order on the counter.

'Could Hedricks have a part in this?'

Arturus frowned.

'I've considered it. The highborns want another Hedricks to captain the next ark for mankind. I doubt Vadim would turn the *Archangel* against them, let alone the Orionis government. The simplest explanation is that he wants a war to hang his legacy on, and to vindicate the existence of that awful ship.'

Vespa shook her head.

'Tomorrow I expect he'll tell us that an invasion is just business as usual for the Navy and nothing to concern ourselves with.'

'If he even shows,' Arturus said. 'What do you hope to gain by confronting him?'

She washed the first batch of pills down.

'Only to remind him that the Navy serves the people of Orionis, and is accountable to the government they elected.'

'I think he knows that.'

Vespa shook her head.

'I've ordered Augustus Tyrell to launch a treason investigation against him.'

'That was rather ... bold.'

'No charges to be filed until this Ceti mess is dealt with,' she said, swallowing another batch. 'If we're still here.'

Arturus regarded her as she fumbled for the next set of pills.

'Is it your own death that you're so afraid of?' he asked. 'Or everyone else's?'

Vespa didn't answer, fixating on the remaining line of drugs.

'Did you ever consider the Gift tricked you into *making* the future you feared most?' Arturus asked. 'And that removing old Don from power was what put you on this very path?'

Although she felt no compelling guilt for ending the man's life, her eyes filled with tears.

'Go to hell,' she said.

'If you're so certain the vision will happen,' Arturus continued, 'then all that remains is a clear conscience. What are you prepared to do?'

'I don't know,' Vespa confessed. 'Ceti believes they have nothing to lose.'

'Then petition them for peace.'

That made Vespa angry.

'In the purest definition of the word, they are terrorists,' she said. 'Vladric Mors does not negotiate. He's obsessed with destroying this government. What do you offer someone like that? The man doesn't want peace. He wants … closure.'

'Give it to him,' Arturus said. 'Make him a real offer. Disarm the *Archangel*. Abolish Heritage. Give Ceti no reason to fight.'

'And let them win the war? On principle alone, the prospect is appalling.'

'Ceti would win a footnote in history,' Arturus explained. 'Your name will be disgraced, but the subtext will be that your actions, by avoiding war, undoubtedly saved lives – millions of *Ceti* lives. Address Vladric, but speak to *them*. They're just as sceptical of his ambitions as we are. Force the man to answer them.'

Vespa slumped into a chair.

'"Our dawn and hope for all Humankind",' she muttered, quoting the Earth memorial in Liberty Hall. 'I don't want to be the one who let *Tabit* burn.'

Arturus shook his head.

'Take your pills and rest, Vespa,' he said. 'Be unafraid of the night. But when you awaken, leave your pride behind.'

It was Sunday, and Liberty Hall was nearly empty. While the odd employee or two could be seen at work, the precious space was otherwise deserted, and the press rarely bothered to lurk about this day of the week. Vespa was counting on that. Behind the hall were smaller antechambers for the Senate's six committees, which hosted closed hearings. She never appeared unless invited, and then only virtually.

In private meetings with each member, Vespa had convinced the Military Services Committee to force Hedricks to testify. They shared her concern about the Navy's increasing distance from governance and, as mostly final term senators, they had no political risk in pursuing answers aggressively. From the Chancellor's office, she was virtually seated on the bench with them. Rear Admiral Jang Lao marched through the door precisely on time, drawing mutters from the seven senators glaring at him. He sat at the witness table, posture perfectly straight, and looked up at them.

Senator Alaister Roddick, the committee leader, spoke first.

'You're not the admiral we asked to come here today,' he said.

'My apologies, Senator,' Admiral Lao said. 'But Admiral Hedricks will attend virtually.'

Vespa watched as Hedricks materialised beside Lao. His arrogance came through even in the delayed feed.

'Good morning, your honours. Chancellor,' Admiral Hedricks said, nodding towards Vespa. 'I'm afraid operational responsibilities prevent me from attending in person.'

Senator Roddick was 110 years old and still talked like the twenty-year-old chemical engineer he used to be. His district was the Mulberry Colonies, and although he aligned with the Freetracks Guild, Vespa enjoyed his company and often worked with him to find common ground on issues with her own Genesis party.

'Senate subpoenas mandate a physical presence,' Senator Roddick stated. 'Notwithstanding emergency extenuating circumstances, you are in contempt.'

Admiral Hedricks didn't flinch.

'My primary responsibility is the defence of Orionis,' he said, 'and those circumstances are always extenuating.'

'We'll be the judge of that,' Senator Margaery Brusceau intervened. She was one of twelve representatives from the Vulcan colonies on Eris. 'Admiral, as far as I'm concerned, withholding material information concerning national security is indistinguishable from perjury. Now, is there anything you wish to share with us?'

Again, Admiral Hedricks was completely impassive before the implied threat.

'Ceti is launching an attack on the *Archangel*,' he said. 'Their fleet has already departed Brotherhood.'

Vespa watched the senators' expressions. Hedrick's matter-of-fact delivery infuriated everyone.

'Where is this fleet now?' Senator Roddick growled.

'The Belt, approximately.'

'"Approximately",' Senator Brusceau repeated, shaking her head. 'When were you planning to tell us?'

'I never planned to inform you.'

Vespa was pleased to observe the bipartisan outrage at his answer.

'I beg your pardon?' Senator Brusceau snapped. But Admiral Hedricks remained inscrutable.

'There are skirmishes with Ceti warships every day,' he said. 'This is no different.'

That was the last straw for Senator Brandon Tice.

'No *different*?' he exclaimed. 'With their entire fleet bearing down on us?'

'That is correct, with the exception of the outcome,' Admiral Hedricks said. 'This is our chance to decisively end the war, eliminate the largest criminal organisation in human history, and reclaim Brotherhood.'

'Your arrogance is appalling,' Senator Tice snarled. 'What about public safety? How dare you withhold information like that from us?'

'There is no danger to public safety,' Admiral Hedricks said, 'and I have withheld nothing from you.'

'The attempt to obscure news of an invasion is criminal conduct,' Senator Roddick pointed out.

'I never used the word "invasion",' Admiral Hedricks said. 'I choose my words with more care, lest people misconstrue meaning, or, as tends to be the case in politics, sensationalise reality.'

'Drop the cavalier attitude right now,' Senator Brusceau warned, drawing stares from everyone. 'I'm weighing whether or not to charge you with dereliction of duty. You're under oath. Explain to us exactly what is happening.'

'There are times when the most effective means to crush an enemy is to let them in close,' Admiral Hedricks said. 'The defences at Corinth alone could pulverise their fleet, but with the *Archangel*, Ceti may as well fly into the sun.'

'Do you really need to be reminded of your *obligation* to keep us informed?' Senator Tice said. 'This is a major engagement that puts Ceti weapons in range of civilian targets inside the Belt.'

'I provide this committee with a report that details enemy engagements every week, thus fulfilling my obligation.'

'*After* the fact,' Senator Brusceau fumed. '*After* you've taken the welfare of Orionis into your own hands.'

'The loss of Brotherhood illustrates what happens when politics dictate tactics,' Admiral Hedricks said. 'Had I used your vernacular to describe Ceti's present activity, the politics would have compelled a rush to meet them in the open, which would result in disaster. I swore an oath to protect Orionis, and that includes protecting it from itself.'

'Admiral, your assessment is wrong,' Senator Roddick said. 'Brotherhood was lost because we weren't prepared. This time we are, and your efforts undermine our ability to respond intelligently and with minimal loss of life.'

'Senator,' Admiral Hedricks said, straightening his posture. 'You seem disappointed that Ceti's days are numbered. Then again, twenty-five per cent of the Orionis economy is military expenditure. I suppose I can't blame you.'

Senator Roddick's eyes narrowed.

'What the hell is that supposed to mean?'

'Your constituents build the weapons that your political sponsors sell to the Navy. The relationship has made you a wealthy man. So when you undermine me, you just end up hurting yourself.'

Vespa had heard enough. The case for prosecuting Admiral Hedricks had never been stronger. Now it was time for the hard work.

'Thank you so much for meeting with us, Admiral,' she said. 'I realise the defence of Orionis is a tremendous responsibility. I appreciate you taking the time to answer our questions.'

'The honour is mine, Chancellor Vespa.'

'I have no doubt that you'll crush our Ceti foes,' she continued. 'However, I am disappointed about Captain Lyons's arrest. I would never have known about your future heroics if not for him.'

'Captain Lyons is well, Chancellor.'

'I hope you don't mind my prying,' Vespa continued, somewhat enjoying herself. 'After all, I need to have medals minted in advance of your triumph. You're far too modest about your achievements, planned or otherwise. Much as I loathe the idea of spoiling your glory, I'm going to propose something radical, something perhaps no one on this committee would have suggested, even had we known an invasion was imminent. Admiral Lao, I could use your assistance here.'

The officer was surprised to have been brought into the conversation. 'Chancellor?' he asked.

'Let's say I wanted to communicate with the Ceti fleet,' Vespa said. 'How would I go about doing that?'

Admiral Lao blinked.

'Without a hard fix on their location, secure comms is impossible,' he answered.

'Who said anything about secure?' Vespa asked. 'I don't care who hears this.'

Lao glanced towards Admiral Hedricks before answering.

'They can't respond without giving away their position,' Admiral Lao said.

'I don't give a damn if they answer,' Vespa snapped. 'I hate to ruin the joy of zapping Ceti corvettes, but slaughtering millions just because you *can* doesn't mean that you *should*. Now, that fleet would still hear a general broadcast on the freight channels, correct?'

Admiral Hedricks moved ever so slightly.

'Think carefully upon what you are doing, Chancellor,' he warned.

Vespa smiled.

'Admiral Lao,' she said. 'Ready a general broadcast.'

'You'll be routed through our search and rescue frequencies,' the officer muttered, typing away on his corelink. 'Every receiver from here to the Hades Terminus will hear it. Is that what you want?'

The committee members appeared either aghast or perplexed. Senator Tice was the former.

'Now hold on a minute,' he blurted. 'What happened to trying to avert a panic?'

Vespa looked right at him.

'The more people that hear this, the better.'

Admiral Lao had a resigned look on his face.

'Just a moment,' he said, manipulating the device one last time. 'And ... you're live.'

Vespa glanced at the flashing icon on her corelink for a moment, then picked it up.

'Vladric Mors,' she said, 'this is Chancellor Vespa Jade. I know you're listening. I know your fleet is approaching. And I know that your goals may be achieved without violence. Surely a man charged with the welfare of so many has the courage to try dialogue. For the sake of those under your command, I challenge you to take the higher ground.'

Vespa terminated the connection.

'We'll adjourn for now,' she said. 'Admiral Hedricks, if he hasn't answered by the time he's in range of your guns, then by all means, defend Orionis.'

'Thank you, Chancellor. Senators.'

The moment his image vanished, Senator Roddick slammed his fist.

'I want that son of a bitch thrown in jail.'

Senator Brusceau was shaking her head.

'Chancellor, I wish we had discussed this beforehand,' she said.

Vespa nodded.

'I know how it looks,' she said, 'but this government has a moral obligation to reveal what the Admiral was hiding. Better to pre-empt this on our own terms before someone spots their fleet. Liza is about to release a statement that puts the danger in perspective. She'll answer questions until I can address the nation.'

Vespa breathed deeply.

'I accept full responsibility for Hedricks's insubordination,' She admitted. 'I should have reined him in sooner. It will be dealt with once this invasion mess is sorted.'

Admiral Lao suddenly cursed. All heads turned towards him.

'It's *him*,' he said. 'Vladric Mors. We're tracing it.'

Vespa was shocked.

She picked up her corelink again.

'Vladric?'

There was no video. Only a deep, scratchy voice.

'Chancellor.'

'You heard my offer?' she asked.

'I heard a plea for mercy,' Vladric said.

'On behalf of your own people,' she said.

'My conscience is clear, Vespa. How is yours?'

'You can't win,' she said. 'Not without my help.'

'I've already won,' he said. 'Orionis knows the truth about you now.'

'And what truth is that?' Vespa asked.

'That you believe in ghosts.'

'Don't talk in semantics. I'm trying to save people's lives.'

'Heritage destroyed more lives than I ever could,' Vladric said. 'I've taken every unwanted synthetic foetus of highborn society and raised them as my own. What have you raised?'

'Humankind, in a sensible, sustainable way,' Vespa snapped. 'You know why that policy exists. Years of breathing recycled air should have made the point. There is a solution, and Ceti can be part of it, but it will take time to get there and *war* will put the destination out of reach. Please, Vladric. I'm willing to compromise here. Let me help you.'

'Time, you say?' Vladric said. 'For the longest *time* you refused to acknowledge us. Now that we're at your gates, you'll make the *time* for a ghost? Alright, Chancellor. One more chance. Abolish the Heritage Act, here and now, before all of humanity. Say the words, and the ghosts you care about so much will suffer no harm.'

The fires on *Tabit* were raging in Vespa's mind.

'Abolishing Heritage with the snap of my fingers is impossible,' she said. 'But we can find a way. Walk with me, Vladric. Please.'

For a time, there was silence. Then, he answered.

'Very well, Chancellor. Let us take our first step together by dispelling a myth.'

'What's that?'

'The myth that ghosts can't hurt you.'

30

ANONYMOUS

21 May 2809

Dear Amaryllis,

I have a wonderful vision of you doing something *human* right now.

I picture you brushing your hair, perfectly arranging every detail of your appearance just before meeting a friend for tea, and perhaps a stroll among the shops of Tabit Prime. I imagine your thoughts are consumed by the day's chores and work or family. You have aspirations and dreams, goals to strive for and achievements to celebrate. I hope that you have found love, and that a lifetime of beautiful moments awaits. To me, you will be young for ever.

Those thoughts would make me smile, if only I could.

I am writing from the cabin of a Raothri spacecraft travelling at one-quarter of the speed of light. For unspecified reasons, Ceitus is sending us to the Ch1 Orionis AB system. We will learn our mission after setting orbit around its second planet. There are twelve of us, and for a change we are all sporting vaguely humanoid forms, with a pair of burly arms and legs, elongated heads resembling a horseshoe crab's carapace, complete with fangs and claws for battling and consuming the native mammal species found on the surface of the human-habitable ice world we're visiting.

For nostalgia's sake, I hope we can land there, just so I can breathe the air.

Our ship is travelling to a Lagrange point, at which time it will engage a smaller version of the same 'abaryon drive' that the *Archangel* has. In an instant we'll be vaulted across some immeasurable distance of spacetime; we'll pause to allow the drive to recover from the jump, and then continue our journey across the stars.

As I gaze through a portal at the black veil of nothingness beyond, I see no movement in the stars. The universe taunts my utter insignificance; I am travelling 'fast' yet going nowhere, living a thousand lifetimes while fixating only on the one I shared so briefly with you.

Wherever you are right now, take inventory of your surroundings, and pick a solitary object to focus on. Your stability is an illusion; you and everything around you are moving at dizzying speeds, with no control of the direction or destination. As infants we get our bearings in a world full of stationary objects. Later on we grasp the relativity of existence; that our home is a spinning sphere orbiting a moving sun among countless stars all hurtling towards some 'Great Attractor' of incomprehensible magnitude, an orderly chaos set in motion by the colossal event ingloriously named the 'Big Bang' by humans.

You would be surprised at the reverence other alien species have for that moment. All the good and misery that ever happened to any life form, anywhere and at any time, was born in that instant. Some attribute existence to divinity, others just the pure luck of nature. But the fact is this: in the beginning, we were all dealt the same hand. You and I, the Raothri, the Shadows, *all of us*; we're all different shades of the same life force, made from the exact same stuff.

The twenty-first-century version of humanity was the intellectual equivalent of a delusional teenager convinced he knows everything. Astronomers spotted a few exoplanets in the cosmos and remained unconvinced that alien intelligence existed. Some even postulated that no civilisation could be more advanced than ours, given the amount of time it took for complex life forms to develop from the Big Bang.

Such presumption assumed every intelligent species was just as fallible as our own.

The Raothri didn't make the same mistakes humans did. Their 'Library at Alexandria' never burned. They suffered no Dark Ages.

There were no religions threatened by the discovery of truth in the cosmos. Theirs was a relentless, unimpeded advance towards a super intelligence.

From the beginning, they knew their days were numbered. The parent star that gave birth to intelligent life on their homeworld was a red giant in the final stages of its life. The Raothri rose from a world that was a dark and frigid hell for millennia, thawed only when its solar system literally began to die. Urgency is in their DNA. By the time *Homo sapiens* took their first steps, the Raothri had colonised their own solar system, retreating from a world about to be consumed by the sun. By the time humans learned how to cast bronze, the Raothri had learned to travel between the stars.

Dark energy was born with the Big Bang, and like all the energy released in that moment, it still surges throughout the universe like the waters of a delta. These 'waters' are teeming with Planck-scale wormholes that appear and disappear at random. But some become stable, and part of what humans infer from observable space as the presence of 'dark matter' is in fact a sea of pathways connecting remote locations of the universe.

As masters of femtotechnology, the Raothri manufacture exotic matter that can expand these wormholes large enough for ships to travel through – and can keep them open indefinitely. For millennia, they have sent starships staggering distances to trawl the cosmos for sites to build these 'abaryonic gates': non-baryonic conduits of baryonic matter that any starship with adequate shielding can use.

Ceitus tells us that in several years, the dark matter "tides" of our galaxy will shift, engulfing Sol. When that happens, the birthplace of humankind will become the Orion Arm waypoint of an interstellar transportation network that spans the Milky Way. If this is true, then you should take heart, Amaryllis. There are other worlds, and they are within reach.

We don't miss Earth because it's home. We miss it because it's all we know.

As we approached the final jump in our journey, I learned that Vladric Mors and his entire fleet have slipped undetected into the Inner Rim. They will be within strike range of Corinth in hours. Against my judgement, I asked Ceitus if we could intervene. She said there are too many forces at work to make any difference.

I am scared for you, Amaryllis.

Please, don't end. Not like this.

- A

31

WYLLYM

All throughout the evolution of weapons technology, the fundamental objective of combat has remained the same: deliver some quantity of force to a specific location at a precise moment in time. When applying that principle to scales on the order of solar systems, the distances and velocities involved provide ample opportunity to manufacture apocalyptic destruction.

The Battle of Brotherhood left millions of individual bits of shrapnel hurtling through space at blistering speeds. From grains of scrap to freighter keels a kilometre in length, every fragment was a lethal satellite packing a terrifying amount of kinetic energy. The largest such concentration of debris was trapped in high, unstable orbits around the moon Lethe, slowly pulling away towards Zeus. The second largest field was close to the inner boundary of the Belt itself, where the Navy had clashed with Ceti and mercenary privateers, and where Wyllym had made his name as a warrior.

With the right timing – and an added quantity of directional thrust – a body forced from either debris cloud could intersect with orbits in the Inner Rim. Had their contents been catalogued only months ago, even a casual observer today would have noticed a substantial loss of inventory.

The opening shots of the Archangel War were not fired from cannons; they were fired from the depths of history. In one last stab from the grave, the ghosts of Brotherhood lashed out, slamming their dead, twisted starships into Navy targets with enough force to atomise metal.

Wyllym was aboard a Navy Police gunship when he learned the war had begun.

'*Fuck*,' Augustus fumed, banging a heavy fist against his knee. 'Another Big Eye just died.'

Three hours earlier, Wyllym had been awakened in his cell by a middle-aged soldier dressed in a combat exosuit who identified himself only as 'Mike'. He had brought a Gryphon flight exosuit with him; the electronic nametag embedded within would identify the wearer as one Lieutenant Vronn Tarkon.

Mike was quiet but moved with urgency, speaking only to issue terse instructions to other guards. They journeyed to Corinth's hangar bay, where they were met by Augustus and twenty police Omniwar Specialists. These soldiers, called OMSPECs, had been wearing combat exosuits nearly identical to Wyllym's and were carrying enough firepower to level a city block.

'Rail fire?' Wyllym asked, squirming. Outside of a Gryphon, his flight suit was uncomfortable and cumbersome, especially within the confines of the Navy gunship. It dawned on him that the exosuits everyone was wearing reflected the grim likelihood that they would all end up in space at some point.

'Collision,' Augustus spat, pressing his earpiece in as he listened to the comm chatter. Like the other soldiers, he was wearing mechanised ballistic armour.

Wyllym had to turn his shoulders to look at him.

'With what?' he repeated.

Augustus tapped his earpiece.

'The ONW *Auckland*, apparently.'

Wyllym blinked.

'The *Auckland* was lost at Brotherhood twenty-five years ago.'

'That is correct,' Augustus said, handing him his corelink. 'Here.'

The former Navy frigate had been one of the last pre-colonial UNSEC designs in the fleet, refitted a dozen times and scheduled to be decommissioned. Its hull was conspicuously unique among the arsenal of modern warships; a flying crucifix in which each arm was a rotating engine and its 'head' was the primary weapons bay.

A Navy captain assigned to patrol the Big Eye platforms between Eris and the Belt witnessed the *Auckland* – what was left of her – hurl past his position on its way to impacting with the sensor post, utterly pulverising it and the eight-man crew stationed there. Radar logs confirmed that it was indeed the *Auckland* that had struck the fatal blow.

'Big Eyes aren't the most agile things,' Augustus grumbled. 'Point defences popped off a few rounds. About as effective as throwing turds at a mech.'

Wyllym was incredulous. Five Big Eyes had vanished in the last twenty minutes. Somehow, they had missed an incoming spread of junkyard buckshot a hundred kilometres across whose contents included a *frigate*.

'This is impossible,' he said, reading the captain's report. 'Those mirrors are half a click wide, they should have seen this coming from—'

'"Should" and "have" are the operative words there,' Augustus said, unholstering his sidearm and making sure a round was chambered. 'Right now I'm wondering if they ever worked at all.'

Wyllym eyed the weapon.

'You don't think you're going to need that, do you?' he asked.

'Getting you into a Gryphon might require some persuading,' Augustus answered.

Wyllym opened his mouth to speak, then thought better of it.

'What?' Augustus asked.

'Nothing, this is just ...' Wyllym started. 'I'm a soldier of Orionis, for God's sake.'

'You were,' Augustus corrected. 'Now you're an enemy of the state.'

'What does that make you?'

'An oath keeper,' Augustus said.

Mike's eyes were closed as he listened to the chaos on the comm channels. The general alarm had been sounded – all Navy personnel were reporting to battle stations, and the *Archangel* was priming her engines to leave port.

The Gryphons, now following orders directly from Admiral Hedricks, were preparing to scramble.

'You can't persuade anyone that I'm Vronn Tarkon, even with that,' Wyllym said.

'You two are the same height, the rest is easy,' Augustus joked. 'Relax, my techs put a filter in your mask. You'll modulate to sound just like him. Just keep the damn helmet on.'

The gunship rotated on its wing several degrees; Wyllym felt the retro thrusters fire. They were close.

'Where is Vronn now?' Wyllym asked.

'On his way to the medbay with a very serious medical condition.'

'What?'

'It's a diversion,' Augustus said. 'Gave him a pill to take. The medbay personnel are mine and telling Hedricks he'll be good to go momentarily. Flight ops is holding his wing on deck, so we're in great shape.'

The pilot interrupted him on the intercom.

'Sir, *Archangel* Harbour Control is challenging us,' she warned. 'You're up.'

Wyllym froze. Augustus snatched his corelink out of his hands.

'Control, this is Commander Tyrell, Navy Police,' Augustus growled. 'Let us on board. Government business.'

'Your craft is not on the flight manifest—'

'We are boarding the *Archangel* by order of the Chancellor on official government business. Clear our approach or you'll be in a brig.'

A different voice jumped on the channel.

'What's with the hardware, Commander?'

'Chancellorship orders to take Vladric Mors *alive*, if possible. We'll brief Hedricks on board.'

'Cleared two-two-west.'

'*Thanks.*'

Wyllym exhaled nervously as the gunship executed another turn.

'You're not remotely worried about this?' he asked.

'I've spent the last thirty years infiltrating Ceti,' Augustus said. 'I'm sure I can sneak you onto a Navy ship.'

Wyllym nodded towards the soldiers, most of whom were leaning back in their armour catching some last-minute rest.

'Then why do they need to be here?'

Augustus smiled.

'Like I said, for the possibility of taking Vladric Mors alive,' he said. 'Make him face justice.'

Another burst of deceleration rattled the hull. Wyllym didn't feel like he was about to land on a friendly ship. He felt like he was readying to invade a hostile one. The *Archangel*'s looming, colossal, *alien* appearance was more menacing than ever before: its ebony armour was glowing white in places as energy coursed through it, and the massive rings in the centre were spinning in counter-rotational directions as occasional electrostatic arcs ran up the four towers.

Wyllym still had trouble accepting that this was a ship at all. Even with the mothership classification, the *Archangel* was just *huge*; it seemed larger than Corinth itself. As the gunship aligned with an open hangar bay, he could see orderly processions of shuttles and freighters approaching other hangar bays on the ship, their navigation lights casting hull strobes all the way back to Able Station.

'Personnel transfers,' Augustus remarked. 'The beast is getting her crew. Couldn't ask for better timing. It's going to be crowded down there.'

Gravity tugged on his muscles as the gunship flew past the mysterious barrier into the *Archangel*'s hangar. For the first time that he could recall, Wyllym wished he was in a Gryphon right now. The world just made more sense from the inside of a cockpit.

'Ready up, OMSPEC,' Augustus announced, and the soldiers awoke to immediate alertness, stood up and grunted enthusiastic 'hoo-ahhs' in unison. The gunship had landed. 'Move out!'

'You'll remain here with Mike for ten minutes while the rest of us secure the medbay,' Augustus said. 'Then he'll take you to us, and then escort you to the flight deck. We'll be able to communicate through your helmet. If you're addressed by anyone else, keep your answers short, and *relax* before you speak – the modulator can't keep up with fast talk. You can disable it anytime by saying the code word "*viceroy*".'

'Why that word?' Wyllym blurted.

Augustus lightly slapped him in the head.

'Because there's zero chance it will come up conversationally,' he said. 'The flight deck is expecting Vronn Tarkon to leave the medbay any moment. We're sending you out instead.'

'What's going to happen to Vronn?'

A hint of graveness crept into Augustus's bravado.

'I need to get him off this ship,' he said. 'You alright?'

Wyllym exhaled forcibly, shaking his head.

'We came all this way to kill Vladric Mors,' he muttered. 'Why do I feel like we're going after the wrong man?'

Augustus regarded him for a moment.

'No wonder they put you in jail,' he said, offering his hand. 'Good luck, man.'

Wyllym shook it.

'You too.'

The airlock opened, and Augustus was through.

With a thin carbon dioxide atmosphere and a toxic layer of fine dust coating the entire planet, the planet Eris was uninhabitable, despite its prime location in the circumstellar habitable zone of the Orionis sun. Yet Vulcan Industries had invested heavily here, manufacturing biodomes for food production and deep core drilling sites to harvest precious metals and common ores.

The vast industrial infrastructure made for ample business opportunities with privateers, especially among heavy dropships and freighters. Eris was served by a single space elevator, and its orbital terminus was busy at all times. Cargo transfers and maintenance craft serviced the heavy haulers queuing to transport their spoils to eager buyers throughout Orionis. Once loaded, the encumbered freighters unlatched from the yard to await the proper rotational window to fire their main engines and begin their long, slow journey.

Navigating a freighter required more precision than flying smaller, nimbler craft because there was no room for error, especially when travelling great distances. Captain Jon Sanderson, a privateer and veteran hauler who owned the freighter *Audrey Pat*, knew this better than most, squeezing every last CRO from the margins by running heavy loads with minimal fuel reserves to maximise space for cargo. The *Audrey*, whose holds were packed with iron and nickel ore, had just reached maximum cruise velocity en route to Tabit Prime when her radar sounded a collision warning with an exceptionally large, unidentified object that was still more than six hundred kilometres away.

In the estimation of the *Audrey*'s navigation systems, it was impossible to avoid an intercept given the Audrey's present mass, fuel, and available thrust.

Captain Sanderson's demand for answers from Vulcan Harbour Control was pointless; they had no radar coverage this far from Eris, and nothing in their flight log should have been in his path, let alone something so large.

There was enough time to board a life pod and eject. There was also time to jettison cargo, thus shedding mass and giving his beloved *Audrey Pat* manoeuvring options. But Captain Sanderson was a principled man, and refused to relinquish his precious load without at least understanding what exactly was about to claim it.

His stubbornness, while ultimately fatal, benefitted the Inner Rim. As the distance between them closed, the *Audrey*'s radar was able to resolve the large object into hundreds of smaller returns, each of which happened to be a Ceti warship. To his credit, Captain Sanderson had the presence of mind to broadcast the radar image along with his distress call.

As the *Audrey Pat* was torn apart by Ceti missiles, word quickly spread around Tabit Prime: Vladric Mors was coming, and he was less than a million kilometres from Corinth.

The Navy, meanwhile, was trying to understand how Vladric could have hurled so much space junk at their vaunted Big Eye network, which was now completely obliterated. They correctly determined that his fleet alone – as depicted in Captain Sanderson's radar image – was incapable of such a feat, unless their numbers had been greatly underestimated.

Mike spoke with startling intensity.

'Remember your cover,' he said. 'You are an OMSPEC operator under my command. Don't act nervous, don't speak unless you have to, and stay one pace from my heels at all times. Do you understand?'

'Yes,' Wyllym acknowledged.

'Let's move.'

Mike opened the airlock hatch, peering in both directions before stepping down onto the tarmac. Stiff from the journey, Wyllym nearly stumbled when he landed. Gathering his armoured legs beneath him, he stood tall like a soldier, only to find Mike glaring coldly at him.

Augustus had not been exaggerating when he said it would be crowded. From behind his mask, Wyllym watched crewmen disembark from a nearby transport by the dozens. Cargo mechs marched about carrying crates unloaded from a freight shuttle beside the transport. Small platoons gathered around staff sergeants for a few brief instructions before filing out. Organised chaos was a mainstay of Navy life, but there was a frantic current in the atmosphere. Everyone was focused, like him, following the instructions of leaders acting as if they knew what to do.

Wyllym wondered how many of them were seeing the *Archangel* for the first time. Like the outer hull, the deck was an ebony sheen, but with thin venting and lighting panels lining the pathways where it was safe to stand without getting run over by a mech or dismembered by a freight crane. There was no view of space from here; ships landed on a retractable platform two decks above them and were lowered to the pressurised bay for refuelling and cargo management.

Red battlestation lights a hundred metres overhead cast eerie god rays through the thick air. A file of crewmen jogged by Mike as he walked towards a large, hexagon-shaped hallway. When they passed beneath the entrance, they were stopped by a young Navy major.

'Why aren't you with the rest of your group?' the officer demanded.

'Which group would that be?' Mike asked.

'Don't play dumb with me, Captain,' she snapped, obviously checking some manifest on her own AR.

'Commander Tyrell instructed us to continue mission planning while the rest of my squad stows their gear,' Mike said.

The officer – Wyllym saw the name 'Dominguez' on her uniform lapel – narrowed her eyes.

'What's the matter with him?' she demanded. 'Why is he wearing a helmet?'

'Major, if we capture a Ceti ship, this man will be the first one through the breach,' Mike said calmly. 'Do you know what his survival odds are?'

'No, Captain, I don't,' she hissed.

Wyllym had been holding his breath for so long that he had become dizzy.

'One in ten,' Mike said. 'But he's survived nineteen straight raids. *Nineteen.* He follows the same pre-mission ritual every time. The helmet's working for him. Don't fuck with his odds.'

'You OMSPECs think you're so special,' she growled.

'Only because we always win,' Mike said. 'Excuse us, Major.'

She glared at him, then stepped aside.

'As you were,' Mike said.

Wyllym exhaled quietly.

They approached the entrance to the *Archangel*'s rapid transit system. The elevator car was small – perhaps four people could fit inside.

'We're in,' Mike said, presumably into his comms receiver. 'Two coming up.'

Wyllym felt a hint of movement as the elevator began climbing.

'Is everything okay?' he asked.

'The medbay is secure,' Mike answered, 'but you'll only have a few seconds up there.'

Wyllym breathed a sigh of relief.

'How long have you been doing this sort of thing?' he asked.

'Eight years with OMSPEC,' Mike said, glancing at Wyllym a moment. 'This is my first op against the Navy.'

When the elevator door opened, Wyllym could scarcely believe his eyes.

Six men, all wearing Navy uniforms, were on their knees, bound, gagged, and blindfolded. OMSPEC soldiers with drawn weapons were patrolling the hall leading to the medbay entrance while Augustus and another soldier dragged a very pale and haggard-looking Vronn Tarkon forward to meet him.

'Captain,' he breathed. 'Lieutenant Ruslov is your wing command. He was briefed directly by Hedricks ... he's been on at me all week about "being with us or against us". I don't know what they're going to ask of you, but watch yourself out there.'

'Hedricks is partitioning the crew,' Augustus warned, motioning towards the prisoners. 'These men came in to relieve the doctor and his staff – they're all ghosts from Able. We hacked their corelinks and checked the ship manifest. They aren't even in the Navy. You have to get off this ship right now.'

Wyllym's head was spinning as Admiral Hedrick's voice cut through his comms.

'What is the status of Lieutenant Tarkon?' he demanded.

Wyllym heard the medbay physician's response.

'He contracted a stomach virus,' he answered. 'Very contagious. So many new faces aboard I'm not surprised. We'll be watching them for symptoms.'

'Can he fly or not?'

'Yes, if his helmet and mask stay on,' the physician said. 'I've provided antiviral inhalants and an IV through his flight suit to deal with dehydration. He should be symptom-free in an hour, maybe less.'

'Lieutenant Tarkon?'

Augustus motioned for Wyllym to talk. Vronn just nodded.

The AR inside his helmet sprung to life. He was now broadcasting himself as Vronn Tarkon to the *Archangel*. He cleared his throat.

'I'm ready to go, sir,' Wyllym said.

'Then report to Gryphon Bay at once,' Admiral Hedricks ordered. 'Lieutenant Ruslov is your wing command.'

'Yes, sir,' Wyllym said.

The connection dropped. Augustus looked at Mike.

'Whatever it takes,' he warned.

'Understood,' Mike acknowledged.

Thanks to the *Audrey Pat*, the Orionis Navy had a general idea where the Ceti fleet was. But they had yet to make contact with it. Navy assets from Tabit Prime all the way to the Belt were scrambling in anticipation of the order to intercept the invaders before they could reach Corinth.

Except no such order was given, which sowed even more confusion.

Grand Admiral Hedricks was not responding to calls from the Chancellor's office or the OPCOM admirals in the field. This was especially alarming given that the *Archangel* was about to depart from the Corinth Shipyard.

The next casualties of the war belonged to the ONW *London*, a frigate returning from a Zeus deployment that was approaching Corinth for shore leave. By sheer bad luck, its deceleration manoeuvres placed it squarely in the path of nine Ceti corvettes.

They engaged from a distance of three hundred kilometres. The *London*'s belly was opened by a penetrator round, and all hands on board were killed when a Ceti missile got past her point defences and exploded inside her hull.

Before it perished, the *London* accurately returned fire, with the onboard 'Starburst' Navy weapons management system confirming that their rounds scored direct hits on three separate Ceti corvettes. But no damage effect was detected, and the captain died wondering how that could possibly be.

When the steel blast doors peeled apart, they were met by a Navy ensign.

Wyllym stared past him at the hulking Gryphon parked fifty metres beyond. The bay was well lit, but the fighter's dull, greyish-black surface drank in the brightness like a shadow. The numbers '1-3' were stencilled in red on its four sloping wings, and the Orionis Navy emblem was emblazoned in yellow on the craft's main engine nacelles. Beneath every weapon hardpoint was a cluster of oval-shaped 'Harpoon' anti-ship missiles, and all eight of the fighter's vectored exhaust ports were already flexing in their sheaths as part of the automated pre-flight routine.

Several flight deck crewmembers were waiting to secure him inside the retractable cockpit. The three other Gryphons of his wing were positioned in their departure spots on the platform that would transfer them to the launch hangar. Their pilots were already inside, impatiently waiting for Vronn Tarkon.

'Who are you?' the ensign asked.

'Captain Mike Vogel, Navy Police, escorting Lieutenant Tarkon to the flight deck,' Mike said. 'I was hoping to speak with the loadmaster while I'm here.'

The 'ensign' was a large man, taller even than Wyllym in his flight suit. He also carried himself with more authority than any ensign he'd ever met before.

'You don't have any business with the loadmasters on this deck,' the ensign said.

'OMSPEC is here for SAR and raid missions,' Mike said. 'We brought a lot of gear. I need to speak with a loadmaster. Now.'

Wyllym heard Augustus in his earpiece.

'Act impatient,' he warned.

'Do you guys mind?' Wyllym said, taking care to keep his words slow and distinct for the modulator. 'We got a war to fight.'

The ensign stared at him, and Wyllym wondered if he had just said the wrong thing.

'Feeling better, Tarkon?' he asked. 'Well, hurry up!'

Wyllym began walking, then trotting, towards the waiting deck personnel, trying to control his breathing.

There was another burst of static in his earpiece.

'Move it, Wyll,' Augustus warned, as another ensign – shorter and stockier than the brute confronting Mike – joined Wyllym at the hip.

'Where did that MP meet you?' the ensign asked, referring to Mike.

'Outside the medbay,' Augustus said. There was shouting in the background.

'Right after I was discharged,' Wyllym said, lowering himself into the cockpit module. The other crew went to work securing him inside.

'Why didn't you say anything?' the ensign demanded. 'He's not on the list.'

Other members of the flight deck were converging on Mike.

'He's … an MP,' Wyllym said. 'I didn't think anything of it.'

Wyllym flinched as shots rang out inside his helmet. The OMSPECs were in a firefight.

'Leave him,' Augustus shouted over the gunfire. 'Get into the fucking ship!'

While his heart pounded, the crew closed and sealed the compartment. As the cockpit rose into position, Admiral Hedricks spoke on the flight ops channel.

'Remember, Lieutenant Ruslov speaks for me,' he said. 'Follow his orders.'

The Gryphon platform rotated as it ascended towards the launch deck, giving Wyllym his final glimpse of Mike, who had his rifle trained on the crowd swarming towards him.

At this point, mass confusion was spreading throughout the Navy as mid-level officers – those with the most direct control of warfare assets – struggled to get clarity from the superior chain of command. News of the *London*'s destruction was fuelling a dangerous sense of initiative that was too easily corrupted by impulsiveness.

Making matters worse was the open and flagrant dissension at the OPCOM level of leadership. Grand Admiral Hedricks controlled the task group stationed at Tabit Prime. That group, led by the cruiser flagship *Sacramento,* was ordered to stay put – which made sense. But Vice Admiral Kristjan Larksson, the Belt OPCOM, received no assignment despite his relative proximity to Corinth and ability to bring decisive firepower to the fight.

Rear Admiral Jung Lao insisted that all was well and ordered everyone to remain where they were.

Wyllym didn't realise the *Archangel* had left her birthplace until after his Gryphon cleared the hangar. The mothership was completely clear of the shipyard scaffolding, its aft hull glowing an azure blue from her impulse drives. Wyllym had always assumed there would be a grand celebration to herald the *Archangel*'s maiden voyage. Instead, she was stealing away under the cover of night.

'Gunfighter one-three, cleared for flight vector navpoint alpha,' the *Archangel* tower commanded. 'Engines go for intercept. Ruslov, he's your bird.'

'Thank you, *Archangel,*' Ruslov said. His Gryphon was just one hundred metres ahead. Jans Orpyk and Cassius Adams were the other wingmen, positioned sixty metres to Wyllym's two and ten o'clock in a diamond formation.

'Wing, set to alpha,' Ruslov instructed. Wyllym pointed his craft towards the designation on his HUD. 'Nine-zero burn in three, two, one, *mark.*'

Wyllym opened the Gryphon's throttle to ninety per cent of maximum thrust, and the craft smoothly accelerated to 12,000 metres per second relative to Corinth.

All he could think about was Augustus.

'Tarkon,' Lieutenant Ruslov said. 'Maintain speed and heading. Do not deviate.'

The three Gryphons slowed and took position close behind him.

'Now,' Ruslov said. 'What were you doing in Corinth last month?'

Wyllym paused, hoping that either Vronn or Augustus would answer. They didn't.

'Testifying against Wyllym Lyons,' he decided. 'Typical ghost shit.'

'That's not what you said the last time I asked,' Ruslov growled.

'I was instructed by the police not to talk about it.'

The weapons radar announced a warning: sixty, then ninety, then two hundred new contacts ... with every sweep, the number increased.

'Retroburn to flank,' Ruslov ordered, meaning to steer wide of the contacts, reduce forward vector and accelerate to match the Ceti fleet's speed. Wyllym frowned: an intercept would fly directly at the enemy, fire weapons, then break and reassess.

These orders were more fitting for an *escort*, not a kill mission. Including his own, there were just seventeen Gryphons in space right now, most covering the far side of the inbound Ceti fleet, all within firing range, and they had yet to fire a shot.

But Wyllym did as he was told anyway, and the Gryphon's engines rotated forward. A gruelling high-G burndown ensued, pushing him forward into the harness. A surge of painkillers flooded into his system; he felt no ill effect from the aggressive manoeuvring, but knew his body was already protesting the abuse.

'I will assign targets,' Ruslov said. 'You will attack *only* those ships. Understood?'

Wyllym's weapons system was now 'painting' several Ceti corvettes, all in rearguard positions relative to the fleet's vector.

It made no tactical sense at all, and he had seen enough to start challenging Ruslov.

'Any reason why we're ignoring the leads?' Wyllym asked.

He was answered by the Gryphon's threat indicator, as Ruslov and his two wingmen targeted him.

'Play along, Tarkon,' Ruslov growled. 'Or this ends badly for you.'

Wyllym felt a deep, cold rage take hold of him, and his Gift began calculating possibilities.

Admiral Hedricks cut through the audio.

'Gryphons, new targets will be in range momentarily,' he said, his voice as nasal as ever. 'Ruslov, they are priority.'

Wyllym's search radar picked out a host of new contacts: Navy warships, all executing a textbook intercept on the Ceti fleet. It was the cruiser ONW *Gettysburg*, escorted by the frigates the ONW *Rio* and ONW *Cologne*, and at least one hundred corvettes.

'Gryphons, this is Admiral Larksson,' the scruffy old man announced from the *Gettysburg*. 'I seem to have misplaced my invitation to this reception. We are here to assist.'

The Ceti fleet maintained its deadeye course straight for the *Archangel*, now some twenty thousand kilometres behind the Gryphons.

'New targets for you, Tarkon,' Ruslov announced. 'Think you can handle it?'

Wyllym's HUD was now instructing him to attack the *Gettysburg*.

'Gryphons, please respond,' Admiral Larksson said.

Wyllym closed his eyes for a moment, asking some invisible power for strength. Then he switched channels.

'Augustus, if you can hear me, I'm breaking cover,' he said. 'Hedricks just ordered me to fire on the *Gettysburg*. The Gryphons are fighting for Ceti. I'll do what I can. Send word to Tabit Prime. Lyons out.'

Then he switched back to the Gryphon comm channel. The Ceti fleet was in visual range, a distinct patch of glitter in the black eternal distance.

'*Gettysburg*, this is Gunfighter One-Three,' Wyllym said. 'I'm with you.'

'Big mistake, Tarkon,' Ruslov mocked. All three of his wingmen were about to open fire. 'I'm sending you back to Mama Cerlis in a box.'

'Lieutenant Tarkon would be intimidated. *Viceroy*,' Wyllym growled, disabling the voice modulator. 'I'm not.'

32

JAKE

The worst part of cryosleep is waking up with the same exact thought you had when the lights went out. In the darkness, you feel the deepest chill you've ever known. By then, the journey is over, and experienced voyagers know they're being thawed out. Months could have passed, and mentally you feel like nothing's changed beyond the fact you're suddenly freezing and sick to your stomach.

But your body knows otherwise. And substance abuse issues make the experience a lot worse.

It's been more than forty-eight hours since the icebox pumped my veins with chemicals to kick-start my metabolism. I've been tethered to a bunk ever since, and I have no desire to leave it. Although the *Breakaway*'s viewports are covered for battle, it's all I can do to push all the visual cues of space travel out of my head.

Honestly, I'd rather be dead than aboard this ship.

I fell asleep thinking three things: the annoyance of being unable to control my shaking; that I would absolutely murder Dusty if he was standing between me and a joint; and that Vladric Mors was nearby, plotting to kill me.

Inexperienced travellers panic when they wake from cryo because that's when the reality of their commitment hits. You sleep to speed up your perception of time during a long journey, and there's no going back. My commitment was boarding a ship running head first into a war we can't win. And since Vladric was leading the charge, I fully expected *Griefmaker* to turn her guns on us. It was just a matter of time.

I would welcome that. If only the bastard had found the mercy to do it while I was sleeping.

'Jack, get up here!' Dusty shouted. '*Now!*'

My only friend, and I hate him. His bossing, my claustrophobia, the irritating sound of his nasal little voice. Anger and fear make a dangerous combination.

'Hurry up!' he hollered. 'We're close!'

The *Breakaway* was decelerating hard; I knew because I was getting pulled towards the front of the ship.

'C'mon Jack, shake it off!'

The fucking bastard. Right on cue, I'm literally shaking again. I'm craving drugs so badly that I can *see* myself smoking. It's so real I can taste the bitter, beautiful smell in the back of my throat.

Then I realise it's just bile, and that no one can help me except the prick screaming at me like a drill sergeant.

By the time I made it to the bridge, I could barely fit through the entrance. Dusty, who was plugged into the *Breakaway*'s command module, was secured to the captain's chair in a four-point harness. His head was covered with a bulky helmet that gave him a virtual simulation of the space outside, which he manipulated with a combination of thoughts and hand gestures.

Beneath the helmet, he was just wearing a T-shirt, overalls, and flip-flops.

I was wearing an EVA suit.

'Seriously?' Dusty asked, shaking his head. 'Whatever. Hurry up and plug in, I need you.'

'For what?'

'To man the guns, dude! Wake up already!'

The instrument panels surrounding the captain's chair were lit up like the place was on fire. Reluctantly, I sat in the seat next to Dusty, fantasising about throat-chopping him.

'There are four Gryphons stalking us out there,' he said, excitedly.

'That's just great,' I mumbled.

'Don't worry,' he said. 'They're not crazy enough to engage.'

When I pulled the VR helmet on, I found myself staring into the Minotaur's furious yellow eyes. I shrieked and ripped it right off.

'*C'mon, Jack!*' Dusty protested. 'Pull it together!'

Trembling, I put the helmet back on. This time I was transported into the black of space, engulfed in volumetric displays of nearby contacts and their vectors through space. The entire Ceti fleet – roughly three hundred corvettes of numerous different shapes and classes – was packed together in a cloud of firepower a hundred kilometres across. The closest ship was the *Pretoria*, less than two kilometres to our starboard. Vladric's *Griefmaker* was ten clicks ahead of us; her three engines were alight but facing opposite the direction we were travelling, and her weapon bays were open and ready for business.

'There he is, the crowning failure of your life,' the Minotaur growled, full of venomous disgust.

'What?' Dusty asked.

'You should have ended this when you had the *fucking* chance!' the Minotaur shouted.

'Ended *what*?' Dusty asked. 'Dude, you're freaking me out. It's going to be alright! The *Archangel* is half a million clicks dead ahead. We've got the numbers and the element of surprise.'

I tried to ignore the horse-man.

'Why haven't we shot the Gryphons?' I managed.

'They're too far away,' Dusty said. 'That's what they want, to draw us out of formation, thin us out …'

'Or they're waiting for the *Archangel* to warm her guns on us,' I suggested.

'Or maybe you should just chill out,' Dusty said. 'Fuck, man. Get a grip.'

My hands were shaking so much that the excess movement was confusing the *Breakaway*'s weapons system.

The Minotaur snorted his approval of Dusty's assessment, and I coughed hard to clear the stench of his breath from my sinuses.

'I don't understand,' I muttered, feeling the stab of a very potent migraine at the top of my head. 'Where's the Navy? How did we get this close?'

'I told you to *believe*, man,' Dusty assured. 'We're gonna do this!'

A few moments later, the radar warning system blew up his pathetic optimism. An entire Navy task force suddenly appeared: the *Gettysburg*

– the Navy's newest and most lethal cruiser – plus two frigate escorts and at least a hundred Keating-class corvettes. The group was six hundred kilometres away and burning very fast to intercept us. The *Gettysburg* had the longest-ranged guns in space – non-negotiable 500mm bores – ready to put chunks of tungsten into us.

In space, 'weapon range' is subjective. Technically, a gun has infinite range if nothing interacts with the projectile. In naval combat, 'effective range' described the combination of distance, vector and velocity at which a projectile became impossible to avoid or defend against.

The *Breakaway*, along with every ship in the Ceti vanguard, was seconds from reaching that threshold. And the four Gryphons, emboldened with Big Brother on the grid, were now aggressively closing the distance between us, now less than two hundred kilometres away.

Horse-man snorted, chuckled, and then broke into outright laughter. I felt the migraine stab all the way to my chest.

'Stop that!' Dusty snapped, flustered at the horse-man's throaty guffaw. 'Get a lock on those Gryphons!'

Something very strange happened as he said that. I felt a rush of premonition, almost like a dance, and gasped at what was about to happen.

Flying in a tight diamond formation, the lead Gryphon abruptly pitched its nose downward so that it was flying perpendicular to the craft behind it.

Then, in a devastating braking action, all her burners ignited at once.

The four fighters merged. Before I could blink, there were ten contacts spinning violently away from each other in a cloud of debris.

Two of the new contacts were broadcasting automated SOS signals. These were presumably ejected pilots. The rest were Gryphon chunks.

Even the Minotaur was shocked.

'Wha—?' Dusty breathed. 'What the hell just happened?

One of the contacts – the lead Gryphon that caused the collision – suddenly sprung to life, her thrusters sputtering to stabilise a nasty spin. There were probably thirty Ceti ships illuminating the expanding debris field with fire control radar now, and all that return energy give the *Breakaway*'s sensors a very good picture of its condition. The Gryphon's ventral side was dented up badly, and her starboard engine nacelle was a tangled mess of electrical carnage.

Judging from the condition of the other fighters, the lead pilot had presented the strongest structure of his craft as a battering ram to the Gryphons behind her. Two of the fighters crashed into each other attempting to evade, and the cockpit area of the trailing craft was grotesquely caved in.

The lead Gryphon was now burning towards the Navy fleet, presumably for protection, trailing bright hot debris behind it like a comet.

Its tail marking read One-Three.

'That's impossible,' Dusty mumbled. 'There can't be anything alive in there.'

He had a point. By all reason, there shouldn't be anything in that Gryphon cockpit but a film of red paste.

But I knew the pilot was alive. Critically injured, but alive. And the more I thought about him, the harder the icepick drove into me.

'You're wrong,' I muttered, barely keeping my own nerves together. My teeth were clacking together like a jackhammer.

The Ceti ships around us were starting to drift out of formation.

'How do you know that?' Dusty said nervously.

Before I could answer, the *Gettysburg* opened fire with all eight of her rails.

33

AUGUSTUS

Blood and bone fragments were still seeping into the deck grating when the OMSPECs resumed their work on the rapid transit controls. Augustus didn't know who the intruders were; only that they had burst into the room shooting, and that they were using weapon technology he didn't understand.

The OMSPEC who had been standing next to him just vanished in a burst of light. Completely absent were the kinetic effects of projectile impacts. All he saw was a strange flash erupt from the intruder's rifle; then the OMSPEC turned into a rising apparition before disappearing for good.

A stray round – or blast, Augustus wasn't sure which – struck one of the bound prisoners on the deck. He did *not* disintegrate, and barely flinched from the impact.

Fortunately, the assailants – all wearing Navy uniforms – were clearly not trained tactical operators. Wild, sprayed rounds vaporised random equipment throughout the medbay, *except* when they struck that eerie black armour on the *Archangel* bulkheads. Those rounds simply vanished into the surface without leaving a scratch.

OMSPEC gunfire was far more precise, shredding the intruders in the manner Augustus was accustomed to: via the forceful displacement of flesh, bone, and blood. When the last assailant fell, the OMSPECs sealed the deck entrance shut. They did not pause to mourn the loss of one of their own, nor did they lose their composure at the prospect of facing an enemy with superior firepower.

Vronn Tarkon, on the other hand, was huddled on the deck covering his head.

'I'm sorry,' he said, with considerable effort. 'I've never been in a real firefight before.'

'I'm not sure that's what I'd call it,' Augustus dismissed, kicking over a corpse whose face had collapsed around a bullet hole in the cheek. 'Do you have any idea who the fuck these people are and why they're shooting at us?'

'No,' Vronn said. 'We were always kept isolated from the crew.'

Augustus eyed the strange rifle lying beside the corpse. It had a short, hexagon-shaped barrel surrounded by concentric tubes on both sides of the action and 'magazine', which was likely an energy source. The weapon had no stock, and its colour was metallic-ebony, with deep purple trim along the grip.

'I'd stay away from that if I were you,' Vronn warned.

'Why?'

'If it doesn't recognise you, you might disappear.'

Someone shouted, and the OMSPECs scurried away from the hatch. Loud, deep bangs rang from the other side, and then a small explosion followed by a thin line of white-hot plasma broke through.

'Persistent bastards,' Augustus growled. 'Vronn, I hate to tell you this, but there are no good options for getting you off this ship.'

The remaining prisoners, now unconscious thanks to sedatives found in the medbay, had provided little information. They claimed to be dock workers confined to Able for the duration of the *Archangel*'s construction, and recently given orders by Rear Admiral Lao to report for active duty on board this ship.

Augustus didn't believe a word of it, but there just wasn't time for a proper interrogation.

Their DNA was unregistered with the Navy and general Orionis archive. They were ghosts in every sense of the word.

Augustus looked towards the OMSPEC tech working on the Rapid Transport controls.

'How are we doing?' he asked.

'Not good,' the tech said. '*Archangel* rejects police authentication, and I can't bypass locally. I don't even understand the wiring.'

As the torch line reached a third of the way around the hatch, OMSPECs took up firing positions, this time selecting bulkheads with black armour for cover.

'Just blast the thing,' Augustus said, raising his voice to a shout. 'Hey! You men get claymores in front of the hatch! Get these prisoners behind them! We're climbing up!'

'What's the plan?' Vronn asked.

'We'll fight our way to the Gryphon deck,' Augustus said. 'There has to be something else there you can fly yourself out in. Then we're going after Mike.'

There had been no radio contact from the OMSPEC operative since the ambush, but his exosuit was still broadcasting vital signs.

'There is another option,' Vronn said. 'The life pods. If we reach those, we can all eject.'

'That's pointless, we'll just end up getting caught,' Augustus said. 'We need a real ship to escape.'

'You can't get that elevator to work,' Vronn snapped. 'What makes you think they'll open the hangar bay for you?'

Augustus nearly lost his temper, but he knew the Gryphon pilot was right.

'She's not going to let us out,' Vronn said, clearly distressed. 'We should find Mike.'

The OMSPEC tech signalled that he was finished placing charges.

'Do it,' Augustus ordered.

A muffled blast followed by snapping metal rung their eardrums. The Rapid Transit car fell a metre, got stuck for a moment, and then fell away. The elevator shaft was fully exposed.

'Masks on! Get in there!' Augustus shouted, hoping his *Archangel* schematics were accurate. They were facing a two-hundred-metre vertical climb, assuming the gravity vectors remained aligned all the way up.

'The nearest life pods are above us,' Augustus said, as OMSPECs filed past. 'We'll get you inside one.'

Wyllym broke through on his comms.

' … I repeat, the Gryphons are with Ceti,' he said, his voice laboured. 'Ty, please acknowledge.'

Augustus paused by the shaft entrance, waving Vronn inside.

'*All* of them?'

'They're attacking the *Gettysburg* group now,' Wyllym said. 'I'm ... doing what I can.'

'Where's the rest of the Navy?' Augustus asked, as the last soldier filed through. The torch line was past the halfway mark. He ducked inside and began climbing, hoping not to get run over by another car or blown to bits by a sentry system.

'Don't know,' Wyllym stammered. 'You have to broadcast for help ... use civilian channels.'

'Help? From who?'

'Anyone,' Wyllym breathed. 'Their shield tech works ... rail fire ineffective ...'

'You're kidding me ...'

'They're not all protected,' Wyllym said. 'Can't tell which. We need he—'

Augustus felt a dizzying wave of sickness overwhelm him. Gravity abruptly vanished, and the transmission from Wyllym dropped.

The quick-thinking OMSPECs above him seized the opportunity and began pulling themselves 'upwards' as fast as they could.

'... God in heaven,' he heard Wyllym breathe. 'Are you alright?'

Augustus was still feeling a little queasy.

'I'm fine, why?'

'The *Archangel*,' Wyllym said. 'It's here!'

'What do you mean, "here"?'

Gravity suddenly returned, and an OMSPEC tumbled past Augustus as he held on for dear life.

34

JAKE

For several moments, the fighting ceased.

The *Archangel*, which had been half a million kilometres from us just moments ago, was now less than ten kilometres away.

We had been fighting for our lives when a disc brighter than the sun opened in the black of space. The *Archangel* emerged from a womb of light, the mysterious radiance centred on the gap at the mothership's core.

Time stopped. I think everyone – Ceti, Navy, ghost and highborn alike – understood the significance of that moment: humans were in possession of a ship that could bridge the stars. The hopes and dreams of a race at the brink of extinction sailed through that seam in the fabric of spacetime.

It was like witnessing the birth of God.

But since we are His flawed, imperfect creatures, the killing resumed.

Before the *Archangel*'s surreal entrance, the opening salvo from the *Gettysburg* – eight independently targeted railguns launching tungsten sabots at *twelve kilometres per second* – shattered the spines of five ships. One of those was the *Pretoria*, whose exploding hull riddled the *Breakaway* with blistering fragments of molten shrapnel, disabling the port thruster and sparking an internal fire.

The remaining rounds also landed direct hits on three Ceti corvettes in the vanguard, including the *Griefmaker*. I know this because I saw the same line of shells that obliterated the *Pretoria* intersect with her conning tower, except the *Griefmaker* was unharmed.

With rail fire raining down on the fleet, Vladric Mors ordered the rearguard to engage the attacking Navy task force – all *except* for the Gryphons, of which there were now fourteen. Inexplicably, those fighters began attacking *Navy* ships, destroying a dozen Keating corvettes before the *Gettysburg* captain fully understood that the Gryphons had changed sides.

Dusty's faith in Vladric Mors began to falter when he realised no *shielded* Ceti ship made any attempt to defend the ones that weren't. In fact, some were openly attacking unprotected Ceti ships as they turned towards the *Archangel*, *which had opened every one of her bay doors*.

Rank madness had descended on Corinth. It was every ship and every man for himself. Ceti fired upon Ceti; Navy upon Ceti; Gryphon upon Navy; and all against the unshielded.

But Dusty wanted to believe. Still thought he could trust Vladric.

'*Griefmaker*, I could use cover from this rail fire,' he said. 'Can you come left thirty degrees to assist my approach?'

I felt another stab in my skull and tried to warn him.

'Dusty, don't—'

He saw it a fraction of a second after I did, recognising the danger as the *Griefmaker*'s turrets swivelled aft and opened fire. I felt my stomach rise into my throat as Dusty pushed the *Breakaway* away from the line of fire.

A terrifying shudder rocked my seat. I heard groaning metal and the scream of fire alarms. We were hit.

Dusty was devastated.

'*Griefmaker*, cease fire! Friendly at your six!' he pleaded.

One of the rounds penetrated our damaged engine and nicked its confinement generator, releasing plasma before the automated shut-off could engage. Superheated matter struck the main hull, triggering an explosion that sent the *Breakaway* into a yawing spin. As Dusty fought the controls, the Minotaur, overpowering the centrifugal forces hammering me into my seat, leapt into action.

For a horse-man, he moved with surprising grace, pulling himself through the narrow, red-tinged corridors with speed and precision, following the rush of air towards the danger. Plummeting cabin pressure signalled a general containment failure, and that the fire – also following the air – would meet him head-on.

Past the galley, the corridor branched around the reactor compartment, sealed within bulkheads a metre thick. Armoured conduits jutting out from the compartment like spokes served power to the engines; the Minotaur was getting pulled towards the blue flames undulating like waves along the deck grating to the right.

Shielding his face from the heat, the Minotaur saw the problem: one of Dusty's hobby projects had wedged itself into the track beneath a containment hatch, preventing it from sealing. The mutant grabbed a fire extinguisher, planted himself against the hatch, and wailed on the debris with all his might, even as flames oozed up his hooved legs. With a final, desperate blow, it dislodged, and the spring-loaded hatch slammed shut.

Turning the fire extinguisher on himself, he cursed furiously at Dusty, vowing that he would make him beat out the next fire with his goddamn flip-flops.

But the young, naïve captain never paid attention. He was too desperate.

'Can anyone tell me what's happening?' he cried on open comms. The space outside the *Breakaway* was a treacherous debris field of lifeless or dying starship hulks spinning out of control. In front of it all, the crowning blow of Vladric Mor's betrayal of Ceti was laid bare for all to see: the *Griefmaker* and a parade of Ceti corvettes – all shielded, no doubt – were landing inside the colossal hangar bays of the *Archangel*.

Before I could react, the Minotaur seized the gun controls from me, and the *Breakaway*'s four cannons began spitting shells towards the *Griefmaker*.

'Die!' he howled. 'You fucking bastard! *Die!*'

Dusty was unhinged, muttering something unintelligible.

'*You wanted to follow him,*' the Minotaur accused. 'Here we are! Now savour the *fucking* moment.'

I couldn't tell if our shells landed. It would make no difference if they had. Others followed our example and fired at the *Griefmaker*, stabbing for revenge before a Gryphon or Navy warship blotted them from existence.

I imagined our own end was imminent.

'Oh, God!' Dusty cried, nearly throwing me off balance as he turned the *Breakaway* hard. I couldn't remember when I had stood up. 'That Gryphon's coming for us!'

Without looking, I knew he meant One-Three.

Throughout the chaos, the damaged fighter was performing an incredible feat of ship combat. Manoeuvring with preternatural dominance, it was using the *Gettysburg* and her rail fire as cover, from which it would emerge to unleash weapons, firing thrusters to yaw, pitch or roll away from counterattacks at precisely the right time.

In a span of seconds, I watched One-Three destroy four Ceti corvettes, all while being chased down by another Gryphon, who was simply unable to hit it.

A Navy frigate ended the Gryphon's pursuit with cannon fire as One-Three continued its rampage through the Ceti fleet.

No one had ever seen anything like this. It was spiritual to behold. I shared a bond with the pilot of that Gryphon. I knew he was dying; I could *feel* his heart struggle to continue beating. He was determined to take as much life with him as he could, including ours. We were in his sights, and reflexively, I put the *Breakaway*'s cross hairs on him.

'Jack!' Dusty shrieked, as he swung towards us from just sixty kilometres away. 'Shoot him! *Shoot!*'

And that was when the Minotaur said:

'Enough, Jake. It's time.'

A moment of clarity. Every part of me was in agreement with the horse-man, even as the missile flew off the Gryphon's rail.

A lifetime ago, a police academy instructor had told me what to say, when the moment arrived.

'Gryphon One-Three, renegade, renegade, *renegade*!' I said, alerting every Navy asset on the battlefield that I was an undercover agent. 'Ident Nine-Three-Six-Oxide at your twelve, cease fire, renegade!'

The bright red icon of death on my weapons display converged on us, and I closed my eyes as Dusty flung the *Breakaway* over in a desperate bid to evade.

'Nine-Three-Six-Oxide, tally,' the cool, laboured voice said. The missile passed over the *Breakaway*, seeking another target. 'Name and rank, please.'

'Reddeck,' I said. 'Lieutenant Jake Reddeck.'

'What … what are you doing?' Dusty asked.

'Reddeck?' the voice repeated. 'Tyrell's son-in-law?'

Was I?

'Yes, sir,' the Minotaur said. 'That's me.'

35

AUGUSTUS

Mike was dead, and Augustus would never know what had killed him.

Whatever his fate, the climb lasted just twenty metres – two deck levels – before the missing soldier's vitals flatlined. Then the adversary began firing at them from above, leaving him no choice but to abandon the plan and breach the first deck they could.

That placed them on the *Archangel*'s bioreactor lab, an open deck the size of a football pitch with rows of canisters containing everything from slush tank bacteria to human heart cell tissue. Several greenhouse enclosures lined the perimeter, above which hung an overhead deck gantry with four exits to the main concourse, making the area completely indefensible from any location within.

Men with strange rifles were already darting into the lab. As the OMSPECs tried to find cover, Augustus considered that this would be the exact setting his friend Wyllym wanted for himself: dying among a lot of plants.

'Buy me some time,' he said to the nearest soldier.

'Yes, sir,' the lad said, without a trace of fear in his voice.

Augustus looked towards the firstborn Gryphon pilot who had sacrificed so much.

'Vronn,' he said, offering his sidearm. 'Don't let them take you alive.'

The lieutenant took the weapon without saying a word, then flinched as the first gunshot rang out beside him. OMSPECs fired rifles and heaved grenades from behind thin metal bioreactors. Augustus hunched beside one and activated his broadcast comms. Over the sounds of desperation, he spoke as clearly as he could.

'Attention Orionis civilians and friendly forces. This is Commander Augustus Tyrell of the Navy Police. The *Archangel* is no longer under Navy control and should be considered hostile. Civilians should avoid travel to Corinth or Tabit Prime. Any warships loyal to the Orionis government are encouraged to assist in the protection of civilians from Ceti forces. All ships are cautioned to exercise extreme vigilance at this time.'

An OMSPEC was knocked off his feet by a blast; he disintegrated before he could hit the deck. Enemies were so close that Augustus could hear their voices.

Wyllym confirmed what he already suspected would happen.

'They've landed on the *Archangel*,' Augustus heard in his earpiece. 'You have to warn the Chancellor!'

Augustus switched channels. Vronn was seated with his back to a bioreactor – frozen, ineffective, resigned to his fate.

'Chancellor, the *Archangel* is lost,' Augustus said. 'Advise you recall all loyal Navy forces for the possible defence of Tabit Prime. Make secure preparations to be evacuated for your own safety. It's been an honour to serve ...'

'Ty, your son-in-law is here,' Wyllym said. 'He's on a Ceti corvette. I'm escorting him now.'

'Sir?' he heard. The voice was painfully familiar.

A Navy crewman with no name stepped around the reactor and levelled a rifle at him.

Augustus smiled, summoning the gentlest voice he could.

'You were good for Danna, son,' he said. 'I'm sorry for everything.'

The weapon stock struck him, and there was darkness.

36

JAKE

'Sir?' I heard myself repeat. 'Dad?'

'This is Captain Wyllym Lyons,' the voice of One-Three said. 'What ship is Vladric Mors on?'

'The *Griefmaker*,' the Minotaur answered.

'Then it's too late,' Wyllym said. 'Jake, you have to disengage *now*. Set course for Eris or Helena.'

'He called me "son",' I said.

'You can't help him,' Wyllym said. 'Stay with me, Jake.'

I looked towards my friend. It was hard to see or breathe. Dusty's hands were still on the controls. They were keeping us alive.

'Dusty?'

'That's some cool shit you said there,' he said. 'Real fast thinking, man. Bought us some time.'

His breathing was shallow. And I no longer had control of the *Breakaway*'s weapons.

'My name's Jake,' I said. 'I'm a cop.'

'There's a lot of metal out here,' Wyllym warned. 'Change course or I can't cover you.'

Dusty was frozen.

'Are you in command?' Wyllym demanded.

'He's our only way out,' I said.

'Is he?' Dusty asked.

I felt the warning as he said it; the exact moment he gave up.

I lunged for him as the *Breakaway* lurched towards the *Archangel* on

346

a suicide run. My actions were reflexive; one hand pushed the control stick over; the other punched Dusty in the helmet.

Lyons yelled something on the radio. I don't know what.

Dusty was limp in his harness. Collision alarms sounded. I didn't care. I didn't want to hurt him. But he was broken, and so was I.

Then I heard – felt – the most awful noise you could hear in a ship: metal striking metal, a deafening, lingering *crack*. My inner ear sensed the ship take on another spin; whatever we had struck was a glancing blow somewhere aft.

I unstrapped Dusty, pushing him aside as I scrambled into the captain's chair. Ripped his helmet off, put it on. Tried to make sense of the world. The *Breakaway* had lost her damaged thruster completely, leaving us with the centreline main and one manoeuvring jet. And I couldn't fly worth shit in the best of times.

'We're alive,' I said, fighting the controls as we corkscrewed forward. 'I have command.'

'The *Gettysburg* can cover an egress towards Eris,' Wyllym breathed, his voice very laboured now. 'I … can't do anything else for you. Stay on my six. Good luck.'

I tried to keep the *Breakaway* on the Gryphon's damaged rear as it turned and accelerated.

Rolling a few degrees per second, fires were raging inside the *Gettysburg*; there were more holes in her than I could count. She was so damaged I couldn't believe there was any fight left in her at all.

The *Archangel* was just a bystander in this fight, but her bay doors were closing. If any more Gryphons had survived, they were aboard. The remaining Ceti ships were engaged in life and death struggles with Navy corvettes; the frigates *Rio* and *Cologne* were both dark and lifeless, drifting along the same path they had entered the fray from.

'*Gettysburg*, I'm towing a Ceti corvette into your coverage,' Wyllym announced. 'Call sign *Breakaway*, she's one of ours.'

As the battered cruiser turned towards us, I noticed the Minotaur watching me. He was horribly burned; skin was sloughing off his face. But there was no anger. He was thoughtful; introspective; admiring the human in me.

The *Breakaway* was a runaway dead shot now, burning towards the *Gettysburg*, where good people were dying to save my dreadful life.

I saw her break in two, and for a moment, I saw Danna in the light.

37

VESPA

Behind the brave face of a leader navigating a crisis, Chancellor Jade was resigned to defeat. Moving briskly from one decision to the next, the nightmares had prepared her for this moment for years. The Gift, she now understood, was a curse. Glimpsing the future was pointless without the means to change it. The *Archangel* was just one variable in the calculus of causation, a distraction from countless unknown, vital details she had missed – the greatest of which was herself.

By taking the Chancellorship, Vespa had assumed responsibility for the fate of humankind. Failure was not supposed to be an option. If she survived, she would have to accept the possibility that her premeditated actions had done more to doom Orionis than anything Vladric Mors had already done.

On the *Tabit Genesis*, the War Room was located on the main centre-line of the original mothership. The microgravity environment was ideal for expediting the evacuation of government VIPs if necessary; a police gunship was docked directly outside the hull.

Real-time information from every Navy asset in Orionis was routed to this room. Unfortunately, the emergency response team of her government relied almost entirely on the Navy OPCOM leadership tier for strategic insight, and the members of that tier were either unresponsive or confirmed dead.

As the most senior Senator in the Orionis parliament, Brandon Tice was in attendance, assuming Augustus Tyrell's responsibility for civilian safety. A Navy Police technician, Lieutenant Marson Andrews, was coordinating the intelligence feeds and deployment logistics. Colonel Haley Tors led the Chancellor's security detail, and attending virtually was Captain Samson Jankovich, captain of the ONW *Sacramento* and commander of the battle group charged with the protection of Tabit Prime.

'Contact with the *Gettysburg* has been lost,' Lieutenant Andrews reported. 'TACLNK command now transferring to the *Brisbane*. Captain Dodson, do you read?'

The ONW *Brisbane* was one of six frigates assigned to Admiral Larksson's group, and had only just arrived as the battle was winding down, far too late to help.

'*Brisbane* copies,' Captain Dodson said. 'The *Gettysburg* is down … no beacons …'

Vespa felt a pang of dread. To a man, Admiral Larksson and his crew had fought to the end.

'Where is the *Archangel*?' she asked.

'Same location,' the *Brisbane* captain answered. 'No activity since the hangars closed.'

Vespa felt the only aspect of the crisis she had managed correctly was approving Commander Tyrell's plan to get Wyllym Lyons into the fight.

'Captain Lyons, have you heard from Commander Tyrell?' she asked.

There was no answer.

'Chancellor, we lost contact with Gunfighter One-Three and Lieutenant Reddeck when the *Gettysburg* exploded,' Captain Dodson finally said. 'No beacons from either ship. The debris field is too expansive to scan at this time.'

'What about Augustus?' Senator Tice asked.

'Unreachable since his announcement,' Captain Andrews said.

Vespa waved for both of them to be silent.

'Is the *Archangel* communicating with anyone?' she asked.

'Negative, no comm emissions,' Captain Dodson reported. 'No search or fire control radars either. She's just sitting there. The orphaned Ceti ships are fleeing. Some have surrendered. We've taken massive casualties and shifted our priority to rescue and recovery.'

'We're going to send help,' Vespa said. 'Proceed with caution, but move your fleet away from the *Archangel* as soon as you can.'

'Wilco,' Captain Dodson said. 'Chancellor, if I may, those Ceti orphans thought they were boarding the *Archangel*. Vladric hung them out to dry. I'd swear on it.'

Vespa understood the implications.

'Thank you, Captain,' she said. 'Now, why is it just sitting there?'

'The leading theory is she's crippled,' Senator Tice said. He would know, considering he had oversight of distributing government subsidies to contractors who had participated in the *Archangel*'s construction. To get the funds, the corporations had been forced to disclose all the building plans and supporting technology. 'The engineers we've spoken with all said that drive was at least a year away from live tests.'

'Well, clearly they were wrong,' Vespa said.

'In any case,' said Captain Dodson, 'we think Admiral Larksson forced the hand of whoever is in command of the *Archangel*. Shielded or not, the Ceti ships that boarded her wouldn't have survived otherwise. Not against the *Gettysburg*'s firepower.'

'Hedricks,' Vespa hissed. 'He'll answer for this. If he's not dead already.'

'Whatever his fate, we have no friendly assets left on the *Archangel*,' Captain Jankovich said from the *Sacramento*. 'The ship is lost.'

'Can it be boarded?' Vespa asked.

'We're the only group that can even consider it,' Captain Jankovich said. 'But getting close enough to breach is a different story.'

The Sacramento Task Force was ferrying one mechanised division. Supporting that group in combat required a cruiser and six frigates, plus a host of corvettes. To put the *Archangel*'s size in perspective, all twenty thousand of that division's troops, including their armour, mechs, gunships, and supporting logistical equipment wouldn't even fill a single deck level on the mothership – and there were thirty-five of them.

'Captain Dodson, how many Gryphons are left?' Senator Tice asked.

'We tracked seventeen when the fight began,' he said. 'Eight landed. Lyons shot the rest down.'

Vespa blinked.

'Captain Lyons shot down *eight* Gryphons?' she asked.

'Chancellor, I've never seen anything like it,' Captain Dodson said.

'Hell … I've never even *heard* of anything like that,' Senator Tice grumbled.

'The *Archangel*'s point defences were designed to blast asteroids out of the way,' Captain Jankovich said. 'If they're operational, we'll get real bloody on the approach.'

'That's the problem,' Captain Dodson reiterated. 'There are no good options for determining if she can fight or not.'

Vespa shook her head.

'The *Archangel* was built for the future,' she said, refusing to lavish feminine reverence upon the mothership like the others. 'New technologies were to be developed during its mission. Now if I'm not mistaken, Ceti just brought Basilisk shielding technology aboard. It's only a matter of time before it's completely impervious to our weapons.'

'So if boarding isn't a "good" option, what is?' asked Senator Tice. 'Nukes?'

'And draw the Raothri's attention?' Vespa asked. 'Out of the question.'

'They already know we're here,' Senator Tice said. 'Why bother coming after us now?'

'It's pointless to debate their rationale,' Vespa said, drawing a deep breath. 'All we know is nuclear weapons brought them to us before. I'd rather take my chances against the *Archangel*. Captain Jankovich?'

'Chancellor?'

'Please lead your task force to Corinth. Link with the *Brisbane* group, assist in recovery operations and prepare your troops for assault.'

'Yes, Chancellor,' Captain Jankovich said.

'That leaves Tabit Prime undefended,' Senator Tice warned. 'I hope the *Archangel* isn't bluffing.'

'We can always ask the corporations for help,' Vespa said, knowing full well they wouldn't respond. 'We'll rely on you to convince them.'

'They're more likely to court whoever they think will win,' Senator Tice said, with a hint of disgust. 'They've been fortifying their own property ever since this started. None has offered assistance.'

'Please ask them again,' Vespa said. 'If we have to make it worth their while, so be it. Just make it happen.'

Lieutenant Andrews gasped, his eyes wide with surprise.

'Chancellor,' he breathed. 'Harbour Control is tracking hundreds of new contacts approaching from Ares. They're inside our orbit and heading for Tabit Prime.'

'It can't be more Ceti ships,' Senator Tice said.

'Whoever they are, they're ignoring standard harbour approach vectors,' Lieutenant Andrews said. 'Eight *hundred* unique contacts and climbing ...'

'Chancellor,' Colonel Tors interrupted. 'I'm obliged to advise you of security protocol in the event we have to evacuate.'

'I'm not going anywhere,' Vespa snapped. 'New orders, Captain Jankovich: *defend Tabit.*'

'One *thousand* contacts,' Lieutenant Andrews said. 'Orbital guns are tracking, but there are too many to defend against.'

Vespa's corelink rang – an emergency message from ORPHUS. There was only one word:

Obyeran.

38

MAEZ

Lightspears were stealthy ships, Maez thought, but the lack of vigilance in Tabit Prime was appalling. The mission flight plan took them on a wide course skirting the Inner Rim, passing Eileithyia a week ago, then slinging around the sun and slowing at Ares until the time was right. Maez had always assumed the heart of human civilisation would be protected by layers upon layers of defences. Not so. Maez was beginning to realise that Vladric Mors's ambitions were more plausible than anyone imagined.

The taste of cryo chemicals lingered in his mouth, and a wisp of fog glazed his helmet as he wrenched it free. His genetically engineered body was invigorated by their proximity to the sun; not since his father left the Inner Rim had any Obyeran been this close. Beyond the bridge viewport, the marble-white crescent of Eileithyia loomed. Countless points of light blinked around the world, its space littered with hab modules, machines, and wasteful rubbish.

Maez had never understood why Myrha always spoke so reverently about this place. 'Because this is where it all began,' she would say, usually as a lead-in for showering their father with praise. 'He started there with nothing, and look at all he's accomplished.'

Maez was less appreciative. As far as he was concerned, the origination of all modern achievement was thanks to rampant sex among primates, and no one considered building them any monuments. People either exploited their potential or they did not. His father deserved no special accolades for being born with genes that would let him accomplish more than the rest.

A devious grin spread across his cheeks as the bright points of light began reacting to their presence. He imagined the spectacle of a thousand warships in one place was causing some concern. As X-band radars painted his ship, Maez prepared for the dirty work ahead.

'Vanguard lances to point defence positions,' he ordered.

The Lightspears were approaching Tabit Prime in a 'lens' formation one hundred kilometres in diameter, where the deepest part of the lens was furthest away from the fleet's forward direction. Each point on the periphery was a 'lance' consisting of six corvettes flying in close formation; at Maez's command, heavy beam cannons dropped from the fuselage of these 'vanguard' ships and rotated forward. If anyone in *Tabit* lost their senses and fired a railgun, three hundred heavy lasers would melt the slug before it could do any harm.

Reviewing his targeting information, Maez noted with amusement that the corporate ships were vacating first. For good fun, he considered broadcasting 'Take me to your leader' on a loop. Their cowardice was making it easier to justify what he had come here to do. Humanity was past due for another round of natural selection. Perhaps this bloody venture would benefit mankind in the long run.

The brightest point of all was taking shape; the ugly *Tabit Genesis*. If only Myrha could see it. She would certainly attempt to say a few inspiring words, to which he would roll his eyes in derision. He missed her deeply. It was time to get on with the ugly business of getting her back.

'Orionis,' he began, channelling the diplomatic verbiage he thought Myrha would use. 'My name is Maez. I am the son of King Masaad, ruler of House Obyeran. I must speak with Chancellor Jade.'

And no, he thought, I don't have an appointment.

Some elements of Tabit Prime's meagre Navy were coming into view – a cruiser, numerous corvettes, a handful of frigates, and a ship-yard with six half-stripped destroyers in the process of being refitted.

'Spear Lances, passive locks on that cruiser,' he instructed. 'Target its weapons only. The rest of you, steady as you are.'

Maez could sense the weakness of his opponent. They had no idea how to respond.

'This is a public channel,' *Tabit*'s Harbour Control replied. 'Do you wish to move to secure comms?'

'There is no need,' Maez said. 'Your people should hear what I came here to say.'

Several more moments passed.

'Prince Obyeran, this is Chancellor Jade,' the brittle voice said. 'Welcome to Tabit Prime. We are honoured by your presence.'

'The honour is ours,' Maez said. 'My King has sent me on a mission of mercy. He has no quarrel with you, nor the good people of Orionis. However, unfortunate circumstances have compelled him to make demands that he concedes are unjust, and evil. At such time as these matters are resolved, he swears, on the honour of our great House, to make amends.'

'Wouldn't you prefer to join us here in person to discuss your … offer?' she asked.

'That is most gracious of you, Chancellor, but time is of the essence.'

The Navy corvettes were changing course, and the frigates were drifting away from the cruiser.

'It usually is, whenever weapons are drawn,' she said. 'What can we do for you, Obyeran?'

Ah, finally. Some defiance, a little backbone. Good.

'We demand the following,' he said. 'First, do not, under any circumstances, send additional forces to Corinth. This is to spare your Navy any more loss of life. As a token of my respect for your armed forces, I will send ships to assist in your search and rescue operations, and return all recovered property to the nearest Navy asset.'

'That's kind of you,' Chancellor Jade said. 'Anything else?'

'My final demand is that you evacuate the *Tabit Genesis* at once. You can guess the reason why. I have no desire to harm anyone, but it would be unwise to challenge my resolve. You have sixty minutes to move your people out, starting now.'

There was no answer. Maez smiled as the queued shuttle traffic outside of *Tabit*'s hangar bay began to increase. Smaller personal craft were already darting out in streams.

'Chancellor,' he said. 'King Masaad wishes to express his deepest apology for these heinous demands. In exchange for your compliance, he offers to help rebuild – no. Not rebuild. *Replace Tabit* with another ship, a station, whatever you wish. You know he has the resources to achieve this, and he vows to commit them to Orionis. But time is counting down, whether you take his offer or not.'

The Lightspears were decelerating rapidly, but his Obyeran engineered musculoskeletal body was easily withstanding the pressure, no doubt alarming the Navy ships foolishly contemplating their options.

'Those are indeed cruel demands,' Chancellor Jade said. 'I've never met King Masaad, but by all accounts he is a decent man. But this isn't diplomacy. It's extortion.'

'Fifty-five minutes, Chancellor.'

'What compelled him to do this?' she asked. 'Is there anything we can do to help?'

Maez had to stifle a laugh.

'You can help by evacuating that station,' he said. 'There is no other solution. Given your inability to keep motherships from falling into the wrong hands, I'm sceptical of your ability to help. Gracious of you to offer, but I won't discuss the King's business. However … if you are as wise as the legends say, I think you can surmise that we share a mutual enemy in Vladric Mors.'

Scanning his active targets, Maez noticed the House Alyxander pleasure barges in their remote orbit, a third of the way to Amnisos. Anger twisted at his heart.

'The company you keep says much about you,' he said. 'Fifty-two minutes.'

'Do you think we're going to remain passive while you raze the single most important ship in human history?' Chancellor Jade said.

'History? Is that what's most important now?' Maez snapped. 'Chancellor, I am not a patient man. History mattered when we lived on Earth. Today, it prevents us from making difficult choices. Would you really risk the lives of your people for the sake of nostalgia? *Get off that ship!* It's a monument to failure. Build something truly great in its place. We'll help.'

'You are attacking the capital of a sovereign government,' she said. 'We will defend ourselves.'

'Chancellor, don't be a fool,' Maez growled. 'Does the captain of the *Sacramento* have a family? Do you think he would like to see them again? Ask how he feels about facing a thousand Lightspears. You cannot win, your soldiers know they cannot win, *and you will die if you remain on* Tabit. Forty-nine minutes!'

Maez slammed the seat rest. No wonder his father had left these Luddites to start his own empire. As he watched the panic unfold at the *Tabit* hangars, he shuddered at the prospect of butchering civilians. He had warned his father this could happen, and now bloodshed seemed inevitable. His Lightspears, and the crews that flew them, would follow him across the galaxy. But he did not want their first combat experience under his command to be against unarmed ships.

'Blades, go to delta,' he ordered.

'Blades' were the Lightspears assigned to the long-range damage-dealing segment of the fleet. The 'delta' configuration linked five ships with each other, bow to stern, with their beam lens aligned and inter-linked. The rear ship would fire the beam, and each successive ship would amplify its intensity to the highest power the lens could stand. Maez was going to use these 'blades' to carve up the *Tabit Genesis*, and anything else in his path.

When this ugliness was done, he would devote all his energy to finding Vladric Mors. No matter what happened to Myrha, that bastard needed to die. And before he did, Maez would make him reveal everyone that had assisted him – especially the traitor who had learned where to find Myrha during The Rites.

That was the greatest concern. It had to be someone within; someone very close. The game of Outer Rim influence was tilted towards House Alyxander, and they had deep pockets. Maez prayed they were involved. That was the battle he wanted to lead.

And as if some god heard his prayers, he noticed the House Alyxander pleasure barges were accelerating. If they stayed on course, their trajectory would lead them directly to the *Tabit Genesis*.

Maez was considering the implications of that when a new voice joined the channel.

'Hello, Maez. I am Arturus Jade, Ambassador of House Alyxander. Since you took to public channels, I see no reason why I can't join the conversation.'

'We have no business, Ambassador. I will speak only with Chancellor Jade.'

'I imagine she's indisposed at the moment,' Arturus said. 'Since she happens to be my sister, I feel I am the next best person to ... assist.'

'Forty minutes left.'

'Oh, she's aware, as is everyone else within a million kilometres of here. We have noted your actions, Maez. House Alyxander will assist the Orionis government in the evacuation of civilians.'

'Thirty-nine minutes.'

'So relieved the Prince knows how to read a clock – an essential skill for one who commands a thousand ships. One needs to be able to count them all. Orionis is watching you, Maez. Speculating on why Lightspears, Ceti, and the *Archangel* are all in bed together. Speaking of guilty pleasures, we have many beds on our barges. Won't you join us to, say, get your mind off things a bit?'

The last time Maez had felt this humiliated was when Myrha had taken off his hand.

'Save one for your own corpse,' he growled. 'I'll send it back to Alyxander with the King's regards.'

'How is the old man doing?' Arturus asked. 'Off crafting some new technology while you misbehave? Pity, I always thought he was someone who wanted to do some good here.'

Maez took a breath. He would not be provoked.

'King Masaad is deeply apologetic,' he said, 'and vows to help the Orionis government rebuild.'

'Sure he does,' Arturus cooed. 'You know, Maez, I always imagined your sister leading that fleet around. One has to wonder: you're here, with the crown jewels, so to speak ... and your father is sorry? What could Vladric possibly take to make him send a thousand Lightspears all this way to do harm? By the way ... how *is* Myrha these days?'

The pleasure barges were closing at terrific speed, turning their bulks around to burn and decelerate. At their current velocity, they would be almost impossible to avoid hitting when the attack commenced.

'Don't put your barges between us and the *Tabit*,' Maez warned.

'I bet Myrha isn't well at all,' Arturus said. 'So, Vladric found the King's weakness. I'm sure you've asked yourself by now: is she really worth what you're about to do?'

Seven thousand Obyerans were listening to this. Maez was moving beyond anger, surrendering to the rationale that he had been sent here to do violence.

'She's out there somewhere, suffering,' Arturus pressed. 'All that strength and intellect rendered moot as she lies bound, gagged, and violated by someone weaker than her, afraid of her, threatened by her greatness. Imagine, to be denied what she was literally born for. And here you are, the beneficiary of her torment. Here's a thought: perhaps *you're* the one who gave her to Vladric. We're none the wiser, Prince.'

Maez snapped.

'Target that lead barge and fire,' he ordered.

39

VESPA

Laser fire is visible only when the medium it travels through is filled with dust.

An observer from one of *Tabit*'s rings might have seen several points of light in the black of space, each lasting a second or two. They would have also seen the simultaneous obliteration of a House Alyxander pleasure barge as its unarmoured hull plating vaporised in a spectacular plume of white-hot debris. A secondary explosion from within broke the barge into three incinerated segments, each one hundreds of metres long.

Two more points of light appeared, and the largest chunks were blasted into clouds of shrapnel hurling towards the *Tabit*.

'That debris field will hit us in twelve minutes,' Lieutenant Andrews warned. 'Ring One and bow-ward. Too much for point defences.'

Vespa's teeth were clenched tight.

'How many are still on board?'

Senator Tice was beyond livid.

'What was that asshole brother of yours thinking?'

'*I said how many!*' Vespa shouted.

'Twelve thousand,' Lieutenant Andrews said. 'Excluding Navy personnel.'

Thirty-three minutes remained in the deadline. They had managed to get forty thousand off, but the hangars were overwhelmed. It was time for the triage to begin.

'That's not enough time,' Vespa grumbled. 'It was never going to be enough time. Lieutenant, start directing people in the rings towards the life pod batteries. When those are expended, it's survival suits for everyone else. Make sure some of the queued shuttles are prepared to make EVA pickups.'

'Yes, ma'am,' Lieutenant Andrews said.

Vespa glared at Senator Tice.

'My brother provoked Maez to discover their weakness,' Vespa said. 'Now we know what to shoot at. We're going on the offensive to buy ourselves more time. Captain Jankovich, focus on neutralising those Lightspear clusters. You now have total control of Orionis's arsenal – don't make it easy for the bastards. If they want to hurt the *Genesis* they'll have to get in close to do it. I never dreamt I would say this … but the *Tabit Genesis* is indefensible. Abandon ship.'

There was a chorus of solemn, affirmative responses.

'Agreed.'

'Chancellor,' Colonel Tors said. 'We have to move you *now*.'

'Not yet, Colonel,' Vespa said.

Another barge exploded. Then another. The House Alyxander ships were vaporising at random as the entire Lightspear fleet unleashed beam fire upon them.

'You're not a military officer,' Colonel Tors insisted. 'The rules are clear on this. Let's move.'

Vespa sighed, taking a look around.

'The toll will be more than any of us can bear,' she said. 'But Orionis shall persevere.'

'*Sacramento* here,' Captain Jankovich said. 'It's been an honour to serve.'

40

THE BLOOD PRINCE

Maez enjoyed watching those barges die.

Their destruction served notice for those Orionis 'firstborns' to take him seriously. And who better to warm the Lightspear's guns on than House Alyxander? But the time for games was over. It was time to prosecute the King's business and then start the journey home. If Myrha was not released, they would be making stops along the way, perhaps even paying the *Archangel* a visit. Now there was a challenge worthy of House Obyeran ...

... Maez happened to be looking at the danger just as it happened.

Six, eight, and then an entire squadron of his Lightspears exploded as a hail of rail fire converged on four separate deltas. The Navy cruiser *Sacramento*, which had moved close to the *Tabit* to help ferry passengers, instead decided to fight. She was supported by the moored Geneva-class destroyers, still in port, their guns coordinating as a single battery.

Tabit's orbital turrets had fired as well. Each delta had faced a minimum of ten shells per ship, all approaching from different trajectories. The Lightspear point defences were overwhelmed. Maez could see the rounds heat up as they approached, streaking across space as the Lightspear beams tried in vain to vaporise them before impact.

Now one hundred and forty Obyerans had died under his command.

Maez channelled his rage into the skills his father had programmed him with.

First, he disarmed Orionis. Lightspears decimated the orbital turrets, then filled space with electronic noise to fool Navy sensors, blinding the frigates and corvettes. One by one they were melted into slag, withering under the staggering firepower of the Lightspear fleet. They swarmed the *Sacramento* with surgical precision, melting her railguns and missile bays. They razed the destroyers, severed their moorings and sent them adrift, crashing into the fragile shipyard that had constructed them.

By the time the last Navy gun ceased, the *Tabit Genesis* was unapproachable. Debris clouds from the decimated House Alyxander barges hammered its hull with deadly shrapnel. Huge strips of metal plating, some of it welded when humans still walked the Earth, were blasted away from the superstructure; ominous jets of gas sprouted from ruptures on all three of the *Tabit*'s rings.

Soon, only the crippled *Sacramento* and the *Tabit* remained. The space around her hangars was littered with destroyed shuttlecraft; people died as cloud after cloud of debris struck. Maez tallied his own losses: ninety-seven Lightspears destroyed, and just five survivors among their crew.

He turned his fury towards the crippled Navy cruiser, limping just a few hundred metres from the *Tabit*'s hangars, surrounded by tugs and shuttles of her own, desperate to save themselves.

Vladric Mors had demanded that the *Tabit Genesis* be destroyed. How convenient then, Maez thought, that the *Sacramento* and her fusion reactors were so close by.

41

VESPA

Vespa's last memory was authorising transfer of the government capitol to the Navy shipyard at Amnisos. And before that, the declaration of martial law for the Inner Rim.

She was about to address the people of Orionis when a horrible sound burst her eardrums. Twisted metal fell from above; then a revolting, nauseating feeling rushed through her as the station's rotation changed direction, yanking everyone and everything off their feet; the floor dropping away and then rushing up to meet them over and over.

Colonel Tors had been begging her to leave. One minute sooner would have been enough. Vespa saw the colonel slammed against the ceiling; her head flapped against her shoulders, held in place only by skin.

Then, the terror of pitch darkness, and the roar of air escaping a breach.

When her eyes opened, the first colour she saw was gold, then the upside-down face of torment: the Angustia of House Alyxander, embracers of human suffering. The comforting blue light of ORPHUS was among them.

Darkness again.

Vespa awoke, as she knew she would, to catch her final, familiar glimpse of the *Tabit Genesis*: her rings breaking apart, and the entire ship twisting in a lazy corkscrew; a massive metal tomb devoid of light and life, a silhouette set against the dead skies of Eileithyia.

'Rest, sister,' she heard Arturus say. 'And let the new dreams come.'

42

ADAM

For a time, the *Lycidas* fascinated Adam enough to make him forget that it had killed Pegasus. But now, as he coasted through the circular hallways leading to the observation bubble, he felt the same suffocating anxiety as he had when his father was dying. He would trade all the luxurious amenities of the *Lycidas* to return to those humble days, when he was just a miner providing for his family.

The source of his angst was the three-hundred-cubic metre steel tank currently being lowered into the Zeus atmosphere. Nicknamed 'Orpheus', the Merckon scientists intended to capture a live hunter with it.

Using Viola's research of the creature's anatomy, they had worked day and night for weeks to build it. The main caveat for the trap's design was the Arkady's hypersensitivity to electromagnetic fields: active emissions could not be used to target them. Every drone that used a radar or radio frequency was attacked by hunters and destroyed inside an hour. Drones with passive sensors could never find targets. And pilotless, AI-controlled mechs angered the hunters; one was snatched from the rig and hurled down into the depths.

As far as anyone knew, the only reliable method for drawing hunters to the rig was to use Adam as bait.

The next design challenge was an arrest mechanism that could stop a hunter within the high gravity, high wind environment of Zeus *without* using conventional power-assisted projectiles. Arkady hunters repeatedly demonstrated their cunning ability to evade fire-control systems; thus Orpheus could not use electronic tracking systems or 'active energy' delivery mechanisms. So Merckon's engineers built a harpoon system that relied on a multitude of nanoscale spring coils that, in aggregate, stored enough mechanical energy to launch the grapple and tow cable with as much force as a subsonic railgun slug.

The catch, however, was that the weapon would have to be manually aimed and fired.

After analysing the radar imagery of the Pegasus 'incident', the scientists concluded that a mature hunter could survive a puncture wound – and that several thousand volts of sustained electrical current would paralyse the specimen without killing it. When the harpoon struck the target, the voltage would be applied; then the winch would pull the crippled beast inside and seal. A turbine-driven air filtration system attuned to the local atmospheric molecular composition would pressurise the tank and simulate a jet stream inside to keep the creature from asphyxiating.

The goal was to keep the hunter alive for ten hours. It was not expected to survive longer. A host of passive *and* invasive scientific instruments designed to study the creature's unique biology lined the inside of the tank.

To Adam, this plan amounted to the human equivalent of kidnapping, torture and murder. Viola also loathed the plan but was powerless to stop it. The *Lycidas* was not their ship. Merckon had the numbers, the incentives, and the weapons to put a stop to anything that would interfere with their interests.

Adam would have to play his part whether he wanted to or not. So instead of trying to fight the plan, he and Viola secretly planned for its failure.

Their preparations began with Adam learning how to fly the MGX-10 Avalon inside the *Lycidas*'s ventral hangar bay. Excluding his family and Viola, the security detail was the only crew that tolerated his company. When Adam expressed interest in the gunship, they let him sit in the cockpit and explained the craft's capabilities. With their blessing, Viola gave him access to a training sim and encouraged him to learn how to fly it.

Since then, he had spent nearly all his time on board mastering the Avalon, and hardly any on the rig itself. Merckon owned the trawler, and the *Lycidas* had enough *Three* on board to burn non-stop to the Inner Rim and back. There was little else he could do to make himself useful, and the scientists had no time for his questions. They were too busy transforming the rig from a mining station into an armed research platform.

That was just as well. Adam hadn't been able to bring himself to return to Zeus since Pegasus had died, and Viola was the only person on board who didn't think of the Arkady as monsters. There was no one else to turn to, his mother least of all. She had become even more unavailable, absorbed in her own dark thoughts, losing weight by the day and obsessed with her new habit of smoking narcotics. Whenever Adam asked what was wrong, she claimed to miss his father, which angered him since he knew that was a lie.

Ever since Merckon had entered their lives, his mother had never spent another moment alone with him or Abby. Both had sensed on numerous occasions that there was something urgent she wanted to tell them. But she never did ... because of Captain Mohib. He held some power over her, and it was clear that power extended beyond the traditional role of starship command. Everyone on the *Lycidas* who was enthusiastic with their work and the mission got along with the captain. Abby worshipped the man to a sickening extent.

But Adam didn't like him. Neither did Viola nor his mother. And no one had the courage or even the desire to challenge him, especially now that his moment of triumph had arrived.

'Adam?' a familiar voice called out behind him.

He turned and saw Abby floating there, dressed in her Merckon uniform.

'I'm not going to be late,' Adam said, rolling his eyes.

'I didn't come here to nag you,' she said, looking sheepish. 'Can we talk for a minute? Before we go in?'

'Now?'

'It's never a good time,' she said, lowering her voice, glancing around. 'Or place. Ever, with Mom. And now, I think I know why: Captain Mohib isn't who he claims to be.'

'Well, duh,' Adam said.

'I know you *suspect* they have a history, but he slipped. He said to me, "You have your mother's eyes."'

'So what?'

'Well, it really bothered me because—'

'That's really creepy, you know that?'

Abby sighed impatiently.

'Mom despises him but still does everything he asks,' she explained. 'She denies ever having met him before, but ... she's never been a good liar.'

'Your eyes are green,' Adam suddenly realised. 'Hers are dark brown.'

'I took some of Mom's hair and sequenced it,' she whispered, gently letting her greaves make contact with the deck. 'The *Lycidas* taught me how. She was born with green eyes. Like mine. So was Dad.'

Adam blinked.

'Are they really our parents?' he asked.

'Biologically, yes,' she said. 'But ... I don't believe the surname "Lethos" is ours. Adam ... they had their appearance *changed*. The *Lycidas* told me something else. We aren't ghosts. We ... are *firstborns!*'

She paused to let it sink in. But Adam didn't care. His father had once explained what amniosynthesis was. It was just a different way for people to be born.

'So what if we are?' Adam said.

'Don't you see?' Abby implored, eyes darting around again. 'It explains why they always discouraged any talk of travelling to the Inner Rim ... why Mom refused help for Dad even near the end. They were *running* from something to protect *us*. Something even worse than Ceti. And I think Captain Mohib knows what. I have memories from before we settled here ... just flashes here and there, but I always felt we used to have a better life. Mom always told me I was mistaken. But we weren't meant to be miners.'

'Speak for yourself,' Adam said. 'So who's Captain Mohib, really?'

'I don't know,' Abby said. 'But he has far too much influence with Merckon to just be a freight captain.'

'This doesn't change anything,' Adam said. 'We've never been able to trust anyone but each other.'

'About that ...' Abby said, looking downwards. 'I haven't been the best sister to you. I'm sorry for my behaviour. Some of the time, anyway. When you weren't acting like a little—'

'—Brat Face,' Adam offered.

She flashed a brief grin.

'For what it's worth … I don't agree with what they're doing here either.'

She pushed herself forward, latching onto him in an embrace that left them both floating through the hallway.

'I love you,' she said, squeezing tight. 'You'll always be my little brother. Please be careful.'

'Ladies and gentlemen?' Captain Mohib announced, his champagne pouch raised before him. 'Orpheus is in place.'

The bubble observatory erupted in cheers. All the mission personnel were present, dressed in white and green jumpsuits, embracing one another beneath the distant glare of the Orionis sun.

Adam tethered his greaves near the entrance and kept quiet.

'We don't normally throw early celebrations,' Captain Mohib said, as the voices lowered. 'But your effort deserves an exception. Corporate is so pleased with your progress they've upped the ante: for every hour we keep our specimen alive, each of you will earn an additional *ten per cent* of your base mission pay.'

Excited murmurs filled the room.

'Some of you are about to become very wealthy,' Captain Mohib announced, 'and your discoveries will keep paying dividends – *Merckon* dividends – once the Arkady's secrets are unlocked.'

More cheers and backslapping ensued. Adam suppressed a yawn.

'Now, every mission has its doubters,' Captain Mohib said, looking towards Viola. The room silenced. 'But we should *welcome* scepticism. It inspires diligence in our preparations. Our mission does raise ethical questions … Dr Silveri is right to ask them. Is it ethical to capture an alien life form so we can learn more about it? I'll answer simply with this: the Arkady have a homeworld. We don't. In the universal ecosystem of life, we are but one small creature in a galactic sea, and we must feed. Life is an invasive species. It began on Earth when a comet brought microorganisms that spawned from elsewhere in the cosmos. What we do, we do for our own survival. We *must* unlock the secrets of the Arkady. Our lives depend on it. Gavin and Karyn? Please join me up here.'

370

Adam frowned as they walked to the podium. These two had allegedly demonstrated the highest piloting proficiency in the EVAM simulator, and would be the ones who manually aimed and fired the harpoon. Of course, the training was in itself a competition that had brought out the worst among the scientists, because the winner would draw additional 'hazard pay' for taking the risk.

To help mitigate the danger, the EVAM mechs were armed with 30mm Gatling guns that fired hollow-point slugs, plus white noise pulse emitters that would cause the same carnage the *Lycidas*'s radar had wreaked on Pegasus.

To Adam, the measures were illusory compensation for the electronic blackout requirement of the mission. Nothing, not even the new security cameras Merckon had installed, could be operational. And the manned EVAMs themselves would have to be placed on passive standby, running life support and little else. Adam had tried warning them that even with the reduced EM signature, the Arkady would see the EVAMs as clearly as they had his own mech. But no one took his opinions about anything seriously.

The *Lycidas* would be unable to see or hear what was happening on the rig until contact was made, or a 'contingency' forced them to abort the mission. Only then could radio silence be broken, at which point the research vessel would activate its powerful radars to drive the Arkady away.

Captain Mohib raised a hand towards the two beaming scientists.

'To the best of the best,' he said. 'We're in your capable hands. You are leading Merckon – and all of mankind – into a new frontier. Cheers!'

The group shouted encouragement as they converged on the pair with celebratory hugs. Viola moved away from the crowd, towards the exit.

'Hey,' she said, with a warm smile. 'You okay?'

'I'm fine,' Adam replied. 'Just don't know what the point of me being here was.'

She nodded towards the podium.

'Control,' she said. 'That's all.'

'I'm tired of it,' Adam said. 'When this is over, I want to leave. Or for the *Lycidas* to go.'

She gently turned his shoulders away from Captain Mohib's stare.

'Good things come to those who wait,' she said.

Whether the implication was really there or not, a glimmer of hope rose in Adam's heart.

'How long?'

'Let this run its course,' she advised. 'Never quit on hope, Adam.'

Captain Mohib nearly startled him.

'And how is our little mech pilot doing?'

'Fine,' Adam said.

'Let's have a chat,' the captain said, forcing him away from Viola. He placed a hand on Adam's shoulder as they walked.

'You've always provided for your family,' he said. 'I admire that. This is a chance to secure their welfare permanently. Your mother and sister could live more comfortably than they ever imagined. But that depends entirely on you. Do your part and they'll never have to worry about money again. Cross me, and I'll make them suffer.'

Adam could only nod.

'I'm glad we understand each other,' the captain said, before frowning suddenly. His eyes were darting back and forth as though reading something. Then he left in a hurry, pulling himself briskly away.

Viola said nothing, motioning for Adam to keep silent.

He looked up towards the Orionis star. The Inner Rim was out there somewhere, huddled close to her for warmth. Adam wondered if he would ever see it, that faraway place that produced monsters such as Captain Mohib.

'Come on,' Viola coaxed, tousling his hair. 'Let's get ready.'

Dawn Lethos/Dayla Straka was smoking in her cabin; green smog streamed from her mouth, snaking towards the air ducts above. She needed more of the drug to get high, and wished something stronger was on board.

Captain Mohib walked in without knocking. He sat at the table, while she kept staring blankly at the bulkhead in front of her.

'Something's happened in Tabit,' he said. 'The Orionis government has fallen. House Oberyan destroyed the *Tabit Genesis*. The *Archangel* has been overrun by Ceti. And the corporations are scrambling to protect themselves.'

'Oh?' she responded, cocking her head to one side. 'You should be well informed.'

'As you were, once,' Travis growled. 'What do you think is happening?'

'I've been exiled for a long time,' she said. 'You really must be desperate to be asking me.'

'Tell me why you and Tomas left,' Travis demanded, his voice thick with annoyance. 'Why did Titan go after you?'

Dayla turned slowly, exhaling a long line of smoke.

'You rub shoulders with Argus Fröm, right?' she asked. 'Ask him.'

Travis stared at her for a moment, then struck her face with the back of his hand. The impact bent her sideways in the microgravity, but not hard enough to break the grip of her greaves on the deck.

She straightened up, rubbing her cheek, her eyes dark. But the slightest hint of a smile was there.

'When the *Archangel* was commissioned, there were two hundred living highborns remaining,' she began. 'Even then, Argus Fröm was the most influential among them. His vision for the *Archangel* wasn't a ship that could just *reach* another world. After Eileithyia, he wanted a ship that could *create* one.'

'What do you mean, "create one"?' Travis scoffed, watching her gather up the burning joint that had been knocked from her lips. 'Who else was involved with this?'

'Lance Alyxander, Franz Hedricks, and his son, Vadim. They were members of the *Archangel* consortium, including the Orionis government. But they disagreed with its charter, which vowed to leave the indigenous, intelligent life forms of any discovered world undisturbed – even if that world was habitable. To Franz, that was madness. Argus concurred. So they conspired to build support for their position. Not only were they willing to eradicate alien life to make room for humans, they wanted to reformat the new world itself.'

'How?'

'With biotech,' she said, stabbing the joint out. 'The forbidden weapons of the Third World War. Lance was a headstrong fellow with his own ideas for a mothership and ran off to found his cult. But he claimed to know how to get the *Archangel* into Fröm's hands. So they struck a deal. Argus and the rest agreed to acquire the entire Catalogue, including the biocybernetic weapon sequences. In return, Lance would deliver them the *Archangel*.'

'And that was what made you run?'

'No,' Dawn said. 'Tomas had discovered that Fröm succeeded in stealing the weapon sequences. But he couldn't understand what there was to gain from it. Titan was already the wealthiest corporation in civilisation. He didn't know what Fröm planned to do with them, and we didn't find out until after it was too late. Had he not gone to the police, things might have been different for us.'

'Poor you,' Travis spat. 'Was Ceti in on this deal?'

'I don't know.'

'Well who else was?'

Dawn smiled as she lit another joint.

'All I know for certain is that Argus asked the founders of Iopa, Dyselan … and Vulcan.'

'He asked *Cerlis*?' Travis fumed.

'Mhmm,' Dawn acknowledged. 'But she refused. Imagine, saying "no" to Argus Fröm *and* Franz Hedricks. The most powerful men in existence. And yet, helpless before her.'

Travis stood up.

'Is she the one who told you all this?'

Dawn smiled when she noticed his eyes.

'Wondering why *you* weren't asked?' she cooed.

His expression told her everything and more.

She turned her back as he rushed out, and resumed getting stoned.

For all their meddling on the mining rig, the Merckon people had the decency to leave his beloved Pegasus mech alone. And they'd given him access to the EVAM hangar on the *Lycidas*, with his pick of spare parts to nurture the old mech back to health. She was as good as new – in fact, better than new. Adam had replaced the entire electrical system, including life support. A new Merckon fusion reactor sat in its engine housing, making her overpowered for her size. But he left a few things untouched, especially the limbs and main chassis. They were worn and dented, but now had shiny accents from all the joints he had replaced.

Adam liked the rugged look of it, especially in the company of the white-plated EVAMs travelling down on the rocket sleds. With the new optics system he could zoom across the cloud vapour and see them on the cables from hundreds of metres away. Viola's was the only one that was unarmed. He focused on her face inside the reinforced glass. She was scared. They all were.

As the sled plummeted through the cloud ceiling, Adam glimpsed Orpheus rising from the centre of the platform, a trapezoidal monstrosity ringed with spherical tanks. The rig looked nothing like the one he had left weeks ago. Everything was different.

The braking rockets fired, sending a shudder through the mech. Now the reality hit home, twisting his conscience in knots. As the sled gate opened, Adam caught himself staring at the rails surrounding the platform perimeter.

Violence had never entered Adam's mind until now: he envisioned Captain Mohib trapped in the grasp of his mech, savouring his pleas for mercy as he hurled him over the side.

The flash of Gavin's floodlights from afar broke his dark fantasy. Viola's EVAM did the same.

It was time.

He walked towards the leading edge of the rig, where the atmosphere scrubbers had been.

He thought of his father, back to better days when there'd been no context for understanding how little they had, or how dangerous their work was. When there was only each other, and the rig, and learning how to make it all work.

Adam switched on his radio. Set it to the same frequency he always used.

'I miss you, Dad.'

Panning left and right, he gazed upon the dark clouds rising in the yellow sky.

'If you're out there, listening,' he said aloud, eyes filling with tears. 'I love you. I wish we had had more time.'

The wind was howling; wisps of vapour zipped over the deck.

He walked along the former intakes, scanning the horizon. There was nothing left to say. If they didn't come, that was fine. Eventually he reached the inert EVAM piloted by Viola. She was looking at him, her violet eyes glistening with empathy.

Then they opened wide in terror.

A sole hunter flew low over the rig, soaring just a metre or two over their heads. Extending its flaps, it slowed as it passed, regarding Adam for a moment. Then it dipped beneath the downwind rail and out of sight.

Two hundred metres upwind, he saw Karyn signalling with Gavin. Neither had seen a hunter in its element before. They were trying not to panic.

The hunter reappeared upwind. Karyn's mech was already powered up, moving towards the harpoon.

Adam's heart filled with grief.

'I'm sorry,' he breathed, thinking of Pegasus, and of the hunter that was about to die. 'Please tell Mother I'm so sorry.'

Swooping towards him again, the hunter braked and halted directly above the mech. Flaps opened in its gelatinous skin to bleed off more air; thick tentacles lashed onto the railing, anchoring it in place.

Then premonition struck Adam like a bolt of lightning, and there was death in the vision.

'Karyn, *now*!' Gavin shouted, breaking comm silence.

The hunter turned in Gavin's direction. Karyn raised her weapon. She couldn't miss.

Before Adam could blink, the spear impaled the creature, deploying its grapple on the far side of its body.

The hunter arched in agony, subdermal lightning bolts of pain shooting away from the entry wound. Karyn hooked the end of the spooling wire to the winch.

Then she activated the current.

Thousands of volts seared through the hunter, turning its belly into a coruscating chaos of suffering.

Adam had seen enough, and sprang to action.

It began with a march – then a sprint, as fast as the mech would allow – around the perimeter of Orpheus, rounding the bend just as a tentacle knocked Gavin's EVAM over, sending several large tanks of compressed oxygen flying across the deck.

'Gavin!' Karyn screamed. 'Do it!'

Adam wasn't sure what he was doing; pure instincts compelled him. But before he could reach him, Gavin's EVAM was up, aiming the harpoon.

Again, the hunter recoiled from the impaling shot, then froze as more current flowed in.

Adam accelerated his charge, but Gavin timed a perfect swing of the EVAM's powerful arm at him, connecting at the shoulder and knocking the Pegasus clean off its tripeds. Adam was slammed into his harness as he crashed into the deck.

'Little shit,' Gavin said. 'Karyn! The winch!'

Flipping himself over, Adam saw the cables begin to retract, hauling the struggling hunter towards Orpheus.

Viola, who had been trying to reach Adam, was in the wrong place at the wrong time.

In a desperate spasm of pain, the hunter flailed a wild tentacle. It smashed into her with such force that her EVAM tumbled end over end before smashing into the deck. The Orpheus winches were working hard, but the beast was tiring.

Adam rushed towards Viola's downed mech, checking it for damage. As he did, Karyn gasped.

'Holy God,' Karyn whispered, when a great shadow fell over Adam, just like it had before when …

He reeled around, full of hope.

There, looming above the rig and surrounded by a furious pack of hunters, was …

'… *Pegasus*!' Adam exclaimed.

The beast's underside unleashed an angry pulse of light.

NO

The hunters attacked, lashing at the deck. Some had attached themselves to the suspension cables. Others were ripping anything that resembled a transmitter off the deck.

'*Lycidas*, abort, abort,' Gavin cried. 'Send the pulse!'

Adam turned over and shielded Viola with his own mech.

'Don't look,' he said. 'You can't help them.'

Gavin switched on his fire control radar. The hunters had blocked their routes back to the sleds.

'*Lycidas*, come in!' he said, panic in his voice. 'We're under attack! Send the pulse!'

Captain Mohib's cold voice answered.

'What do you mean, abort?' he said. 'Why can't I see what's happening? Is the specimen trapped or not?'

The last camera on the rig was ripped from its post by enraged hunters. Adam saw Viola's eyes regain focus; she was breathing fast, and then shrieked as the booming sound of an EVAM cannon cut into the Zeus air.

Adam saw its tracer rounds chase a hunter across the sky.

'Run!' Gavin cried.

Karyn switched on the white noise emitter, freezing some hunters midflight. They convulsed helplessly as the current swept them past the rig; others began hurling themselves at the deck, sending metal skidding with each terrifying impact.

'*Lycidas*!' Karyn screamed. 'Help us!'

'Did … you … capture one?' Captain Mohib repeated.

Suddenly, Viola stood upright and marched towards Orpheus. Before Adam could warn her, she had ripped open its panels and plunged the mech's hands inside. After a moment, the electrical current paralysing the trapped hunter ceased. It went limp, flapping in the wind, held in place only by the harpoon tethers.

Adam heard the horrible sound of shrieking, snapping metal; the entire deck shuddered beneath his feet as Pegasus wrapped its enormous tentacles around the radio tower and ripped it off, hurling it over the side.

Then Karyn *really* screamed.

A tentacle had lashed around her EVAM, raising her high above Orpheus. Pegasus brought her close to its skin, regarding her as Gavin raked cannon rounds across its flesh.

Karyn tried to defend herself with her own guns, firing wildly as Pegasus shook her.

Then Adam's vision exploded into stars; his lungs suddenly had no air. A devastating blow to his midsection had knocked him flat on his back. Wet, excruciating pain spread through his legs and hips.

The mech's UI warned that the leg actuators were destroyed; severe structural damage had been incurred in the torso; but the reactor was unaffected, and there was no breach. The stray cannon round had pushed the armour plating in, displacing everything in front of it, including Adam's pelvis.

'Adam!' Viola cried, rushing towards him.

'No!' Adam croaked, his teeth clenched in agony. 'Stay there!'

Blinking through pain, he looked up in time to see Gavin torn in two. Then Karyn was thrown over the rails.

'*No!*' she cried in terror. 'Oh my God! No! *No!*'

She screamed and screamed, falling towards oblivion.

The hunters came for Viola next. She stumbled backwards, arms raised to protect herself.

'Stop!' Adam cried. 'Please, *stop!*'

Angry tentacles stopped just centimetres from Viola's faceplate. Agony was overwhelming Adam. His vision tunnelled as he fought the urge to sleep.

The bottom of the leviathan's belly was flashing furiously.

'The pulses …?' Viola whispered in terror. 'What's it saying?'

Adam struggled to reach the console.

'Use … this,' he said, sending her the translation algorithm.

ADAM
YOU ARE INJURED
RETURN TO THE VEIL

Viola's EVAM was now reading this as well.

'Please don't hurt her,' Adam stammered.

THIS FEMALE
WHY PROTECT

'She's a friend,' Adam said.

TRUST HER

'Yes,' Adam stammered. 'I'm … so sorry about … Pegasus.'

WE KNOW
WHAT PEGASUS
KNEW
WE ARE
PEGASUS
NOW

Viola was breathless, her eyes filling with tears as the beast hovered directly over her.

ADAM MUST LIVE
HELP HIM

Every transmitter except the radios in their EVAMs was gone.

'*Lycidas*, we have injuries,' Viola said, glancing towards the rocket sleds. They looked intact, if slimy from the entrails of dead hunters. 'Ready the trauma centre – we're coming up.'

As the strobes of light illuminated the deck, tentacles gently embraced Adam's mech.

The EVAM's display made Viola's heart sink.

LYCIDAS
DEPARTED

'What do you mean ...?' she asked.
Adam cried out in pain as his mech was lifted.

TO THE VEIL
THEY RETURN

'Leave me here,' Adam said, his voice barely a whisper.
Viola had never been more scared or more amazed.

YOUR TABIT GENESIS
HAS FALLEN

Hunters moved Adam to the sled; he groaned every metre of the way. Viola struggled to keep up, marvelling in terror as they placed him inside. She detached the refuelling hoses as quickly as she could.

'I don't know what's waiting for us up there,' she said.

Adam's eyes were blank, his breath laboured. He was too weak to speak any more.

'You're strong, Adam! Stay with me!' Viola encouraged, closing the gate and stepping back. 'I'm right behind you!'

He cried out as the rocket motor ignited. Then there was silence.

Viola didn't watch it ascend. As she turned towards the rocket sled on the far side of the platform, grey-black translucent tentacles swooped her off the deck.

They set her down before the sled with startling gentleness but didn't let go.

Pegasus was speaking.

As the words typed out on her screen, she saw hunters sever the cables holding their now deceased sibling in place. The current and harpoon wounds had been too much for the creature. It vanished into the jet stream.

Then Pegasus reached *inside itself* and extracted something, cradling it with care.

Viola saw another life form resembling a tiny scyphozoan the size of her fist.

Pegasus placed it inside Orpheus. The tentacle withdrew as the tank sealed shut.

LEARN ITS SECRETS
USE THEM
TAKE US TO THE VEIL
SAVE ADAM
DO NOT BETRAY US
GO

The tentacles released. One struck the launch key.
Viola ascended.

43

AUGUSTUS

Five Years Earlier

'Augustus,' Katrin Tyrell said. 'I'm leaving.'

Days of grieving had left her eyes red and swollen. Friends helped her stand from the pew, but Augustus said nothing, even as they led her away. He had no comfort to offer. Instead, he kept staring at the back of Jake's uniform. The young man had been kneeling before the casket for an hour. The Tabit Prime chapel had emptied long before.

The Orionis government had provided a state funeral with full military honours for his daughter and unborn grandson. No one from OPCOM attended, as they were busy patrolling the Belt in search of the scum that had murdered her several days earlier. There wasn't much to 'bury'. Just a bloodstained piece of metal and a shred of hair: all that could be recovered of the shuttle that had been carrying Danna before it was destroyed by a Ceti bomb. The casket would be set adrift on a symbolic course for Earth. Before it reached the orbit of Ares, it would disintegrate from the heat of the Orionis sun.

And then, all that would be left of his daughter's life was Jake. His proud son-in-law. The son he always wished he had, until he lost Danna.

Augustus couldn't have asked for a finer man to marry his daughter. He had hated him at first, of course. Nearly threw him in the brig on learning Danna was pregnant, and this was in spite of the fact that he was already at the top of every ranked competition and skill set in the

Navy – as a *recruit*. And then less, when he established himself as one of the most promising cadets ever to graduate from the academy. 'Gifted' was an understatement. Jake was a superior marksman, unbeaten in close quarters combat, and possessed superb detective skills.

And he was polite to an absurd extent. The man could beat down anyone in the Navy but acted like a sheep in front of him. Jake was the classic gentleman, and it was impossible not to like him. For Augustus to say that about anyone was a first.

Katrin was fond of him as well. Jake was the first thing they had agreed on in decades. Katrin and Augustus had stayed together, as firstborns tend to do, no matter how bad the marriage. She did her thing. Augustus did his.

But without Danna, there was nothing left for them at all.

Augustus stood, looking around to make sure no one was left. The chapel guards, normally posted inside at the entrance, had taken up their positions outside.

He walked to Jake.

'How long are you going stay on your knees?'

Jake, his face moist and sullen, didn't move.

'Tears won't bring her back, boy,' Augustus said. 'Move on from it.'

Augustus encouraged his military peers to prepare for loss. To survive in Orionis, they had to learn to compartmentalise it.

'*Hey!*' he shouted, giving Jake a hard shove. 'I'm talking to *you!*'

Jake jumped.

'Don't you get it?' Augustus demanded, grabbing him with both hands. 'This is what they want! Don't give in to it! *Get up! Stand on your own feet!*'

His son-in-law was confused. Incredulous. Still grieving for his wife and unborn son.

'You are *not* beaten!' Augustus shouted.

The lad had the skills. Now he had the motivation. He was going to win this war no matter what it cost.

'Are you prepared to do what is necessary?' Augustus demanded.

Jake turned away. Augustus bent to talk into his ear.

'*Justice,*' he growled, 'is the only way you'll ever move past this.'

Jake stood up straight. Took one last look at the casket.

'Tell me what I have to do,' he said.

Present Day

Throbbing pain spread across his face and neck, waking him from the dream.

His last memory was of speaking to Jake, hearing his voice for the first time in years. Realising he should have been proud to call him a son all this time.

Accepting that he had ruined the man for nothing.

His wrists and ankles were bound, his back was resting against a black bulkhead, his eyes coming to focus on a shiny onyx deck.

Lifting his head, he noticed someone else sitting across from him, also bound. Vronn.

'Are you hurt?' Augustus croaked.

The Gryphon pilot shook his head. Motioned with his eyes to warn Augustus they weren't alone.

A thin silhouette was facing a spectacular view of the Milky Way. It was Grand Admiral Vadim Hedricks. He was not restrained.

'You ...' Augustus said. 'What have you done?'

'I am imprisoned, just like you and Lieutenant Vronn.'

'Bullshit,' Augustus snapped. 'You're a traitor.'

The admiral acted surprised.

'I beg your pardon?' he demanded.

'You let them into the Inner Rim—'

'When I believed I had the upper hand, of course.'

'You ordered the Gryphons to attack the *Gettysburg*.'

'When I didn't know which of my admirals had abandoned me.'

'You didn't attack Ceti when you had the chance!'

'When the *Archangel*'s weapons failed after her first jump.'

'You let them fucking land!'

'When I no longer had control of this ship.'

Augustus spat.

'You're under arrest,' he said. 'On suspicion of committing treason against Orionis and mankind. You have the right to—'

384

'I look forward to my day before a judge,' Vadim said. 'Make it a show trial. Let the secrets spill forth and may every highborn tremble in fear.'

'You'll answer for this,' Augustus said. 'One way or the other.'

'We will *all* answer,' Vadim said. 'The bell tolls for Orionis. We swore oaths to men that never honoured one themselves. That will not do, for the people who took the *Archangel*. Don't you see? This ship belongs to men like Wyllym Lyons. Not highborns. They'll kill every man in uniform, saving us for last. Look ...'

Vadim walked over and heaved Augustus upright.

'There,' he said, pointing towards the Milky Way.

Just below the galactic centre was a teeming mass of bodies floating listlessly against the hull of the *Archangel*. Augustus estimated there were dozens, perhaps hundreds. All were dressed in Navy uniforms.

'Every single one a firstborn,' Vadim said. 'I imagine a similar fate awaits us. Though Lieutenant Tarkon may be spared. Cerlis has more favour among ghosts than you or I do.'

He turned towards Vronn, who said nothing.

'She's out there, now,' Vadim said. 'Looking for you in the wreckage. It's remarkable, the tenacity of maternal instincts. The bond between mother and son is the strongest in creation. Do you know what the second strongest is? Brotherhood. The *human* brotherhood.'

Twenty-Five Years Earlier

The *Pantheon* was a Keating-class corvette in name only. Beneath its Navy white and grey hull, she was faster, stronger, and more powerful than any other corvette in the fleet. As the ordained successor to the ailing Grand Admiral Franz Hedricks, Captain Vadim Hedricks was afforded the best technology that money could buy.

Vadim intended to leave Corinth alone. But he was intercepted by his relentless shadow, Lieutenant Jang Lao, the man appointed by his father to be his bodyguard. Thirty-six hours and a quarter billion kilometres later, they were inside the Echo Ring of the Inner Belt, where the largest and thickest concentration of asteroids was. Besides being treacherous to navigate, the area had increasingly become the site of Ceti ambushes.

Whenever the *Pantheon* flew, Navy escorts launched to accompany it. Losing them was no easy feat for Vadim, requiring a combination of skill and pulling rank. By now the officers assigned to his protection were on the verge of panic, and the fleet would soon be coordinating their efforts to find him.

But for Vadim, the risk was worth taking. More importantly, he was the only one who could.

Just beyond the *Pantheon*'s bridge, a large asteroid rotated into view, matching the navigation coordinates he had been given. A Ceti corvette was affixed to its surface, with her running lights turned off.

Its name was the *Aria Black*.

'Sir,' Lieutenant Lao insisted, blocking the exit from the bridge. 'I can't allow you to go out there.'

'Lieutenant, step away from the hatch,' Vadim said. 'That's an order.'

'I swore to your father – we all did,' Lao said. 'You're putting your life and the Navy succession in danger.'

'My oath is to Orionis, not my father,' Vadim said. 'If I'm gone longer than thirty minutes, assume the worst. This is the only chance I have to end a war before it begins.'

Vadim leaned forward and grabbed the lieutenant's shoulder.

'No one can learn about this, Lao,' he said. 'And if anyone does, I wouldn't want to be you.'

He left the bridge, pulling himself towards the gunship hatch in the rear of the ship. The lieutenant was close behind.

'This is treason,' he said.

'No,' Vadim said, entering the cockpit. 'It's *courage*.'

He shut the hatch and settled into the controls.

As the craft detached from the *Pantheon*, its radar immediately picked up the *Aria Black*. Following the instructions he received, Vadim landed his craft on the corvette's docking collar. When the airlock had pressurised, he could hear classical music playing from the other side.

Vadim checked his weapon, a railgun that fired a seven-millimetre poisoned hollow point. The tiny weapon was concealed on the inside of his sleeve. He was 'advised' to come unarmed, but his instincts said otherwise. The stakes were too high.

Vadim swung the hatch open. And there, waiting for him, was Vladric Mors.

'Captain,' the Ceti leader said, bowing slightly. 'Welcome. Please, right this way.'

Vadim followed.

'Have much trouble sneaking away?' Vladric asked.

'Nothing that wasn't anticipated,' Vadim answered, admiring the artwork adorning the wood panel bulkheads. He was led into a cabin that resembled a seventeenth-century stateroom.

'Thank you for leaving your weapon behind,' Vladric said, motioning for him to take a seat. 'I know it took a leap of faith. Your Navy colleagues are searching for you. I estimate we have thirty minutes before they make contact. I hope we reach an understanding by then.'

'It was bold of you to ask me to come here,' Vadim said. 'I can't say why I agreed.'

'As in, unable to articulate why?' Vladric asked. 'Or because your oath prevents you?'

'I'm here because I want to avoid a war,' Vadim said. 'I know what you're doing. I've seen the change in tactics. Where your ships are patrolling. And I know that Zeus's present position relative to Corinth makes Brotherhood especially vulnerable to an attack.'

'A fact no doubt recognised by your peers,' Vladric said, beaming a smile. 'The question is, do they believe we'll try?'

'No.'

'But you do. Which is why you're here.'

Vadim studied his arch-enemy. He wanted to hate this man. Vladric Mors had murdered civilians, Navy personnel, highborn officers, men Vadim's own father relied on. And yet, there was something about him, a charisma that contradicted his reputation as a monster.

'What has to happen to avoid conflict?' Vadim asked.

'Do you speak on behalf of the Navy and Orionis?' Vladric asked.

'I am a person of considerable influence in those domains, yes.'

Vladric leaned forward, and his pleasant demeanour transformed to that of a stern, hard man.

387

'Because you're a *Hedricks*,' he said.

It was an uncanny imitation of his father.

'Does that amuse you?' Vadim asked, his face reddening.

'No,' Vladric said. 'Just clarifying I understand the source of your "influence". Carry on.'

'There is nothing more to say,' Vadim said. 'I contacted you because I believe you can be reasoned with.'

'I knew you would contact me,' Vladric said. 'And you know there is nothing anyone can do to stop me.'

'Then what is it you want?' Vadim demanded.

'Brotherhood,' Vladric answered.

Vadim laughed.

'The station?'

'And brotherhood for mankind.'

'I suppose I've wasted my time,' Vadim said, standing up. 'Good luck.'

'What's the real reason that brought you here?' Vladric asked. 'You know you can't dissuade me. It had to be more than just ... intuition, right?'

Vadim paused.

'I don't know what you're talking about.'

'You're a Hedricks,' Vladric said. 'Born with disabilities and disease. A lowborn with your afflictions would have been tossed into a slush tank. But you are your father's *son*. He invested so much restoring you to his expectations, didn't he?'

Vadim tried to salvage something from this visit.

'I have a list of personnel accused of crimes against Orionis,' he said. 'Extradite them and I'll push to allow Ceti to lease space on Brotherhood once construction—'

Vladric interrupted him.

'It wasn't your name or cybernetics that got you to where you are,' he said. 'It was something else. You can read people, you know their intentions. Your instincts are a *Gift*. And they led you to me. Why? Because it runs in the family.'

'What?'

Vladric smiled.

'My mother had fair skin, like yours. Dark hair, like yours. Eyes like

388

yours, before your father had them augmented. She was very beautiful. Strong, but kind. Nurturing. As every mother should be.'

'What are you talking about?'

'No other species stays at the breast as long as humans do,' Vladric said. 'The memory of our mothers stays with us. May I guess the year yours died?'

With a flick of his wrist, Vadim drew his weapon from his sleeve.

'What a shame,' Vladric said. 'I guess you don't trust me after all. And yet you still came all this way to make peace. Your mother died in 2712. Or to be precise, that was the year she disappeared. Old Franz was so disappointed, wasn't he?'

'Shut up,' Vadim warned.

'What did the Navy tell you?' Vladric persisted. 'Is she still officially a "missing person"? Well, I'm sorry to inform you, but your mother was a murder victim.'

'Shut your mouth!' Vadim shouted.

'She died on a ship called *The Baxley*,' Vladric said. 'Right before my very eyes, she starved to death. Your father told you, what … she decided on her own not to return? Did he cite irreconcilable differences as well? At least that wasn't a lie.'

'I'm going to count to three,' Vadim said, tightening his grip on the pistol.

Vladric raised both hands over his head.

'Franz Hedricks: Captain of the Tabit Genesis, architect of Orionis society,' Vladric said. 'All he ever wanted was a firstborn son to take his place in history.'

'One …' Vadim said, taking aim.

'All your mother wanted,' Vladric continued, taking a cautious step forward, 'was a child that would survive. Was that such a horrible crime?'

Vadim flicked the safety off.

'Two,' he said, through gritted teeth.

'To Franz Hedricks, it was unforgivable,' Vladric said, slowly kneeling, his arms still raised overhead. 'Losing you was not an option. To put his genetic legacy into a machine … this was sacrilege. The Hedricks name would not be carried on by a *ghost*. And he vowed to never allow his firstborn son to learn of his mother's disgrace.'

Vadim tried to say the word 'three'. But he couldn't.

'I have not lied to you,' Vladric said. 'I can't prove your father was responsible for making sure *The Baxley* couldn't land. But *you can*, and when you do, *please* ... we need closure.'

Slowly, Vladric rose and stepped away from the gun.

'Let me show how I know these things,' he said, rolling up his sleeve. Then he withdrew a curved blade from behind his back. Vadim took aim. But Vladric put the blade to his own forearm and sliced deeply.

A stream of crimson globules emerged from the wound, scattering throughout the stateroom.

Vladric pushed himself behind the hatch frame of the adjacent compartment.

'Take some back with you,' he said. 'It's yours as much as my own.'

Present Day

Augustus now understood the end of his life was near.

'My own blood,' Vadim said, concluding his story. 'My father disowned his second son to preserve the tyranny of highborn control over the fate of humanity. Men like him are a bane to us all. And now, the worst of them are gone.'

Vladric Mors stood in the doorway. Augustus had to blink to make sure it wasn't an illusion.

The Ceti leader walked to Grand Admiral Vadim Hedricks with a broad, warm smile on his face.

They shook hands. Then embraced. Tears were in the eyes of both. Vronn's face resembled Augustus's own: utter disbelief.

'We did it,' Vladric said, patting Vadim's shoulders. 'We did it!'

The brothers looked upon Augustus with a hint of amusement.

'I had planned to meet you under different circumstances,' Vadim said. 'The restraints should not be necessary. You would have come here of your own volition.'

'Sure,' Augustus growled. 'To cut your throat.'

'You are a worthy adversary,' Vladric said. 'There is a place for you in the new world.'

'Society needs a lawman with your tenacity,' Vadim said. 'For decades you've enforced the will of highborns. Now we need you to enforce the law of *man*.'

'You see those corpses?' Vladric said. 'They pulled every firstborn privilege they could to be assigned to this ship. Vulcan, Merckon, Iopa, you name the corporation, there's a dynasty floating there. All believed they were laying claim to the world we'll find with this ship. Now we have the means to reach it. *All of us*. Not just the entitled.'

'We followed the wrong people, Augustus,' Vadim said. 'Men who disguised their interests as the betterment for all—'

'Both of you, *shut up*,' Augustus snapped. 'You are not heroes. You are murderers. And you will burn.'

'In all the years you hunted me,' Vladric said, 'did you never once question what you were defending?'

'I defend the Orionis democracy,' Augustus said. 'It's ugly but it's the only path forward. You two are deranged, sadistic fucks. Sooner or later people will see you for what you really are. They'll never bow to tyranny, and neither will I!'

The brothers looked at each other. Their disappointment was evident.

'That is tragic,' Vadim said.

'Please, Augustus,' Vladric said. 'Choose the manner of your execution.'

Augustus glared at him.

'You know my response to that.'

'I do,' Vladric said, removing his coat.

Vadim unlocked the cuffs on Augustus and stepped away.

'Farewell, Augustus Tyrell,' he said. 'You're a good man.'

Vladric unhooked one of the curved blades at his hips and tossed it to Augustus.

'Or would you like them both?' he asked, waving the other one.

Augustus snarled and launched himself towards Vladric, swinging the blade with all his might.

It was parried and he was steered harmlessly aside.

Channelling all his rage, Augustus slashed again. He missed, and this time Vladric countered with a palm strike that struck his chest, blasting him backwards towards the bulkhead.

The impact made him drop the weapon.

Vladric waited patiently for him to retrieve it.

Augustus picked it up slowly. He decided to take his chances with Vadim instead.

As Vladric rushed to intercept, Vronn kicked himself forward, tripping him.

Primal, desperate adrenaline surged through Augustus. And then, with his hand drawn back to strike, Vadim vanished.

There was just enough time to feel a hand push his back, redirecting his trajectory towards the bubble room glass.

His head struck. There was pain and disorientation. Perhaps a moment of blackness before realising he had been spun around.

The brothers were standing before him. The knife was no longer in his hands.

He tried to ball his hands into fists. But his fingers wouldn't move.

There was blood at his greaves.

His knees buckled, but the brothers caught him. A tyrant at each shoulder, they gently set him down.

Augustus saw deep cuts in both wrists, down to the bone. His life was rushing out from within.

'I'll never forget you,' Vladric said.

Augustus wanted to lash out. But his body had already surrendered.

44

CERLIS

Cerlis Tarkon was seated within the cockpit of a VMK-5 'Arbiter' class gunship. It was nestled within the open dropbay of the Vulcan Dynamics frigate *Odessa,* and before them was the greatest ship graveyard since the Battle of Brotherhood.

The *Archangel* was barely visible from here, but the *Odessa* and her escorts were well within reach. No one in the Vulcan chain of command was comfortable with her decision to lead the expedition. But none advised her against it.

'Possible contact at zero-one-five,' the *Odessa* navigator said. 'Eighty per cent probability.'

'Shift course to intercept,' Cerlis ordered, her hands tightening around the gunship's controls.

'Brace for manoeuvres.'

The *Odessa* fired her vectored thrusters in precise sequence, combining several degrees of pitch and roll. Cerlis felt her body compress and stretch, but was determined to persevere.

'Five hundred metres, drift rate of two metres per second,' the navigator announced. 'Probability is ninety-nine per cent.'

Cerlis slammed the release switch in the cockpit. Four small bursts of gas pushed the Arbiter out of the bay. She wobbled the stick to confirm control; the craft responded nimbly. The contact was straight ahead.

'Ma'am, we have eighteen minutes,' he resumed. 'Your contact is on a collision course with more debris tracking in.'

'Then shoot it down,' she grumbled, easing the throttle forward. The contact was visible already, throwing off glints of reflected sunlight.

'We can't,' the navigator said. 'It's too big.'

Cerlis didn't even hear him. Her heart was beating in her throat; before her was the blackened ruins of a Gryphon. Its strong contours were twisted and bent; sharp, serrated frame pylons jutted out like compound fractures from where an engine once sat.

The tail marking was the most unblemished part of the wreck. Its number read 'One-Three'.

Vronn's Gryphon.

'Tally,' she said quietly, flying as close as she dared.

'Matching thrust sequence sent,' the navigator said.

'Acknowledged, firing,' she said.

The gunship's autopilot engaged the manoeuvring thrusters; she felt herself tumbling in three dimensions. But through the cockpit canopy, Gryphon One-Three appeared stationary.

Instead of deploying towing grapples as the navigator expected, Cerlis landed the craft's magnetic skids directly onto the Gryphon.

'Ma'am, that is not advisable,' the navigator warned.

She began scanning the wreck with X-ray and terahertz, building a three-dimensional image of what was inside.

The armoured cockpit was intact, but the ejection mechanism had failed. Structural damage had prevented the egress plating from detaching, and the trapped rocket motors had burned the surrounding housing into molten slag that had since cooled and hardened.

Life support power reserves were still running. The pilot was entombed in the flight seat, frozen solid but intubated by cryonic feeds. No heartbeat was present.

X-ray imagery cast serious doubt he could be revived. The spine, skull, and almost every bone in his body had the consistency of powder. Massive organ trauma was evident, frozen in place before it became systemic.

But frozen didn't mean dead. Not yet.

'*Odessa*, ready the hangar,' Cerlis ordered, pushing the Arbitrator away from the wreck. 'We are bringing this on board.'

'The entire thing?'

'Affirmative,' she said. 'Deploying tow cables now.'

As the grapples made contact, a new voice entered the channel.

'Cerlis.'

She clenched her teeth.

'Vladric.'

'That is not your son,' he said.

She looked towards the wreck.

'Vronn is well,' Vladric assured. 'And I'd like to propose a trade.'

45

ANONYMOUS

13 July 2809

Dear Amaryllis,

I finally understand why I never hear back from you.

It is because no one can say with any certainty if you still exist. When we said goodbye all those years ago, I asked which Genesis was yours ... the Tau, or the Tabit. Knowing that we would never see each other again, you answered, 'Both ... because I want both stars to remind you of us.'

I have been writing these letters to hold on. To me, you *were* the last of us. It's time to say farewell. I've been grieving at your grave long enough.

You died on a Sunday. Somewhere in the spinning bowels of the *Tabit Genesis*, your body rests, awaiting its final descent to Eileithyia's scorched surface. There at last, your journey will end.

What a tragic voyage it was. And, so fitting that it should end the way it did. Aboard the very ship where the genesis began. The rebirth of our species under the glare of another sun. Murdered, in cold blood, by the next generation of mankind. The survivors of an ancient hegemony, side by side with their synthetic offspring, seeking out new worlds to burn.

Humans are better at nothing else.

We started our journeys in this universe at the same time. Yet I will live on and on, as many different living things. But none of them will ever be human again. At least, not in spirit. That part of me died along with you.

I no longer need or want the memory of you. I begged Ceitus to remove it. But she refused. She has, however, instructed my colleagues not to speak with me about anything other than the mission. Most are concerned that I have been compromised by the fact that the *Tabit Genesis* is no more.

They have nothing to fear.

Yesterday we arrived at the Ch1 Orionis AB system. An Oberyan Lightspear is orbiting the second planet. There is no one aboard. The aft dropship pad is empty. But there is evidence it was launched from this system for a probable surface landing. With the exception of a temperate band surrounding the equator, most of the planet is buried in ice. Ceitus has narrowed the range of possible landing sites, factoring in favourable survival conditions, weather patterns, and dropship range. It will take us months to search them all.

The ship logs have been deleted. Whoever did this took great care to remove the entries from every datacore on board. Power still flows from the reactors but all systems, including life support, are idle.

The vessel is designed to be run by a crew of seven, but is completely sterile. There is not a single trace of biological evidence to indicate that any humans were ever aboard.

Our mission is to learn what happened here.

Goodbye, Amaryllis. Forever.

- A

ACKNOWLEDGEMENTS

Thank you so much for reading this. The Tabit Genesis is the first work I can truly call my own. Of those which came before, this one means the most to me.

Many themes in this story are drawn from the world we live in today. Climate change, war, the rule of oligarchs, cancer and race have a part here. All I did was sprinkle in Murphy's Law with a dash of rail guns and I ended up with a space opera.

To me, the perseverance of these issues in the fictional world of Orionis is entirely plausible because we still allow them to exist today, here on Earth, despite having the means to act decisively on them. We are, without question, a greater enemy to ourselves than the Raothri ever could be.

This part of the journey ended much the same way it began: surrounded by the people I love the most. To my beautiful children, my beloved bride, and my wonderful parents: I am truly blessed. It may sound cliché, but this work would not be possible without you. Thank you for being the rock of my life.

In memoriam, to George: You were taken from us too soon. We miss you.

Finally, to Ben: You are always with me. This one is for you.

TG

15 February 2015

ABOUT GOLLANCZ

Gollancz is the oldest SF publishing imprint in the world. Since being founded in 1927 Gollancz has continued to publish a focused selection of bestselling and award-winning authors. The front-list includes **Ben Aaronovitch**, **Joe Abercrombie**, **Charlaine Harris**, **Joanne Harris**, **Joe Hill**, **Alastair Reynolds**, **Patrick Rothfuss**, **Nalini Singh** and **Brandon Sanderson**.

As one of the largest Science Fiction and Fantasy imprints in the UK it is no surprise we have one of the most extensive backlists in the world. Find high quality SF on Gateway written by such authors as **Philip K. Dick**, **Ursula Le Guin**, **Connie Willis**, **Sir Arthur C. Clarke**, **Pat Cadigan**, **Michael Moorcock** and **George R.R. Martin**.

We also have a strand of publishing in translation, which includes French, Polish and Russian authors. Gollancz is home to more award-winning authors than any other imprint, with names including **Aliette de Bodard**, **M. John Harrison**, **Paul McAuley**, **Sarah Pinborough**, **Pierre Pevel**, **Justina Robson** and many more.

The SF Gateway
More than 3,000 classic, rare and previously out-of-print SF novels at your fingertips.
www.sfgateway.com

The Gollancz Blog
Bringing you news from our worlds to yours. Stories, interviews, articles and exclusive extracts just for you!
www.gollancz.co.uk

GOLLANCZ
LONDON